TRINITY TRILOGY
BOOK ONE

PRAISE FOR BODY

"Seriously there is EVERYTHING to like about this book. Hot blooded Alpha Male who wants his woman and decides he will protect her at all costs."

~ Not Another Damn Book Blog

"FIVE STAR REVIEW I recommend this book to anyone looking for a sweet, fierce love story. It takes a lot to write an original story that takes twists and turns you won't see coming."

~ Give Me Books Blog

"I want more Chase! I will definitely be getting the next book in this trilogy. I give this book 5 stars."

~ Obsessed by Books Blog

Body

TRINITY TRILOGY
BOOK ONE

AUDREY CARLAN

WATERHOUSE
PRESS

This book is an original publication of Audrey Carlan

Cover Design by Waterhouse Press, LLC

Cover Photographs: Shutterstock

Paperback ISBN: 978-0-9905056-5-5
PRINTED IN THE UNITED STATES OF AMERICA

For my mother, Regina…
Because you never received your happily ever after.
I miss you every day.

SPECIAL ACKNOWLEDGEMENT

To my soul sisters Dyani, Nikki, and Carolyn

Without you, I am not me.
Without your love and undying support, this novel wouldn't have been published.
Without you Dyani Gingerich, there would be no Maria De La Torre.
Without you Nikki Chiverrell, there would be no Bree Simmons.
Without you Carolyn Beasley, there would be no Kathleen Bennett.
Without soul sisters this book wouldn't be as special.

I'll always love you more.

BESOS

Bound - Eternally - Sisters - of - Souls

CHAPTER ONE

I just want a normal life—one without pain. I've experienced more physical and emotional pain in my twenty-four years than most women experience their entire lives. People take for granted how easy they have it, running around, never worrying about when it will all come to a burning, crashing end. I envy those people, and am determined to one day be like them. My new motto is to live for tomorrow. Every decision will move me toward a future filled with light, one that cannot be dulled by harsh realities and unplanned inconveniences. I am the maker of my dreams. No longer am I the wallflower who allows myself to be hurt.

My position as fundraising manager for one of the largest charitable organizations for women in the United States brought me to where I am today, sitting in this bar. After a long travel day with two layovers, I sink into the plush cushioned seat that forms to my curves. Looking around, I'm glad I threw on my work blazer and dark trouser jeans. The sky-high BCBG peep-toe shoes and a long beaded necklace spruce up the business casual look.

I'm a little out of my league. Men and women in pristine suits and cocktail dresses congregate in small groups of people to enjoy "Happy Hour." This is not my scene. If the Safe Haven Foundation board of directors meeting weren't being held in this hotel, I'd be sitting at home in comfy pajamas, sipping wine, and watching a chick flick with my roommate, Maria.

The deep grooves in the bull nose edge of the bar are perfectly etched in a swirling pattern. The bar is backlit and shines light through each liquor bottle like a sunbeam shooting through a crystal. The different rays of colors scatter, looking more like art than glass shelves filled with a variety of alcoholic beverages. A tall ladder climbs each side so the bartender can reach the "top-shelf" liquor. The stuff that's a few hundred dollars a bottle, possibly even per glass, is placed on those shelves of honor.

Scanning the wine list, I'm reminded of my station in life. Living in wine country, I have a pretty good grasp on what's good, fair, and straight vinegar. Everything on this menu is priced by the bottle, the cheapest close to a hundred dollars—nowhere near my pay grade.

A furry little man behind the bar smiles at me, wipes the space in front of me with a damp cloth, and sets down a coaster. "What can I get for you?" His accent holds an Italian Chicagoan inflection.

"Um, not sure. Do you have wine by the glass?"

"You're not from around here are you?" His question is genuine and friendly.

I figure honesty is the best policy. "Nope. Here on business."

"Excellent. I'll hook you up," he says, smacking the bar. "White or red?"

"White, please. Thank you."

The bar is something else. I had reservations about coming down, but I'm glad I did. My weariness from today's travel starts to wear off. The bartender sets a generous glass of wine in front of me. He gave me well over the customary four ounces. I smile wide, probably all teeth and gums. He grins and sets off to assist another patron.

Hidden speakers play Amy Winehouse's lilting voice crooning softly about her being no good for her man. People chat among themselves. I take a sip of my wine and am assaulted by the burst of the smooth, buttery notes in the Chardonnay. Reminds me of a little winery my soul sisters and I visited last year in Napa. Their wine was just as satiny smooth on the palate. It's the taste of money. My only hope is that my bill isn't over twenty dollars. Otherwise my little *per diem* splurge is toast.

Turning sideways, I take in the eclectic mix of contemporary art coupled with dimmed track lighting. A pristine black grand piano sits off to the corner. A soft light shines on it as if awaiting some lonely soul to tickle its ivories. A man places his hand on the glossy surface, breaking my trance. Following the hand up the arm, I find it's attached to the most striking male face I've ever seen. His image could easily grace the cover of any high fashion magazine. Strong dark brows define what I suspect are dark eyes. Sculpted cheekbones rise as his head tips back in laughter. He's the epitome of tall, dark, and handsome in the inky suit that sits on, quite possibly, one of the most perfect forms I've seen. He's magnificent.

I skim his body from his leather designer shoes up to the most exquisitely tailored slacks, which hang on a trim waist in that sexy way you only see on men gracing the silver screen. I gulp down the wine, letting the burn of the too-large drink pierce my consciousness as my eyes continue the journey up a very broad chest. I imagine that underneath the silky fabric is a chiseled chest and abdomen. His tie is loose. He probably just finished his workday, in a hurry to meet the guys in downtown Chicago for a beer.

No, that's not right. He's too elegant for beer. That would be the type of guy I usually date. This man, Mr. Superman, is far too classy. His tumbler is filled with a honey-colored liquid, confirming his taste. Scotch or whiskey on the rocks.

He's sex personified as he sips the liquid. I imagine it burns as it rushes down his throat. I'll bet the harsh alcohol warms his belly and soothes the trials of the day away. I'm thinking corporate lawyer or banker. Maybe he had a meeting in this very hotel and is schmoozing the men standing around him. Better yet, they could be trying to impress him. That's more like it.

I settle my gaze on his face and am shocked to find his eyes boring intensely into mine. I want to look away, but can't. It's as if he's holding me tethered to his focused stare. Heat swirls in my gut as our gazes meet and we dance around one another, assessing, considering the other. I try but fail to look away. After what seems like an eternity, one of his dark brows tips, and a sly grin slips across his face. Magnificent wasn't the right word. He's splendid.

Long fingers brush his dark hair. It falls in sexy layers that I'd give anything to comb my own fingers through. Chills run up my back as we continue our mutual staring contest. As I'm about to pass out from holding my breath so long, he looks away. It's like tossing sand on a burning flame. The fire is out. Gone. Cold. Nothing but ash remains.

What the hell was that?

The day must have done a number on me. I've never

scoped out a man before at such great length, nor have I been so taken with one. *I'll bet he's good in bed.* The thought flits across my mind, and I squash it. There be dragons in thoughts like that. It's a good thing he looked away. Even better that he didn't hear the silent siren's call summoning him over to fill the desire pumping through my every pore. All he'd need is one match, and I'd go up in flames like a pile of fallen dried leaves.

With every fiber of my being, I face the bar and do everything I can to focus on anything other than the man in the corner. Delicately, I trace the rim of the wineglass, seeing if I can make it sing along with the music filtering through the room. Satisfaction flourishes when I'm able to circle out a soft hum, a tiny pitch to match the lyrics.

"Neat trick," a deep voice booms behind me. It's one of those voices that settles in your belly and tickles you from the inside out.

I twirl so fast my wineglass skitters across the bar. A quick arm reaches across me and catches it before a drop spills. I'm caged between a broad chest and the bar behind me. Instinctively, I balance my hands on the hard surface pressing into me. My nose is stuffed into a crisp shirt. Sandalwood and citrus permeate the air with a heady scent. I take a deep breath, sucking the flavor of nature and man into my being. The smell reminds me that it's been far too long since I've been this intimate with the opposite sex.

A rumble destroys my happy place. The chest I'm wedged against is laughing. I push lightly and the wall moves to reveal stunning Caribbean-blue eyes. The light was playing tricks on me before. They're not dark at all. I look from feature to feature. From those blue eyes, to the sculpted cheekbones, down to the heart-shaped pout. The sexy Superman is here, right in front of me, looking down at me. A halo of light behind him accentuates every delectable feature. He's…laughing.

I wrinkle my nose and push hard against his chest to secure some much-needed space. In mere seconds, this stranger has completely invaded and caged me like an animal, saved my drink, and left me without the ability to speak.

"Cat got your tongue?"

"No!" I roll my eyes at how ridiculous that sounds, even to me.

He laughs and gestures to the open seat next to me.

"May I?" He sits without waiting for an answer.

"No, you may not. I'm expecting someone." Perfectly reasonable reply. It's a fat lie, but it always works when an unwanted suitor tries to saddle up next to me.

"They can sit in the chair on the other side of you." He grins.

Damn his sexy face. I could look at it for days on end and still not understand how God could create something so perfect. That's probably all he has going for him.

He snaps at the bartender, and he comes running.

"How rude. Do you always treat everyone like a dog?" I'm not even sure why I opened my mouth. I should have ignored him, finished my drink, and left. But no, I had to poke the sexy Superman.

He looks at me as the bartender waits patiently. Seems odd from a bartender. Why not just butt in and ask what Superman wants? He searches my face with his ocean eyes and speaks to the bartender without looking at him. Again, rude!

"Sam, I'll have another. As will she." He gestures to my mostly drained wineglass.

"Yes, Mr. Davis. Right away." The bartender practically bows before running off to make the drinks.

"Mr. Davis? I take it you come here often?"

"Chase Davis, and yes, I own this hotel. It's important to check in on my investments."

My cheeks burn. I'm not sure if it's from embarrassment or irritation. Maybe a little of both. Besides being distractingly beautiful, he's pompous. I don't care for it.

"I'm sorry if I appeared rude, but a snap did get Sam's attention. I wanted to order you another drink before you ran off."

Seems reasonable enough. "And why are you interested in buying me a drink, Mr. Davis?"

"Chase. You can call me Chase."

"I get the feeling you're used to being called Mr. Davis." I use my most seductive tone. "You like the respect it gives you?" Where in the hell I'm coming up with this shit is beyond me. I feel like I'm playing a game I've never played before, and I have no idea if I'm winning or losing. Something about this man taunts my defenses to prickle and strike, but not in an uncomfortable way. More like I want to get a rise out of him.

"In my professional life, Mr. Davis is appropriate, yes. Privately, as in this conversation, I'd like you to call me Chase." His eyes sparkle, and when he smiles, I'm gifted an even set of white teeth. Breathtaking.

I nod, not sure how to keep up the sparring. Every bit of his essence exudes confidence and control, and I'm wilting under the pressure of being near him. He's the sexy Superman, but it seems as if he's becoming my kryptonite.

"In answer to your question, I bought you a drink so I could get to know you better."

My insides quiver as he skims my face and then moves down, his gaze landing on my chest. I'm so thankful I wore the tight tank top under the blazer. It accentuates my breasts, yet leaves just enough to the imagination. Thank you, *What Not to Wear*, for the fitted jacket and sexy tank technique.

I lick my lips and bite the bottom one, trying to decide what to say or do next. He inhales, and I see the rise and fall of his wide chest. Those blue eyes swirl with color and dilate.

"What's your name?" he asks.

"Gillian Callahan, but my friends call me Gigi."

"I will call you Gillian or Miss Callahan." He clasps my hand and brings it to his lips for a kiss. "Pet names are earned. I prefer to choose my own."

His husky tone sends bouts of pure lust twisting and curling in rivulets through me.

Jesus, this man is sex incarnate. It oozes through his words, the twinkle in his eyes, and the sly grin attached to a delectable pair of lips. I want to kiss, bite, and savor those lips. In that order. He yanks at his tie and pulls the knot free entirely. With a flick of his fingers, he undoes the top two buttons at the collar, exposing a nice tanned piece of flesh. I lean closer to him, riveted to that speck of flesh. Desperately, I want to reach out and give it a lick. Just a quick little taste. That's all I'd need.

"You like what you see, Gillian?"

Before my brain connects and filters my reply, I nod

dumbly. With the full spirit of a teenage girl with a crush, the lame drawn-out response slips out. "God, yes."

"Mmm, I'm so glad. Shall we continue this conversation somewhere else?" His eyes go from Caribbean blue to black in seconds.

One large hand strays to my knee, and his thumb traces an infinity symbol there. With each small press of skin to denim, I feel his touch as if it is searing my skin with his mark. Ribbons of excitement rush out through my limbs until what he said crashes around me.

"Excuse me. What?" I jump from my seat, which takes a bit of effort, as my legs have turned to jelly. Take this somewhere more comfortable? Like I'm a whore ready to hop into bed with a man, albeit a sexy as hell one, ten minutes after meeting? I am not that girl. Well, I could be, but that's not the impression I want to give.

His face twists into a confused grimace. He reaches for me, but I step back, escaping his grasp. Big men reaching for me often trigger a panic attack.

His eyes narrow. "You want me. I can see it very clearly. It's written all over your gorgeous face, and you wear your emotions on your sleeve."

Tingles of fear prickle my spine and shoot up to raise the tender hairs at my neck. I shake my head. "You must have misunderstood. I need to go. It was nice meeting you." Turning, I clear my head and make for the lobby bar's exit.

"Gillian, wait!" he calls from behind me.

I debate breaking into a full run, but I know I'm safe here. This is a five-star resort hotel in the middle of downtown Chicago. People are milling around everywhere. With a deep breath, I turn and face the most beautiful man alive. Superman doesn't do him justice. He is just...perfect.

When he catches up to me, he hands me a white card. "My business card. My cell is on the back. I'm not really sure what happened here, but I'd like to see you again."

Fat chance. "I'll think about it."

He tilts his head in a way that makes me believe he's never been let down by a woman before. He probably hasn't. It would take a certifiable woman to turn down a romp with this sexy stranger, but I'm living for tomorrow, not today. A slow grin slides across his face. He leans forward and places both hands tentatively on my biceps. It takes everything I have not to panic. I instigate touching. It is part of my coping mechanism. I close my eyes as he leans close and kisses my cheek.

Sandalwood and citrus permeate the air around his large frame. God, he smells good.

Chase whispers in my ear. "Until we meet again." Then he drags his lips along the side of my chin before he pulls away.

I could melt on the spot. He winks, turns, and walks back to the bar.

★ ★ ★ ★

Stupid. Stupid. Stupid.

The internal rant runs in a constant loop as I pull off my heels and chuck them across the room. Poor beautiful shoes. They don't deserve such treatment, but I have to get the aggression out somehow. Smacking my head against a hard surface is very appealing at this moment. It is concussion or shoe abuse.

Ugh, why can't I just be normal? Walk into a bar. Sit down. Have a drink. Meet a beautiful man. Flirt. He asks you out. That's how that meeting with Chase *should* have gone. But no. Not for Gigi Callahan, the broken girl from San Francisco. The man makes one overtly sexual suggestion, and I crumble into a weeping willow. Worse, I scamper off like a frightened little puppy. I should have stayed and given it back to him in spades.

It's not as if I'm a prude or a saint. I've been approached sexually plenty of times. Even considered it a time or two. But with him, it was as if I couldn't get my brain together long enough to put two sentences together. My lack of a filter egged him on, gave him the green light. He probably beds a different woman each night. With a face and body like Adonis, who wouldn't want to fall into his bed? Hell, if I weren't such a scaredy-cat, I'd be scratching at his leg right now, begging for a petting.

Chase. Just thinking about him has my stomach in knots and my panties moist. *Arrrggghhhhh.*

I flop down on the bed and stare at the ceiling in defeat. When am I going to learn how to control my fears? Doesn't matter. I'm here to focus on my work with Safe Haven, and that's it. Though, maybe if I do unto others, eventually someone good will come unto me. Like someone tall with dark hair, ocean-blue eyes, and warm hands.

Stupid. Stupid. Stupid.

My cell phone buzzes on the end table, bringing me out of my reverie. It's my roommate. Thank God!

"Ria! I'm so glad you called," I screech into the phone.

"*Mi Amiga!* What's wrong? You don't sound like yourself."

Maria De La Torre is one of my best female friends and my roommate. We've been through hell and back and own matching T-shirts. Over the years, we've grown especially protective of one another. Her love and support got me through many nights full of tears and self-loathing. I've been her rock just as many times. Together, and with a great deal of therapy, we've learned to cope and be more open about our feelings. I'm still closed off, but there are a select few people in my world I trust. Maria is one of them.

"Girl, I met a man." I sigh into the phone, disgusted with myself.

"So why do you sound like your dog just died?" She laughs.

"I don't know. This man is different. He's intense." Intense is an understatement.

Maria sighs over the line. "Gigi, don't tell me you met another bastard who just wants to get into your pants. I mean, you're pretty bangin', but you have to stop attracting these *pedazos de mierda!*"

I laugh. She thinks all men are *pieces of shit.* Useless. Her use of Spanish intermingled with English makes her incredibly endearing. It's unique to her, and it's taught me quite a lot about the language.

"He's not like that. Well, actually, I don't know much about him other than he's hot. When I say he's hot, I'm talking movie star quality, *People's* 'Sexiest Man Alive' kind of hot. Women everywhere probably drop their panties without question for him." He probably knows it, too. Smug bastard.

She giggles. "Nice. So are you going to?"

"Am I going to what?"

"Drop your panties for him, silly." Her laughter gets louder, laced with a "duh" tone.

"No! I met him, had a conversation with him, and then ran off. I completely embarrassed myself. I doubt he'd want to see me again." It's true. Besides, if he knew my past, he'd take that sexy suit-wearing Superman body of his in the opposite direction.

"*Cara bonita*, no. I'm sure you didn't."

I cringe. She has always called me "beautiful face." It's her personal pet name. She busts out with the endearment when she feels I'm down or need encouragement.

"Did he ask you out or ask for your phone number?"

A spark of hope glitters in the distance. "Well, yes, kind of. He gave me his business card with his cell phone number on the back. Asked me to call him." Technically, he did give me the card after the idiotic behavior, so maybe he is interested. What does that say about him though? I acted like a complete wackadoo, but he did make an overture as if he were soliciting me. That was uncalled for too.

"See, obviously there was something there. Are you going to?" She sounds hopeful. "You deserve a little fun while you're in Chicago. Besides, when was the last time you got laid, anyway?"

Her question is rhetorical. She knows it's been months.

"Ria! I just met him. You're suggesting I fall into bed with him?" The girl has no limits. Though I can't say the thought didn't wiggle its way into my mind, especially when he loosened that silver tie, exposing a stimulating patch of skin.

"Yes, I am. You need to get fucked!"

I gasp at her crassness.

"You've been uptight lately. You said yourself he's the kind of guy women want to bed. Just think about it. You're young, *mi amiga!* Start acting twenty-four instead of forty-four."

I sigh and blow out a long breath. "You've got a point. I'll think about it. How 'bout I call you tomorrow after my first board meeting? I'm going to head to bed so I can hit the gym first thing." I yawn loudly and realize I'm spent.

Maria really does have a point. I have been way too uptight. The last relationship I had, if you could call it that, was with Daniel the wimp.

That's unfair. It's not really that he was a wimp. He was just too sensitive for me. Treated me like a princess and cried at chick flicks. I rarely cry. He was also really boring in bed. Only interested in the missionary position, never straying from the norm. He freaked out when I suggested he take me from behind. His shocked voice rumbled in my brain, *"You want to be fucked like a whore, Gigi? Jesus, what's wrong with you?"* The thought of the jerk makes me ill. I need a man who knows his way around a woman. One who will excite me, make me come regularly without fearing being hurt. Daniel never gave me much pleasure, but he never once touched me in anger.

Ria's disgruntled voice brings me back from my reverie. "Ugh! You are always hitting the gym. Bree would be proud though. Me, I'm going to sit down and enjoy a fat dinner with Tommy. Things are heating up, and I think I'm finally going to get him to take me to bed!"

Watching Maria fawn over a man is completely new territory. Most men fall all over themselves to be near her, not the other way around. "Anticipation makes the experience all the better," I remind her. "Enjoy the attention he's lavishing on you. At least he actually wants to be with you, not just jump your bones." I laugh and hear her frustrated growl.

"I want *mis huesos* jumped!"

"Good luck with that. Enjoy your dinner. I'm exhausted from traveling, and it's two hours ahead here," I remind her with another loud yawn.

"Goodnight, *Cara bonita. Te quiero. Besos.*"

"I love you too. *Besos.*"

I hook the phone to the charger and slip into a nightgown. After scanning my texts, I decide to do a mass text to the girls and Phillip. My other soul sisters will want to know I'm safe and sound in the Windy City. Phillip comes unglued if he doesn't hear from me. One quick text to the group stating I'll reach out tomorrow after the board meeting, and I'm ready to hit the hay.

I'm nervous about the day, never having been to a Board of Directors meeting for the Safe Haven Foundation. My hope is that I can impress them with my campaign statistics and fundraising accomplishments for the year. Closing my eyes, I slow my breathing, allowing my jumpy nerves to relax. I fall asleep dreaming of Caribbean-blue eyes and strong hands caressing me into oblivion.

CHAPTER TWO

My heart pounds and my muscles scream while a fine layer of sweat slowly trickles down the valley between my breasts. Every breath I take comes in harsh, heaving, gusts of air. I'm close, so close, just a little further, and I'll be there. Euphoria hits, and I push that extra bit harder, taking me right over the edge. Runner's high. Sweet baby Jesus, it's so good.

My feet pound against the treadmill, and I smile in victory. A loud whoosh of breath, almost a moan, escapes me. I close my eyes in pure bliss, relishing in the feeling of being completely alive.

"Incredible," someone whispers behind me.

I'm startled out of my nirvana. My foot hits the rubber at a slant, and I'm falling. In a useless attempt, I grapple for purchase against the metal bars of the treadmill, but my sweaty fingers slip and my body flies backward. I tumble over myself, limbs flailing. Strong arms grip my waist and haul me off the machine. I'm crushed against a solid wall of hard muscle.

"Jesus, Gillian! You could have been seriously hurt!" Chase Davis's worried eyes search my face.

I'm stunned into silence. I feel dazed and confused. My heart is pounding a mile a minute, legs weak and wobbly, and my breath comes in huge panting gasps. I grip the skin of his back tightly, trying to get my equilibrium back. He caresses my face with his right hand and firmly holds me around my waist with his left. If he weren't, I don't know that I'd have been able to stand on my own.

"Are you okay?"

"Um, yeah. I think so." I shake my head and bring my hands to his shoulders to steady myself. They meet naked, moist flesh, and my body becomes all too aware of just how close Chase is. Our bodies are plastered against one another. His stomach touching mine, skin to skin, as I take deep breaths. Every part of him is warm, from his hard abdominals to his strong shoulders. Sweat trickles from his hairline, dripping down his neck. I want to lick that drop of sweat off just to see how he tastes.

Having his arms around me feels safe, as if nothing could harm me, not even him. It's a feeling I'm unaccustomed to, but one I crave deep down to the depths of my soul. I've always believed those were feelings I would never, could never have, after what I've survived.

"Are you okay? You scared the hell out of me."

He continues to hold me while things around me slip back into focus. He caresses my cheek with his thumb, and I look up into his eyes. I was not prepared for his level of concern or the worry furrowing his brow. Maybe he's not just an overconfident man with a pretty face and slick words. Begrudgingly, I realize that it's a definite possibility that strong, dominant males don't all use their strength to hurt others.

The pad of his finger sweeps my bottom lip. I gasp, and his eyes go dark. He licks his lips. His grip tightens around my waist and his hand presses against my back. He's going to kiss me. *Oh my God.*

Frantically pushing away from him, I step back and hunch over to take in huge lung-filling breaths of blessed air. I peer up and stand again.

His eyes question mine, and a sly grin adorns his beautiful face.

The man was going to kiss me. I know it. Did I want him to kiss me? *Hell, yes!* my mind screams. Then why the hell did I pull away?

As I come down from panic-induced delirium, I finally notice him in all his glory. And oh, what a sight. Glory, glory, hallelujah. Can I get an amen? Wow. Just wow.

He's wearing gray sweats slung low on his hips and nothing else. He bends and picks up the shirt he must have dropped when he caught me. His chest is bare, and I look my fill. He is in amazing shape. His shoulders and chest are large, strong, and all sinew and muscle. He has a perfectly defined V-shape with a trim waist and flawless abs. This man works out…a lot.

A smattering of dark hair below his belly button trails down and dips farther into his pants. *Oh my, what I wouldn't give to scratch my nails along that patch of hair dipping lower…*

I realize he's still waiting for a response, and I say the first thing that comes to mind, "You're fine." His shocked expression reaches my frazzled brain. "I mean, uh, shit. I mean, I'm fine."

His laugh echoes throughout the space, reminding me where I am. I scan the hotel gym. I'd be mortified if anyone else witnessed my not-so-graceful fall. It seems Chase and I are alone. Groaning, I walk over to the implement of my embarrassment and slap the "Stop" button more harshly than necessary. It comes to a screeching halt. Taking my frustration out on exercise equipment isn't going to assuage my burning pride. I turn and place my hands on my hips in a defensive pose. Chase is leaning against one of the pillars next to us, his arms crossed over his chest. He's completely at ease baring that golden naked skin.

His eyes fill with mirth to accompany that sexy grin on his smug face. It's obvious he finds the situation funny, which irritates the hell out of me. And why the hell hasn't he bothered to put his shirt on? It's distracting. All I can think about is gobbling him up, starting at the delectable patch of skin slick with sweat right under his hip bone. When I'm done with that, I'll drag my tongue across the wide expanse of his chest from his clavicle to his belly button and lower.

God, I'm frustrated, sexually and mentally. Maria was right. I need to get laid. Makes his offer last night seem even more desirable.

I blow out a harsh breath and pull on my ponytail holder. My auburn hair falls around my shoulders.

Chase watches me like a hawk, tracking my clunky movements. I pull my hair back up and sweep the length into a messy bun piled on top of my head. His gaze roams over my form, but he says nothing. The heat I see in those steely orbs is fierce while he takes in every inch of me, from the bottom of my Nikes, up my bare calves and tight workout shorts, over my naked midriff to my sports bra, and back to my face. I tremble under his scrutiny. I wonder if he finds me lacking.

"You're a beautiful woman, Gillian."

I let out the breath I didn't realize I was holding. "That's very kind of you, especially considering my tumble moments ago." Cringing, I look down at my feet. The Nike swoosh is suddenly the most interesting thing in the world.

In two strides, he's beside me, cupping my chin, tipping my face up to his. Those aqua eyes are steely. "You need to learn how to accept a compliment."

I nod, self-preservation instincts coming to full alert. When a man grips a woman, he means business. He searches my eyes once more and releases my chin. The hands at my waist clench into fists, and my gut churns. I'm about to hightail it out of there when his thumb grazes my cheekbone lightly. Last time a man did that to me, it was to check his handiwork.

Breathe, Gigi. I promised myself I would start trusting men again. Start allowing them to touch me. Chase comes off domineering, but I don't think he means to add an element of fear. My own insecurities crop up and twist beautiful moments like these into something they're not. I force myself to relax and take a clarifying breath.

"Good. Now, I'd like to see you this evening."

I tilt my head as my mind tries to make sense of what he's saying. "You mean, like a date?" I watch him closely as the corner of his lips tip up. That small grin is lethal. So much so, I want to see it on his face again and again, preferably while naked.

He shakes out the tank top he is holding, adjusts it, and lifts his long arms over his head to pull it on. It feels like it happens in slow motion. I stare at his muscles as they ripple and stretch while he pulls the tank top over his wide expanse of chest. My body thrums, nipples growing erect and pressing tightly against the flexible fabric of my sports bra.

"You could say that. Unfortunately, I have a dinner engagement, but after, I'd like to share a drink with you. I'll send a car for you at nine p.m."

I'm still stuck on his body. "You work out a lot," I say in awe.

His gaze pierces mine. "When I'm not in a relationship, the need to work out is exemplified." He grins.

My panties moisten. I take a slow breath and lick my lips. "And when you are in a relationship?" *Oh Gigi, you're asking for it.*

He cradles my neck with his large hand. I inhale and crane my head to the opposite side, offering the white column for his taking. The move is instinctual. Usually, I flee when a man puts his hands on me before I'm ready for it. His hand glides down my neck, over my shoulder, as his fingertips trail featherlight along my arm. The limb is thick with sweat from my workout, but he doesn't seem to mind. Quite the opposite. Chase's eyes are dark and hooded as they zero in on my mouth. His pink tongue barely juts out to wet perfectly plump lips. Gooseflesh spreads along my arm. His hand stops at my wrist, and he caresses the pulse point there slowly in a figure eight. Over and over. Eternity.

The action makes me twitchy, needy, and on edge. Chase likes to touch, and often. It's not something I'm used to. He's practically a stranger, but my body bows and arcs towards his as if it's always known his touch. *Traitor.*

"When I'm in a relationship, I'm too busy fucking what's mine to need to work out."

Those words settle deep into my belly like a warm soup on a cold day. A new sheen of sweat breaks along my skin, heat building white-hot within my core.

Does he want to fuck me?

No. Something deep in my subconscious awakens to remind me of my goals. I've made a solid vow not to get swept away in a man again. Here I am, hanging on every word, every tilt of his perfect face, losing myself in his eyes. Jesus. This isn't me. I've learned my lesson. The past taught me that you can't trust men. They are out for one thing and one thing only. Control. But what do I really have against sex? No, *fucking*. That's what he's after.

I've never been in a relationship that was just about physical needs. Frankly, it scares the hell out of me. What if he *needs* to throw me against a wall and take me against my will? Not a chance. Since the moment I met this man, my libido has been in overdrive. All I think about is what it would be like to be surrounded by this perfect male specimen. Consumed.

I know this is dangerous and he could easily break me, yet I still *want* him beyond reason. It's illogical. I'm officially losing my mind. Bat-shit crazy.

"Just a drink," I finally answer his earlier request.

Chase's smile at my agreement could light up a room. Perfectly even teeth sparkle and shine under the harsh fluorescent lights of the gym. "I will send my driver promptly at nine p.m. just outside the hotel lobby. Do not be late. I detest tardiness," he says. "As much as I'd like to stay and chat"—he raises his eyebrows, scans my body once more, and bites his lip—"and look at your half-naked body, I confess, I must go."

Before I can respond, he turns and strides off, leaving the gym and a stunned redhead in his wake. I watch the exit long after he's gone. *Did that just happen?* What is it about

Chase Davis that continues to stupefy me? Is it as simple as being wildly attracted to him? Can't be. A connection perhaps? My girlfriend Bree would tell me it's the universe forcing us together.

I spend the next few minutes going over our two encounters again. My mind wanders as I enjoy the view from the windows overlooking the Chicago skyline. It's breathtaking. This hotel provides for extreme luxuries. Patrons are able to view the entire city while they burn calories on a treadmill or elliptical.

"Too busy fucking what's mine." His words burn a path through my subconscious. What if I were his? The simple thought makes my belly go warm. I squeeze my thighs together to relieve some of the pressure building between them.

He's obviously successful. If you consider the meticulously tailored suit he wore last night, the air of authority around him, and the fact that he's going to send a driver for me this evening—plus the little tidbit of owning this lush hotel. Definitely the type of man who can take care of himself. *And me.*

Though, I don't need to be taken care of. My mother taught me long ago to never count on a man.

"Take a look in the mirror, Gigi. You see that person? That's the only person you can count on in this world. Never expect a man to be your everything. He will fail miserably. If you want something in life, you must go after it."

She was right. Men have done nothing but harm and prevent me from reaching my goals and dreams. Not anymore. My cell phone alarms on the treadmill. I've got to get ready for this board meeting. It's six thirty a.m., and

I'm meeting my boss in an hour. Scurrying out of the gym, I leave my thoughts of Chase for the birds.

After a lightning-fast shower, I dry off and pull out the clothing I set aside for the meeting. I look at myself in the floor-length mirror in my room. I'm wearing a form-fitting black pencil skirt that falls just above my knees. It fits like a glove. I turn to view my backside. The slit up the center of the back hits mid-thigh. Respectable, yet feminine. I've coupled the skirt with an emerald-green silk blouse. It's sleeveless and gathers at the front, keeping my breasts away from any unwanted attention. My hair is up and away from my face in a sleek chignon, leaving a delicate swooping layer of hair running across my forehead like a strip of fiery red across a white canvas. I slip stocking feet into black suede four-inch Guess heels. They have this enticing cutout right at the arch that makes me feel innately sexy, even though the outfit puts off a smart vibe. I shrug into my matching blazer, and I'm out the door.

★ ★ ★ ★

My boss, Taye Jefferson, waits in the hotel lobby Starbucks. He sits sideways in one of the small chairs, holding a white foam cup. It is barely visible under his large paw. Taye is an African American SUV-sized man in his late forties and the Director of Contributions for the Safe Haven Foundation.

I love working with Taye. He treats me as his equal and hates yes-men. He wants to know what I'm thinking and genuinely appreciates my opinions. We make a great team and have been very successful. I've only been at the company a couple years, working my way up from assistant to manager. In that short time, we have found an easy partnership in our charitable work.

He checks his watch and looks up with a big smile. "Right on time as usual, Gigi. Woman after my own heart."

"Uh-huh, that's what you tell all the ladies, especially Mrs. Jefferson," I tease him.

Taye smiles wide. When his wife is mentioned, he gets this cheesy grin across his face. He truly loves her. What I wouldn't give to have a man appreciate me like that, but it's likely never to happen. A good man wouldn't want a woman with my history—damaged goods as Justin would say.

There's a Starbucks cup across from Taye and a crusty, crunchy muffin that looks delicious.

"For me?"

He nods. "A little welcome to the world of board meetings and proving yourself accountable to the bigwigs."

I take a sip and the creamy, hot liquid surges over my taste buds. I want to bow down and worship the Starbucks Gods for making such a perfect combination of espresso, cream, and vanilla goodness. "Mmmmm, Taye, you know what I like. Thank you." I break off a piece of the crunchy muffin and take a bite. It's as satisfying as the latte. Well, almost. "So what's the plan for this morning?" I ask around a mouthful of muffin. Not exactly the best manners, but Taye is used to it. We're like family, rather than boss and subordinate. There's an ease about being around him. Most big men make me uncomfortable. Taye has always made me feel the exact opposite. I feel safe around him. Much like I did when Chase's arms were around me this morning.

He shuffles through his briefcase and hands me something. "I just received the agenda last night from the president's secretary. We're on the schedule just after lunch. President's Office speaks first, and then Business Development runs through their latest plans for new affiliations. Then lunch, Contributions, and the Volunteer Department will go over their recent cases. Tomorrow, there's Marketing, Finance, and general Board items."

"Do you have any pointers you want to share? I'm afraid I'm going to make a complete fool of myself. This morning I tripped and almost killed myself on the treadmill." I chuckle and shovel in another bite.

He shoots me a worried look. "Are you okay, Gigi? Did you hurt yourself?"

"Just my pride. A man caught me." *Chase.* He keeps popping to the surface of my mind. It's official. I'm a lunatic.

Taye continues to stare. He tips his head to the side in one of his "tell me, my child" gestures that usually has me spilling my guts. Not this time.

"It just rattled me, and I was already nervous about today." I pat his hand with affection.

"Just do what you always do." He smiles and sips his coffee. "Dazzle them with your statistics and campaign numbers. You have the Midas touch when it comes to direct mail and tele-fundraising. Just explain what you've done differently and the outcomes." I nod. "Just be yourself."

I roll my eyes. "Oh, come on, Taye. A cliché, really? Just be yourself? Did you not eat your Wheaties this morning, big guy?"

He laughs and leans back in his chair. "I need to work on my pep talks. You ready? It's ten to eight. From what I remember, the Chairman despises people who are late."

Someone else recently mentioned not being tardy.

Wonder what Chase would do if I didn't show or was late to his little nine p.m. command appearance. We grab our things and shuffle toward the large bank of elevators. The boardroom is on the third floor with the other convention and meeting rooms.

"At the last board meeting I attended," Taye says, "the chairman made a board member wait outside until the first break in the schedule. Then the board member had to apologize to the entire room for being late." He stabs button number three on the brightly lit panel inside the elevator, and the car rises.

"You're kidding? The chairman treats a colleague like an errant child?"

"Well, he's the founder and chairman. He's crazy rich. Donates over half our foundation's budget each year. Forty million annually."

I whistle. The elevator dings. We step into the corridor, and a sign on a pedestal states, "Safe Haven Foundation Board of Directors Meeting." An arrow points down the hall.

"Forty million dollars? Damn!" That's an obscene amount of money. Anyone who can donate that kind of capital to one foundation can't be all bad. People don't just hand over millions to a charity without having a huge heart, especially since the work we do is so personal. We protect and help battered women. I shake my head before going back to my indignation. "That doesn't give him the right to humiliate someone publicly."

"Agreed. He's a bastard for sure—a filthy rich one. You know, he pays for all the board members to stay here in the lap of luxury."

I wondered how a charitable organization could afford such a swanky location.

"Word is, he didn't want to be seen in a low rent hotel. Would ruin his image."

It's impossible to stop the grimace spreading across my face. "Yikes, the man sounds like a jerk."

Taye laughs. I'm more nervous than before. The chair sounds like a barbarian. We make our way to the open door at the end of the corridor. Several men and women in dark suits of varying shades of black and gray mill around the entrance. It makes the emerald green I chose pop in contrast to the funeral vibe.

Taye introduces me to four men and two women in the span of fifteen seconds. I shake their hands and smile politely. He ushers me into a large room where more individuals, also in sharp suits, are already seated, preparing for the meeting. We find place cards with our names and take a seat.

"Gigi, I'll set up the laptops if you get us another cup of coffee." Taye gestures to the sideboard with the coffee pitchers. "I'll have decaf."

Nodding, I head to the table. I'm careful to walk slowly, with my head held high, trying valiantly to hide my nerves. This is the first meeting I've been invited to since my promotion to Contributions Manager. I want to make a good impression. My future with the Safe Haven Foundation depends on it.

I fill two small coffee cups with decaf. Each cup has a tiny gold trim along the rim. I'll bet they're real china. Everything in the hotel seems top-notch. Even if the chairman is paying the bill, it seems frivolous. Turning, coffee in hand, I take one step into a rock solid chest. Luckily, I'm still holding the two cups out to my side and don't spill them.

Slowly, I look up, ready to apologize, when I'm stricken by the distinct, heady smell of sandalwood and citrus. *Oh, no!* Aquamarine orbs prettier than an open blue sky bore into mine. The beauty steals my breath. Excitement and fear scream through my veins in equal parts. Rigid hands hold me by the waist. His presence surrounds me, and the room fades into nothing but him.

"Miss Callahan. We meet again." A smug grin adorns his chiseled features.

I'm disheartened that he didn't use my first name.

CHAPTER THREE

"You've got to be kidding me!"

Chase grabs the coffee cups and gives them to a hotel steward who hovers nearby. "Put these next to Miss Callahan and Mr. Jefferson's name plates," he instructs.

Based on his obvious knowledge of Taye, and now me, he had to have known who I was when we met at the bar last night. He never said a word. Frustration and anger war within me.

Chase grasps my hand and brings it to those plump lips. Electricity zaps me the second his lips touch my knuckles. His expressive eyes darken, pupils dilating. I swear I feel the lightest sweep of his tongue in between my middle and ring finger with that kiss. I gasp, and his eyebrows rise. He watches me intently, sending me crazy mixed signals.

I hear the softest "Mmm," and I'm lost in the sensation of his nearness. His body dwarfs mine by a good half foot, even in heels. I zero in on the bit of flesh still pressed against my hand. The air around us is sizzling, and I'm once again breathing in his woodsy fruity love potion concoction. Finally he lets go as Taye joins us.

"Gigi, I see you've met Mr. Davis, the chairman of the board," Taye says.

The. Spell. Is. Broken.

Hazarding a glance at Chase, I'm certain my bafflement shows in my widened eyes. *I am so screwed!*

"You're the chairman of the board?" I close my eyes and attempt to piece the puzzle together. How the hell did I not know this? Recognition slaps me against the forehead. The company letterhead has "C. Davis, Chairman of the Board" listed prominently at the top. I sigh. *So stupid!* I should have been smart enough to put two and two together. Now the joke's on me.

Chase shakes Taye's hand. "Mr. Jefferson, good to see you again. I trust you're well?"

"Yes, Mr. Davis. Thank you. I've brought along Gillian Callahan, our Contributions Manager," Taye says with pride.

Chase looks at me and discreetly skims me from head to heeled toe. A flicker of heat fills his blue gaze. "We've met, briefly. I look forward to your presentation this afternoon, Miss Callahan."

He acts as if nothing happened between us. Technically, nothing has...besides a few caresses and a near kiss. Now that I know who he is, that kiss will never happen in this lifetime, and neither will the non-date only "drinks" that were supposed to happen tonight.

I cannot believe my luck. My mystery man, my tall dark and handsome, is the chairman of the board of my foundation. I want to crawl under a rock and die. Instead, I pick up my bootstraps. This is not the time to crumble. I've been through much more embarrassing and harrowing days over the past several years. This is but a bump in the road. A sexy-as-sin-man is just gum on the bottom of my shoe. I'll scrape off the feelings I have for him and move forward with my plan to secure my future.

A lovely blond woman taps Chase's shoulder. "Excuse me, Mr. Davis. It's eight o'clock."

He clasps his hands together. "Excellent. Let's get started then." He winks and turns toward the head of the table.

Taye grasps my elbow and leads me to our table closer to the end of room. I fall into my seat rather clumsily. Chase starts the meeting, and I hunker down, taking notes and trying desperately to clear my foggy mind of all things sexy-man-in-nothing-but-workout-sweats-and-washboard-abs-you-could crack-a-tooth-on.

The rest of the meeting is spent paying close attention and doing my best to avoid looking at Chase. I already feel better about my decision to blow him off. We break for fifteen minutes, and I rush out of the room. I need the space.

Entering the solace of the women's restroom, I lean against the cool multicolored tile. The washroom has a quaint sitting area with large puffy couches. A mirror spans an entire wall. A large square sink fills the space, almost like an ornate trough. Turning on the water, I chill my hands, wrists, and the crook of my elbow like my mother used to when I was child. The cooling of my pressure points does wonders at calming rankled nerves. He's the fricking chairman of the board. I refrain from slamming my head against the mirror to knock the stupid out of me. *Break all ties and run.*

Behind me, I hear two women enter the sitting area giggling. "Did you see how perfectly those slacks fit that tight ass?" one of them says.

"How could you not? Makes you just want to wrap your legs around that cowboy and ride him into morning!" the other woman drawls with a southern accent.

"Maybe you should make a go for Davis, Claire. He seems to like tall blondes." The first woman laughs.

Peering around the wall that separates the two spaces, I see Claire Dalton, the board member from Texas. The other woman I haven't met yet. They adjust their hair and makeup in the vanity mirror. I plaster myself along the wall, staying out of sight, and listen.

"I think I will. Maybe at tonight's dinner I'll make a move on him," Claire drawls.

No, no, no, no! I want to scream! Wait. If he goes for the blond Barbie doll, he'll forget about me. My job won't be at risk, and my sanity will stay intact. It's a win-win.

My job at the foundation is more than just a position or somewhere I pull a salary. The past few years have been rife with hard work while I tried to piece my life back together after the *Justin Period*. I'm not letting anyone take me away from my goal. Especially not a man. Even if he's disarmingly handsome and makes me quake with desire. Nothing matters except securing my future.

The two women leave the sitting area. My fifteen minutes of freedom are up. Sighing, I square my shoulders. I can do this

Outside the bathroom, I see that Claire doesn't waste time. She and Chase are standing not ten feet from the bathroom door. His back is to me and Claire is laughing, batting those long eyelashes of hers. I inch my way around the two of them, careful not to interrupt.

A firm hand grasps my wrist and tugs me to a halt. "Miss Callahan, may I have a word?" His eyes pierce mine.

Taken away by his essence once more, I'm rooted to the ground where I stand, awaiting his next request. It's annoying the innate control this man has over me.

"Claire, it's a very nice offer, but I have plans after dinner. I'll be just a moment."

Claire looks deflated at his dismissal. I have an evil desire to stick my tongue out at her retreating form. *He doesn't want you! He wants me.* Not the frame of mind I need to have right now.

I pull my hand from Chase's grasp. "Don't manhandle me," I whisper in an irritated voice. The man is constantly touching me. It needs to stop.

"I didn't want you running away." He takes a deep breath.

Knotting my fingers together, I look down at my heels to calm my nerves.

"I just wanted to remind you about this evening."

Looking up, I meet his gaze. "You still want to meet me?"

"More than anything," he says with confidence.

I fully expected him to come to the conclusion I had. Our pseudo-date was a no-go. I inhale sharply and shake my head.

His eyes graze over my body like a caress. "Nothing's changed."

He looks around the hallway. The rest of the group has returned to the meeting room, leaving us alone. The pace of my heart picks up. He leans, and his lips lightly stroke the shell of my ear. A tremble runs from my head to my toes. A warm wet sensation tickles the curved flesh of my ear. His tongue. Liquid fire spreads from my ear down my neck, through my chest, settling in my belly. The tender space between my legs feels heavy, aching to be touched. I clench my thighs. Zings of pleasure shoot through my body.

"You're stunning in green," he whispers. "Brings out the color of your eyes. I could easily get lost in them."

Chase's words, his nearness, the breath against my ear, all compound to make me dizzy. I steady myself against the solid wall of his chest with a shaking hand. I curl my fingers around his tie and tug him toward my mouth. All rational thought is gone. I want him more than I want my next breath. I reach up on my toes to bring our mouths closer. He pulls away, the silky fabric slipping through my fingers.

Reality crashes in, and once again the spell is broken.

I was going to kiss him! Right here. Right where anyone could see us. Jesus, what's wrong with me? This is not who I am. It's him. He makes me feel needy, wanton, and sexually depraved. Prickles of embarrassment coat my skin.

"Another time," he says, though his smile is wicked and would drop the panties of any female in his presence.

Thank God one of us has his wits about him. I must have left mine in the box marked "Private" under my bed.

Chase sets his hand against my lower back as he leads me towards the boardroom. "Nine o'clock," he reminds me. His hand falls away as I enter the room to take my seat.

The meeting continues and the business development director drones on and on about the new affiliations and business arrangements he's negotiated this past year.

"Thank you, Mr. Howe, for your update." Chase cuts off the director somewhat abruptly, noting the allotted hour he was given has passed. "I believe we have lunch, and then the Contributions Department will give their presentation." He looks at Taye and then me.

Taye smiles confidently. I'm trying in earnest to snag the confidence I had before I learned my Superman is the chairman of the board.

Taye pats my shoulder. "You're going to do great," he whispers.

Nodding, I smile.

When I look up, Chase is blatantly staring at me, his features pinched. He seems to be assessing the communication between Taye and me. Whatever Chase is thinking, he doesn't seem pleased. I continue my conversation with Taye and ignore Chase's stare until lunch arrives.

Watching Chase in action today has been quite a treat. The questions he asks each presenter are calculated, to the point, and innately brilliant. His expectations of his peers and the foundation staff are high, ones he seems to have also given himself.

A hotel server sets a silver tray in front of me. "The filet, miss, is seared and broiled with a blue cheese butter crust, coupled with hickory smoked bacon mashed potatoes and seasoned sautéed vegetables."

"Thank you." My mouth waters at the sight of the food. The muffin this morning was tasty but pales in comparison to this feast. I can't recall the last time I had filet mignon. Must have been prior to my mom's passing. She always did love the finer things in life. Not that we ever got to indulge much on our little family's budget.

I take a bite, and the taste explodes like a firecracker on the fourth of July. The texture of the meat is utter perfection. It's a soft melt-in-your-mouth bit of heaven. I moan in contentment, closing my eyes to enjoy the experience. When I open them, Chase has his eyes on me, but they are no longer the stunning blue of the ocean. They are black as night. His pupils are dilated, and he's gripping his fork so tightly his knuckles have turned white. His jaw is clenched and so taut I wonder briefly if he's angry. He lets out a deep exhale that I can almost feel against my skin even though there's a ten-foot gap between us.

I know that look. I've seen it on men several times in my life. He's turned on. He shakes his head and tunnels his fingers through his hair haphazardly, giving it that sexy, tussled, just-got-out-of-bed look. He's clearly affected by me physically. As much as I need to avoid starting anything with him, the sexual tension I feel in his presence is stifling. I bite my lip and look anywhere but at his heated gaze.

"Are you about ready?" Taye's voice startles me.

"Yeah, I think I am. The numbers don't lie. Time to blow them away." I smile widely at my colleague and friend.

Sitting straighter in my chair, I look at Chase, pleased that I've gotten under his skin a little. Chase's subtle smile fills me with light. Regardless of what's going on between us, I came here to prove my worth to this foundation, and I'm going to do just that.

Taye gives his update on major giving donors and quite a few of the board members seem impressed. "At the Chairman's Giving level, Mr. Davis, we request that you sit down face-to-face with the donor. It would be at a time and place of your choosing, based on your schedule."

Chase tips his chin, an air of authority surrounding the movement. "And at what level would that donor be giving?"

"Miss Callahan and I have done a great deal of research and secured recommendations from a national philanthropic organization—"

"Brass tacks, Mr. Jefferson," Chase warns. "What does one pay to have the pleasure of my company?"

Several board members snicker, and he grins, merriment taking over the all business fierceness in his eyes.

"Six figures, Mr. Davis." A couple of people gasp. "You are a very desirable man, Mr. Davis."

Chase's eyebrows shoot up. He flicks his gaze flicks to me and then back to Taye as he continues his spiel.

"Direct access to one of the wealthiest men in the United States can be very valuable to anyone with that kind of disposable capital. I imagine anyone's access to you on a regular basis is limited." Taye smoothes down his jacket. "Is that not the case?"

Chase looks at a hulk of a man standing near the door. I hadn't noticed him before. He's almost as broad shouldered as he is tall. Looks like an NFL football player. He's stoic, unmoving, his arms firmly planted across his chest. Slicked back black hair adds to his very Italian mafia-type features. I wonder why he's here and who he is.

"You are correct," Chase responds. "Access to me is strictly on a needs basis outside the foundation."

"So a donation in the six figures would be worthy of access to you?"

Everything is riding on the answer to Taye's question. He's been preparing this moment for three months.

"I'm agreeable to it," Chase says.

I release my breath in a whoosh. Taye got him. Slam dunk! I was proud. Taye worked so hard on this proposal, and Chase's agreement to visit top donors face-to-face is the last piece of the puzzle. The Leadership Society would move forward.

"You won't regret it, Mr. Davis." Taye beams.

"Don't let me, Mr. Jefferson. Great work. I look forward to seeing how this pans out." Chase smiles at me. "I believe Miss Callahan has some information to share with the board."

His smile, coupled with his agreement to Taye's request, gives me the confidence boost I need.

Over the next thirty minutes, I dazzle them with glossy charts and graphs showing in great detail how the Contributions Department has met its revenue goals for the fiscal year in charitable gifts. Not only met, but also exceeded it by forty-five percent.

"Miss Callahan, what did you do to make these numbers increase so drastically?" asks one prim and proper-looking board member.

"Well, Ms. Conrad, I took a different approach." I pace the room. "The foundation had been sending out mailings that were about the foundation and the work we do in a generic professional way. However, it lacked sincerity. The stories of the women who so desperately need our help on a regular basis show a more personal aspect."

A couple of the board members nod.

"I interviewed some of the women who had been battered and were having trouble seeing the light at the end of the tunnel until they found us." I clear my throat but my voice cracks and shakes. "I shared how we helped save their lives. It spoke volumes to the donors."

I choke up again when I remember my last interview of a woman who had suffered a brutal beating. She couldn't walk for a week afterward. The foundation helped her cut ties with her attacker and to start a new life. I held her hand

and cried right along with her.

Tears blur my vision. I dab at them before taking a deep breath. Chase stands, goes to the drinks table, and brings me a glass of water. I gently sip while getting my emotions in check.

Now is not the time to relive the past. Chase's hand warms my shoulder as he tips his head to the side. "Okay? Need a moment?" He searches my face, clearly showing his concern.

I nod and plaster on the fakest smile I can muster. The last thing I need is to breakdown in the middle of the most important presentation of my career.

"Thank you." I clear my throat and shift my shoulders back.

"Wow, Miss Callahan. I don't think anyone here had any inkling you wrote those letters. We also weren't aware they were about real women the foundation had saved." Chase's voice holds adoration. He wasn't just saying it to win over the group, or me.

I feel nothing but a deep respect for him in that moment. I nod and set down the glass of water.

"Well, let me be the first to congratulate you on a job very well done. Please continue with your presentation."

"Thank you, Mr. Davis." I watch him walk back to his seat.

He focuses solely on me as he gracefully sits. His intensity may get to me, but I'm thrilled that he's seeing my work and the value I have to the organization, not just someone he wants to bed.

"The next area our department focused on was tele-fundraising." For the next fifteen minutes, I hit them with the results of our successful calling campaign. "If you would be so kind as to review the information and the additional fundraising options, I believe we could save a lot of women with the money we'd raise." Scanning each member of the board, I can tell that I'm making an impact. "We understand these massive changes take time, and we appreciate the board's consideration. Thank you."

"Very impressive, Miss Callahan. You have given us a great deal to think about over the coming weeks," Chase offers. He glances at his colleagues. "I want each of you to review the information each department has brought to the table today and come to our next board meeting with your list of questions, concerns, and your initial decision on whether to move forward with the recommendations from our staff. We will take a vote at the next meeting."

The board members nod, write notes, and the board secretary rapidly taps out her transcription of the action.

Taye nudges my shoulder as I sit down. His full pearly white smile beams, the one he says is the only way to find him in the dark. Under the table, he holds out his hand. I smack it lightly. We both quietly snap. It's our mini-high five "won and then done" victory bump.

As the meeting concludes, I'm thinking of a nice hot bath to end the intense day. I'm about to leave with Taye when Chase grasps my hand and pulls me to his side. I wave off Taye and feel the jolt like two magnets reaching for each other. My body flows toward his so easily. I've known him for twenty-four hours, but the pull is undeniable.

"Gillian, I'd like to introduce you to someone." He guides me to the burly man in black. "Gillian, this is Jack Porter. My bodyguard, driver, my safety net. He will be picking you up this evening."

"Good to meet you." I hold out my hand.

Instead of taking it, Jack looks me up and down. I'm not sure if he's assessing me as a woman, or checking to see if I have any conspicuous bulges that could hide a concealed weapon. I tilt my chin defensively and place my hands on my hips. "Take a picture, it will last longer," I say to the huge man.

He grumbles, but doesn't respond.

Chase laughs a full-bellied laugh as he leads me away from the mob boss. The man didn't say two words to me. Strange company Chase keeps.

"He didn't even shake my hand. And it's rude to stare like that."

Chase continues to laugh as we walk briskly out of the room, his hand at my lower back. A girl could get used to being led by Superman. Maybe Lois Lane purposely put herself in all those dangerous situations so she'd be saved by the man of steel.

We're a good distance from everyone else when I realize I'm being propelled into another small meeting room. Jack comes and stands in front of the door and guards the entrance.

"Chase," I say in warning, not altogether comfortable with being guided into a dark room.

"Trust me." He ushers me farther into the room. And without question, I do trust him. There's no rhyme or reason to it. The man has done nothing but put me off kilter since the moment our eyes met across the bar last night. I should be more circumspect, but the prevailing feeling I have near him is "cherished." I'm not sure why or where the feeling comes from, but it's filling the doubts that usually control all my decisions with something other than fear.

As my eyes adjust to the dark, I notice a normal-sized conference table with a bunch of cushy leather office chairs. I'm about to ask what we're doing here when Chase grasps my arms, whirls me around, and pins me against the closed door.

A protest sits on the edge of my lips until his mouth prevents speech. The moment our lips touch, it's magic. I lose all thought. His fingers intertwine with mine, palm to palm. Electricity sizzles between our clasped hands as he holds them over my head, pressing his large body against me. The power behind his kiss, the wet heat, fingers clutching, chest pinning me to the door is exhilarating. It's like a fast car racing around the track, going the distance right before crossing the finish line in an explosion of excitement.

The forbidden nature of his passion has my mind in a drunken tizzy. The realization that I've allowed him to control me is disconcerting, but it feels too good to stop. His lips nibble and pluck, and a delicious sensation ricochets through every pore as sparks of lust race through me. I need more. Of him. Of his mouth. Just more.

I suck his tongue greedily and am rewarded with a guttural groan. Chase pulls away to catch a breath and then delves in deep, leaving no space uncharted. God, the man knows how to kiss. He tastes of coffee, the tiramisu we had for dessert, and something darker, richer. My entire body is on fire. Every nerve ending is hypersensitive, anticipating his next touch. He lets go of my hands and brings one to the side of my neck, tipping my head where he wants, and then he plunders again, taking total possession. I can feel the weight of his body pushing me harder against the door. The thick length of his erection digs into my hip.

His left hand burns a trail from my neck, over my breast, and settles at my rib cage. I want to tell him to go back up where I need him most, but he steals my breath with his searching tongue. I can do nothing but grip his back to keep him firmly pressed against me, rubbing my body along his, trying but failing to assuage the burning desire ripping me apart. He sweeps his thumb across the silky fabric at my ribs in small massaging circles. The touch fills me with want, with the need to take him, right here, right now. My brain tells me to stop this, let go. Walk away. It's too much. My body, however, has different plans. I arch into him to feel more, to get closer.

Both of his hands encircle my hips as he thrusts his erection against me. I moan into his mouth, loving the fact that I please him, make him hard. He devours me with his tongue, teeth, and lips. He moves his hand lower, pulling one leg up and hooking it over his hip, holding it there. The angle is sublime. He grinds in the perfect spot between my thighs, captivating me with every stroke. Desire shatters through me, soaking the wisp of lace between us. My entire focus is on the press and release of his body as he pushes me to unbelievable heights of pleasure. Taking advantage of my hiked leg, he glides his fingers to where my thigh high is held in place by the thin strip of fabric attached to a black garter.

"Jesus Christ, you're wearing thigh highs," he says in a strangled voice against my mouth.

His teeth nip my swollen lips to the point where pleasure and pain mingle. I grin against his teeth. Some of my secrets are good ones. My penchant for sexy lingerie is a favorite. He comes in for another scorching kiss, pressing his turgid length deep against my clit. Tingles of pleasure ripple out from the sensitive nub. I fear I may come here, against this door, like a common hussy.

Chase kisses his way down my neck, and I'm lost in the sensation. His natural woodsy and citrus scent is stronger as his skin shimmers with sweat. It's intoxicating, pulling me further into the abyss that is Chase. I tremble with need, my breath ragged as I grip and claw, trying to pull him deeper against me. Merge as one.

His lips brush my ear, sending chills down my spine. I hear his intake of breath as he drags his warm tongue down the column of my neck, tasting, devouring. He moans and bites down hard on the ball of my shoulder. Excitement builds between my thighs, moisture pooling and soaking my panties. No man has taken control of me and my body in this way before. I want to bottle it whole, spray it on every surface in my bedroom so I can revisit it…often. It's unusual, frightening and freeing at the same time. I want to beg for more, not run in fear. Chase brings out a side of me I don't recognize, but am desperate to release.

Chase nips at my ear. I can feel every breath as his words caress the skin of my neck. "You're driving me mad." He bites my earlobe and I gasp. Then he pecks my lips with a kiss.

"I won't be able to make it through dinner"—kiss again—"without thinking about you"—kiss—"against this door, wearing those fucking thigh highs"—kiss—"and how I'm going to remove them with my teeth." His hips rhythmically circle and press harder into me with every staccato kiss.

"God, Chase," I moan.

He dips his tongue into my mouth as he presses against me exactly where I need it most. A cry tears from my throat. I bite my lip, almost drawing blood. He soothes the hurt with his tongue. I reach down and squeeze his tight ass, bringing him closer. It's too much. I have to have him.

"Please," I beg shamelessly and punctuate my need by digging my stiletto into the tender meat of his thigh.

He winces, hissing through his teeth. "God, I can't wait to get you into my bed." He finishes his statement by sealing his mouth over the skin of my neck.

I'm sure he'll leave marks. I almost hope he does. That thought is a first for me. I've had a man leave too many marks. Never have I wanted them to be there.

Chase picks up the pace of grinding me into sexual oblivion. His cock perfectly presses against my clit. All thoughts of the past are gone. I'm plowed right back into a haze of need. The pleasure almost reaches the apex, a few more strokes and I'll fly—

A brisk knock on the door behind me startles us both. We both jump away from one another and scramble to readjust our clothes like two teenagers caught by the adults.

"Just a moment!" Chase says to the closed door.

My heart races as I smooth my skirt with shaky hands. Our breathing comes in tight bursts. I'm trembling, and the knowledge of what was about to take place is like an ice pick to my chest. The chairman of the board was dry humping me against a door. *Shit!*

Chase scans me while smoothing his suit coat and tie. He grips both the lapels of his jacket, shaking it in place before buttoning the jacket over a very impressive erection. I cringe as he covers his need for me. He catches me sizing up his package, shoots me an impish grin, and finger combs his hair into that sexy tussled look, which this time is actually from a sex act. Chase reaches out and glides his fingertips down the side of my face. He clasps my chin and tips it up. He pets the cheekbone and pulls me into a simple, reaffirming kiss.

"Tonight. I will have you," he promises, and then opens the door.

His cell phone rings, bringing me out of the sex-induced coma. With a flick of the wrist, his phone is to his ear and he barks into it, exiting. He takes one look back and shoots me a saucy wink that I can feel from the tips of my toes to the ends of my hair.

I wait a respectable amount of time until I can't hear any voices outside. If I am honest, I'm really waiting to make sure I can walk without having to hold myself up using the wall like a drunken college student on frat night. I'd be mortified if anyone caught me coming out of a dark room with Chase. I can only imagine what they'd think. Probably assume I'm sleeping my way to the top or something equaling demoralizing.

Venturing out, I see that Jack is waiting for me. He has my laptop and purse. He hands me my cell phone.

"Mr. Davis asked me to wait for you to ensure you got your things. He also said to give you his personal cell phone number and asked that you text him that you still plan to meet him. I've added it to your contacts. Do not share it with anyone," he warns.

"Thanks," I say to his retreating form. The man is so on

edge. I wonder who pissed in his Cheerios today.

How odd. Chase had his driver, bodyguard, whatever he is, wait for me and ensure that I text him about a meeting that's less than three hours away. Looks like Mr. Chairman of the Board has a few insecurities of his own. The thought makes me feel a little better, but not by much.

I open my contacts and find him. Of course the mob boss entered Chase's information in perfect text, appropriate capitalization on the C and D. He added his cell, business, and home numbers. He also provided his e-mail. I guess that leaves no possible reason for me not to reach him in one format or another.

I pull together a quick text.

To: Chase Davis
From: Gillian Callahan
Your linebacker expressed your wishes. I'll meet you.

Immediately I receive a reply.

To: Gillian Callahan
From: Chase Davis
I'll be waiting.

The thought of what will likely take place tonight makes my stomach feel tight and fluttery. Anxiety swirls and festers, pricking my skin as if I were getting acupuncture. I want this man. Really want him.

In my bed. In my body. In every way possible.

I'm torn. A man has never made me feel this high or want to fall so hard. Chase brings out desire in me so fierce I can barely avoid its burn. After the conference room escapade, I know we'll set the sheets ablaze. *I want you in my bed,* he said. That one sentence has me twitching with longing and impatience. His need for me makes me want to weep in frustration. Regardless of how bad it will look if people find out, I've got to have him.

Lord help me, I'm about to make one beautiful mistake.

CHAPTER FOUR

Three hours have passed since the dry hump against a wall with the sexiest man alive. Three whole hours to find every excuse possible to prove that Chase Davis is a bad idea, probably fatal to my career.

Yes, he's unbelievably gorgeous, with kisses that make me weak in the knees. He can bring me from zero to sixty with an intense gaze across a crowded room. How many men have the capability of doing that to a woman?

Attraction aside, I won't ruin my chances for success with the foundation. Years ago, Safe Haven scraped me off the floor, brought me back from the dead, and gave me life. After Justin, I cannot afford to let my life get off track.

Justin. Deep, utter revulsion at the thought of that name makes me queasy. Taking a few deep breaths, I count to ten. Slowly, the swill of disgusting thoughts of Justin leaves, readying me to let down a man whose body was crafted by angels. Chase is definitely a catch. Doesn't matter. This girl is throwing this particular fish back into the sea of distracting, beautiful men.

Chase could have any woman he wants. With that face and wallet, he could point and click the perfect woman and she'd appear. I'm nobody special. Besides, from what I found online, he's had several perfect pieces of arm candy in the past year alone. Lengthy model-thin beauties, perfect trophy material for a man like Chase. My Google kung fu is dead on. Besides, I'm not even his type. He likes perfectly tan statuesque blondes, not pale curvy redheads.

With my decision made, I walk briskly toward the glass double doors leading outside the hotel. The wind whips my hair, and I clutch my blazer tightly to ward off the chill. Like a shiny black ghost, a sleek pitch-black stretch limousine parks in front of me. Wow. Hadn't expected that. I've never ridden in a limo before. The little girl in me wants to squeal with delight.

"Miss Callahan, Mr. Davis is expecting you." Jack holds the car door open.

I slide along the smooth leather seat. It's cool against the skin of my palm. The interior is lush. Cherry wood panels span one side, hosting an array of glass tumblers and amber-colored liquids in crystal decanters. Jack drops his huge form into the driver's seat. "Feel free to have a drink."

"No, thank you." I lean back into the supple leather, resting my eyes as he turns out onto the busy street.

Downtown Chicago is alight with the sounds of the city. People mill along the concrete streets, taking advantage of the hodgepodge of stores mixed in with restaurants. We pass an elevated train, sitting high above the ground a couple stories up. I've heard of the L, but never seen it in person. The skyscrapers spanning the city jut up into the sky in varying shapes and sizes, reminding me of stacked Legos. San Francisco seems relatively sleepy compared to this eclectic mix of modern and old-school. Most of the people who live in San Francisco are commuters who work in a city they can't afford to live in. By six, it is a ghost town, everyone having gone back to his Bay Area or Valley residence. Here, the city is alive and thrumming, matching my rapid pulse as we near our destination.

"Where are we going?" I ask my quiet companion.

"Mr. Davis has requested your presence at the Sky Lounge, one of his bars. We will be there in less than five minutes."

His driver, someone Chase claims to be a friend, is not the friendliest guy. I guess that's part of his job. He's supposed to be as scary as hell so that no one messes with his charge.

Am I supposed to sit quietly and let him drive Miss Daisy? Or is he supposed to keep me company? My natural inclination is to talk, and I'd like to find out more about his boss. Hell, *my* boss.

"How long have you worked for Mr. Davis?"

"Five years, but I've known him his entire life." He frowns.

I don't think he meant to share that last bit. "Oh, really?" I'm confident now that I'll get a sneak peek into the enigmatic man.

"We're here." He expertly evades my question without much effort. I force myself not to pout.

Jack gets out of the car and comes to open my door. To my surprise, he dips a hand towards the entrance. "Right this way, Miss Callahan."

He leads me to a bank of elevators and presses the button. A grim line sets his mouth, insinuating that he's not interested in chitchat. I roll my eyes and take a breath.

"You know, I can take it from here. If you just tell me what floor, I can find my way."

"Mr. Davis requested I bring you directly to him," Jack

says.

"Oh, okay." *Control freak.*

On the way to floor sixty, my palms sweat and I wipe them against my skirt. Maybe I should have changed into something else? No. This is not a date. Changing into something more feminine and pretty would give the impression I want more. *Letting him hump you against a wall, his tongue down your throat, gave that impression already.* I sigh, letting those thoughts leave me before they twist and turn into something more.

I'll sit with the man, have a drink, and explain that this is the last time we're going to see each other outside of work. That shouldn't be too hard. Before today's board meeting, I never so much as cast a glance at him, and I've worked for the foundation for over two years. Decision made, I remind myself that this is the way it has to be. A relationship with him would be career suicide. I've worked too hard to lose everything now.

We reach our destination, and I swipe a hand through my hair to make sure no loose strands are out of place from the wind earlier. I didn't change clothes, but I did pull my hair down and curl it into soft waves around my face. My appearance reflects back at me in the mirrored elevator doors. The bright red pop of color across my full lips adds drama to the look. My pale skin, red hair, and the emerald of my eyes and blouse make the ruby lipstick a perfect contrast. I feel brazen, bold. It gives me the courage to let down the world's most eligible bachelor. Closing my eyes, I take a deep breath and remind myself that we are from two very different worlds that, if pressed together, would collide and implode. If he really knew me and the details of my past, he wouldn't want me anyway. There's also the giant elephant-sized issue of him being my boss.

Jack walks me through a crowd of people talking and laughing at intimate tables. The centerpiece consists of three wineglasses at varying heights filled with a blue liquid. There's a delicate flower-shaped tea light floating on the surface of each. Such a simple but unique concept. It would be smashing at a donor fundraising dinner. I could even use food coloring to change the color of the water. I store the idea in the back of my mind for future reference and look around the lounge. It occupies the entire floor of the building. Glass walls enclose the space from floor to ceiling, providing a 360-degree view of the Chicago skyline. The view of the city from this height is breathtaking and dizzying. I sway, and Jack plants a firm hand on my elbow.

"It's a rotating floor. It's designed to allow the patrons to see the entire 360 view."

"Beautiful." I pay closer attention and feel the slight movement. He keeps his hold of my arm as he leads me to the bar, dead center of the room. Blue lights glow behind frosted glass. The bar's surface is black and shiny like a grand piano. The entire place is very chic. I can see why Mr. Megabucks would own something so opulent. Another reminder why I, who live in a shabby apartment with a roommate, could not possibly fit into his world.

Chase's presence is like a current that tingles down my spine, tickling the hair at the nape of my neck before I even see him. Jack leads me around a divider. Chase swivels on a barstool as if he can feel me, too. No preparation, not even the serious pep talk I gave myself before coming tonight, could prevent me from eye-fucking this beautiful man. He has removed his tie and blazer. The crisp white dress shirt he's wearing pulls against his broad chest and is rolled up at the sleeves. A couple buttons are undone at the collar. His hair looks like he's combed his fingers through it a million times, giving him that just-rolled-out-of-bed rugged appeal. His come-hither look and crooked smile are almost my undoing. I stand stock still as he appraises me. I *feel* his eyes glide over me as if they were his hands.

"Miss Callahan as requested, sir." Jack pushes me toward Chase.

Chase's eyes soften. He stands and pulls out the chair next to him. "Thank you, Jack. That will be all. I'll ring you when we're ready to leave." Jack exits. No goodbye, no see you later.

I sit down in the chair he offers. "Interesting company you keep." I gesture toward Jack as he walks away.

Chase laughs. "He's rough around the edges, but he gets the job done. I trust him to protect me. We've had some close calls, but he rises to the challenge."

I swallow the golf ball that gets stuck in my throat as he mentions the "close calls." I want to ask him about his experiences, but choose to hold my tongue. Learning too much about him when I'm going to give him the "it's not you, it's me" talk wouldn't help my situation.

"Thank you for meeting me, Gillian. I was looking forward to seeing you."

His smile puts me at ease, even though I'm about to tell him we can't take this thing between us any further.

"Would you like a drink?"

"That would be lovely, thank you."

Chase waves at the bartender, who bustles over at

breakneck speed. "Yes, Mr. Davis. Sir, what can I get for you?"

"A bottle of the Caymus Special Selection 2010 Cabernet Sauvignon."

He doesn't ask what I'd like, but it doesn't bother me. He's comfortable taking the lead, and it gives me a few moments to figure out what to say.

"Figured you'd appreciate a wine from our backyard." He smiles and turns his chair toward me as he did the night we met. Was that only just last night? Jeez. Time definitely slows in his presence.

"I'm sure anything you pick will be great."

"So, Gillian, tell me about yourself." He turns his body toward mine.

His focus on me is absolute. For a moment, having this much of Chase's attention is disconcerting with a twinge of exhilaration. What would it be like to be the center of such an intense man's world? I'll never know.

The bartender sets two bulbous glasses in front of us and busies himself opening our wine.

"What do you want to know?" If he keeps looking at me like I'm the most interesting thing in the world, I'll be happy to pull out my diary and read it to him.

"Everything." His eyes light as he reaches to twirl a few fingers through one of my locks. "You have gorgeous hair. I love redheads."

"Really? I thought you preferred blondes." The comment slips between my lips before I can take it back.

He frowns. "What would give you that impression?" One brown eyebrow rises to a point.

Might as well go for broke. "I looked you up before I

came."

"Ah, I see. So you saw pictures of me at events with blondes, and you surmised that I have a type?" He gestures using air quotes when he says *type*. I nod.

"Those women were not mine. They meant nothing to me." He grabs the wine the bartender poured for him to taste.

Watching him hold the delicate stem reminds me of his hands trailing down my neck with the barest of touches. A shiver runs through me. Cupping the glass, he circles it, swirling the wine. He inhales before he puts the glass to his mouth and sips. The burgundy liquid kisses his full lips. He makes an "mmm" sound, and the tone goes straight to my core. I cross my legs, and his hand covers my knee. He drags a thumb across the silky nylon surface and starts mimicking figure eights or the infinity symbol. It's maddening, but I don't move it. I like his hands on me too much to stop him.

"The wine is fine. Thank you, James."

"When you ordered the wine, you said from *our* backyard. Are you from California too?"

He nods. "I have homes in all the major cities, but I leave my heart in San Francisco." His eyes twinkle.

I laugh. Cheeky fella. He'd be so easy to fall for. The bartender half fills our glasses and meanders away. I get up the nerve to ask the question I really want to know. "So what do you mean when you say those women weren't yours?"

He continues to rub circles across my knee, rising higher at each turn. It's a slow, quiet seduction of my senses, but it's working well. Each pass stokes my desire, ramping it up until I'm a tight ball of need.

He ignores my question at first. "God, Gillian, I can't stop thinking about what's under here." Now his entire hand is gripping my thigh and creeping up until the tip of his fingers reach the garter clasp. He growls quietly and focus his attention on my leg. "I, uh, I hire them to go to those events with me."

I can't hide my shock. "Why? You could have anyone?"

"Thank you, but I have very little time to woo women. Except you. You are something else." He shakes his head. "Something else entirely." He squeezes my thigh.

I imagine him squeezing me somewhere else, preferably with his cock buried inside me. *No, no, no! This is not supposed to be happening. I'm supposed to be cutting him loose.* I lick my overly dry lips. His eyes go dark, and I glance away. Looking into those hungry eyes will be my undoing.

"So you weren't with those women?" He's feeding me a line. No woman in her right mind would go out with him and not try to bed him. He'd be a major win for anyone. *Just not me.*

"I fucked them, if that's what you're asking."

Holy moly, he's crass and dangerously effective at making me hotter.

"But I was never in a relationship with them."

I narrow my eyes, completely disbelieving the line of bullshit spewing from his mouth.

"Gillian, I never lie. Dishonesty is the worst kind of weakness." The smile that has me captive turns into a frown, and his tone sounds irritated.

He slides his hand to the outside of my thigh. I look at his hand clutching me possessively and see how very right it is there, how right his touch feels. Warm and safe. Feeling safe with a man is foreign to me. Panic wiggles into my subconscious and twists at my gut. I can't look at his hand on my body anymore. I grasp for the wine, needing the distraction.

Deep breath, Gigi. You're fine. You like his touch. You want his touch. It feels good.

"You had sex with those women after paying them to attend a function with you?" Disdain creeps into my tone. "You know what that's called?"

He nods and grins. "Does that shock you?" he asks with a seductive lilt. He toys with the strap of my garter, slipping two fingers under and sliding them up and down, pushing my skirt to an indecent height.

His touch is like molten lava, but I can't push him away. I crave the intense heat, need to feel the burn. When his hands are on me, I feel alive.

"Y-Yes, it does," I stutter as his hands wickedly seduce me. "Why?" I whisper.

"Why not? Sometimes I need an escort to a function."

"I'm not asking why you took them. I'm asking why you paid them for sex!" The words spill softly from my lips to ensure none of the other patrons can hear.

Chase grins and takes a swallow of his wine. He leans close to my ear. "I didn't, nor would I ever, pay for sex. I paid for the escort. The sex was completely their choice, optional on their part." He drags his lips along my ear, inhales deeply, and groans before sitting back upright.

Oh, thank God! I almost believed he was paying prostitutes, which seems just as ridiculous as his need to hire an escort. Any woman would want to date him. He could literally walk up to a woman sitting alone in the bar, and she'd fall all over herself to entertain him. *What do you care? You're bailing on him anyway.* I adjust my shoulders, readying myself to cut and run.

He brings his hand to smooth down the length of my back. The simple caress is relaxing, and I'm still no closer to telling him I can't see him. My mind races to come up with a way to manage both my job and him. Is it possible?

"Your turn. Where did you grow up?" He trails his hand along my spine in flourishing sweeps, almost as if he's coating my lust like an artist with a paintbrush.

"I grew up in Northern California. Sacramento and the surrounding cities, mostly. Went to Sacramento State, got my degree in Business Administration with a focus in Marketing a little over two years ago. Moved to the Bay Area just out of college and was hired on by the foundation right away. Been in fundraising ever since."

"Wow, that was the abridged version. Do you have the spiel memorized?" He laughs.

"I don't like talking about myself. Where did you grow up?"

His smile fades. "I lived most of my life with my uncle and four cousins in Beverly Hills. I lived in Boston during my days at Harvard."

I'm certain my eyebrows are reaching for the sky. He's an Ivy League boy. *What the hell is he doing here with me?*

"Before I finished at Harvard, I amassed my own small fortune investing in broken bankrupt firms that cost me next to nothing. My uncle helped, bankrolling my first acquisition. Then I built each company up from the ashes and made them profitable again. After doing that a dozen times, I built my own company and slowly my empire." He's proud of his achievements but doesn't come off too smug.

"A phoenix rising from the ashes."

His surprised eyes meet mine. He's clearly delighted and wickedly handsome when he's happy.

"Exactly." He nods and smiles.

"Why did you create the Safe Haven Foundation?" It makes no sense why he would create a foundation when it's obvious he's in the business of making money, not giving it away.

"I saw a need. I had the capital, and it was important to me." He shrugs and looks away for the first time this evening.

He swirls his wine and then refills his glass and mine with the remaining crimson liquid. I can tell he doesn't want to go into additional detail.

"Tell me about your family, your parents?"

I go cold. The hairs on my forearms rise. "My mother passed away from cancer a few years back. I don't really know much about my father. He was never around. Once in a while he'd send Mom money to help out, but I've only seen him a handful of times. Last I heard, he was working construction for a company that travels from site to site around the nation. I'm an only child. My parents didn't have siblings, so I don't have extended family either."

He looks at me to gauge my emotions. "I'm sorry." His hand covers mine, and he brings it to his lips and kisses it.

It's an old-fashioned gesture for a man so young. It almost makes me forget why I'm here. A deep ache settles into my gut. I pull my hand away and prepare to stop this pseudo date right here. I have to tell him we can't continue to see each other.

Behind me, a sultry voice calls Chase's name. "Mr. Davis! Fancy seeing you here." The woman has a thick Puerto Rican accent. She circles around me, insinuating herself between Chase and me. She slides one small hand up Chase's forearm to his shoulder. Miss Puerto Rico is long, lean, and all mocha-colored, satiny-looking skin. She's wearing a slinky swath of a dress that barely covers her ass. It's fuchsia with little glittering beads all over it. Two diamond strings run around her neck, holding the tiny garment up. With little effort, she brings her body to Chase's and boldly hangs both arms over his shoulders, grasping his neck. "Where have you been all my life?"

Chase looks shocked to see her, but doesn't immediately pull away. Even if this is a casual date or drinks, the woman is rude. Fawning all over a man I'm sitting intimately close to is disgusting and pisses me off!

"Tatiana? I wasn't expecting to see you here. I thought you were in Peru."

He puts his hands around her waist, maybe to move her, maybe to bring her closer. I don't know, and right now, I don't care. I watch with sick fascination as the woman practically rubs her body along the juncture between his thighs. He grips her hips, and I want to vomit. Getting the hell out of here is the only thing I can think of. Moving from the opposite side of my chair, I try not to jostle the tanned bimbo rubbing his lap.

I've had enough when she slides her hand down his chest several times in a very lover-esque manner. Quickly, I turn my chair to the side and slip off. I pull my purse onto my shoulder and take a few steps away from the scene unfolding in front of me.

"I have to go, Chase."

He snaps his head up.

"I was just going to tell you that this thing between us—" I flip my hand at him as his eyes shoot from the girl hanging all over him to me. Ms. Puerto Rico grins and winks at me. "It won't work out. You're my boss. End of story."

Chase's eyes bug out, and his jaw drops open on a gasp.

The leggy brunette sidles in closer and kisses his neck. That's it. I've had enough. I turn and beat feet out of the bar.

"Gillian, wait!" he calls.

I chance a glance back and find the brunette is kissing him. Ridiculous. Invite me out on a date and then kiss and rub all over another woman? Good riddance. I don't need him or his distracting beautiful body trying to sway me into being another one of his bimbos. I dart from the bar and to the elevators as quick as my heels will take me. Chase yells my name as the elevator doors close.

In what world does a sex kitten climb her way up a man who is clearly on a date with another woman? A world I'm not meant for. One that involves incredibly good-looking, rich men who own swanky bars, limousines, and have linebackers as drivers. Before the bimbo broke the trance, I was actually having a really nice time. Even started to believe he was genuinely interested in getting to know me. *So stupid!* It's for the best. So why do I feel like my heart was ripped out and served to me on a platter? That's insanity or maybe lust talking. The door of the elevator opens, and I step out and collide with Jack.

"Get the hell out of my way," I grate through my teeth and rush toward the building's doors.

"Miss Callahan. Mr. Davis has asked me to detain you." He grabs my arm.

I yank it out of his grasp so fast he steps back. "Don't fucking touch me!" I run out the door and down the street. My strides are long, and my skirt bunches up with each step. After several minutes of running, my lungs are on fire, heart jack hammering in my chest. A piercing ache throbs just under my ribs. Coming to a screeching halt, I suck down precious air and try to calm down. Large heaping breaths rack me as I try to gain back control. Stupid man. I should go back there and thank the slut for saving me from heartache down the road. The phone in my blazer's pocket buzzes angrily. It's Chase. I hit the "talk" button and bring it to my ear, not waiting for him to speak.

"You don't have to apologize or answer for anything. Enjoy your real date!" The shrill tone surprises even me as I hang up on him.

Immediately the phone rings again and I ignore it. It keeps ringing and ringing until I smash the power button and turn the damn thing off.

In my desire to bolt, I wasn't paying attention, just following the need to get away. *To escape.* The darkened section of the city I find myself in isn't exactly appealing. Why the hell do I always get myself in these situations? Did I do something to someone in a past life to have such crummy karma? Glancing around the dark street, I realize I'm lost. Running blindly in varying directions so that I wouldn't be followed seemed like a great plan at the time. Now, not so much.

Ahead, a streetlamp illuminates a small area and looks like the best place to stop and call a cab. Pressing zero on the phone, I get the operator. The woman is helpful, and I look up at the street sign to tell her where I'm stranded. She connects me to a cab company that assures me they will pick me up in fifteen minutes.

This night went from good, to bad, to worse in what seems like a nanosecond. The thought of having to sit in the same room with Chase tomorrow at the meeting, knowing what he and Tatiana are going to do all night, makes me want to hurl. I place my phone in my pocket and lean against the chain link fence behind me to riffle through my purse. Maybe I can find a loose hair tie and get the sweaty hair off my neck. Crazy ending to what started out to be an amazing day.

Crunching leaves and the sound of footsteps behind me make the little hairs on the back of my neck stand at attention. Without warning, a large hand comes around my neck and pulls me against the fence. The metal digs into my back as my feet flail and kick out. Reflexively, I use both hands to yank at the hand restricting my breath, but it won't budge.

"You fucking scream, bitch, and I'll kill you," says a man's voice next to my ear.

The stench of sweat mixed with cigarettes is revolting. I stiffen and tremble. Instantly, I'm taken back to a memory of when Justin held me down. I remember the glazed faraway look in his eyes right before he struck. Panic rips through my chest, and fear takes over my defenses.

The attacker's voice rips through all thoughts. "You listen to me, you little cunt. Hand me your purse now, and I won't kill you."

The cold, hard steel of a gun presses against my skull as

his other hand squeezes the tender skin at my neck, cutting off all air. I gag and choke at the viselike grip around my throat. Oh God, please no!

"Okay, okay. Whatever you want." I'm barely able to get out through his snakelike constriction on my neck preventing much sound.

His hand grips my neck like a steel claw, nails digging in and piercing the flesh. I feel blood pool and drip down my neck in little streams like the legs of red wine dancing along a swirled glass. Pain sears through my neck and chest, black-and-white stars pop in my peripheral vision like flashes of a camera. I'm going to die. I remember the feeling all too well when Justin left me on the cold hard floor of our apartment a few years ago to bleed out.

"You can have whatever you want!" A choked, raspy sob spills from my lungs. I hold up my purse.

The man squeezes the tender flesh of my neck so tight I can't breathe. "Good bitch!" he says from over my shoulder. He snatches the purse from my hand.

He lets my neck go long enough for a blood-curdling scream to roar through the empty street just as he strikes my face with the hard metal of his gun. The world goes black.

★ ★ ★ ★

Beep. Beep. Beep.

Someone turn off the alarm. The beeping continues like Chinese water torture against the frayed edges of my consciousness. My eyelashes are heavy and my eyes hard to open. It's as if the lashes are weighed down by tiny manacles holding onto each strand. The sickening smell of bleach and antiseptic fills the air. A hammer knocks against my forehead. *Bam. Bam. Bam.*

The pressure above my eye feels like someone hit me with a baseball bat. With shaking fingers, I feel my face. A large bandage covers the tender spot above my eye. My cheekbone is twice its normal size.

The memory of what happened slams me into the here and now. *Oh God.* Bile rises in my throat, leaving a sour taste. I was robbed. At gunpoint. I had been waiting for the taxi. I open my eyes, and the haze and cloudiness of the memory slowly fades. When I get my eyes open and blink rapidly, I'm able to look around. The white room is dimly lit from behind my bed. As I make my visual trek around the room, my gaze settles onto the very pissed-off face of one Chase Davis. Anger pumps off his large form in waves, and I start to shake. I've seen anger like that in the eyes of another man. I don't care to ever experience it again. He stands and pulls the blanket over me more tightly, tucking the sides around me. I have to hold my breath, trying desperately not to flinch. Panic rises like a high tide at sundown.

"How did I get here?" I croak, voice thickened by drugs.

He grabs the pink plastic water cup sitting on the side table and brings the straw to my lips. I sip. Pure heaven. He sets down the cup and takes a seat next to the bed, arms crossed defensively.

"You were mugged. The taxi driver found you and called 9-1-1." Chase's eyes narrow, and he holds his chin tight, teeth clenched. The man is *really* upset.

The evening's events come back to me. Tears well, and I grip the blanket tightly.

"You could have been killed, Gillian." His voice is horrified, perhaps even emotional. "You were accosted, roughed up, and left in a very tough neighborhood. I am so angry with you."

Tears slide down my cheeks, and he wipes them away with both of his thumbs. His touch is so light against my skin I can barely feel it.

"Why are you here?"

He winces at my question.

"The nurses searched your clothing. My business card was in the pocket of your blazer with your cell phone. My call was the last you received." He gets up and paces the small space like a caged animal. "You have no idea what it was like being told that you had been attacked." He takes a harrowed breath and roughly shoves his fingers though his hair. "Then, I come to the hospital and see you like…like this! You could have died!"

He holds my gaze with a questioning look. I have no answer.

"I'm sorry you had to leave Tatiana for me," I grumble and look away. I wish he'd just leave.

He grips my chin and lightly tugs it back so he can look me in the eyes. "Tatiana means nothing to me. You on the other hand…" He sighs heavily and slumps back into the chair next to me. He's too far away to reach.

"Tell me…" I urge, desperate to find out what he was going to say.

The nurse walks in, destroying the moment. "Welcome to the world of the living, Mrs. Davis."

I'm certain the look on my face is one of complete confusion. Chase leans forward and clasps my hand. It's warm and comforting. I latch on to his lifeline as it if will disappear at any moment.

"When can I take my wife home?"

Maybe that blow to the head was worse than I thought?

"Once the doctor looks her over, checks the stitches, and gives you the okay. Then you can take her home." She smiles at Chase, but he's staring at me. "You gave this man quite a scare, young lady." The nurse gestures to Chase.

He shrugs and looks away.

"You should have seen the way he burst into the ER, roaring, demanding access to you immediately. Like he was a real-life Superman." She clucks her tongue.

The image makes me snicker a little. He is a real-life Superman. Chase squeezes my hand and the nurse leaves.

"Your wife?" I ask.

"They asked if I was next of kin. I told them we were married."

"I thought you never lied. That dishonesty was weakness?" I stare deeply into his eyes.

He looks away. "It is. I had a moment." He won't look me in the eye.

The doctor comes in and explains that I have a concussion, a bruised cheekbone, five crescent-shaped cuts in my neck, and a few stitches above my right eye where the gunman hit me with the butt of the weapon.

Chase grips my hand so tightly I almost cry out as the doctor revisits each wound. I clasp Chase's hands in both of mine and pet the top one. He traces an infinity symbol over my wrist with his thumb while the doctor explains that a concussion is a traumatic brain injury that alters the way your brain functions. The effects are usually temporary, but can include problems with headache, concentration, memory, judgment, balance, and coordination. I will need to be awakened every two hours, asked to remember three items, and then to repeat them at the next waking. He also informs us that the police want to take a statement.

"Not tonight," Chase interrupts. "I'm taking her home. She's had a traumatic evening." He pulls me against his side and I snuggle in.

The nurse brings me some scrubs and hospital slippers, and I slip into the little bathroom, changing out of my hospital gown. When I return, she hands Chase the bag with my soiled bloody clothes in it. Might as well toss the entire lot in the trash. I'll never wear that outfit again.

"Gillian, I have my people on this. That fucker won't get away with hurting you."

He embraces me, his strong arms enveloping me. Warm and safe. In his arms, I lean my head against his chest and listen to his heartbeat. It should calm and soothe, but it does the exact opposite. The tidal wave of emotions, as I remember the night's activities, rips through me. Tears form and spill unchecked onto his shirt. Deep gut-wrenching sobs roar from my scratchy throat as the realization of what happened truly invades me. Chase's arms hold me tight, gifting me his protection and solace as I weep.

"Baby, it's okay. I've got you." Chase pets my hair. "I'm taking you back to the hotel."

I nod into his chest, not capable of speech.

We leave the hospital, and he ushers me into his limo. I don't see the scenery on the way back. The pain medication they filled me with starts to take effect, and I lean heavily into Chase's solid form. I must have dozed off because we're at the hotel and Chase is lifting me from the limo. I lull against his chest as he carries me through the hotel. I can only imagine what we look like. Hopefully, people don't notice much at this time of night. Really though, I'm too far gone to care.

"Mr. Davis, sir, do you need a wheelchair?" a man asks in the background.

"No. I'm not letting her go."

His comment makes me feel warm and snuggly. I hear the ding of the elevator, and soon we're rising. Moments later, I'm on a big, soft bed. Chase pulls off my scrub pants and tucks my legs under the silky soft, cool linen sheets. He goes to the dresser and pulls out a white V-neck T-shirt. I watch in a daze, unable to do much other than stare. He drags the scrub top over my head, careful of my swollen face.

I wait in my black lacy bra for him to put the shirt on me.

"Jesus Christ, Gillian. What did that fucker do to you?" His tone is strained.

His fingertips are featherlight on my neck. Moving my hair to the side, he turns me toward the lamp light. He's seeing the marks left by my attacker's nails embossed into the tender skin of my neck. Chase surprises me by bringing his face close and trailing soft kisses along the entire surface. The gesture is incredibly sweet. He's such a dichotomy. One minute he's challenging and demanding, the next, gentle and tender.

"Never again will you be hurt, Gillian. I'll make certain of it," he promises between the soothing pecks of his lips against my flesh.

I shiver from the feel of his mouth on me, more than

from the trauma I experienced. A traitorous tear escapes and drips onto his face.

He grabs the soft white T-shirt and lightly pulls it over my body. It smells of fabric softener and laundry soap. I lean back and rest my head against the pillow.

"Rest, baby, just rest. I'll wake you every two hours as the doctor ordered." He kisses the part of my forehead not ensconced in a bandage.

I'm fading fast. Without opening my eyes, I whisper, "Thank you. I'm sorry for all the trouble."

"My pleasure. Taking care of you is my pleasure."

CHAPTER FIVE

True to his word, Chase wakes me two hours later. I expect the hotel alarm clock, not soft soothing fingers caressing my face and hairline. A bone-chilling cold creeps along the sensitive skin of my cheekbone. My eyelids flicker open, and I gaze into sleepy half-hooded azure eyes. His features are different under the muted glow of the bedside lamp, more comforting, less intense. I could get used to seeing these bedroom eyes. He holds an ice pack against my swollen cheek. The icy chill sends shivers through me.

"Gillian, what's my name?" he asks in a hushed voice.

"Chase," I say groggily. The pain medication makes my tongue feel thick and swollen.

"Here, baby, take these." He puts two small white pills on the tip of my tongue and hands me a glass of water.

When did he start calling me baby?

"The doctor said it will help with the swelling and the pain from your stitches."

I swallow the pills and lie back down. He sets the glass down, brings the covers back up to my chin, and puts the ice pack on the bedside table. He clocks every inch of my face, a mercurial look fastened to his features. I smile dreamily at him. Chase is pretty.

"Why, thank you," he says, amusement in his tone.

I didn't realize I said the thought aloud, but don't take it back. It's the truth.

He plants a soft kiss against my lips. He cradles the undamaged side of my face in his right hand. I return the kiss as he slides satiny lips against mine. He continues the slow assault on my mouth, not increasing the pressure or taking it further. Just kissing me how he wants. Like a man who cherishes his woman. This is dangerous territory we're entering.

He strokes my bottom lip with his tongue, and I slide my fingers into his hairline, tickling his scalp and increasing the pressure. That's all the permission he needs. Taking the invitation greedily, he uses his mouth to swallow me whole. His tongue sweeps past my teeth and against my tongue in long unhurried swipes. A moan leaves me on a rasp of breath. He tastes good, rich and utterly male. I want his body on top of me, coating every surface with his warm skin. Tugging at his shoulders, I attempt to bring him against my chest. It doesn't work. He's a solid rock, unmovable. I grunt in frustration, scissoring my legs to aid in my goal. Unfortunately, Chase does the exact opposite of what I want and pulls away.

"God, what you do to me, Gillian. It's never... Let's just say I'm not used to this." He pulls completely away and walks to the other side of the bed and gets in.

The rumpled sheets and imprint of his head in the pillow tell me he's been sleeping next me. In my drug-induced state, I didn't notice. I frown, wishing I could remember the exact moment he lay down next to me.

"Not used to what?" I turn on my side, resting my head on the pillow, and stare at him in the soft light.

He's lying on his back, breathing deeply. His white T-shirt stretches across his broad chest, accentuating the hills and valleys of a perfectly sculpted frame. I want to scrape my nails against the fabric to see how he responds. He's contemplative and brooding. Instead of touching him, I wait, keeping my distance.

"This attraction. It's maddening." He frowns.

I stare. Chase is panty-melting good-looking. Everything about him attracts me. From the tip of his dark hair, down his beautiful face, and over his broad chest, to the parts of him I haven't yet been introduced to. I'm not sure what he is talking about, but my head is heavy and I'm losing the battle to keep my eyes open. I feel him turn towards me.

"Gillian, look at me," he says sternly.

I open my eyes and focus with a great deal of effort. I'm fading fast.

"Can you remember these three things? Vanilla, emerald, and Popsicle. You got that?"

My head feels as though it's a water balloon, filled to the brim, as I nod.

"No, say it," he demands.

Closing incredibly heavy lids, I attempt the list, trying not to slip into dreamland. "Um, vanilla, emerald, and a Popsicle," I repeat like a good girl.

The next time I wake is to heat, a veritable inferno. A body surrounds me, large legs and arms enclosing me tightly. The room is bathed in black, and strong arms hold me fast against a wide chest, preventing much movement. I can't remember the last time I woke in a man's arms. The feeling of being so sheltered, so secure, is heart-melting. I can feel Chase's breath quicken and his chest rise and fall against my cheek. If only I could bottle this feeling for eternity.

"Baby, what are the three things I asked you to remember?" Chase asks in a low, gravelly voice.

"Um, green, vanilla, and Popsicle." I snuggle into his chest and start to drift. My head is so heavy it feels like a stack of bricks are holding it down.

He stiffens and pulls away, forcing me to lose my comfy spot. "Gillian, what are the three things in exact order, exactly as I said them?" His tone is harsh, demanding.

I try really hard to think back to what he told me. "Oh. Vanilla, emerald, *not* green, and Popsicle," I say, confident but still exhausted.

A huge breath leaves his chest, but the scowl I can barely see in the shadows of night still mars his lovely face.

"Go to back to sleep." He grips me protectively.

I rub against his side like a cat, stretching and finding just the right position before I start purring.

Gentle fingers glide along my arm, shoulder, neck, hairline, and down along my hip and naked thigh, waking me once more. The caress is repeated over and over, sending dizzying bouts of lust through every limb. The sensation is wonderful, and I roll completely onto my back, opening myself to him in the most vulnerable way. Chase's large hand slips to my bare belly and covers the entire expanse. He's huge compared to me.

An errant thumb lightly circles the edge of my panties. My breath puffs out in tiny frantic bursts of excitement. I feel the heat of his head at the base of my neck, his five o'clock shadow grating along the skin there. His teeth nibble at my chin in a line to my mouth. Once he reaches my mouth, I take his lips into a feverish kiss, never having opened my eyes. His tongue demands entrance. I open for him. In this moment, there's nothing I want more than Chase over me. On top of me. Completing me.

Chase drinks from the well of my mouth, biting into my bottom lip and then moving to its twin. I groan, needing, wanting more. Finally, his hand slides under my shirt to cup one full breast. I arch, pressing the heavy flesh into his strong hand, relishing the tingles that spread through my chest. I taste his minty breath as he moans his pleasure into my mouth. His fingers fondle the globe teasingly. Then utter relief splatters across my senses as he brings the cup of my bra down and grazes his thumb over an aching tip. Bliss.

"Oh, God," spills from my throat, as if ripped directly from the heavens. It's guttural and raw. Chase is doing this to me. Turning me into something else, someone I don't recognize. He swallows my cry as if he's eating it, all lips, teeth, and tongue.

With his thumb, he pulls and pinches the tight peak, elongating it into a tender bit of flesh that's tethered directly to the pleasure building in my core. I grip him hard, pulling him to me, sliding my hands under his shirt to scratch my nails down the fine skin of his muscular back. He takes the advantage and slides my shirt up, exposing my chest. He pushes the bra down to fully squeeze and grope both breasts greedily, flicking and tugging at each tip, driving me insane with lust. I pray that he never stops touching them. I'd willingly serve them up on a platter every day if he would promise me this nirvana regularly.

"Fuck, you have an incredible body!" he says as he pulls my right breast into his warm mouth.

Sparks fly as the wet heat of his tongue sends ribbons

of pleasure down to the ache between my legs. God, I wish he'd touch me there. His other hand plucks and pinches my nipple's twin, adding to the mounting tension spiraling through me. Heat infuses my belly, and I arc my hips against his straining erection, relishing the heavy growl that leaves his lips. As he worships my tits, I think I might actually come from him ravishing my breasts. He sucks and flicks the enlarged peak with the tip of his tongue until it glistens. He moves one hand up to my neck to settle at the nape. His thumb grazes my swollen cheek. I gasp as pain splinters in every direction, dampening my excitement.

"Shit, baby, I'm sorry. Fuck!" He backs away.

I pull him with all my might. He's a wall. An unmovable one with a mighty scowl marring his previously lust-ridden features. I want to throw my hands in the air and flail my limbs in a full soap opera–worthy tantrum. He cannot set me on fire without putting me out.

He sits back on his haunches, watching me seethe.

"Chase, no. No, it's okay. Really, I'm fine." I place soothing kisses everywhere I can reach as I scoot into his lap, my legs wrapped around his waist.

With intent, I've placed my center directly against his raging erection. He slides his hands along my ass and grips me firmly, digging his rock solid cock against my clit.

I moan, head tilting back, baring my neck. "God, yes!"

He slides his hand lightly along the column. I feel the melancholy building in him as he reverently touches the five perfect crescent-shaped indents marring the skin there. They're likely coupled with bruises that would resemble a man's hand, a physical reminder of the torment I underwent only hours ago.

Shivering, I force myself not to recoil. More than anything, I *need* to let a man be close to me again. If not forever, at least for now, with *this* man. Damn, I promised myself I'd never be the victim again, and here I am, covered in bruises, narrowly having escaped death by another abuser.

Chase lays me back against the bed, his soulful gaze filled with pain. "Gillian, I'm going to give you some relief, but we need to wait."

His words are meant to soothe. They only frustrate. I am not a porcelain doll. I can take whatever he dishes out and then some.

Confusion and desire are thick in the air around us as I catalogue his every feature. Before I can fully respond, he slips his hand into my panties and plunges two fingers deep into my wet sex.

I cry out. Ecstasy invades every facet of my being. His long fingers press high and deep, sending waves of pleasure rippling through me. This is exactly what I wanted. Chase touching me. His thumb searches through my curls and finds the little bundle of nerves nestled there, sliding against it perfectly. He pumps his fingers in and out of me as he circles just the outside rim of my clit, driving me wild. I buck my hips and spread my hands across the mattress, searching for something to grab on to. Anything that will keep me grounded to this earth. I twist the bedding in my fingers as he lifts my shirt, baring my breasts to his waiting mouth. He covers one nipple and flicks the tip, sending naughty little pinpricks to the center of my excitement.

"So good!" I gasp.

I move my head from side to side, frantically trying to hold onto this feeling. It's overwhelming and unique, just like the man who's giving it to me. His fingers hook delectably inside me, digging harshly into that effervescing spot deep within. Just when I think I can't take anymore, his thumb presses in tight circles over my clit as his teeth bite down on my nipple.

Gone. Set off into orbit. Pleasure shoots through my core, light explodes behind my eyes, and the sound of thunder pounds in my ears. I scream his name as my body quakes and convulses in a blinding orgasm.

Chase continues plucking every one of my erogenous zones until there's nothing left but the automatic shake and twitch of well-used muscles.

He kisses me with languid slow sweeps of his tongue and lips, his fingers still lodged deep within me, almost as if he doesn't want to leave my heat. I sigh as he gently pulls his hand from my panties. His eyes are so dark it's like looking into a black hole. With his azure orbs laser-focused on me, he brings his fingers to his mouth and leisurely licks them clean of my essence. A low purr resonates through my chest and out my mouth. His eyebrow lifts into a perfect point as he swirls his tongue around the long digits.

I widen my eyes and grow heavy with lust as my hips set up a slow dance, waiting patiently for more of what I know he can offer.

"You taste so good, baby. I can't wait to have you. Here, taste." He kisses me deeply.

I can taste myself on his tongue, and there's something incredibly erotic and forbidden about it. Everything about Chase seems erotic and forbidden. When we're both breathless, he leans over me, his weight held up by the strong muscles in his forearms. I stretch, pointing my toes and reaching above my head until I feel relaxed and sated.

"Good?" he asks. The sly grin and cocky tone only make me want to jump him.

Then it dawns on me that he didn't get anything in return. He goes to pull away, but I reach out and grasp the obvious erection tenting his boxer briefs. Holy shit, he's big. This is going to be so good. I lick my lips in barely contained anticipation and mentally prepare to be blown away. He stills my hand.

Confusion and hurt play havoc with my frayed emotions. "What about you?" My voice sounds almost like a child's.

"That was for you, baby. When you're better, I *will* fuck you good and hard. That's when I will make you mine. Until then, we wait." His words sound brutally honest and shocking said aloud.

I don't think any of his many business cohorts would believe this well put together man had the sexual predilections of a porn star and mouth to go with it.

Somewhat relieved, I nod. More than anything, I want to please him, but my head is pounding, screaming for relief. I cringe and tremble as last night's hell comes back to me in bright Technicolor. Unfortunately, even the big O can't take away those memories. Just one more thing to add to my long list of issues. I shake it off.

Chase cringes but kisses me before getting out of bed. He picks up the medicine bottle, opens it, and shakes out a couple pills. "You're in pain. I can see it all over your gorgeous face." He hands the oval pills to me.

Chase thinks I'm gorgeous. The thought has me feeling shy and womanly.

"Thank you. Thank you for...everything." I look away, avoiding his gaze. I don't want him to see how vulnerable I am right now. Battered, sleep deprived, chock-full of drugs, and sated from the orgasm he just gave me. All of those things on top of knowing Chase thinks I'm gorgeous... It's too much.

"Gillian, stop running from me. From this, whatever it is." He gestures between us.

He waits for me to say something. I don't think he's going to move until I respond. I take a deep breath, adjust my shoulders, and look deep into his eyes. "I'll try." It's the best I can do. Allowing a man inside of my body is one thing, inside of my mind and heart is something I promised I'd never do again.

He must realize it's what I can offer right now because he looks down briefly, tightens his jaw, and nods. Chase leaves me sated and medicated on the rumpled sheets as he heads into the bathroom and starts the shower.

My cell phone rings somewhere across the room. The sound is like a jackhammer being inserted straight into my skull. I make the stupid mistake of jumping up to get it. The concussion sways me, and I almost tumble to the floor. I steady myself against the dresser and glance toward the bathroom to make sure Chase didn't see me almost lose it again. The last thing I need is another man who thinks he can take care of me. Even if Chase helped me last night, I'll be damned if I become this weak little victim in his eyes.

I find my phone on top of my clothes nestled in the sitting chair by the large window. In an unladylike fashion, I drop into the cushy armchair and pull it to my ear.

"Hello," I croak, my voice still raspy from last night.

"Gigi, thank God! I was starting to worry about you."

The sound of my best friend, Phillip's, voice calms me. A huge smile splits my face, and then I cringe at the tight skin pulling at my swollen cheek. I lean back in the chair to get comfortable as I spill my guts, glad it's him and not one of the girls.

"I had a rough night." Like ripping off a Band-Aid, I figure it's easier to just spit it out quick and painless. "Phil, I was mugged and landed in the hospital." Tears pool as I hear him gasp. A few tears build, but I press my little fingers into the edges of my eyes to staunch the flow.

"Gigi, are you okay? Are you still in the hospital?" His voice is thick and gritty. "Do you need me to fly out and come get you?"

Oh, how I love this man. He's one of the good guys. A lightness fills me. I'm so very thankful.

"No, no, I'm fine. Really. I'm being taken care of." *By Chase,* my mind adds wickedly, and I smile. "It was scary though. He held me at gunpoint." A shiver spirals down my spine, and I stiffen it. This will *not* break me. I've been through worse.

"Oh my God, honey, what happened?"

I tell him the entire story, leaving out the part about coming back to the hotel with Chase, my boss. Phillip and I have very few secrets, but I want to explain the situation with Chase to him in person when Phillip is not distraught.

"Phil, I'm fine. Just shaken up." I use my brave girl voice.

"I'll feel better the second I see you, Gigi," he says softly.

I know it is hard for him to hear I was hurt. We've been there for one another since he lost his wife, Angela. He's seen me through the good and the bad, including what

Justin did to me, and then again, after Daniel and I broke up six months ago.

"I'm looking forward to seeing you too. I'll call you when I get home, I promise." I press my head against my arm. The pain meds make it feel like a bowling ball.

"Call me when you land. I'll pick you up," he suggests.

He won't rest until he sees that I'm fine. Only I'm not, and he'll know it. The bruises and marks ringing my neck aren't going to help. At this point I'm not sure what will.

"I'll let you know. I have to go to the police station and make my statement today." I sigh into the phone loudly. So much for the board meeting. I'm going to have to call Taye before I head to the station. I need to update him on what occurred last night and why I won't be present at the meeting today. He's going to be furious that I didn't call him last night.

"I'll be thinking about you. Anabelle misses you. She drew you a picture." He laughs lightly.

Phillip's angelic daughter, Anabelle, is such a light in a dark world. Her blond curly hair and crystal-blue eyes can make any day brighter. I take my duty as her godmother very seriously, especially since her mother died in a car wreck two years ago.

"I miss her. Send her my love and tell her I have a present for her."

"I love you, Gigi."

I hear the fear in his voice. Part of me wants to hide what happened to me from him, but the stitches and bruised cheek would lead to more questions and hurt feelings. Besides, I promised him I'd never lie to him.

"I love you too. I'll see you when I get home, Phillip."

I hang up and exhale. With great effort, I stand and turn around.

Chase is standing halfway across the expanse of the room. His gaze is searing, jaw clenched so tight he could break a tooth.

"Who do you love?" comes out demanding, unforgiving.

I'm caught off guard by the rage pumping off him. I slump against the chair at the angry tone. My hackles rise, and I lift my chin, irritation setting in at his accusatory tone. "Phillip. My best friend."

"Not your lover?" His eyes blaze.

For a moment, I'm lost. He has a white towel slung low over his waist and tied at one hip. Water drips down his muscled torso. Rivulets trail down the square bumps of his tight abdomen, disappearing into the cotton of the towel at his pelvis. Oh, what I wouldn't give to be one of those droplets right now. I lick my lips and bite down on the bottom one.

"I asked you a question. I expect an answer." His voice is cold.

"No. He's not." I leave out the part that he once was. Somehow I don't think that tidbit of information would ease Chase right now. Besides, it was a lifetime ago. Almost as if it were something that happened in a long-forgotten dream.

"I will not share you with another man." His jaw is tight, the muscles flicking with tension like a rubber band being pulled at both ends, just on the cusp of snapping. "Once I have you, you will be mine, Gillian. Think about that before we go any further."

His anger infuriates me. Who does he think he is? My

knight in shining Armani? "Phillip is my best friend. We've been through a lot together, and I will not give him up for any man." I hold my chin up and cross my arms.

He watches me, detached, his gaze frosty. I don't care. He doesn't get to control me. No man does.

"I love him dearly, but I'm not 'in love' with him, nor will I ever be." Now I'm pissed off. "You know what? I don't need to explain my relationship with Phillip to you. I don't even know what this is." I gesture between the two of us.

His towel drops to the floor as he stalks to me.

Holy-Naked-God-Among-Men.

His body is incredible. Tall with broad muscled shoulders that narrow into a tight chest, lean waist and hips, thick muscular thighs, tight strong shins and calves. But nothing is quite as beautiful as his cock. It's semi-erect, long and thick, bobbing as he makes his way across the room. It's as if it's straining to reach me. My mouth waters at the sight, and I want to fall to my knees and wrap my lips around the perfect knobbed head in complete adoration of its beauty.

"You see what you do to me?" He pulls me to him, tightly pressing his naked body against me. The ridge of his now fully erect cock digs into the tender flesh of my belly.

I grapple for purchase on all the slick yummy male skin surrounding me. I whimper. My intense response is carnal, animalistic. I lick his pec, pulling in the taste of fresh water, a hint of soap, and blessed man.

Chase closes me in between the wall of windows and the chair. Standing next to this wide window with a gloriously naked man pressing his tight body to my half-naked one feels electric and exhilarating.

He grasps my nape and kisses me passionately, pressing me against the chair back. Strong hands pull at my thighs, roughly hiking me up to set my bum on the edge. I wrap my legs around his lean waist as he presses his erection against the tiny triangle of fabric covering my sex before deepening the kiss. Chase is all around me and everywhere at once. His sandalwood and fruit scent strong from the shower surrounds me, pulling me into the vortex that is Chase. He wrenches his mouth away roughly. My lips feel prickly and swollen.

"Christ, I could come just from kissing you." His forehead crinkles and he locks his gaze with mine.

There's a raging fire of lust that I desperately want to put out. Preferably with my body.

"Chase," I say breathlessly, nipping at his lips, tugging on the bottom one. He groans and bites back. God, this man makes me insane. One minute he's scolding me, the next he's driving me wild with need.

A knock on the suite's door breaks the spell. I pull tightly against his body, startled by the intrusion. Anger seems to flick on like a switch through Chase as he gives me one last deep kiss, grinding his erection into my parted thighs.

"Soon," he grates through clenched teeth. He unfurls my leg lock from his waist, helping me to stand against the chair. He sweeps his gaze over my bare legs, up his shirt, and to my swollen lips. It's as if he's cataloguing every facet of my body. "You're perfect wrapped in me," he says seductively.

I lean, stunned, against the chair, so completely turned on I can hardly function. That orgasm earlier felt like a tiny miniscule appetizer to a feast of pleasure Chase is sure to provide. He picks up the towel he dropped and wraps it back around his waist to answer the door. I want to hiss and boo at the loss of seeing his beautiful body.

"She'll be ready in an hour," he says to someone, but it's muffled. He saunters back into the bedroom. "Jack is going to take you to the station in an hour for your statement. He will bring you back to the hotel."

I open my mouth to suggest I can take a cab and he stops me.

"Don't argue with me. This is nonnegotiable."

And that is that. Discussion over. He enters the closet and pulls out his suit. I throw the scrub pants from last night back on but keep his shirt. It's nice having something that's Chase's on me right now. I have to go. I need time to think, to process everything that's happened. Last night and this morning. Trying to cope through a mind filled with lust is not doing me any favors. Grabbing my dirty clothes, I venture to the open bathroom door where Chase is at the mirror fixing his hair. The dark layers fall into place as he burrows his fingers through it.

"I'm going to my room to get ready. I'll meet Jack downstairs."

He nods and fiddles with a black textured tie around his golden neck. It lies crisply against the stark white of his dress shirt. His dark charcoal suit brings out the gray flecks in his eyes. He's meticulous in his movements, concentrating on putting on his cuff links. They are small dime-sized circles with a black onyx gem, the sphere lined by silver plating.

"Text me when you're finished." His eyes find mine in the mirror, the look almost pleading. His genuine concern makes me nod.

As I'm about to leave, I remember the question I forgot to ask last night. "Hey, why did you pick vanilla, emerald, and Popsicle as the three words you wanted me to remember?"

He grins wickedly and walks me to the hotel room entry. Jack is filling a giant lounge chair in the sitting room, watching as Chase holds open the door. He gestures for Jack to follow me, and I realize this is going to be my new friend for the day. Chase is not letting me go anywhere alone. Since I'm still shaken, having protection isn't all together uncomfortable. Jack does look like one scary guy.

"You really want to know?" he asks, a sly grin twisting his lips in a way that makes me want to kiss them. I nod and wait patiently.

His smile shows all his pearly white teeth. In a husky voice dripping with innuendo, he says, "You, Gillian, smell like vanilla." He leans down and inhales loudly before kissing my neck. "That's the scent I want surrounding me when I look into your emerald eyes as you suck my cock as if you were eating a Popsicle." He chuckles.

I know my eyes have to be as wide as dinner plates as my chin drops and my mouth gapes open.

"You asked." He laughs.

Jesus, he paints a sexy, illicit image. Then I realize we're not alone. Jack has the good grace to look away, a grin plastered across his square face. Heat fans across my cheeks. Chase grabs my shoulders and hauls me against him. He plunders my mouth, giving me a taste of his minty freshness and something uniquely Chase. My knees feel weak and wobbly when he lets me go.

★ ★ ★ ★

After I dress, I call Taye. He's upset that I didn't call him last night to come to the hospital. I explain that Chase came. Quickly, I detail the oddity of Chase helping me by telling him they found his business card in my jacket pocket from the meeting. The nurses called him, not Taye. It seems reasonable, and technically, it isn't a lie. He says he will touch base with Mr. Davis at the board meeting and hopes I feel better after making my statement and resting.

Jack escorts me to the police station. The visit is horrifying. A wide array of delinquents and degenerates from all walks of life are being dragged around the facility. Even though I get a handful of stares and disgusting grins, none of them dare approach me. Jack, the "Tank," snarls like a possessive dog would, protecting its owner when men look my way. The bodyguard must have instructions from Chase, ones he takes very seriously. The big guy doesn't leave me alone, not even for a minute.

The officer takes me into a quiet room, and Jack follows, standing in the corner watching everything without making a sound. I don't have much to offer. My attacker came from behind, held me immobile, and then knocked me out. Nothing to see. There is little hope of getting back my belongings or finding the man who attacked me. I express my fear that my attacker has my address and personal information. The officer is less concerned because I live in San Francisco. My attacker is in Chicago, over two thousand miles away. The thought makes me feel a bit better. Not much.

When all the i's are dotted and the t's crossed, Jack ushers me to the waiting car. I'm happy he didn't drive the limo today. That would have felt outlandish at a police station in downtown Chicago.

I take out my cell phone to type Chase a text message.

To: Chase Davis

From: Gillian Callahan

Statement made. Nothing more can be done. On my way back to hotel.

My phone dings with a message before I can put it back in my pocket.

To: Gillian Callahan

From: Chase Davis

Are you okay?

Those three little words make my heart jump. In the span of two days, this man has become something more than the Chairman of the Board of Safe Haven. Much more. I need time away from him to figure out just how much, as well as to sort out this strange connection we have. Home. That's where I need to be. Then it dawns on me. How the hell am I going to get home without my driver's license or identification? Worry trickles along the edges of my tired mind.

To: Chase Davis

From: Gillian Callahan

Worried about how I'm going to get home without ID.

I lean my throbbing head against the seat rest and pull the pain medication from my briefcase. It's all I have since my purse was stolen.

"Here's a bottle of water, Miss Callahan." Jack hands me

a bottle over the seat. I take it and smile at him in the review mirror. He doesn't return the gesture.

To: Gillian Callahan

From: Chase Davis

I have taken care of it. You will fly home with me in the company jet. Stop worrying.

"Holy Shit! He has a company jet?" I say aloud while staring at the words on my phone. I blow a puff of air toward my heated forehead. "How rich is this guy?" Who really has their own jet? Donald Trump maybe? The president for sure.

"No, Miss Callahan. Mr. Davis does not have 'a' jet. He owns a fleet of them."

My mouth drops to my chin.

"Mr. Davis is worth billions," Jack adds, very matter of fact.

I start to shake and twist my fingers together. *Billions?* I knew he was rich, but I had no idea. What could a man like that possibly want with a poor charitable fundraiser from a broken home with a jaded past? Besides, I'm a mess. I have more than my fair share of issues and baggage, much more than any man deserves. God, knowing he's worth so much, that he's so valuable, makes me want to run for the hills.

We make our way back to the hotel. My head aches, my heart heavy. The linebacker follows me into the hotel room. He checks the closet, bathroom, under the bed, and behind the curtains. For what, I don't know. How an intruder would be able to get into a locked hotel room is beyond me, but I allow him to do what he feels is necessary before kicking him out.

"Mr. Davis will come for you this evening at six p.m.

Be ready when he arrives. He requests that you not leave the hotel."

"Oh really? Is that right? You just tell Mr. Davis that I don't need his permission, but thanks for the concern." I walk to the door and open it wide for him. The man almost spans the entire space of the door frame. I wonder idly if he used to play football. "Thank you, Jack. For your assistance today at the station."

Jack leaves with a nod and a frown. Is he ever happy? My guess—probably not.

The end result today was a good reminder for me. I answer to no man. Even if Chase has some misguided notion that I will fall in line like everyone else does around him, he's dead wrong. I'm no longer the type of woman to bow down to a man's every whim. I learned that lesson the hard way.

My cell phone pings, and I pluck it out of my briefcase and see his name.

To: Gillian Callahan

From: Chase Davis

Dinner at 6:00 p.m. We head home first thing in the morning. Have your bags ready.

Even from his board meeting he's trying to control me. Unbelievable.

To: Chase Davis

From: Gillian Callahan

I'm tired. No dinner. I'll be ready in the morning. See you then.

Space from Chase Davis is necessary. He makes me all googly-eyed and filled with feelings I can't control. Last night, though, he took care of me. I haven't been taken care of by a man in years. My last boyfriend Daniel tried, but ended up making me feel smothered. He was just too damned nice all the time. His voice never rose once until the night I asked him to try a different sexual position. That's when things started to fall apart. Good riddance. He was a lousy lay. I've had more pleasure from Chase's fingers just the once than I had in the better part of a yearlong relationship with Daniel.

Even though Chase is trying to be nice, he doesn't own me. *But you'd like him to,* my traitorous subconscious pipes in. I groan, knowing I just need to sleep. My head is killing me and I've suffered through a lot. Between the board meeting yesterday, the emotional roller coaster, being mugged, a stint in the hospital, waking up next to Chase, having Chase get me off, and making my statement at the station, I'm a mess. A tired, broken-down mess. Once I've rested I'll be as good as new. Unlike Humpty Dumpty after he falls off the wall, I'll be able to pull myself together again.

I yank off my jeans and sweater and let them fall to the floor in a clumsy pile. The sheets are crisp and cool as I crawl into the plush bed in my bra and underwear. Sleep takes me instantly.

CHAPTER SIX

Silk whispers across my forehead, against my temples, down the side of my face. I try to stretch and realize I can't. Something prevents me from moving. The blankets are pinned on either side of me. I can't move. *I can't move!* I gasp for breath and scream. My heartbeat speeds up, and I start to panic and struggle.

"Shhh, baby, there you are. You're finally awake."

Chase's voice penetrates the layer of fear, calming me instantly. I breathe in and out a few times. The panic eases. For a scant moment, I was back *there*. Back to when I awakened tied to the bed against my will. The room is dark, though I can still see Chase's sly smile. He's in the same suit from this morning and distractingly handsome. I take a deep breath and exhale slowly. The rest of the anxiety trickles out the edges of my pores as I inhale his woodsy scent. His fingers slide along my temple and he cups my chin. He pets the apple of my cheek, which is probably still twice its normal size.

"What time is it?"

"It's six. I'm taking you out. Get up. Get dressed."

A sigh escapes. "I told you, I was tired. I'm not going out." I stick to my guns, though Chase's nearness sends all pretense of a defense crumbling into a pile of mush. When he's close, I just want to be with him. Alone, it's easy to pretend what's happening between us isn't real.

He brings his mouth down for a slow luxurious kiss. Mmm, this man can kiss. He slowly sweeps his mouth across my lips and nibbles on the plump lower one. I groan as he deepens the pleasurable assault. His tongue enters my mouth, sweeping along mine. He tastes so good. Like a perfectly ripe strawberry. I know he's using my lack of restraint when he's touching me to get what he wants. *Sneaky bastard.*

I twine my fingers through his thick dark hair, scraping his scalp lightly. He groans while sliding one hand against my chin to turn my head, delving deeper. He swipes his tongue languidly against mine, and I feel that tingling down low in my belly. God, I want this man. Just as I grip at his waist to pull his shirt out of his pants, he pulls away.

"Seriously?" Frustration seeps out in a snarl.

"Gillian, as much as I'd like to fuck you right now, you're in no state."

I roll my eyes in disbelief. He's the only man in the universe with a conscience.

"Believe me, I want to sink my dick so far into you, you won't know what hit you, but it would be taking advantage." He stands and tucks his shirt back into his slacks. "I'm taking you to one of my restaurants this evening. I've had a dress sent over." He grabs a box that he must have brought in because it wasn't there when I went to sleep.

"How did you get in here?"

He shrugs. "My hotel."

"Do you ever take no for an answer?"

"Rarely," he admits. "Now slip this on."

He holds the box out, but away from the bed, so I have

to get out of bed to retrieve it.

Two can play at this game. I smile coyly, and his eyebrows rise into sculpted triangles. He has no idea what he's in for. I pull back the covers and stand tall in a royal blue bra and thong matching set and nothing else. The cups of the bra are see-through, leaving nothing to the imagination. My pale pink nipples have hardened and puckered through the sheer fabric. His mouth opens and closes on a gasp. He takes a deep breath, and those ocean eyes scan me from head to toe before zeroing in on my chest.

I grab the box from him and delight in the knowledge that the second I turn around, he's going to see bare ass with only a tiny wisp of lace above my tailbone and a string across each hip holding the garment in place. I turn and sashay toward the bathroom.

"God, woman! You're going to be the death of me!"

In a second flat, he's behind me, one hand on my ass gripping and squeezing the cheek, the other cupping a breast, pinching the nipple through the sheer fabric, elongating it further. My back is smashed against his front. He kisses the side of my neck, across my shoulder blades, ending at the opposite shoulder, where he bites down, leaving a slight indentation in the skin. I moan and melt against him as he soothes the bite with his tongue and lips.

"You smell so good. Baby, I've never held back before, and it's killing me."

The breath against my ear sends shivers down my spine and a new bout of need through my core. His fingers do wicked things to my nipple, and I moan, leaning against him harder, pressing and rubbing my ass into his growing erection.

"Then don't hold back," I goad.

He pulls back and slaps my ass. I shriek and jump forward.

"Get dressed," he says with finality, and adjusts his crotch.

Gritting my teeth, I enter the bathroom. Closing the door, I take a firm hold of the sink, gripping the tile. I have never wanted to make love to a man more than I do right now. He's driving me insane waiting. After a few deep breaths, I've cooled the fevered emotions and hormones his mere presence sends raging. Looking in the mirror at my reflection, I go cold.

I haven't really looked at myself since the attack. Unfortunately, I've seen this woman before, and she's hideous. My cheek is still swollen, though it is not nearly as noticeable as last night. There's a garish purple-and-yellow bruise forming and spreading along my cheek into my hairline and up to the bandage over my right eye. I pull at the sterile strips, removing the bandage completely, and take a good look at the stitches. There are five stitches accompanied by a sticky dark orange substance surrounding the area. It's the iodine they used to prep the area before stitching it. It's not the first time I've been sewn up after an attack. Hopefully, the last though. I sigh. How many times have I looked in the mirror at this ugly woman? Too many to count.

I wash away the iodine, and the area looks better. The doctor did a good job stitching up the wound. Maybe it won't scar. Concealer helps to hide the bruise and discoloration. I pull up my hair and pin it into a messy bun with the longer layers sweeping across my forehead and cheek. That serves as a nice cover to the wounded area and hides the stitches quite nicely. It's the best I can do. I hate that I'm an expert at covering up bruises and wounds. Too many years of practice. But not anymore. I shake the thought away. Now's not the time to go digging into the past.

Opening the box, I pull out the garment Chase brought for me. Extravagant would describe it best. I'm pretty sure I've never worn anything so exquisite. It's a deep chocolate with a high neck that will cover the cuts and bruises at my throat. I slip it on, clip the back, and the dress falls to just above the knee. It delicately hugs my curves. The silk fabric feels like flowing water on my skin, it's so soft. I look at myself in the mirror and do not recognize the woman staring back. The dress is stunning and makes me look elegant. Chase might actually be proud of having this woman on his arm.

The entire back opens in a cowl-style hanging just above my bottom. The little dips above my sacrum wink into sight as the fabric sways over them with the slightest movement. Awkwardly, I remove my bra.

I'm happy he came for me, even though I tried to push him away. In this dress, I feel like myself. The pounding headache from earlier is gone, thanks to the long nap and double dose of meds, but now I'm ravenous. Hungry for both food and Chase. Though, if Chase sticks to his ridiculous no hanky-panky policy, I'm only going to be satisfied with one.

I slide a sheer glistening gloss over my lips and exit the bathroom. Chase is sipping a glass of wine. He hands me a glass and grasps my hand, twirling me around to inspect the dress.

"You're an incredibly sexy woman, Gillian." His voice is seductive as he trails one finger along the open back, caressing my spine from nape to tailbone.

Goose bumps appear across my flesh, and I hold in a moan, biting my lip instead.

Boldly, he dips his fingers into the back of the dress to trace the tip of my thong. "I love that I'm the only man who gets to do this."

"Chase, the things you say," comes out breathy and labored. I go to the closet and pull out a pair of nude peep-toe heels, relieved that I packed the perfect staple shoes. They go with anything and everything. I step into them, and the additional few inches of height make me feel better immediately.

"I have one more thing for you," he says.

I take another sip of the wine and set it down on the side table. He hands me a bag with Louis Vuitton emblazoned on the outside.

"Why are you buying me things? You hardly know me," I ask nervously.

"Because I want to. If I want to buy a beautiful woman nice things, I will."

I gaze into his eyes and see honesty there. "Thank you," I reply, not knowing what else to say. Mom always told me that when someone does something nice you, just say thank you. Don't question it. Just be grateful they thought of you.

I open the bag and find a sleek black midsized purse. It has medium-length handles and is square. Very minimalist. It's exactly what I would have picked for myself. The style and color will easily go with most outfits. He has excellent taste, and it is a lovely, thoughtful gesture after mine was stolen last night.

I smile and look at him grinning. "This is amazing,

Chase. Really, thank you." I pull it out and hold it next to me. The price tag drops over the side of the strap and I catch the amount. Oh. My. God. "You spent eleven hundred dollars on a purse! This is too much." I push the bag toward him as if it has suddenly grown teeth.

He doesn't take it and it drops to the floor in a beautiful leather heap.

"Chase, the purse that was stolen probably cost me fifty dollars. This is more than my share of rent for a month!" I'm breathing too fast. I swallow slowly and try to avoid the mini-panic attack. I look up at Chase. His teeth are clenched and that little muscle in his jaw is ticking.

"You deserve nice things, Gillian. I can afford it," he says almost mockingly.

"I don't want your money!" I stare at him in disbelief.

"I know." His statement is matter of fact. "Boggles the mind." He shakes his head and smiles. "Come. Dinner waits." He picks up the purse and hands it to me.

Chase is a man used to getting his way. I don't stand a chance against him. I'm going to need a new strategy if I'm going to guard my heart and my morals. We are so not done with this conversation though. I cling to the purse and grab a light jacket.

In the limo, I'm still flustered and irritated. Now I'm wondering how much he spent on this dress. It would probably horrify me. *Does he typically just burn money?* There are so many better uses for it than material things. It is a lovely purse, though. The leather is buttery soft, the style perfect to go with any dress, and it even has a name written on the inside lining. *Madeline*. I guess if you're going to charge eleven hundred dollars for something, you might as well name it.

Chase twines his fingers with mine, bringing our hands palm to palm. Energy buzzes between us instantly.

He leans over and whispers, "I can't stop thinking about your ass in that blue thong. I'm looking forward to licking and spanking every inch of it when you've healed."

He bites the tender flesh of my earlobe, sending a zing straight to my core. Did he say *spank*? I've never been spanked before. Hit with intent to harm, but never spanked for pleasure. Not sure if I'd like it, but if Chase is naked and doing the spanking, I'll give it a whirl. He places a leisurely kiss against my shoulder. It's an intimate gesture from someone who's only known me a couple days. I'm having a hard time with how much of my attention this man has in such a short time.

We reach our destination, and I am wired for sound. With little touches and caresses, the man has me on sexual pins and needles. Men have not paid attention to me the way Chase does. Maybe because I never let them. Chase seems to watch every move, every subtle nuance—the flick of my hair, the shake of my foot. Everything. It is as if he is intimately in tune with my natural self.

Sex spills from his lips as he speaks and in the way he inches his body closer to mine. I want to climb into his lap and stay for a week. There is this heavy, needy ache that fills the air around us, stifling with its unfulfilled intent. If he doesn't put me out of my misery soon and take me, I fear I'll explode. Icarus flying to close to the sun. I look at the flesh of my arms and legs to ensure they aren't sizzling and burning already, sitting so close to white-hot fire.

We arrive at the restaurant, and Chase escorts me up a

narrow staircase, his hand firmly planted on the bare skin of my lower back. I can hear the melodic lull of a piano playing as we enter a large space filled with white columns and hardwood floors. My heels click against the dark surface. A catacomb of open rooms makes each dining space seem small, intimate. The walls are a soft, buttery yellow, the light so low that the room glows. The walls have few adornments, only a couple of pieces of large art hanging on one wall. Tall skinny vases stand like sentinels along the wall, and giant sticks poke out in every direction. A simple frosted glass lights each table with a small orchid lying alongside it. Golden leather high-back seats nestle against a cappuccino-colored table. It's very simple and a complete contrast to the bar we went to last night. It has an Asian-inspired spirit to it.

People talk quietly at their tables. Everyone is dressed impeccably. Chase caresses my lower back, his palm pressing lightly against the naked flesh to usher me forward.

"Mr. Davis, it's lovely to see you tonight," says a man in a structured black suit.

"Thank you, Jeffery. I would like my table. We will be staying for dinner. Please tell the chef to prepare a seafood dish for two."

I tug on his suit coat. He leans in. Whispering into his ear, I respond, "I don't eat seafood."

"Really? None at all?" He looks at me quizzically.

"No." I bite my lip and check my pedicure. Yep, still looking good. No chips in the pink paint.

"Hold that, Jeffery. This stunning lady does not eat seafood. What would you like, baby?"

Baby again? A girl could get used to that endearment. "I'd give anything for some pasta." I grin and lick my lips.

He brings his thumb up to gently pet the moist flesh, stealing my breath. His eyes go dark, his gaze intense as he studies my face.

"Don't lick them, or I will," he warns.

I nod. Excitement swirls in my gut at his words. Would he lick me right here in the middle of a restaurant with everyone watching? If I were a betting woman, I'd say the odds are a complete and resounding yes.

"Apparently the lady would like some pasta, sans the seafood. I will have the same." He makes a tsking sound. "What this woman does to me." He shakes his head and leads the way with his hand splayed along my back.

I can't focus on anything because his finger is distractingly close to the fabric of my thong. He's definitely ramping up the seduction. I'd give in with a loud "take me" if I thought he would go against his earlier decision to wait.

The maître d' leads us to a secluded table set apart from the other patrons. It's separated by a wall of dark plantation-style shutters. Chase pulls out my chair. I don't think in all of my twenty-four years I have had a man pull out my chair. It's so noble and old-fashioned. It's part of what makes this mercurial man unique, so...special.

Wine appears without Chase ordering it. "I took the liberty of bringing you the newest selection, sir," Jeffery says confidently.

"Have at it, my friend."

I love how Chase is jovial and respectful with his staff, especially after what I thought was rudeness to the bartender the other night. He claims it was his impatience to ensure I'd have a drink with him. I choose to give him the benefit of the doubt.

Jeffery pours the wine.

Chase sips it. "You've done it again. It's perfect and will go well with the pasta."

The maître d' fills our glasses and exits, closing the shutters, providing complete privacy.

He clinks our glasses together. "To us," he says.

My cheeks heat as I tap his glass then take a sip. The wine is to-die-for splendid. This is the third time I've had a glass of wine in Chase's presence, and every last one was incredible.

Chase smiles as I assess the legs in the glass of red. "So, Gillian, what does a typical day for you look like?" he asks and takes his own sip of wine.

I'm about to answer but am interrupted by the buzzing of my phone from the new purse. "Just a sec." I check and realize I have six missed calls. Not good. The text display is from Maria.

To: Gillian Callahan

From: Maria De La Torre

Dios Mio, are you okay? Call me. Now!

Oh, no. She knows. Shit! This is not going to be good.

"Everything okay?" Chase asks at the same time another ping rings out from my cell phone.

I glance down, reading the text.

To: Gillian Callahan

From: Bree Simmons

What the hell happened? Where are you? I'm freaking out! Call me.

I look up at Chase with what must be a miserable

expression because his gaze fills with concern. "Um, looks like the girls found out about last night?" Another ping. I roll my eyes. *Not now!* I look down. It's Kat. I sigh loudly.

To: Gillian Callahan

From: Kathleen Bennett

I just heard. We're worried about you, Gigi. Please tell me you're okay. How can we help?

"What the hell is going on?" Chase's voice rises above the static of irritation swirling around my subconscious.

Damn that Phillip!

I turn my phone off and concentrate on him. "They found out. I'm going to kill Phillip tomorrow," I say, annoyed. Phillip can't just leave well enough alone. I should have never told him. No, that was never an option. I should have told him *not* to say anything to the girls so that I could tell them first. Preferably after they've had a couple glasses of wine. None of us take kindly to the other being hurt and being mugged at gunpoint… I take a huge gulp of my wine and am momentarily assaulted by the lush berry notes. It's delicious.

"Who found out? What did they find out?"

I wasn't planning on going into detail about my family. Technically, they're not my blood, but they are the only family I have and they are fiercely protective.

"The girls. Phillip must have told Maria what happened. Now they're all freaking out and blowing up my phone."

"Gillian, back up. Who are the girls?"

I light up at the mention of my soul sisters. I miss them terribly. My huge grin must have set him at ease because his eyes twinkle as he smiles at me. "This could take a while,"

I joke.

"I've got all night, especially when you have that gorgeous smile on your face. Tell me about them."

Jeffery brings a cheese, olive, and meat appetizer that pairs perfectly with the wine. After a few nibbles, I explain the loves of my life.

"Maria De La Torre is half Italian, half Spanish. Very feisty. She's the most incredible dancer you've ever seen. Watching her dance is like"—I fan my hands and arms out, trying to show it—"watching a painting come to life. It's breathtaking."

He nods.

I continue, "We're roommates. We've lived together the past couple years, but have been friends for half a decade." I stop a moment when the memory of that first meeting invades my mind.

We were both black-and-blue, sitting quietly with a group of other battered women who'd escaped their bad relationships. The other women were there to coach us. But neither of us felt a connection to them. They looked perfect, didn't have a scratch. Even though they said they'd been in our same chair a time or two, Maria and I looked at one another and clasped hands. Right then and there, I knew we'd support one another for life.

"You've got this glazed look in your eyes. Tell me." Chase breaks into the memory.

I smile, trying to recall where I was before I took a detour down memory lane. "Maria just has a fire in her. When you're near her, she's warm and comforting. She traveled the world dancing until she had uh…an accident." I settle on accident. I don't intend to go into the details behind the particular event that almost ruined her career. "But she's back to her old self and working at the San Francisco Theatre with one of the local dance companies."

"Incidentally, I know the company and the theatre well. Beautiful architecture," he says.

I nod. "You should see one of her shows. Everyone is impressed when they see her talent."

"Looking forward to meeting her. Maybe tomorrow when I take you home from the airport?"

"Sure."

He smiles before plopping in a bite of meat and cheese. "Continue."

And I do because it's fun and easy to talk about my girlfriends. "Bree Simmons owns 'I Am Yoga' in downtown San Francisco. We met several years ago when I took up yoga. She's absolutely gorgeous, flexible." I waggle my eyebrows at him.

He laughs.

"She has the voice of an angel. She will bring any grown man to his knees through her songs, flexibility, and huge heart. But what is so amazing is that she doesn't even have a clue about her beauty."

"Neither do you."

I tilt my head to the side.

"Gillian, you're gorgeous. You have no idea of your own beauty."

I'm fairly certain my cheeks are back to being rosy as I smile shyly, take another bite of Brie cheese, and think about how funny it is that I'm talking about Bree and eating Brie at the same time. I tell Chase, and we both laugh.

"Is that all of them?" he questions.

I shake my head. "You know about Phillip, now."

His eyes darken, almost slamming a shutter down over the easy conversation but I forge on, determined to bring it back.

"Last, but most certainly not least, is Kathleen Bennett, otherwise known as Kat. She's reserved, quiet, and the most talented costume designer in the business. She does the costume work for the San Francisco Theatre. I met her through Maria. I like to think of her as my tree-hugging comrade because she cares so much about the earth and the environment. We both do, but she's very green."

"Being green is excellent," he says.

"True. I like doing my part."

"Is that all of them?" he asks with the most stunning smile.

"Those are my soul sisters." I grin and twirl my fingers around the stem of my wineglass.

His eyebrows knit together. He waits for me to continue but it's hard talking about my family, or lack thereof.

"I don't have any siblings or family besides my biological father. I don't see him much. They are all I have. We support one another through everything."

Chase sips his wine. "They sound wonderful. I'm looking forward to meeting them." His tone is sincere.

I wonder if he will really be around long enough to be introduced. "Wait until they get a load of you. You might want to go after those three beauties. Two hot blondes and a brunette. More your speed?"

He frowns. "Don't compare yourself to any woman. I. Want. You." His eyes are heated, daring me to comment.

"Why, Chase?" I hate how small my voice sounds.

"A woman hasn't caught my eye in years. I don't date, never bring them to my home."

My mouth drops.

He looks away. "Hell, most women I meet I bed within hours."

I can imagine how any woman would fall willingly into bed with him. Also it explains why he assumed what he did when we met. He's the real living version of Superman. Hell, bedding him is all I can think about right now. I squeeze my legs together, relieving a bit of the throbbing ache he's left me with since waking me.

Chase continues, "Gillian, I take women to one of my hotels, fuck them, and go home."

I process this information and shake my head. It doesn't make sense. He took me to his room last night. Lay in bed with me. Took care of me through the night. That's the sweet knight in shining Armani I know. Not this callous womanizer.

Chase takes a deep breath. "All I can think about with you is bringing you to my penthouse in San Francisco and locking you away with me for a week. I'm not sure what is between us, but I'm committed to finding out why I'm so drawn to you." He frowns as if he doesn't like what he said.

"And then what? Are you going to love me and leave me too?" My voice is meek, so unlike the strong person I'm trying to pretend to be.

He shakes his head. "I haven't yet, and I've had ample opportunity." His gaze is intense, daring me to argue.

He could have had me several times and didn't. What does that mean?

"I slept better next to you last night than I have in years, even waking every couple hours to take care of you. I'm still trying to understand it." He covers my hand with his, and his thumb caresses the pale skin, tracing smooth circles.

I shiver and pull away, feeling a bit awkward and insecure.

Jeffery comes in with our pasta dishes. They're beautiful. The pasta has a cream or white sauce with sprinkles of fresh herbs and sits in a square plate. A perfectly white orchid nestles at the side with a sprig of rosemary. It's almost too pretty to eat, but I twirl a long noodle around my fork and taste anyway. It's out of this world good. I moan around the cheesy goodness. The food is indescribable.

Chase watches me intently. "I love watching you eat. The sound coming from those ruby lips makes my dick hard." He licks his lips solicitously.

Will I ever get used to him, his candor, and the intensity? I feel like I'm standing on the edge of a cliff. A subtle gust of wind will topple me over the edge at any moment.

"Tell me about your family, Chase."

He wipes his mouth with his napkin, sips his wine, and rests his elbow on the table. "I spent most of my childhood and teen years living with my Uncle Charles on my mother's side. He was a widower taking care of my four cousins, Craig, Carson, Cooper, and Chloe."

I giggle and he stops, that sculpted eyebrow going into a curious point. "You all have a name that starts with C?"

"Yes, and we all share the surname of Davis."

That's odd. He said his uncle was his mother's brother. Wouldn't Chase have his father's name?

"My uncle and his nannies raised me from the time I was seven until I was eighteen and went off to Harvard. My cousin Carson was already there. He's two years older than I am."

"So what's the difference between the ages of the five of you?" I take another bite of the creamy pasta.

"Craig is thirty-five. Carson, thirty-two, Cooper is thirty. We're about the same age. I turn thirty this year. Then Chloe is the baby. She's twenty-seven."

"Are you close to them?" His large family sounds interesting. I've never known the love of a big family. It was mostly just me and mom growing up. Now, it's me and the girls, and of course Phillip.

"I respect them. I'm close with Carson. Craig is married and living in New York. I see him when I'm traveling for business or checking on one of my companies. Chloe is a fashion designer and in and out of Europe, so I don't see her as much as I'd like. She has an incredible eye for detail. I have a couple suits she designed for me when she was dabbling in menswear. Mostly, she designs for women."

"I'd love to see her work."

He smiles and nods.

"What about Cooper?"

He looks away, his teeth clench, and his jaw muscle starts to twitch again. "Coop and I used to be very close, but not any longer." He twists noodles around his fork and eats them.

I expect him to continue after he's done, but he doesn't. Sipping my wine, I wait patiently, hoping he'll finish what he was saying. An uncomfortable vibe crackles in the space around us.

"I don't want to talk about Cooper." He looks down and fiddles with the pasta on his plate.

I'm not going to press it. I'd rather he not press me for information about my past either. "Okay." I shrug, trying to be nonchalant.

The tension dissipates as we grin over our wineglasses and eat. It's comfortable sitting with Chase, talking about our upbringing. My belly has warmed from the wine, and I take a moment to analyze his features. The way his dark brown hair whisks across his forehead makes me want to brush my fingers across it. His eyes gleam like a multicolored opal. He has a five o'clock shadow, making him look edgy. I'd like to drag my tongue across that lower lip and feel the prickles of the overgrown stubble. Chase's gaze catches mine, and power exudes from him like a tornado. I'm powerless against the pull.

His large hand comes over mine on top of the table and he turns it over, running his index finger from the crook of my elbow to my palm. A tremble runs through me at the simple touch. He trails his fingers along the expanse of skin again as I look into his eyes. They burn with intensity and—as he's told me not to do—I lick my lips.

He stands with a jerk and is around the table in a nanosecond. He hauls me out of my chair and against his chest. One large hand cups the back of my head, and he crushes my lips to his. I open my mouth to allow him access. He plunders my mouth fiercely with deep swipes of his tongue. We're all lips, teeth, and tongue, arms desperately pulling at one another. His left hand trails warmly down my bare back and dips into the opening of my dress. He slips under the fabric of my thong to grip my sex from behind while he grinds his erection into my belly. When he slips one long digit into my center, I cry out. Before I can object, he adds a second finger and thrusts in and out. Instantly my sex clenches around the intrusion. His mouth swallows my cries of passion and desire.

Chase pulls away and trails wet kisses along my hairline, behind my ear, punctuating his movement with a nip to the chin. Talented fingers continue their glorious torture, and I grind against his hand.

He laughs as he whirls his tongue around the edge of my ear. "Eager to come, are we?" he says huskily.

"Yeah." It's the only coherent thought I can mutter. My eyes are tightly closed, my mind solely focused on those fingers delving so deep. In and out, tug and clench. My pleasure soars and hits that effervescing peak. I'm ready to explode at any moment. I feel wanton and desperate for release, even with the knowledge that at any moment Jeffery could enter and catch us in a compromising position. The exhibitionist in me moans and gasps at a particularly hard thrust. It feels as though he's reaching to the farthest depths within me. He crooks his fingers, rubbing against the inner wall. Bursts of need spike in all directions, and I become a lifeless doll, clinging to his shoulders, my body shaking all over as he jerks and tugs at the tiny knot of nerves, as if he is wringing it out of me by force.

Chase's other hand covers my breast, and he zeroes in to pinch and twist the nipple. Fresh ribbons of heat fly down to my sex, coating his fingers with my essence. The fabric of my dress adds an extra layer of tension against the tight peak he's plucking. I groan and slide my hands up his back into that sexy hair. I drag his mouth to mine and bite his plump lower lip, sucking it inside. His hand leaves my breast, and I groan in frustration. His fingers steadily pump into me.

Wetness drips around the apex of my thighs.

"You are so wet. God." He inhales, his nostrils flaring. "I can fucking *smell* you," he growls and nips at my neck.

I moan and gasp when he speeds up. I'm so close, but I need something more to tip me over the edge. "Are you ready to come for me, my lovely?"

"Chase, please!" I beg.

"Look at me, Gillian."

My eyes meet his. He's stunningly beautiful. His brow is tight, jaw clenched as he focuses on my pleasure. Slowly, he trails the hand that was twisting my nipple down the front of my dress. He scrunches up the fabric, finding my wet center. He winks and opens his mouth on an exhale as his fingers press down on my clit. He twirls two fingers around the hardened nub.

"Come for me, baby."

He presses hard on my clit, his fingers reaching so far into me I scream out in release. It's too much, too good. His kiss swallows the noise, and I ride the ephemeral waves, gripping him tightly as my entire body detonates. It goes on and on as he pinches my clit and tickles my insides, extending the orgasm while wave after glorious wave consumes me.

When those beautiful fingers leave my sex, he holds me against him, both of our chests moving up and down with great effort. I lean my face into the crook at his neck, the woodsy citrus scent so strong I stick out my tongue and lick along the tendon. He groans and hugs me tighter to him. God he tastes good. Like man and sex.

"It's mesmerizing watching you come," he whispers in my ear. "I plan on seeing that expression a lot more in the very near future."

Someone clears his throat behind me, but I don't turn around. I have no idea how much he may or may not have seen or heard. Instead, I choose to keep my heated face cowering in Chase's neck where I kiss and lick the surface as I breathe deep, letting my heart rate slow.

"Dessert, Mr. Davis?"

I look into Chase's face. His desire shines strongly in those beautiful orbs. He brings his fingers to his mouth, and I watch with intense fascination as he sucks the two digits that were inside of me clean. He closes his eyes as if he's in pure bliss.

Finally he answers Jeffery. "No, thank you. We'll be leaving shortly."

My heart may have actually stopped. Never in my years of having sex has a man been so blatantly graphic or sexually stimulating. I knew in that moment, he was going to take me to heights I'd only ever dreamed of experiencing. I could hardly wait.

"It was lovely having you visit, sir. Until next time," Jeffery says with his eyes down as he leaves.

"Nothing will be as sweet as you." Chase kisses me languidly.

I'm sure a blush is roaring across my cheeks and down my neck. The Irish blood in me does no favors at hiding the way I react to him.

As we walk through the restaurant, Chase holds me tight to his side. Several patrons wave, but he doesn't stop. He's on a mission. I can only hope it's to conquer *me* back at the hotel.

CHAPTER SEVEN

Complete and utter frustration permeates my entire body and mind. I'm sitting next to Chase in the limo on the way to the airport. Last night he received a call and jetted off to his room to deal with a situation for work. He even had his henchman walk me to my room to ensure I got there safely. Probably had Jack waiting outside my room all night to make sure I didn't leave unattended.

After he manipulated my body in the restaurant, I was certain he was going to take me to his room and make good on what he started. No, he just kissed the daylights out of me and shoved me in the arms of his bodyguard. Told Jack to make sure I was safely escorted to my room.

I'm used to Phillip being protective of me, but not Chase. I've known him all of three days, and in that span of time, he's frustrated me mentally and physically, taken care of me after the mugging, and showered me with gifts. He's a tornado of contradictions. And this raw sense of ownership Chase seems to have over me is downright shocking and uncalled for. It's as if he's decided he has control over me because of his warped perception of this attraction between the two of us.

I called each of the girls last night. It was like visiting my esthetician and getting a bikini wax. Each strip hurting more than the next because you know exactly what the pain is going to feel like once that glue hits and that sterile strip is pulled. Telling my best friends one by one about the attack brought a lot of old wounds I had buried deep down back to the surface. All three of them know about Justin and the volatile relationship we had, so going over the mugging in striking detail left me feeling damaged and split open emotionally. Couple that with sitting next to Chase in a small car after three days of unresolved sexual tension, and I can officially add tortured to the list of twisted feelings. I want to snuggle up to his side and rub along his strong frame and find that sense of comfort, the one I had when he held me in his arms in bed, that safe and warm feeling I was just starting to appreciate.

"Not acceptable. I want that property for less than fair market or we walk." Chase's tone is sharp, biting as he responds to the individual on his cell phone.

He's facing away from me, his focus on a spot outside the window. His jaw tightens as he clenches his teeth, and that tic I've become fascinated with makes its appearance.

"I understand they are in a position. I want that property for less than twenty million. Make it happen," he says and clicks off without saying goodbye.

"Everything okay?" I wade into unfamiliar waters, wanting to be there for him but not knowing how to be.

He throws me a life raft. His eyes soften and he curls his hand around mine. The simple touch makes me melt.

"Your being here makes it a lot better." He brings my hand to his lips to kiss my palm.

I smile as he rests our entwined fingers on his thigh. His phone rings again, and I stare out the window, enjoying the simple comfort of holding hands with a man. Not any man... *Chase.*

We reach the airstrip, and I am in awe. A large white plane with "Davis Industries" scrolled along the side awaits. Jack opens our doors, and I go to the trunk to get my luggage.

Chase clears his throat, and I look up at him.

He grins like a schoolboy. "Gillian, Jack will handle the bags." He holds out his hand.

I shyly come around the car and take it.

"You're so cute," he says as he drags me to the stairs of the plane.

We board and settle into large beige leather chairs. We are given the flight information and told to sit back and enjoy. Chase's cell phone rings again, and he looks at me in apology.

"I understand. You're a busy man. Do whatever you need to do. I'll be fine," I assure him.

He nods and takes his call.

I settle into the large cushy chair, lean my head back, and close my eyes. I didn't get much sleep after dinner and am exhausted today. The dull ache in my head from the wound isn't helping. Neither is being sexually starved and emotionally spent. Ripping open that can again brought up too many memories of the past and made me toss and turn all night. Someone drapes a blanket over my legs. I sigh in contentment. Warm lips brush my cheeks, and I lean toward the soft touch.

"You're beautiful, baby," Chase says.

I hear him walk away. His footsteps get lighter the farther away he goes. I don't bother to open my eyes. I settle further into the warmth and am fast asleep before we take off.

In what feels like seconds, a featherlight sensation trails along my hairline and along my scalp. I lean into the touch.

"Baby, we're here." Chase's voice reaches through the sleepy fog.

I open my eyes and am gifted his dazzling blues.

"Didn't you sleep last night?"

I shake my head and he frowns. "I would have slept better had you joined me," I challenge.

"You're a little vixen, aren't you? Makes me want to take you right here." He leans forward and kisses me hard. I don't have the chance to respond before his lips are gone. Then he's pulling me out of my chair and out of the plane.

Jack has our bags on a cart and follows as Chase leads me off the tarmac and into the airport. Hand in hand, we walk toward the exit when I hear a child's squeal.

"Gigi!"

A bouncing girl with curly blond pigtails runs toward me. I lean down and pull her up into my arms, spinning around in a circle. She squeezes me as tightly as a four-year-old can.

"Anabelle." I hug my angel tightly. "I missed you, Belle." I bring her down to the white laminate floor and come down to her level to peer into her smiling face. She's looks exactly like her gorgeous mother.

"Dad said you had a present for me!" she exclaims excitedly.

"I do, but honey, what are you doing here?"

Strong familiar arms encircle me from behind as I stand. Phillip. A big grin splits my face, and I twirl and hug my dearest friend tightly. "Phil, what are you doing here?"

He cups my face and frowns. "Not again, Gigi." He's looking at the stitches above my brow. His fingers graze my bruised cheek, inspecting the damage. He shakes his head.

I turn away from his ministrations, not able to look at him. I know what he's thinking. A throat clears behind me and a hand settles on my waist. I'm pulled toward Chase. His body plasters along my back.

"Introduce me," he growls into my ear.

"Oh my God." I got so swept away in seeing Anabelle and Phillip I forgot Chase. "Phillip Parks, meet Chase Davis." I gesture to Chase behind me.

Phillip's eyes widen as he looks down and clocks Chase's possessive hand around my waist. "The Chase Davis? As in Davis Industries?" Phillip asks as he holds out his hand.

Chase nods and grips Phillip's hand in a firm shake.

"Wow, Gigi, I didn't know you were arriving with anyone. I came to pick you up as we discussed yesterday."

I frown. If I remember correctly, we didn't confirm anything officially. "Oh, I completely forgot you offered. One too many hits to the head," I joke.

Phillip frowns and Chase's jaw clenches.

"Bad joke," I say miserably.

Chase's arm comes up my back and encircles the nape of my neck where his thumb makes endless infinity symbols. "Shall we go?" he asks softly nuzzling into my cheek.

Phillip eyes the exchange warily.

This scenario is not something I anticipated. As much as I'd love to take Chase back to my apartment and convince him to have his wicked way with me, I can't leave Phil and Anabelle. This is not going to go over well. On the other hand, Phillip is my best friend, and Chase is… Well, I don't really know what Chase is right now. I shake my head. Chase's eyebrows rise—I'm not sure whether in surprise or in question.

"Thank you for the flight, Chase. I'm going to head home with Phillip." For some insane reason, I'm nervous about how he will take the news. He's been so incredibly possessive over the past few days, but the last thing I need is a scene.

Chase nods, seemingly unfazed. "Phillip, good to meet you." He shakes Phil's hand once more. "I'm sure we'll be seeing *a lot* more of each other in the near future." His blue gaze bores into mine.

He says so much with that one look. I imagine it's something like: *We will discuss this. You will be mine. You will not escape me.*

Chase turns me around and cups both cheeks. He sweep his thumbs along the apple of my cheekbone. Slowly he brings his lips to settle over mine. I inhale the intoxicating sandalwood and citrus scent, trying to capture it within me. He increases the pressure on my lips, and I'm unable to fight the charge between us. He slides his tongue across my lower lip, and I open my mouth. He enters with his warm, wet tongue, and I grip his shoulders. Chase alternates between nipping my lower then upper lip. Then he tunnels his hands into my hair as he holds me against him, sliding his lips over mine. That spark between us ignites, and I press against his body, forgetting where we are. Everything disappears as I'm swept into the vortex that is Chase. I moan and he growls as I try to pull away. He won't let me. I can feel the hard evidence of his desire and thrust my hips against it. He grins against my lips, peppering my mouth with sweet baby kisses. In my periphery I hear giggling, the kind that can only come from an angel.

"Aunt Gigi is kissing that man, Daddy!" Anabelle exclaims loudly, breaking my trance.

I pull away and swipe the back of my hand against my swollen lips.

Chase looks at me with that devastatingly sexy grin, and I want to jump him all over again. He was staking his claim, and from the look on his face, he's very proud of himself. I'm certain my face is beet red. He pecks my lips once more.

"I expect a call later," he stresses. "Jack, her bags," he says over his shoulder.

Jack. I completely forgot the linebacker was waiting and watching the exchange.

Phillip is waiting rather impatiently. I didn't exactly go into any detail about Chase and the relationship we've formed in the short time I'd been away—if you could call what's happened between Chase and me a relationship. I'm still confused about the entire thing.

Jack sets my bags at my feet and looks at me with a scowl. I don't think the linebacker appreciates me leaving with another man. Chase obviously means a great deal to him. I sigh and thank him.

Chase and Jack saunter towards the exit and I look into Phillip's worried eyes.

"You have some explaining to do," Phil admonishes.

I nod miserably and we head to the exit. I clasp Anabelle's hand and smile as she skips alongside me, happily swinging my arm. What I wouldn't give to be a carefree child instead of a confused twenty-four-year-old.

Phillip puts my bags in the trunk when we get to the car while I buckle Anabelle into her booster seat. Phillip hands her a portable DVD player, and Snow White springs to life on the screen. He places the earphones over her ears. I know he's ensuring we can talk without worrying about what she might hear.

We settle in and head out onto the highway. He waits for me to say something, knowing I won't share openly with him unless it's on my terms. Damn him. It's annoying that he knows me so well.

"Phil, I don't know what you want me to say."

"How about telling me about the man who had his tongue down your throat and his hands all over you?" he says with a twinge of anger.

A quick look out the window shows the gray misty skies of downtown San Francisco. The streets are teaming with cars as we crawl towards our exit. "Chase and I met at the meeting. He's, uh, he's the Chairman of the Board for the Foundation."

"Are you kidding me, Gigi? You're fucking your boss?" He frowns and shakes his head.

"Hey, that's not fair and you know it. And I haven't fucked him!" I cringe and look over my shoulder to make sure Anabelle isn't listening.

She is happily nodding along with the movie, eyes glued to the screen.

"Yet. You haven't yet!"

"You're right, Phil. I haven't yet. But I *want* to, and I will!" I admit without apology. Who does he think he is anyway? Questioning the men in my life. He's not my boyfriend or my father.

"I'm sorry." His tone softens.

I take a deep breath.

"I just…I don't want you to get hurt. A man like that? He's insanely rich and very powerful."

He makes a good point, and I get where he's coming from. Simply, he doesn't want me to lose myself in a man again. One that could destroy everything I've rebuilt since Justin.

Shaking my head, I try to explain. "Phil, this is different. There's something about him. I know it's wrong to date your boss, but he's never at the office. This is the first time in two years of working there that I've seen him." I'm grasping at straws. We both know that dating one's boss isn't a good idea.

"You know what's funny, Gigi?" He laughs. "He's my boss, too." He snickers.

I know I must look like a fish out of water. My head starts to pound. "What do you mean?" I rub at my temples. It's as if I can feel the thud of my heartbeat at the site of my wound. Between the flight and now an annoying conversation with my brother-esque best friend, I'm exhausted.

"He owns the architectural firm I work for. He even has a big office on the top floor of the building, which he also owns."

This new information is hard to assimilate.

He continues, "Chase Davis is a billionaire many times over. He owns the fucking skyscraper and every company in the building I work in. You know that big shiny sign outside of my building?"

I nod. "Yeah?"

His gaze cuts to mine, humor making his eyes a dazzling shade of chocolate. "It says, 'Davis Industries' on it." Phillip snort-laughs.

I cringe feeling ridiculously naive. "I had no idea. Jesus, this is getting complicated." That's the trouble with liking a man. My radar on men hasn't always been trustworthy. They either beat me, call me a whore, or love me and leave me. One way or another, they all seem to want to own me. Chase is no exception. I just wish the connection between us wasn't so strong. It would be easier just to blow it off as a little fling.

Phil brings his hand up to his face and worries his thumbnail. He always does that when he's about to tell me something I don't want to hear. He looks at me sideways then takes a deep breath. "He's also known for being a player. Bedded a couple of the girls at my firm and never called them back. He uses women and throws them away like trash. I don't want that for you."

It's sweet how he's genuinely concerned. I'm lucky to have him.

"I'll be careful. I know he has a history. He told me as much."

He's looks surprised Chase admitted his philandering to me.

"I'm okay. I don't even know what is between us, but I can say that I'm intrigued and fascinated by him. Not to mention, the man is hot."

Phillip laughs loudly as I pretend to fan myself. "I've heard that a lot," he admits. "Just promise me you'll safeguard your heart and be careful. That's all I ask." He grips my hand in a reassuring squeeze.

"I'm a big girl, Phil. I can handle this," I say with all the confidence I can muster. It's a total lie.

Chase is an enigma. One that has me tied, twisted, and feeling uncertain about my surroundings. All I know is that I want to be near him. Want to be with him. Want him in whatever capacity he'll have me.

Phillip drops me off at the apartment after I present Belle with a glittering snow globe from Chicago. It has a few skyscrapers and Navy Pier alongside Lake Michigan. She's instantly fascinated by it. I wave Phil off. He doesn't need to walk me up. I tell him I'll call him tomorrow and we'll meet for dinner later this week. He agrees, and I head up to my building.

I enter the apartment and hear bare feet slapping the wooden floor as Hurricane Maria comes barreling down the hall and captures me in a fierce hug.

"*Dios Mio*! Are you okay?" Maria studies my features, moving my hair to the side to check out the damage. She clucks her tongue and shakes her head. A look of deep concern mars her brow.

"Fine, I'm fine. Though I've missed you, girl." I mean every word.

She gives me a sad smile and traces the bruise along my cheek. Her eyes mist up.

"I'm okay, really. Chase took excellent care of me."

With the strength of her dancer arms, she drags me to the puffy eggplant-colored couch and we plop down, still holding hands. I grip one of the sari-covered throw pillows to my chest.

"Tell me, did you?" she asks.

I know what she's dying to know. Maria is laser-focused

on sex most of the time. She's our resident nympho.

"No," I say miserably and rub my temples.

"What the hell? Is he gay?"

Of course she would go there. I laugh. "He's most certainly *not* gay." My face heats as I recall our rendezvous in the restaurant. My sex clenches at the memory of his long fingers piercing me. "You're never going to believe this."

She waits patiently, her ice-blue eyes focused on me.

"He wants to wait until I'm healed to have sex." Her head imitates whiplash.

"*Como*?" she says in her native tongue.

"I know, doesn't make any sense." I blow a breath over my hair, moving the wisps out of my eyes. "And I've made it very clear that I want to be with him." I pout and cringe, once again annoyed that things didn't go further in Chicago.

"*Estúpido,*" she says. "He has a willing hottie and he's being chivalrous?" She shakes her head. "*Estúpido, cara bonita.*"

"Right! Guess what else?"

She pulls her long raven waves off her neck. Her perfectly sculpted eyebrows knit together.

"Phillip came to the airport to pick me up."

Her eyes widen, delight clearly visible in them.

"There was some serious battle of testosterone going on between them."

"Oh, this is too good." She pulls her legs under her bottom and waits. "Don't leave me hanging, *bonita. Continuar*," she says. Continue.

"Chase all but mauled me in front of Phillip and Anabelle."

"No, he didn't!" she says, throwing her hand over her

mouth.

"He did! And I totally let him. I sucked his face like it was the last drink I was going to have and a drought was coming."

She howls and grabs her stomach in laughter. "What did Phillip do?"

"He gave me a talking-to in the car. Oh, and there's more."

"No, no, I can't take it. This is like Jerry Springer live!" She laughs, leans back, and kicks her legs in the air dramatically.

"Chase owns the building and the firm Phillip works for!" I laugh hysterically.

"Oh, *Dios Mio. Mierda,* shit! I can't believe it. That's crazy!" She shakes her head and puts her hand over her eyes.

"I know, I know. This is becoming really complicated." I lean back on the couch.

"What did Chase do?" she asks.

What did Chase do? I ask myself. He staked his claim as surely as a dog urinates around a tree to ward off other dogs. "He was cool and calm. Though he demanded I call him later. I'm not looking forward to it."

She nods, pursing her lips in what I've come to know is her thinking pout.

While she mulls over the crazy that is my life, I remember she had her big weekend. "Hey, what happened with Tom? Did you?" I waggle my eyebrows.

Her head bobs up and down happily. "*Hermana*, he was amazing. He made me come twice!"

I laugh, and she continues with the gory details. She's as dirty as Chase. I think they'll get along well in that arena.

They are both very sexual creatures and seem rather proud of it. "He was *dulce*...sweet. Though, girl, that man pounded me so hard I think I felt my teeth rattle!"

Like a ninja, I smack her lightly on the leg. A snort bubbles up, and out, when I laugh too hard at the image she portrays. "Good for you! When are you going to see him again?"

She smiles brightly. "This weekend. He's taking me to a baseball game. The Giants."

"Do you even like baseball?"

"Not really." She shrugs. "But I like him, so I'll go."

I giggle and then stop when she becomes quiet. She focuses on my neck. She reaches out and pulls at the collar of my shirt, exposing the glaring bruises and scabs. "*Cara bonita*, are you *really* okay? This had to bring up some bad memories."

Inhaling full and deep, I ponder her question. "It did, I have to admit. Looking at myself in the mirror after the attack reminded me of all the times I was tending to my bruises in the bathroom after one of Justin's tirades."

She grips my hand, and sister solidarity and support covers me like a warm blanket.

Tears fill my eyes. "After two years, it shouldn't come back so easily, should it?"

"*Cara bonita,* we will always have to deal with the fact that we were battered women." Her face tilts to the side, and she clutches my hand. "Remember in group therapy where they made us talk about each experience we could remember so we could flush it out? You talked about the time Justin beat you so badly your face was unrecognizable for weeks?"

I nod. How could I have let him hurt me for so long? The guilt of taking those beatings still haunts me.

"I think you need to go see Dr. Madison," she says. "Talk about what happened so that it doesn't consume you."

"You're right. I'm stronger now. I can talk about the attack. Mostly because it wasn't with someone I trusted. Now that some time has passed, it's a lot easier. That first year of therapy..." I take a deep calming breath. "Having to talk about my relationship with Justin, what he did to me..." I shake my head and pinch my lips together. "Fucking torture."

"It was for me too, *hermana*. I didn't want to admit to what Antonio did to me, but talking about the experiences has made us both stronger. And remember, we got out." She hugs me.

Her familiar floral scent reminds me of all things good in the world. I grip her tightly. We made it out of those diabolical relationships alive when many didn't. Several of our group went back to their men. The next time we saw them, they were in the hospital or a casket. I shiver and Maria holds me tighter. God, I love this woman.

"I love you, Ria."

"*Te amo, cara bonita*." She tucks my hair behind my ears. "Looks like you cleaned up the bruises pretty good. When are the stitches coming out?"

"End of the week. I have to make a follow-up appointment with my doctor."

She gets up and goes to the side table to grab her keys. "I have rehearsal." Her smile drops into a frown. "Are you going to be okay?" She looks at me worriedly.

"Ria, I'm fine. I've been through worse," I remind her

with a wink.

She grins. "I'll be home this evening. Make me dinner? *Por Favor?*" The woman is a glutton for my meals.

"Yes, of course. I'll make dinner. I need to invite Bree and Kat over, too. Thanks to Phillip, they were blowing up my phone yesterday, and they'll want the details."

She throws on a cardigan and nods while pulling her thick dark hair into a knot on the top of her head. "I'll be home at seven. I expect my women to be loaded with vino and ready to grub when I return."

Maria is a riot. She always refers to the girls as "my women." It's an endearing quality that makes me feel needed.

She's out the door in a flash, and I'm back to being alone with my thoughts. I decide to take a shower and unpack. I check in with Taye and confirm that I'll be at work tomorrow at ten. After working the weekend and dealing with the attack, I'm taking a little time for myself. Besides, I need to file for a new license. I've already cancelled my cards and notified the bank. Such a mess. When will my life feel like it's back to being mine?

CHAPTER EIGHT

Bree arrives first. The woman is striking. I'm always shocked by her beauty. Her long blond hair hangs like a golden sheet down her back, almost touching her bottom. Her eyes are a cerulean blue that instantly reminds me of Chase's ocean eyes. Like that of any true Californian girl, her skin is sun-kissed and glowing. Bree's wearing yoga pants and a knit tank top. Even in her work attire, she's all tight muscles and lean curves. At five-foot-two, she's the smallest of all of us, but her strength makes up for her tiny frame. Her pouty lips turn into a wide smile, and I grab her into a hug.

"Gigi, you had me so worried," she whispers against my ear. The smell of rich incense permeates her hair.

"I'm okay, I promise."

She nods and continues to hug me. Her hands encircle my waist. "You look like shit," she says, lightening the heavy moment. I turn and lead her in. "And your ass is getting big. You haven't come to class in a whole week. You owe me three days this week."

Bree is committed to keeping us all fit and flexible. She believes that toning the body and mind is the cure-all for any ailment. She's our resident New Ager from the tips of her pink painted toes to the top of her golden locks.

"I haven't gained a pound, so shut up!" I warn jokingly.

"Suit yourself," she says in mock horror, "if you want Chase to see your sagging ass."

"You bitch!" I scold and we both get lost in a fit of laughter. The doorbell rings again, and I run to open it.

Kathleen is a vision. Her curly blond hair is a halo around her face, reaching just past her shoulders. She slides her hand through it to remove it from her eyes. She's wearing a long, flowing skirt in summery orange hues. Several necklaces in varying lengths hang from a long swanlike neck. Her caramel-brown eyes gleam as she takes me in. Dozens of bangle bracelets tinkle as she pulls me into her arms.

"Oh, Gigi, you gave us one heck of a scare," she says.

"I know, but Kat, I'm okay. Really."

She kisses the side of my hairline and grabs my hand to squeeze it.

We enter the kitchen hand in hand. Bree is already sneaking bites of the salad I prepared. She plops a cherry tomato in her mouth. "What? I haven't eaten all day. And unlike you flabby bitches, I work out all day long!"

We all laugh. "Actually, Kat has been killing it in the studio," Bree says. "I saw you almost every day last week. I'm proud, girlie."

Kat beams. "Unlike Gigi, I have to work hard to keep my girlish figure. The long nights in the theatre hunched over a sewing machine are killing my back." She brings her hand to her slim hips and stretches her back. "The yoga is almost a requirement. And it's not like I have a man to go home to." She sighs.

Kat and Bree have been going through a dry spell with men and complain about it often. I giggle, and they both look at me, waiting.

I tell them what they want to know about Chase and the happenings in Chicago. By the time Hurricane Maria crashes into the kitchen, they are fully up to date and on their second glass of wine. I left out some of the ultra-embarrassing parts, like him getting me off in the middle of a restaurant. Some things are sacred and these girls would never let me live it down if they knew the finer details.

We sit at our quaint kitchen table in mismatched chairs. Maria and I couldn't agree on a table so we refurbished a table we found at a yard sale and scouted out individual unique chairs to go with it. The four of us always sit in the chair we've designated "our" chair. I'm sitting with one knee up on my wooden teal chair. It has cutouts and grooves in the wood where mustard-yellow tones peek through the grain. It has rounded swirling arms that I can rest my palms on perfectly. It's just my size and fits me like a glove.

Maria sits on her deep blue wooden chair with little red flowers indented into every surface. Kat is sitting crossed legged in the oak chair with rich browns and purple lines cutting through the wood in natural swirls. Bree is sitting in lotus position in the lone dark red wooden chair. It has incredibly cool dark brown knots in the wood from the original tree it was cut from. All unique, just like my girls.

They each laugh and talk over one another. I watch them in complete contentment. I am so blessed to have them in my life. I don't know where I would be without them. After losing my mother, the only family I had, and the hell I survived with Justin, their constant presence in my life is a true gift.

"Gigi, what are you thinking about?" Kat asks and eats a forkful of lasagna.

"Just how lucky I am to have you guys," I say genuinely.

She nods and pats my hand.

"I don't know about these bitches, but you're lucky to have me," says Bree, making us all howl. "Seriously though, Gigi. Tell us more about Chase. What's he like?"

"He's…intense. A man used to getting his way in all things." I bring my hand up to my lips and pinch them, lost in thought.

"I don't know about you two, but I like a man who takes charge," Maria adds.

"Yes, but he can be very controlling. With my past history, it makes me nervous," I admit.

Kat jumps in. "I'm sure you're feeling gun-shy after Daniel, and of course, Justin. That's perfectly natural, honey." She takes a sip of her white wine.

"Has anyone seen this man yet?" Bree asks. "Is he hot? You said he was hot, but I don't know if I believe you." She smiles that evil little smile of hers.

"Mouth-wateringly so, Bree. He's tall, at least six two or three. Built." I widen my arms out. "His hair is the color of coffee beans, and his eyes, oh Lord, his eyes will be the death of me. They're not just blue, like the sky. No, they look like the ocean water you see on an advertisement for Cancun!" I gaze off dreamily. My mind flits back to his hand inching down my panties, his lips enslaving my nipple, the tender way he bit down on the sensitive flesh. Goose bumps run over my skin at the memory, and I shiver.

"Um, hello. Earth to Gigi?" Maria says. "I've got him on my cell phone right here. Holy *mierda!* Gigi, talk about *caliente*! He's so hot he's on fire!"

I'm brought back to the here and now, and Maria is

passing her smart phone to Bree.

"Oh, my. Girl, you weren't kidding. He's magnificent!" she exclaims and passes the phone to Kat.

I try to grapple for it, missing it completely.

"Whoa, Gigi. And you haven't hit that yet? What the hell? I'd hit it for you!" Kat exclaims.

They all laugh, annoying the bejesus out of me.

Finally, I clasp the phone, pull it away, and look at the screen. It's a headshot of Chase from our foundation's website. Again, I feel so stupid not having known he was the chairman of the board. I sigh and stare at the image of his gorgeous face for much too long before Maria steals it back.

"You should see him naked. He's glorious."

All three of their mouths drop. I guess I forgot to share that little tidbit. I snicker and pat myself on the back subconsciously. Point for Gigi!

"You've seen him *desnudo*! Complete bare-ass naked and you didn't tell us?" Maria says, a slight edge in her tone.

"You're holding out on your best friends?" Bree mocks indignation.

"We have so little to hold onto, Gigi, and you're getting frisky with a hot male supermodel of a man and you throw us no bones?" Kat laughs.

I take a huge gulp of my wine. Three sets of eyes watch patiently. "Well, it happened so fast. Okay, so he was getting out of the shower in a towel, we had a small argument over Phillip, and then he dropped the towel." I hide my embarrassment in another sip of wine. At this rate, I'm going to end up drunk.

"And how was it?" Bree gestures between her own legs.

I can't believe she's asking about his manhood.

"I'll just bet it was *grande*," Maria counters.

"Probably not. Sometimes those rich pricks have pencil dicks," Kat quips while wiggling her pinky finger.

They're carrying on a conversation with each other, back and forth, barbs flying freely.

"Cut it!" I yell.

All three quiet immediately and all eyes are on me.

"He's huge. Biggest penis I've ever had the pleasure seeing. And it was so pink and pretty and ready. Gawwwdddd." I throw my hands over my heated face.

They bust out in raucous laughter. It's infectious, and we're all laughing so hard we're wiping tears from our eyes.

"So when do you think you'll take it to the next level?" Kat asks sweetly.

"I hope this weekend. Depends on his schedule, I guess. I get my stitches out Friday, and he said he wouldn't touch me until I was better."

"That's actually really sweet," Bree says and stuffs her face full of lasagna. For a tiny woman, the girl can eat. Then again, when you're teaching four yoga classes or more a day, you probably need to carb up.

"So what was your argument over Phillip?" Kat questions.

Taking my time, I explain the uncomfortable conversation we had prior to the towel incident and then again at the airport.

"I can understand why Chase would feel jealous about Phillip. He's hot, Gigi. And he adores you," Bree says.

She thinks Phillip's hot? She never mentioned that. I agree that he's good-looking, but I've never considered him hot. Maybe because I've known him most my life and loved his wife so much.

"Phillip and I do not have that kind of relationship, and all of you know that," I say.

"But technically, you did lose your virginity to him. When are you going share that bit of information with Chase?" Kat throws in.

Never. I cringe and sip my wine. Do I owe Chase an explanation on that part of my past? We were in high school. It was two friends exploring one another and being each other's first. At least I didn't lose my virginity to some asshole in the back of a car on prom night. My time with Phillip was sweet. Phillip was gentle with me, treating me like a porcelain doll. Our exploration lasted all of ten minutes.

"I wasn't planning on sharing that information with him," I say.

Bree shakes her head. "You always say honesty is the best policy. So if it doesn't suit you, you're not going to be honest?"

Damn her for using my own morals against me. She definitely knows how to hit home.

"If it doesn't come up, I don't need to bring it up. It was a lifetime ago." I finish my wine.

Maria leans over and fills my glass once more. She winks at me. "Okay, okay, enough. Let's toast."

Every dinner we share a toast. It's tradition. We each raise our glasses.

Maria leads. "Here's to you, here's to me, if we disagree, fuck you, fuck me, we're family!"

We howl with laughter and each take a sip. Maria always knows the right thing to say to get things back to normal. We discuss Maria's newest show and the costumes involved.

Kat is working on those. Then when Bree is nice and toasty from three glasses of wine, the three of us attack with talk about the fact that Bree is actually interested in Phillip.

I'm surprised by the information but excited. I can't wait to match them up. She'd be a perfect stepmother for Anabelle, and the little girl adores her. Phillip hasn't been with anyone seriously since Angela. We all agree Phillip needs to get laid more than the four of us combined. It would definitely keep him from hounding me about Chase. I start devising a plan to get them in the same space. I decide to work with Maria on the finer details. If there ever was a schemer, it is she, and she's damn good at it.

After we clean up, all of the girls leave, and Maria retires to her room. I look at the clock and realize it's almost midnight. Shit! Chase asked me to call him. I head to my room, put on my pajamas, and crawl into bed with my cell phone.

There's a missed call from Chase and a text message waiting.

To: Gillian Callahan

From: Chase Davis

Haven't heard from you. Call me, no matter the time.

The message he left doesn't sound exactly chipper. I dial his number, and he answers on the first ring.

"Gillian," he says in greeting, but there's a slight edge to his voice.

"Hi. I just got done with dinner and cleaning up."

He doesn't say anything.

"I'm sorry I couldn't call you earlier."

"I was worried." He sounds different. Standoffish, but I

can't quite tell. This is our first real phone conversation.

"I'm sorry." I wait.

He sighs loudly into the phone. I pull on my hair and twirl the strands around my finger nervously.

"Were you with Phillip?" His tone is bored, monotone.

"What? No," I respond, not sure why he'd think that. "Phillip dropped me off and left with Anabelle."

"Where's his wife?"

The question surprises me and the little hairs on the back of my neck stand up. Is he seriously jealous of Phil?

"In San Francisco National Cemetery," I say.

"He's a widower? What happened?"

I still don't like his tone. It hints on accusing, and I've got nothing to say to him if that's the case.

"Drunk driver hit her on her way home from work two years ago. She was killed instantly." I swallow the lump in my throat, thinking of the beautiful blonde who was filled with life and taken away from all of us, especially Anabelle and Phillip, far too soon.

"I'm sorry." Another long pause. He sighs deeply and shocks me with his next question. "You're not in love with him?" His voice is a whisper and more telling than I expected from him.

I smile into the phone. "No, Chase. But he is a part of my life. He's my best friend, and his daughter is important to me."

"I see." His tone is lifeless, flat.

That's it. He sees? What does that even mean? God, he's such an enigma.

"When is your appointment to have your stitches removed?"

That was a peculiar transition from Phillip to my doctor's appointment. "Friday morning." I feel a tingle of anticipation. I pray he wants to see me this weekend.

"I'll be there to pick you up at seven." Again he responds with very little emotion, leaving me floundering to understand where his head is at.

It takes a moment for it to hit but finally it dawns on me what he said. "What? No, you don't have to go to my doctor's appointment. I'm not afraid," I assure him.

"I didn't say you were. I will pick you up Friday. Then after, do you have to go to work?" he asks.

"Yes." He wants to take me to my doctor's appointment. Butterflies start in my stomach and I lean back into my pillows and smile nervously.

"I'll have Jack pick you up from work and bring you to my office here. I have a late meeting on Friday."

He doesn't ask to see me and if I weren't so downright needy for him, I'd likely tell him off. But I can't. I want him too much.

"Okay," I agree without question.

Chase sighs deeply into the phone. "Baby, I look forward to being with you," he says seductively.

Finally! A reaction I can get behind. It's like the flame lighting on a gas stove. Chase can turn me on with a few breathy words.

"Me, too." I barely get the words out. His tone, the sound of his frustrated sigh, do wicked things to my lady parts.

"I can't wait to kiss you, run my tongue along your skin," he adds. "I can almost taste you from the other night."

With effort, I bite back a moan. "Jesus, Chase."

"I can't wait to make you mine, Gillian."

What does that mean to a man like him? Mine for the night? For the weekend? Forever? A chill runs through me at all the possibilities.

"And baby?" he says in a deep gravelly voice.

I shudder, and heat fires down my chest to settle heavily between my thighs. An ache for him starts deep in my core, and I squeeze my thighs together and start to tickle the bare skin above my panties.

"Yes?" I hang on his every word, slipping my hand under the lace fabric.

"Don't masturbate."

What the hell? I pull my hand out of my underwear as if it has been zapped by lightning.

"I want to be the one to make you come from now on." His voice is thick, sexy, and dominant.

Chills run up my spine and goose bumps break out across my skin. "Oh, God. You're killing me, Chase." The man has had me on a slow scalding burn since the moment we exchanged glances at the bar a few days ago.

"Friday," he finishes in a husky timber. "Sweet dreams." He hangs up without saying goodbye.

Maybe he never waits for people to say goodbye. So strange. Smart, sexy as hell, and devastatingly hard to ignore.

He asked me not to masturbate. After a conversation like that, the only thing I can think about is rubbing one off quickly to relieve the intense pressure he's built up in me. I'm strung so tight, one strum of my clit, and I'll be humming in orgasm.

Sleep. It's the only defense I have against the raging desire for him. After these stitches are removed, I am not leaving his side until he puts me out of my misery. I don't care if I have to strip naked and beg.

★ ★ ★ ★

Monday comes fast, and I'm back in the real world. Fundraising, donor testimonials, and event planning are on the docket this week, and I jump in with a flourish. Taye and I meet for lunch. We discuss what happened in Chicago in detail. I confide in him that I'm seeing Chase this weekend. To put it lightly, he is not impressed. He's worried about me and my career.

It's not as though he's telling me anything I don't know. I've already been over the pros and cons a million times. Really, though, when it comes down to it, it is none of his business.

Chase and I share a few texts throughout the week, and he calls me Tuesday evening to tell me he'll be out of town the rest of week, returning late on Thursday. I welcome the time to truly collect my thoughts, knowing he's not just a short drive away. I know the situation with Chase is ill-advised. All the warning signs are going off, but the silk of his voice over the phone and the memory of his hands on my body crush those blaring signals, leaving nothing but anticipation in their wake.

Friday morning at seven, someone knocks on the door. Maria springs off the couch like an Olympic runner. She opens the door before I can set down my coffee cup. I snicker at her exuberance. She's on a mission to meet this man, and nothing is going to get in her way. I figured she'll have to wait. Chase typically sends his linebacker.

I'm surprised when Maria and Chase enter the living area arm in arm, speaking in Spanish. Chase is wearing a pristine black suit and pinstriped blue dress shirt with a crisp white collar. His French cuffs peek out of his suit coat, and the light from the kitchen bounces off his silver cuff links, blinding me.

"*Cuándo aprendiste a hablar español?*" Maria asks.

"*Yo aprendí en la universidad, pasó un período en el extranjero,*" Chase responds.

Maria's clearly impressed. Her smile is huge, and she's using her hands animatedly as she speaks. That's a clear signal she's been sucked into Air Davis where there are no stops and everyone collects two hundred dollars.

"Hello? Remember me? I speak English," I chastise them.

"She asked me when I learned to speak Spanish, and I told her in college. That I spent a term abroad." He makes his way to me and leans down to kiss me. His hand snakes into my hair and tilts my head to the side to gain deeper access.

I open for him, enjoying the taste of his peppermint tongue. A long wolf whistle from behind us makes me pull away. Chase grins, his eyes bright with merriment.

"Damn, you didn't greet me like that," Maria complains with a pout.

Chase puts his arm around my waist and pulls me against him. I curl into his side.

"Sorry. I'm a one woman kind of man," he says, and then dips down for another scorching kiss.

Damn he's pretty, and distracting. I push him off me. He chases my lips and settles for a quick nip on the bottom one before bringing his attention back to our admirer.

Maria winks as a wicked grin slides into place. "Gigi, call me later. Let me know whether or not you'll be coming home this evening." She's about to head to her room to change for rehearsal.

"She won't be coming home," Chase says, a hand at my nape, swooping circles drawn into my skin.

Shivers to race along my spine.

We both turn, and he shrugs nonchalantly. Maria grins at me and waggles her eyebrows.

"Shall we go, kitten?" Chase caresses my elbow.

Kitten? I'm going to ensure that nickname doesn't stick. I hug Maria good bye.

Chase holds out his hand to her. "It's been a pleasure, Miss De La Torre."

Maria laughs and pulls him into a hug. She whispers something in his ear before patting him on the back.

Chase coughs. "Understood," he says with a nod.

He leads me out of the apartment and into the waiting car. I give Jack directions to the doctor's office and then lean back into the seat next to Chase. He puts his hand on my stocking-covered knee and slides it down my inner thigh until he reaches the edge of my thigh-high.

"Good girl," he whispers. He traces the edge of the stocking.

I open my legs wider. He doesn't take the bait, which makes me pout.

"All in good time," he says against my ear before nipping the flesh there.

Groaning, I clamp my legs together. "What did Maria say to you?" I ask, trying to tame the wild harlot inside of me.

"She threatened me," he says flatly.

I blink a few times while the words have trouble forming on my tongue. "She didn't!"

He grins and nods. "She said if I hurt you she'd fucking kill me. Her words, not mine." He chuckles.

She's a dead woman. Wait until I get my claws into her. Revenge is a mean bitch, and I intend to invoke mine at the most inopportune time. I shake my head in frustration. So damned protective, my girl. I can't wait to get her back.

"I like her. She's very"—he pauses—"real."

Just then, my phone pings. I pull the phone from my new Louis Vuitton and check the screen.

To: Gillian Callahan

From: Maria De La Torre

Gatito? I hope that means he likes licking the kitty. (-;

"God, she's incorrigible!" I laugh and try to stuff the phone back into my purse. Before I can, Chase swipes the phone and holds it out while I try to grab it. His arms are too damn long!

"What's so funny?" he says. Jeez, the man has no concern for one's privacy. He reads the message and hands the phone back to me with a smirk. It burns a hole through my palm as I wait for his response.

Time has stopped, and I lean my head back and close my eyes, not wanting to know what he thinks. He slides his hand higher up my leg, almost tickling the edge of my panties. His nose brushes my neck, and the small hairs there stand on end. He trails his tongue up the side of my neck and swirls the edge of my ear. The breath I was holding escapes in a whoosh.

His voice is more like a growl than a whisper against my ear. "I plan to lick you *everywhere*, every inch, especially here." He punctuates his statement by cupping my sex roughly.

I bite my lip and thrust my hips forward on a moan. I feel his lips curl into a sultry smile against my cheek.

"I love how responsive you are. How wet you become for me." He slides one finger up and down my cleft.

His breath against my skin sets my nerve endings on fire.

The car stops, and Jack gets out. I curse when Chase removes his hand and adjusts his suit coat over his straining erection. At least I know he's as affected as I am. The outside world will never have a clue he just fondled a woman in his car. He is stellar at keeping his composure.

We get out of the car and walk into the doctor's office. I take deep breaths and hold his hand. It's like an anchor in an oncoming storm.

CHAPTER NINE

The doctor's office is bright and comfortable. Purple chairs nestle against a long wall in the waiting area. Magazines are scattered on top of the lone coffee table. Chase picks a seat away from any of the other patients as I check in. I haven't been to this doctor previously but made sure my past records were sent from the doctor I had in Sacramento prior to my visit. I'm ordered to fill out paper work. Chase sits quietly next to me, his warm hand caressing my back in soothing sweeps. He doesn't know this, but I am not a fan of doctors. Countless visits to hospitals—where doctor after doctor quizzed me about how I got hurt and poked and prodded at me—have made me leery.

In the past I've always lied, made up bogus stories about falling down on my bike, Rollerblades, and stairs—none of which happened but seemed likely. Some of the medical professionals cared very little. Others would notify me they were bringing in a patient advocate. Those words always made me throw on my clothes and escape as if the building were on fire. The last thing I needed then were helpful "advocates" who would end up calling the police on Justin.

I learned that particular lesson the hard way. Justin was a master manipulator. The first time an advocate tried to "help," I was beaten black-and-blue while being fucked brutally. I could barely walk for days after. Justin claimed he fucked some sense into me. It worked. I never spoke to an advocate again. Not until I made the call that saved my life.

Within fifteen minutes of arriving with Chase, I am seated in another waiting room. Chase followed me into the exam room as if he were owed the privilege. I sit on the exam table and twist my fingers together as he sits in a lone chair behind me. The silence between us is comfortable but still heavy with that energy that sizzles when we are near one another. He browses through his e-mails on his cell phone as I try to calm my heart rate with deep yoga-style breathing Bree taught me. Being in a doctor's office with Chase is a bit unsettling. If I'm honest, being in a doctor's office at all is unsettling.

The doctor strides in with his nose in my file. He's a man of about fifty, dark wavy hair, tall, strong build. He wears rimless glasses that add nicely to his features.

"So, Miss Callahan, you've come to have some stitches removed." He looks at me over the rim of his glasses.

"Yes, Doctor Dutera."

He flips through pages in my file, skimming them. It's not a small file. The doctor in Sacramento must have been thorough in sending my past medical history. "Looks like you are no stranger to having stitches removed."

I clench my jaw tightly.

"Let's see here, also broken ribs, fractured wrists, dislocated shoulder, broken arm, not once but twice, black eyes, and a slew of hospital visits." He shakes his head and smacks his lips. "Looks like for a couple of years you were a regular over at Mercy General in Sac." His eyes are kind as he looks from the file to me and then over at Chase. "Do you have any residual pain from those injuries?" he asks.

Residual pain? I glance toward Chase, hoping he isn't paying attention. Instead of being in the chair, he's standing right behind me with his chest a scant few inches from me. I look up into his eyes. They are clouded, unreadable. Tension emanates from him in droves, and I close my eyes. I cannot see anything remotely close to pity ever again in someone else's eyes. Especially from a man I'm so taken with.

"I'm accident prone. Can we get on with the stitches? I need to get to work."

Doctor Dutera slaps the file shut and nods curtly. He pulls on a pair of latex gloves and cleans the area around my stitches. Chase brings his hand to my back and caresses my lower back, up to my neck, and down in a calming motion.

With the first snip of a stitch and the corresponding burst of pain, my mind catapults to another time.

"You're a lying little whore! You think I don't know about you and Todd?" Justin is on a tirade. He's shit-faced drunk with a chip on his shoulder.

I know instantly nothing good will come of this.

"Justin, I would never cheat on you. I love you. You know that. There's no one else but you," I assure him.

The blow comes so hard against my eye I fall to the floor. I clutch the tender spot over my eye in pain.

"You're fucking your study buddy. I know it! The second I leave, he has his hands all over you, doesn't he? Doesn't he?"

I try to stand, but he kicks me in the gut repeatedly. Hot, white pain rips through my chest as I hear the sick crunching sound of my rib breaking. I lose count of the blows. I howl and gasp when he comes down on top of me, holding my arms over my head with one hand. Forcing broken ribs to stretch and arc almost makes me black out. The pain is so intense it's as if I'm being gutted.

"Look here, you little whore, no one is going to want you. You're not worth your weight in shit. You're lucky I've stayed, but you will not fuck, kiss, or touch another man. You got it?" He bangs my head against the wood floor.

I see stars. I nod furiously, but he punches my face anyway, splitting my lip open. Blood oozes down the side of my face. The taste of copper fills my mouth as I gurgle and sputter around a scream.

"Gillian, what the fuck? You're okay, baby, you're okay! I'm here."

I feel Chase's strong arms around me. I clutch his suit jacket. Tears stream down my face.

The doctor has backed away, his eyes wide, mouth agape. Chase has his arms firmly around me as he pets and caresses me. I haven't had a flashback in a long time. Over a year at least.

"I'm okay, I'm sorry. I'm fine." I push Chase away and avoid looking into his eyes. "I'm fine now. Thank you." I wipe my wet cheeks with the backs of my hands. "Doctor, are we finished?"

I sniff and Chase hands me a handkerchief. Of course he would have a handkerchief. Probably monogrammed. I wipe my dripping nose on the soft cotton.

"Yes, but Miss Callahan, I think we should discuss what just happened here," he says.

Hopping off the exam table, I grab my purse. Chase stands behind me. "Not today. Thank you, Doctor Dutera. I'm sorry for the… I'm sorry." I grab the door handle and briskly walk out to the waiting room and straight on out to the city street. Once I am outside, I inhale deeply, taking in my surroundings, trying to let go of the raging past that swarms around my subconscious like a hive of angry bees.

When I catch my breath and shake off the last dregs of the past, I notice Chase leaning against the car waiting patiently for me to address him. I know he wants answers, but right now I don't have them. I don't know that I ever will.

"Look, Chase, I can't explain what happened in there—"

"You can, and you will," he says, his tone firm.

"I can't." Tears stream down my face again as I desperately try to find a way to deal with this.

Chase wipes them away, kisses each cheek and finally my lips. "Later, then."

I nod into his chest as he hugs me. His firm embrace is a haven to my tortured soul. Safe, warm, and solid. I clutch at him, digging my fingers into his muscular back. He holds me tighter and whispers in my ear. "Do you still want to go to work? I could call Mr. Jefferson for you?" he offers.

A bubble of laughter fills me and spills out as I rub my nose against his breastbone, inhaling his woodsy citrus scent. I pull back. "That's rich. Let the chairman of the board call in sick for me from work? Somehow I don't think that would go over well." I smile, inhale, and exhale slowly, letting it all go. Being here, having Chase's arms around me just makes it better. "I'm fine. Take me to work."

We get into the car, and we're off to the Safe Haven Foundation. When we arrive, I jump out of the car before Chase can comment or Jack can open the door.

"The car will pick you up after work, Gillian," Chase

calls.

I turn and look at him as he slowly walks toward me. He really is a modern-day Superman. His lengthy form as he walks toward me is virile, manly. Chase's dark hair blows enticingly in the wind, giving him that rugged sexy aura as he stalks toward me in a black suit that was tailored to perfection. The blue pinstriped dress shirt is making his eyes light up and seem even bluer than what is possible in real life. His sculpted features turn liquid and sensual as he reaches me, places his hands on my shoulders, and slides them up to cup my neck. He caresses my cheeks with his thumbs as I've come to expect from his touch.

"I will take care of you. You're never going to be hurt again," he promises.

If only that were true. He doesn't know me. I'm damaged. I close my eyes, cutting off the sincerity I see in his eyes.

"Tonight." He grins.

I nod. "Tonight."

He kisses my forehead and releases me. I stand with my eyes closed as he walks away.

★ ★ ★ ★

Jack arrives with the full limo promptly at five p.m. I see quite a few stares and mouths catching flies at the front of the building as I scurry into the vehicle. This ought to give the gossip mill new fodder for at least a week.

The drive takes thirty minutes from one side of the city to the other in rush hour traffic. I don't mind. It gives me time to think.

I haven't had a flashback like this morning's in a long time. I didn't realize those old wounds were still so close to the surface. I haven't even heard from Justin in six months. Doesn't mean he's done taunting me. Sometimes I hear from mutual friends that he asked about me, trying to find out my whereabouts. The last time I saw him I was with Daniel.

Daniel and I had been together about three months then. Daniel was larger than Justin and promptly scared Justin shitless. He also helped make sure a restraining order against Justin was firmly in place. He wasn't aware of the details, just that Justin was part of my past and not a pleasant part. The night we ran into Justin, Daniel stayed over after the run in. He made slow, sweet love to me. I didn't orgasm, never did with Daniel, but it was a nice respite from the volatile situation with Justin.

I was content with Daniel. He made me feel safe. He was a large man that I knew could take out anyone who tried to harm me. I met him at the gym, but he was an accountant for a large firm downtown. He worked out as much as I did. It was about the only thing we had in common. Daniel was good to me. Treated me like a lady. Only problem was he did so in every aspect of our relationship. Sexually he was inept at fulfilling me. There was no passion. *Not like with Chase.*

Chase is in a league of his own. I have never felt such a deep-seated attraction to another person. My fascination with Justin paled in comparison. My body gravitates towards Chase, and I'm powerless to stop it. He stirs desire that burns in me like white-hot fire. Just thinking about him has my pulse quickening, my core thrumming, and my thighs pressing together.

Jack stops in front of a tall concrete-and-glass skyscraper. The building is unique from its neighbors. It's sleek and sophisticated but has a charm you don't often see in a concrete jungle. The building is a bluish-gray in color. Red accents surround each window of the bottom floor. A huge waterfall alternates water bursts and then trickles down three tiled tiers. A glowing concrete sign boasts "Davis Industries." I shake my head, laughing at the absurdity that I've been to this building before to see Phillip and never knew the chairman of my foundation owned the building.

Jack ushers me to the wide bank of elevators. We step in and he presses the 50 on the lit display. Under the fiftieth floor is a letter P and a square LCD screen with the word *Thumbprint* on top of it.

"What's the P stand for?" I ask.

"Penthouse, Mr. Davis's private residence." His lips thin into a grim line.

I wonder if he'll ever be nice to me or capable of having a congenial conversation.

"So you have to put your thumb over the screen?" I'm curious. I've never seen anything like it. The movies with the rich billionaires all have some type of keycard or physical key to unlock the magic quarters.

"Yes." His response is curt and devoid of emotion.

"Do I have access?"

Jack smirks. "Very few have access to Mr. Davis's private quarters." He looks at me as if I've grown horns. "His women friends don't typically receive access to his home." He turns back to the closed doors of the elevator.

Women friends. Is that what I am? Would Chase's bodyguard know otherwise?

I remember that Chase mentioned he didn't take women back to his home. I wonder if he'll take me there. He'd said he wanted to, but that could have been a random remark, not really his intention. Do I want to have access to his home? What would that mean for us?

The doors open to the fiftieth floor and a beautiful blond woman greets us. "Miss Callahan."

I recognize her from the board meeting last weekend. She was sitting next to Chase taking notes but didn't participate in the meeting.

"I'm Gillian Callahan." The woman comes around the desk and shakes my hand.

"Jack, I'll take it from here, thank you."

Jack nods and walks down the hall.

"Mr. Davis is expecting you."

"I'm sorry, I didn't catch your name?"

"Dana Shepherd. I'm Mr. Chase's personal assistant." She smiles warmly at me.

She's a very beautiful woman. Probably in her early thirties. Even in heels she's still a couple inches taller than I am. Dana's thin with a runner's long and lean build and is dressed in a fierce black suit, though her gait is much softer. Her blond hair is pulled up into a chignon so perfect I would have thought it was professionally done by a hair stylist.

"Good to meet you." She's the epitome of whom I saw Chase with in those pictures online. Has he slept with her?

She leads me through a long hallway. Several people in suits rush by with jackets and briefcases. I imagine they are heading home for the evening. Even at the late hour, there are quite a few people still in their offices, phones glued to their ears. We end at a section of double doors with a desk sequestered to the right side.

Dana steps around the desk and hits a button. "Miss Callahan is here to see you," she says.

"Bring her in," a curt voice comes through the speakerphone.

She opens the doors for me.

The room is exceptionally large, taking up the entire corner of the building. One wall is glass from floor to ceiling, looking out over the dimming city. The Pacific Ocean can be seen clearly from this height. The view is breathtaking. To the left of the room is a seating area with two long couches parallel to one another separated by a black reflective coffee table. The couches are white with bright blue and black pillows neatly placed. A canary-yellow sculpture stands about two feet tall in the middle of the coffee table. Along the back wall is a sidebar with what looks to be a small bar. The space is decorated well.

To the right of the door is an enormous black desk. Behind it is a matching credenza filling the entire wall with intricate pieces of art. A couple sculptures, small paintings, statues of varying size are precisely placed in specific locations. There are a few framed photos are thrown in between the art, but I can't tell what they are from this distance.

Chase sets down his cell phone and his eyes meet mine. His gaze is predatory. He takes his time dragging his gaze from the tip of my head to the spike of my heels and back again. He saunters over like a wild animal hunting its prey. All stealth and smooth moves. When he reaches me, he slides his hands into my hair, and his lips cover mine. He's gentle at first but increases the pressure, sliding his tongue along the seam of my lips. I open, and his tongue circles mine. I'm lost in the sensation of his kiss. Heat builds from our chests pressed together. My body goes liquid against his, and he holds me up through his kiss. He tastes of coffee and his own intoxicating maleness. He briefly pulls away and nips at my bottom lip.

"I've missed you this week," he says against my lips.

Even though we saw one another just this morning, we both know what he means. We missed the physical nature of our connection all week.

"Me too."

His lips press mine once more. "Dana, I won't need any further assistance. I'll call you in the morning and bring you up to speed on anything over the weekend."

I completely forgot she was standing there. Turning and looking behind me, I can see a huge smile is plastered across her face.

"I'll have clothes sent first thing in the morning." She looks me up and down in a calculating manner.

She smiles, and I cringe. Chancing a glance at Chase, I find him smiling in her direction. Finally Dana closes the door.

"What's that about?" I ask, still in his embrace.

"She's never seen me kiss a woman in all the years of being my assistant. Actually, I don't think I've ever entertained a woman here."

That makes me innately proud. My lips part in an "Oh," and he laughs. I smile up at him.

"Baby, you are so beautiful when you smile."

I love when he calls me baby. Anything that shows his

interest in me on a more personal level. "It's you, you know," I confide shyly.

He slides his fingers up and down my back, ending at my waist. "What is me?"

"You make me smile." I dip my head to avoid his gaze. He seems to see through me when our eyes meet, as if he's gazing directly into my open soul. I'm not ready for him to know so much about me.

"I plan on doing a lot more than making you smile." He punctuates each word with a thrust of his hips against mine.

I feel the ridged length of his erection hard and unrelenting.

"Just seeing you here makes me ache."

His words fill me with uncontrollable lust. "Jesus, Chase, I want you." I haul his face into a crushing kiss. I fiercely try to devour him whole. The time for niceties is over. I've had enough of his innuendo and teasing all week. It's time for him to make good on his promises.

He slides my jacket off my shoulders. It drops to the floor with a thud. I mimic him by slipping his suit jacket down those thick arms, adding it to the pile at our feet. I search his eyes and am shocked to find them filled with intense desire.

"Baby, I was going to wait, bring you to my bed, but hell, I need you now." His head comes down, and he inhales against the tender skin at my neck. "Vanilla..." he whispers in reverence.

His mouth so close to my pressure point sends shivers of lust ripping through me.

His need ramps up my desire a hundred notches. I yank

at the buttons of his shirt, impatient in my need to get him naked, see that golden chest again. Once the shirt is open, my hands are greedy, smoothing along his hard pecs. I pull my lips away from his to kiss every inch of exposed skin. I suck the flat disk of his nipple and bite down. He groans and tugs at my head, keeping me close. I lightly swirl my tongue around it, lapping in a soothing motion. He shudders in my embrace when his shirt falls to the floor. Time seems to stop. His hands are everywhere at once, down my back, tugging the hair at my nape, bringing me closer to him.

The tiny buttonholes on my shirt and his large hands do not work well together. "Fuck it!" He rips the shirt open and buttons go flying.

It's such a cliché, right out of a romance novel, but I don't care.

I tremble in his arms as he strokes his hands over my rib cage to cup my breasts. Both of his thumbs scrape against the swollen hardened nipples. The action forces me to lunge and bite down on his chest so hard I'm sure to leave a mark. I lap and kiss the flesh better.

"Damn it! I need to fuck you!" He slides his hands over my ass and scrunches my pencil skirt to my waist. He grips my thighs and hauls me up as if I weigh nothing. My legs twine around his body, and I clench my thighs around him, enjoying the feel of his hard body between my legs. Chase palms my ass while walking us over to his desk then plops me down onto the hard surface. Before I can make a sound, his lips are on mine.

Through my lust, I fumble to remove his belt and unzip his pants. Finally the button breaks free, and I'm immediately sliding my hand into his underwear to grasp his length.

"God, baby," he breathes.

I stroke him firmly up and down. *He's huge.* I can barely wrap my hand completely around him as he lengthens and hardens further under my ministrations.

Chase trails his lips down my neck and busily pulls my panties from my hips. He lifts me with one hand around my back and yanks the garment from under my ass. When he tugs the lace down my legs, they slip to one ankle, provocatively dangling along the stiletto. He gently pushes me to lie down against the hard surface of his desk, my chest and core fully exposed to his gaze. My breath is heaving, and my hands bemoan the loss of his skin as I tightly grip onto the edge of the desk. Chase takes a moment to just stare at me laid out on his desk, ripe for the taking. I know I must make for a pornographic image. My chest arcs toward him, breasts reaching for the sky and flowing out the cups of my bra as Chase forces the fabric down. He scans the naked skin, a feral gleam in his eyes. I'd be frightened if I weren't so turned on.

He licks his lips as he slides one finger from my neck down between my breasts. Finally, his head comes down and he brings those stunning lips to my navel, swirling his tongue into the indentation. My stomach jumps, and he laughs. He continues down my body, planting kisses on every inch of exposed skin. I'm dying with need and can't stay still. My body twitches and thrums with unquenched desire.

"I can smell your need." He slides his hands firmly down each thigh, as if he has every right to the sensitive bare skin. He grips my knees and stretches each leg out, opening me wide. His eyes are riveted to my sex, and I clench under his gaze.

He says one word, and it blows me away.

"Mine."

Then his tongue is on me, lapping from anus to clit. I howl and try to close my legs. It's too much, yet not enough. Nowhere near enough. His strong hands prevent me from closing them, keeping me wide open to him.

"So good," he mutters, and dips his tongue deep into my center.

Bliss. An overwhelming feeling of contentment flows through me as his talented tongue plays me. "God, Chase." I bite my lip almost to the point of pain.

He brings his hand into play and slides one long digit into my opening. I grip his hair, pulling and yanking as he swirls his tongue around my clit slowly, not allowing too much pressure. My hips gyrate against his face and finger when he adds another digit. It's just the amount of pressure I need. He picks up the pace, fucking me steadily with his hand. My greedy pussy sucks and clenches around the intrusion.

"God, baby, I could do this all day. You're succulent."

His words have me on the very edge of release. He slides his other hand up my body and to my breast, gripping the mound roughly, possessively. The sensation is mind-numbing, and I press deeper into him. He laps at my clit and digs his fingers high and hard into me, hooking them up into that secret spot, one I think is solely for him alone. A few more licks of his tongue and he presses down hard, sucking with all his might on the tiny abused bundle of nerves. I shatter into a million pieces. My orgasm sweeps over me in an explosion of intense pleasure as I convulse on his desk. Chase stays with me, finger fucking me leisurely while I break apart.

He removes his fingers and places his mouth greedily over my sex delving his tongue deep, as far as he can go. A loud groan fills the air as he laps up my release. He licks and pets me with his tongue, milking me for everything I have as I come down from my high.

Best orgasm ever.

He places kisses up my body until he finds one taut peak and sucks it deeply into his mouth. My sex twitches with pleasure. I can't believe I'm responding again so quickly. I'm panting and moaning as he nips at the tight bud. I try to grip his head, make him stop the sweet torture of my oversensitive tips, but he won't stop. He smiles against my breast and continues his ministrations, flicking the edge with his tongue. His other hand tweaks my nipple's twin, plucking it, making it impossibly engorged and hard as a rock.

Finally, his lips find mine. I can taste the tangy sweetness of my release on his tongue. "I need you," I whisper against his mouth.

His eyes pierce mine. It's as if the word "need" trips something inside of him. He grips my hips roughly, digging into the soft flesh, his nostrils flare slightly, and sweat dusts his hairline. He's every woman's fantasy.

"Are you on birth control?" he asks.

"Yes, yes, the pill," I stutter through my sex-induced haze.

An evil grin breaks across his face, and he slides down his pants. His cock springs free, and my mouth starts to water. I cannot wait to take him into my mouth. He spreads my legs so wide my calves knock against the desk. Thank God for yoga. His hand encircles his length and gives it a couple long hard strokes. I moan, watching pre-cum bead at the tip. It makes me salivate. He adjusts his cock at my opening and slides just the head in. I lean my head back against the desk, close my eyes, and arch up on a gasp. He grips my hips possessively, and in one quick thrust, Chase impales me.

"Chase!" I scream at the onslaught. His cock has stretched me wide, the lips of my sex retracting around his girth. I'm filled to bursting.

He holds his position, allowing my body to adjust to his size before sliding out. Then slowly, inch by glorious inch, he presses more into me. It's not enough. I want him hammering me, showing me how much he wants me. That he's as crazy for me as I am for him.

"More, Chase. I need all of you," I say through gritted teeth.

He pulls back almost all the way and slams back against me until he bottoms out at my cervix. It's unlike anything I've felt before. This is a whole new kind of sex. His body comes over mine and he kisses my lips, neck, and breasts while he pistons his large cock in and out of me feverishly. My pleasure builds with each long stroke of his length, and I lift my hips to meet every thrust. He pinches my nipples hard, and lightning shoots to my lower body, preparing me for the mother of all releases.

"God, baby, this is so good. You're so fucking tight!" He lifts my thighs and presses them close to my chest, changing the angle of his penetration.

Split open, I scream out at the intrusion. Every stroke of his thick cock slides deliciously against that bundle of nerves within me. It is almost like he's pressing an elevator button over and over, except it's more like an orgasm button. With every twitch of his hips, I rocket further into the abyss. A few more strokes, and it's as if his name is forcibly ripped from my lungs, the orgasm tearing through every nerve ending in my body, splintering out into a burst of heat and energy.

"Fuck yeah, come for me, baby!" Chase encourages as he strokes that spot with perfect accuracy. "I need one more, baby. I want it all. Your pleasure is mine now."

His words are like a dusting of kerosene on an open flame. My body burns for him. He continues to plow into me, furiously gripping my hips. I know I will be wearing his mark in the morning. I don't care, as long as he keeps fucking me. He nips at my lips, and I put everything into this kiss, holding nothing back. My fear of commitment, of losing myself, of my career—I leave it all behind, content to give him everything. He'll accept nothing less. Chase's hand slips between our bodies, and his thumb crushes my swollen clit. Spirals of light shoot past my eyes, so bright I squeeze them shut. Pleasure skims through every pore as Chase thrusts into me over and over, extending my orgasm to a place beyond reality. My entire body quakes with the viciousness of his lust. He relentlessly gives pleasure, and I take all that he gives and more. I scream his name so loud I'm sure the people in the other offices hear it.

"God, baby, so beautiful when you come..." A few hard strokes and his eyes close tightly, his jaw sets, teeth clenching down.

On a mighty roar, Chase releases into me, his arms tight, the veins on his forearms raised as he pumps into me over and over. I almost come again from the heat washing over my insides coupled with seeing his loss of control. He's more than my Superman. He's a God, lit up from the inside out when he comes. I know I have to see it again. That beauty is as great as a sunset or a newborn baby. It's light and love and all nature's beauty put together. It's Chase, letting go.

For me.

With me.

Because of me.

He melts against my chest, and I grip him to me protectively as he shudders and trembles, his cock throbbing delectably with every breath. I kiss his shoulders, neck, temples, everywhere I can reach. His head is firmly planted in the crook of my neck. I can feel his strangled breath against my skin. It's warm and comfortable. It's everything.

I slide my hands up and down his naked back and relish touching his skin. The man is a work of art in the bedroom.

"Gillian, damn woman. You'll be the death of me. I'm going to fuck you until we both die. It's inevitable."

I chuckle and kiss him as he lifts me upright. His penis slips from me, and I cringe at the loss. His essence trickles out of me, and he watches it pool on the surface of his glossy black desk. A combination of our pleasure. He grins solicitously, clearly fascinated. He likes what he sees. Dirty boy.

We kiss for a couple of minutes, and then he pulls up his pants. I watch as he enters a door I hadn't noticed to the side of his desk. I hear water running, but I'm too far gone to move from my position on his desk. The man ruined me for the evening. I'm completely sated and reeling. *Three times!* My mind sings. Chase returns with a warm washcloth and wipes between my legs, removing the essence of our pleasure.

"Better?" he asks, quietly cleaning me.

"Perfect." I smile.

And it was perfect. I know the sex wasn't conventional. It wasn't in his bedroom after a nice romantic candlelit dinner but the fierceness in the way he took me was intense, incredible, consuming. I loved every moment of it. I stand as he takes the washcloth into what I can assume is his personal bathroom. Must be good to be the king.

I pull on my panties and slide my skirt back in place, adjusting my bra so my breasts are covered. I pick up my blouse. It's completely destroyed. A slow grin smarts across my lips.

Chase returns with a bright white men's dress shirt and holds it out for me with a shy grin. I turn my back and put my arms through the holes.

He turns me to face him. "Let me." He makes quick work of the buttons.

The shirt hangs to my thighs, but I'm completely covered. I roll the arms up to three quarters. If I had a thick belt, it would actually look like I put the look together intentionally.

"Are you hungry?" What an odd question after mind-blowing sex. "My chef has prepared a meal for us."

Oh, dinner. "Starving," I admit. I pecked at my lunch after the horrible experience at the doctor's office. I am famished, especially after the body-melting sex we just had.

He picks both of our suit jackets up from the pile in the middle of his office floor. He grabs my hand and steers me through the building. Most of the offices are now quiet and dark, but the lighting makes the path easily visible. A couple offices still have people hard at work, and they look up as Chase walks me through the halls, holding my hand. Looks like I've managed to stir two gossip mills today.

We enter the elevator, and he places his thumb against the LED computer screen. A light shines red and scans his thumb, and the elevator springs to life, taking us another level up. He's taking me to his home. The place he never takes women. A sense of pride fills me and I feel taller, standing straighter. The elevator opens to a foyer. The door opposite is wide and Jack holds it open as we enter.

"Mr. Davis, Miss Callahan," Jack greets us.

I smile confidently, Chase still holding my hand. It takes everything I have *not* to stick my tongue out at the man like a silly schoolgirl.

"Mrs. Shepherd said the clothes you ordered for Miss Callahan will be here first thing in the morning. I will have Mr. Bentley see to them."

Chase brings me through a cozy living room adorned in rich jewel tones. Bookcases and large paintings fill the walls. An enormous stone fireplace blazes, making the room glow with ambient light. Before I can examine the space, I am led into an elegant dining room. A long mahogany table that seats twelve fills the room. A sparkling crystal chandelier hangs over the center of the table. Silver candlesticks run down the center of the table on top of a gold-threaded table runner. Two places are set, one at the head of the table and another at the seat just to the right. A water glass and wineglass are preset with the finest-looking china. The plates are white with swirling gold trim etched along the edge. Several forks, spoons, and knives hug the sides of the plates. Too many for me to know which ones to use with which course, but I'll watch him pick the right one.

"Sit." Chase holds out my chair for me. "Would you like some wine?"

"That would be heavenly, thank you."

He pulls the white wine from the freestanding ice bucket and fills our glasses. I'm still completely giddy and sated from our rendezvous moments ago.

We clink our glasses together and sip, eyeing one another.

"That was…" Chase exhales deeply and shakes his head. "Being with you, it was unbelievable, Gillian." His eyes hold mine.

My face heats and I nod, not knowing what to say.

"Having you on top of my desk… I'm usually more controlled than that." He licks his lips and sizes me up. "I can barely keep my hands off you now." His eyes burn with desire.

I bite my own lip as I glance at his hands. They are held into tight fists on top of the table, showing the power behind his restraint.

"Will you stay the weekend with me?" he asks.

"Are you sure that's what you want, Chase?" After this afternoon, I'm surprised he didn't run for the hills. When he really gets to know me, learns of my past, he won't want me anymore. Men like him are used to shiny new toys, not damaged broken ones that need a lot of TLC.

"I've never been more certain of anything." His answer is revealing and brutally honest.

It makes me nervous, but looking into his gorgeous face seals the deal. He's too damned pretty. Maybe I'll just do what Maria says and enjoy. If I don't get too attached to the man, we'll both get something out of it.

"Okay," I say with a hint of trepidation and a great deal of excitement. A couple days of having him in every possible way will be like a dream come true.

"It's settled then. Your clothes will arrive in the morning."

"You ordered me clothes?" That's what they were talking about. I'm so dense.

"Yes." He grins. "I have a charity function I'd like you to attend with me tomorrow evening. I'm certain Dana will do you justice."

Dana. The lovely, perky blonde that seems overly familiar with her boss. Hell, I'm overly familiar with the boss right now. "You call her by her first name." It's not a question but an observation.

"Yes, Dana and I have been together for the past several years. I scooped her up right out of college. She's loyal, and I trust her. I trust very few people."

"Were you ever with her?" I hate myself the second the question passes my lips, but the desire to know is overwhelming. I knot my fingers together in my lap.

He shakes his head and picks up his wineglass "No." He laughs. "She's my most trusted colleague and friend, aside from Carson. I'm not attracted to her in that way, but I care a great deal for her."

I wrap my mind around that and realize this is the time to pounce. "So what you're saying is that you love and care for her, but you're not in love with her. Is that right, Mr. Davis?" My question hits home when I see his eyes sparkle and his lips curl into a crooked grin. Now he'll have no choice but to feel ridiculous about his jealously over Phillip.

"Touché, Miss Callahan." I beam with pride and he caresses the side of my face. His thumb brushes against my lower lip.

A short rotund man enters the room with two plates. He's wearing a butler-style suit. "Salmon, Mr. Davis, and chicken cordon bleu for the lady," he announces.

I smile. He remembered my distaste for seafood. "Thank you." I smile at the man.

"Looks amazing, Bentley. You can leave us undisturbed. I've got it from here."

He definitely has me. That's for sure.

CHAPTER TEN

Clouds streak across a summery pristine blue sky. I stare at the fluffy shapes and try to discern objects from them. As a child, this was a favorite pastime, lying in the grass watching the clouds glide along the wide expanse of sky. I would giggle with extreme joy when my mother could name the object I had decided a specific cloud looked like. Now Chase lies next to me, staring at the endless sky. He points to a large cloud and asks me to guess what it is. I shake my head. I can't take my eyes away from him. I'm too enamored with his glee at the passing clouds above our little enclosure. He looks at me warmly, the blue reflecting off his eyes, making them shine as bright and colorful as an opal. Never in my life have I been more content.

"Baby, wake up," he murmurs.

I look at him, confused. My surroundings tilt and sway. I feel featherlight kisses against my temple, cheek, and jaw.

"Gillian, wake up," he repeats.

His face dissipates and my surroundings change. Dream Chase has disappeared, and I'm left with lovely, warm, sleepy Chase.

I stretch and realize Chase is hovering over me. His knees firmly planted on each side of my hips. That's the second time I've woken to him on top of me, but this time

I'm not scared. I run my hands up and down his naked back, reveling in the feel of his warm skin and the joy of waking with this beautiful man. He's kissing along my neck, long languid presses of his lips and tongue. Light fingertips trail along the balls of each shoulder as his head and lips move down to the swells of my breasts. I sigh, appreciating the intimacy. It's not something I'm used to. I pull Chase over me, wrapping arms and legs tightly around his toned form. He snuggles fully into me, wrapping his arms around me. His head rests against my bare chest. I feel so protected. Loved. Nothing can harm me in the cradle of his body. And for a moment, I allow myself to wish it were forever—although a rather large intruder is poking against my hip. I slowly grind myself against the length.

"Happy to see me?" I ask coyly.

He rubs his forehead against my chest, his nose between my breasts. "Obviously." He grinds his length against me.

"Again?" After last night's marathon sex, I'm honestly surprised. After desecrating his office desk early in the evening, he later took me against the dining room wall before we even finished our meal. Then we slipped into a hot shower where he proceeded to soap every inch of my body in a deliriously meticulous manner that had me purring and moaning like a cat in heat. Soapsuds never felt so good.

We fell into bed sated, snoozed for a few hours, and then woke again and made passionate, unhurried love before we both passed out, completely exhausted.

"Yes, baby. You drive me mad with your sexy body." He cups and squeezes my breasts, fingers rubbing little circles around the tightening peaks.

My body responds like Pavlov's dog to a bell. In an instant, I'm needy and wanton, arching into him.

His foot slides between mine and separates my legs in one swift move. He seats himself firmly between my splayed thighs. With no preamble, he centers his cock against my moist opening, and inch by glorious inch, presses his length into me. The deliciously abused and swollen tissues attempt to reject him, but he slides out a couple inches and works his way in, slowly smoothing the way for me to accept his wide girth. Once he's completely imbedded, I exhale the breath I was holding. It's never been more perfect. When Chase is deep inside me, it's as if our souls are connected and always have been.

"So good," he whispers against my lips as he kisses me.

I return his kiss, enjoying this languid lovemaking.

After several long, slow strokes, he quickens the pace, sliding his hands under my back to cup my shoulders, giving him more purchase to pound into me. Sex with Chase is an event, not just a meeting of skin to skin. He does things to me you only see in movies. The feeling is unparalleled, unlike any experience that came before. The way he moves, the sensual caress of his fingers over my skin, his mouth worshiping every inch of me is like art imitating life. Hard, soft, beautiful, aching, devastating…nourishing. With every press of his body, every taste of his sweet kiss, he is healing me from the inside out.

Chase picks up speed, his movements becoming jerky, erratic. The pleasure within me mounts, crawls up that mountain and sits right at the edge of bliss. A couple hard strokes and I barrel head first off the cliff. I muffle a cry against his shoulder, biting the tender skin near his clavicle.

He roars into my ear, his face wedged into the crook of my neck. His body goes tight, ridged with tension as his climax overtakes him and he spills his seed hotly into me. I love the pulsing beat of his cock nestled deep in my core as the aftershocks extend his pleasure. I grip his length in a Kegel, using the muscles along the pelvic floor to clench around him.

Chase moans into my hairline and thrusts his hips. "Whoa, what the hell was that?" A sexy grin adorns his beautiful face as he trails little bites and nips along my neck and chin before sealing his lips over my mouth.

He pulls away and cups my cheek with one hand, sweeping his thumb along the cheekbone. I smile, waggle my eyebrows, and clinch my internal muscles again. His eyes roll into the back of his head, and a quick breath leaves his lips.

"That was a Kegel, baby." I roll the endearment around in my head. I guess if it works for him, it can work for me. I've never been one to dole out terms of endearment.

He grins that sexy sideways grin. I'm proud of my womanly trick, even more so knowing he's never experienced it with anyone else.

Just when I think I've got one over on him, his dick twitches enticingly inside my womb. "Hey! What was that?"

"A bagel," he answers and licks his bottom lip.

"A what?" I slide my hands up his dewy back and massage the muscles.

He nuzzles his cheek against mine. "If yours was a Kegel, mine was a bagel. A boy Kegel."

His eyes dance with mirth, and we both laugh hysterically. So many rounds in the sack have made us silly and I love the carefree side of him. This is the first time I've seen Playful Chase.

He kisses me and sits up. "I have to get a little work done this morning." His eyes seem to search my face, almost as if he's looking for even a hint of irritation. When he finds none, a beatific smile graces his face. I understand. The man has to work. Even if it is Saturday. I can't imagine he makes billions without burning the midnight oil and working on the weekends.

"'Kay. I'll take a shower." I stretch the kinks in my body and nuzzle into his pillow. It smells like him—completely divine.

"Help yourself to a little something to eat in the kitchen." He moves over to a large chest, pulls out a pair of pajama bottoms and a white undershirt.

Damn, the man would look good enough to eat in a burlap sack, but casual Chase is sleepy sexy. My lady bits twinge excitedly as I watch him slip the shirt over his broad chest, his abdomen bunching and twisting with the effort. Next time we're together I'm licking a trail along each and every bump on that heavenly landscape. He's still talking, and I look away from his body to pay attention.

"I don't usually have Bentley come until around ten. I prefer to have something light in the morning and then have a larger brunch."

"Sounds like a plan." I smile.

He leans down to kiss me one last time. "God, you're beautiful." He shakes his head and leaves the room.

Strange man, but I'm into him. At least until he figures out how messed up I am. I take stock of my body as I stretch each limb. Definitely well used. My shoulders are stiff, lady parts delectably sore, and my thighs feel overworked in a delicious way. Overall, I feel damn good indeed. I smile, proud of myself as I saunter into his master bath, completely naked.

Settling under the double-headed spray, I let the hot water massage my sore, underused muscles. I need to hit the gym this week. I only worked out twice instead of my normal three times, coupled with two visits to Bree's yoga or Pilates classes. Although, the sexcapades last night had to count for a serious calorie burn. I grin to myself. Chase is a stallion in the sack. The way he used my body, gave and took pleasure… A shiver runs down my spine. I stretch each arm and fling my fingers out, trying to knock out the sexual energy that surges when I think of him.

Drying off, I evaluate my surroundings and learn a little about the man behind the empire. Chase's bathroom is right out of a *Modern Living* magazine layout. The walls are covered in tiny mosaic tiles in varying shades of green and blue. A large brown star like shape cuts through the middle of the wall and borders the entire room. The intricate design is stunning. It reminds me of the cool calming colors found at the beach. It must have taken days to place each of the one-inch tiles in perfect order in a bathroom this grandiose. I'm sure Chase paid very good money to make it just so.

I blow dry my hair and use Chase's brush. I smile as I see long red strands running through the bristles. If I were considerate I'd pull them out and throw them away, but I like the idea of a physical reminder of my presence here. He said he's never brought a woman home. I wonder why. Would he tell me if I asked?

Opening doors, I make my way into quite possibly the

largest walk-in closet on God's green earth. I'm not sure it can classify as a closet. It's a small men's clothing store. The space is larger than my entire apartment's living room and kitchen combined. The man is a fashion whore. Just like I am with my bargain shoes. The word "overboard" comes to mind. At least thirty feet of suits hang like perfect sentinels in exact order by color, mostly in shades of black, gray, navy, and tan. Tuxedos finish the lineup. The opposite wall holds jeans, dress shirts, and polos in a wide palette of colors. I grab a white pinstriped dress shirt with the tiniest green lines and throw it over my naked body. Since I don't have suitable clothes, this will have to do. I highly doubt Chase will mind. *If he does, he can just take it off me*, the little devil on my shoulder laughs haughtily.

Too hungry to wait for Bentley, I make my way to the kitchen. It's early, and it's another hour or two before he'll make Chase his breakfast. At the very least, I need caffeine. I look through a few cabinets trying to find the coffee and coffeepot. There's nothing on the kitchen counters except a glass dish filled to the brim with what looks like homemade cookies. Crumbs scatter around the edge of the dish. He likes to have something light in the morning, I snicker. Yeah, right. He eats cookies for breakfast. Alpha male, master of his own universe, and sugar junkie. Somehow it makes him more real.

Again, I scan the space. At home, Maria and I have gadgets, trinkets, and papers galore covering the counters. It's strange to see a living space so sterile. I open the bottom cabinets to the left of the kitchen island and find the coffeepot. *Eureka!* I give myself an internal fist pump, wiggling my bum in the air to a victory beat only I can hear. I move things around in the low cupboard to find the coffee.

"Damn!" says a loud unrecognizable voice behind me.

I spring up, nearly whacking my head on the cupboard, and am caught off guard by the smiling stranger in front of me. His eyes are wide and his mouth opens and closes a couple times, but no words come out. I'm certain the look on my face expresses the same shock. The man's blue eyes travel up and down my scantily clothed body, and I pull the shirttails to cover as much skin as possible. It doesn't work. The shirt only covers my naked form to mid-thigh, so I jump behind the island to hide more of me.

The stranger and I stare, saying nothing. He has blond shaggy hair that's sexy in a boyish way. His blue eyes are really light, almost gray, and his smile is bright white as if he had a lot of orthodontia to make it so perfect. Chase saunters in as if nothing unusual is taking place. He sets down an empty glass, and milk residue pools at the bottom. He grabs a cookie from the dish. He's oblivious to the crackling tension between the man and me as he pulls me to his side with a firm hand around my waist and nuzzles my neck. He kisses it lightly a couple times. The stranger's mouth falls open again before a wide grin splits across his handsome face.

"Carson, meet Gillian Callahan."

Oh, thank God! Carson is the cousin, his best friend from what I've gathered in conversations.

"Gillian, this is Carson Davis."

"Hello." I feel weakened by my lack of appropriate attire.

"Red," he says in awe and shakes his head. "You're a

redhead," he says again, sounding astonished.

I grab a lock of hair and self-consciously twirl it around my fingers. He was probably expecting a blonde. Chase eases my discomfort by walking over to Carson and clapping him on the back.

"Close your mouth, Carson." He laughs.

Carson clamps his mouth shut but continues to stare. It's unnerving and rude. First Chase's bodyguard stares me up and down, now his cousin. What is with these guys?

"Gillian, your clothes have arrived. I set them on the bed," Chase says.

"Nice to meet you. So nice," Carson says and turns to follow Chase out of the kitchen.

Thank God! One more minute suffering this man's stare would undo me. I scurry out of the room, holding the dress shirt firmly to my bum just in case he turns around. I don't want the shirt to float up in my hasty retreat. Carson doesn't need another show. Internally I groan, wondering how much of my bare ass he probably saw.

Several bags and boxes are strewn across the king-sized bed when I get there. What did he do, buy out Macy's? No such luck. Every piece of apparel is designer. Gucci, Prada, Chanel, Marc Jacobs, Guess, Versace…*shit.* I can't accept these. I fall to the bed like an elephant and put my head into my hands. Why is he buying me these things? Does he think that will make me happy? Adding up the price tags, I find there are over ten thousand dollars worth of clothes here, not to mention one long evening gown made by Valentino. *Forty-eight hundred dollars.* For one dress. Tingles of anxiety skitter along my nerve endings. *Breathe.* Deep calming breaths.

I look over the side of the bed and see a plethora of shoe boxes all in my size. How his assistant knew my sizes is beyond me. Maybe he owns a private investigator firm as well as his many other large enterprises. Am I one of his large enterprises? Does he think he needs to buy me expensive things to possess me? The thought makes my stomach lurch and churn. *Whore.* We are going to discuss this later. He's waiting with his most trusted confidant—*besides Dana,* my jealous mind supplies unhelpfully. The redhead comment threw me for a loop. I make a mental note to bring that question up when I broach my discomfort with the money he's spending on clothes and shoes for me.

Quickly, I pull out a pair of Guess jeans and a tan cashmere Marc Jacobs sweater. Probably the most affordable items of the bunch. The jeans are a size six and fit perfectly. They snugly encase my ass, and the length hits perfectly on my foot. It will be ideal for a nice bootie with a two or three-inch heel.

I make my way back to the kitchen barefoot and hear the men conversing. I wait behind the entryway wall to eavesdrop.

"Chase! Dude, when was the last time you brought a girl home?"

Chase laughs and I press my ear as close to the entrance as possible.

"I've never brought a woman here. You know that. I'm bringing her to the function tonight, too."

"Seriously? Wow! You like her. You like her a lot!"

I can't hear Chase's reply. Dammit. He speaks too softly.

"Aunt Coleen is going to be there. The rest of the family too."

"I know." Chase's voice is strained. *"I want Gillian by my*

side."

"Cooper will be there," Carson warns.

"I don't want her anywhere near that fucker!"

Whoa. He's got some serious issues with his cousin Cooper. I knew from the conversation at dinner last week that something wasn't right between the two, but this gets more interesting by the minute.

"She's a redhead," Carson mutters in a hushed tone.

"I noticed," Chase says.

That's when I decide to make my entrance.

"You noticed what?" I ask as I saunter in completely dressed, pretending I didn't hear a thing.

"How beautiful you are," Chase says without missing a beat.

Nice save. I warm, knowing that's not what they were saying. I appreciate his compliment anyway. "I was just telling Carson that I was bringing you to the Houses for Humanity charity event this evening. The San Francisco Chapter is hosting quite the posh event to raise money."

"That sounds wonderful. I'm happy to attend. It's always great when I can attend a charity event and make mental notes of how they organized it, what they offered in way of food, how the presentation was done and such."

Both men smirk at me.

"Gillian, this is not work. This is you going as my significant other. You will be meeting my family."

Chase shocks me with that. His significant other. I didn't realize we had reached an official status. I don't really know how to respond.

"Why would you take notes at a boring ass charity event?" Carson asks.

It reminds me that he doesn't know what I do for a living or anything about me really.

"Gillian works for the Safe Haven Foundation. She's the contributions manager there. She makes us a great deal of money." Chase beams with pride. "Her campaigns have been incredibly successful."

"You work for Safe Haven?" Carson asks. "So...Chase is your boss?"

"You could say that," I answer honestly and then hang my head. My hair falls in front of my face, hiding my embarrassment.

"Dude, that's, well, I didn't know you had it in you to break rules like that." He laughs. "Damn, you're smitten!"

"Shut up, you bastard." Chase laughs too.

Bentley makes his appearance, rushing in with a pretty young blonde in tow. Must be his assistant. Are all the women around Chase blond and beautiful? It's enough to give any woman a complex, especially being a redhead against a sea of shiny, perfect blondes.

"So I don't need that extra seat at the event tonight." Carson picks at a piece of invisible lint on his shirt.

"What happened to the girl you were bringing?" Chase asks.

"Didn't work out. She wanted to get married and have babies...yesterday!" Carson cringes. "So I'm going solo."

I immediately think of Kat. She's available and can be ready at a moment's notice. The show she's working on doesn't open for a couple more weeks. Her Saturday should be free, and Carson is just her type. Tall, good-looking, laughs a lot. "I know someone I could invite to be your date." I venture into unchartered territory, wondering if I've suggested a double date too soon. I barely even know Chase, let alone Carson.

"Really?" Carson seems hopeful. "Is she hot?"

A wicked grin slips across my face. Is Kat hot? If I knew him better, I'd gush all over the place about how wonderful my soul sister is. Since I don't, I just nod.

"No, I mean, is she hot like you?"

Chase punches Carson in the arm.

"Ouch! Damn, dude! What the hell?" Carson rubs his arm and looks like a sad little puppy.

"Don't hit on my woman, and you'll live life with a lot less bruises." Chase's hint of humor holds a note of warning.

His woman? I like the sound of that but choose not to let it go to my head. I'm still unconvinced this will go further than a few weeks and a few rolls in the hay once he learns how weak I am.

"I'll call her now! Her name is Kathleen. We call her Kat. She's tall, blond, thin but curvy in all the right places," I tell Carson.

He waggles his blond eyebrows. I think he might be perfect for Kat. She has a soft spot for big, hunky blonds. Carson fits the bill perfectly. Hell, I may get BFF of the year award for this setup. Now I just have to pull my "get out of jail free card" to get her to go on a blind date. Every woman hates a blind date. Once she's there and sees his fine ass, she'll be thanking me!

"I'll be back in twenty," I tell the men.

Chase catches me as I turn to leave. He grasps my waist and pulls me against him. I fall into his lap. One hand strokes my thigh, and the other holds me close. He inhales my scent at the crook of my neck. Carson gets up and leaves the room. I'm not sure where he's going, nor do I care. When Chase's arms are around me, everything and everyone ceases to exist.

"What do you want for breakfast?" he whispers into my ear. He slides his tongue up the curve of my neck.

I lean to the side giving him better access. "Mmm, you?" I breathe seductively against his lips.

He laughs. "Seriously, whatever you want. It's yours." He slides his hands up the front of my shirt and cups my breasts.

I increase the pressure by pushing his hands against me and sigh with pleasure. He tweaks the peaks through the fabric.

"Jesus, I want you again," he says through clenched teeth, thrusting his ridged length against my ass.

I flip myself around and put my legs on either side of the chair, straddling him, and plant my lips over his. He deepens the kiss, and we spend a few minutes groping and kissing like two hormone-driven teenagers.

"Chase! Today!" Carson yells from somewhere outside the kitchen.

Chase pulls away. "If that bastard weren't my best friend, I'd throw him out on his ass."

I laugh and shimmy out of his grasp. I mouth the word "later," and he grins and heads out of the kitchen.

After heavy cajoling and pulling out every trick in the book, Kat agrees to go to the charity function as Carson's date. I'm thrilled. I tell her I owe her one. She reminds me I owe her plenty more than one. I squeal in excitement and then compose myself once more.

Kat is going to evaluate her closet. The woman has

more dresses than a bridal shop, though many are in various stages of creation. I'm sure one of them will do. I remind her that she's the most talented designer I've ever known and she should wear something already finished. I also inform her that Chase's cousin is a designer. I hear her intake of breath when she puts two and two together and realizes that Chloe Davis is Chase's family. Apparently she knows who the young designer is and groans, saying she can't possibly wear anything old. I hang up, leaving her talking to herself and freaking out. She couldn't care less about the date now. She's more interested in meeting the designer.

I go back into the kitchen and realize Chase and Carson are no longer there. I look around perplexed.

"They are in the garden," Bentley informs me.

A garden? We're on the fifty-first floor of a skyscraper. Where the hell would they put a garden?

"Take her to the garden," Bentley tells his assistant.

"Come with me, Miss Callahan," she says.

"Call me Gigi."

The young girl smiles shyly and nods her head.

We walk through the length of the apartment to a spiraling black staircase. It reminds me that I haven't really had the tour of Chase's home. I've seen the dining room, kitchen, his bedroom, and bathroom. I smirk, realizing that Chase and I have been too busy pleasing each other to have a proper look around. I shrug, not really caring.

"Just go up the stairs and you'll be there," the young blonde says.

"Thank you. What's your name?" I ask.

"Summer," she says, looking down and gripping her black dress.

"A beautiful name," I tell her.

She smiles and rushes back to Bentley and her tasks.

The staircase is wrought iron and very intricate. The spindles are swirled metal with curling ends that encircle the railing like a claw. I reach the top and open the heavy metal door. Bright light blinds me as I put a hand over my eyes. *Oh my God!*

The garden spans the entire rooftop. It looks like a huge courtyard with a greenhouse, trickling fountains, shrubbery, pretty much everything you would find in an upscale mansion's backyard but on top of a roof. There's even a lap pool and a hot tub. I let out a wolf whistle as Chase grips my shoulders.

"You like?"

"I like," I say, barely able to speak.

I've never seen anything quite like it. It's out of this world. We've escaped the city and landed in the book *A Secret Garden*. I feel worlds away from concrete and the city, though if you look across the horizon, you can see the entire cityscape in all its glory. There's the magnificent view of the ocean and the bay. It spans the horizon in a perfect line as if the world just clips off and ends where the line stops. The view is incredible.

Chase walks around the garden, holding me close, pointing out different plants, telling me names and whether they bloom or are seasonal plants. His knowledge is telling, and I ask about the greenhouse. He explains that he believes all buildings need greenhouses, and that Americans can lessen our carbon footprint by placing them atop every city building across the nation.

Being green is something we have in common. I make

a mental note to bring it up at dinner tonight. Kat could go on and on about it. Between her and Bree, I've been completely brainwashed. I buy organic regardless of the price because I'm convinced that if I bought otherwise they would know and I'd suffer the consequences. I choose to pick my battles with the lovelies. Then again, I make them feel guilty about not giving to charity every chance I get, so it evens out.

Bentley serves us a scrumptious brunch, including feta-stuffed egg white omelets with plenty of spinach, tomatoes, and honey-glazed bacon. He couples it with homemade hash browns that are cut into perfect squares. How he was able to cut a potato into a square I don't know, but it is delicious. The cook added several different fruits and pastries, and Chase opens up a bottle of champagne. We sip mimosas and gaze out over the city. It's been lovely getting to know Carson and Chase in a casual setting. It's one of the best mornings I've had in a long time.

Carson takes his leave shortly after breakfast, and Chase and I spend the rest of the day getting to know each other better.

I'm not surprised to learn he's involved in a dozen charities. He serves on several of their boards. The others he mostly gives monetary donations to. He also tells me about the different types of businesses he owns, from hotels, to tech-related companies, to fashion stores, to nightclubs and restaurants. His interests are fascinating and broad. He really does have his hand in a bit of everything.

"You know what's funny?" I lean my head against his chest as we sit on a large garden lounge chair not quite designed to fit two, but we make it work.

"Hmm?" He massages my shoulders.

I lean my head back to give him further access to my aching muscles. "You're Phillip's boss, too!" I laugh.

He stops massaging and hums. "Really?"

"Yup, he works for the architectural firm on the twentieth floor." I giggle.

"Small world." He continues the massage, digging into the overworked muscles. "So tell me more about you and Phillip."

I know Chase is worried about my relationship with Phil, possibly even jealous. "We met in high school. I introduced him to his wife, Angela. Stood up in their wedding as maid of honor. Oh, that feels good," I groan as he finds a knot in my neck and works his magic fingers through it.

A sigh slips from my lips when the muscle releases and he smoothes his hands along the base of my neck. "Then they had Anabelle, and I was honored to be asked to be her godmother."

"You love that little girl a great deal." It's a statement, not a question.

I answer anyway. "So much. And since her mom passed, I feel it's more important than ever that I be there for her."

He nods his head and snuggles into the crook of my neck from behind. "So you and Phillip were never in a relationship?"

Closing my eyes, I groan. I really didn't want to go into this. "I wouldn't exactly say that," I admit.

He stops massaging, and his body tenses. The air around us is suddenly thick. Chase pulls me to lean fully against his chest. His arms cross around my front in a hugging manner.

"Tell me," he whispers against my ear, sending chills of

excitement dancing along my nerve endings.

"Phillip and I weren't in a relationship in the conventional sense. We never dated. He never considered me his girlfriend. I never considered him my boyfriend. Nothing like that." I exhale, feeling a bit annoyed that we're even having this conversation.

"What is it, baby? Just tell me what it was." He slides his hands up and down my biceps.

I stiffen, destroying the relaxed place we were moments before. I'm not embarrassed by my relationship with Phillip, but I know instinctively how Chase is going to take this bit of information.

Instead of dragging it out and attempting to walk around how I might think he'll respond, I go for broke. "Phillip was my first, Chase." I turn my head but he doesn't look at me. "It was a long time ago. We were teenagers. I didn't want my first time to be with someone who would take advantage of me."

Gripping his chin, I force him to look at me. I need to see his eyes. He doesn't say what he's thinking, but his eyes tell me what I need to know. They are cloudy and deep blue. Not good.

"He was your first?" he asks through clenched teeth.

I nod as his eyes calculate my features, jumping from one plane to the next.

A deep emotion crosses his features, and then, with finality, he says, "I'll be your last."

The look in his eyes is steadfast and haunting. This is the Chase I don't want to cross. The one who says what he means and means what he says, almost frightening in his intensity.

I don't know how to respond. His words floor me. The meaning behind them, his promise, is startling. "What's happening between us?" I take a shuddering breath, asking the question I've wanted to know since the moment I realized this thing between us wasn't going to go away. If I'm honest, it was the moment I realized the hell we were going to go through when I found out he was the chairman of the board. My insides heat, and anxiety swirls within my gut as I take a deep breath. The words spill from my lips so quickly I'm not able to hold them back. "What I'm feeling… It's too fast." I close my eyes.

He pulls me to his chest and holds me tightly. His gaze pierces mine. "For me, too."

After an eternity of staring into one another's minds, hearts, and souls, he pulls at my sweater and I hold my arms above my head. He slides the straps of my bra down and unhooks the back, letting it fall. My breathing quickens. I can tell he's brooding about Phillip and me, but this thing between us is too strong to ignore. It's like a live wire sparking at both ends, burning us, scarring our souls with an imprint of the other.

Chase doesn't speak. He unsnaps my jeans and gestures for me to stand. I do, and he pulls my jeans and panties down at the same time leaving me bare before him. His eyes scour every inch of my naked form. His fingers trace the sides of my rounded breasts, down each rib, along my waistline before he grips my hips possessively and brings his face to my stomach. He places a hard kiss just under my naval before he pulls my body down to straddle his legs. I pull his T-shirt over his head, leaving him tenting his pajama bottoms, the fabric restricting his manhood. He traces my curves with the tips of his fingers again in the lightest caress. He draws an infinity symbol over my chest and between my breasts. I lean my head back and close my eyes in pure ecstasy as he takes one hard peak into the warmth of his mouth. He sucks the tip and then clamps his perfect teeth against the swollen flesh. The jolt goes straight to my core, and I push my breast against his mouth, wanting, needing more of him. My fingers dig into his shoulders as he places wicked lashes of his talented tongue against each breast with biting precision. He nips and licks until I'm panting and grinding against his cock. I'm coating his pants with the wetness between my thighs.

Finally, I can wait no longer. "Chase, please."

He grins devilishly and bites my breast softly while pinching the other peak to perfection.

I grip his head. "Chase…"

"These are mine." He licks and bites each tip again.

I sigh wholeheartedly in agreement.

"Say they're mine, baby," he urges with a hard suck and swirl of his tongue.

My hips jerk. I'm eager to meet his hardness as I try to force him to touch me *there*.

"Yours." The word slips from my dry mouth as I focus hard on the building pressure his words of ownership send through my body. He has me twisting and rutting on top of him, barreling to the top of the roller coaster, waiting to be pushed off into a free fall.

He slides his hand down to my clit and presses his thumb in teasing circles. I cry out and shudder, wrapping my legs around his waist to thrust harder against his hand. He swirls slowly, just out of the realm of tipping me over into the release I'm dying for. He licks his lips and kisses my throat.

"Look down, baby, see me touching you."

I look down and see his finger spinning in lazy circles over my cherry-red clit, engorged and aching for the pressure only he can provide.

"This. This is mine," he affirms.

I nod, gyrating against his hand, needing more.

"Say it, Gillian." His tone is strong, forceful, demanding.

"Yours, Chase. Yours." I gasp and tip my head back to see the swirling blue-and-white sky above our castle in the clouds.

He removes his hand, and I cry out until he pulls down his pajama bottoms, freeing his thick cock. God, he's enormous. Harder and longer than I remember. I lick my lips in anticipation. He lifts my hips and rubs his dick along my soaked folds. He grins when he becomes slick with my essence before he centers me perfectly and presses just the head in. Teasing me with the beauty of his cock, of the completeness of our bodies joined together.

"More, please..." I go straight to shameless begging. I would do anything to get his dick inside me at this moment.

His hands on my waist bring me down hard as his hips thrust up, tearing into me, splitting me in half with the most obscene pleasure imaginable.

"Chase!" I scream out into the heavens. The enormity of this moment, of being taken so fully, his penetration piercing a part so deep within me it's never been touched before. Chase is a steel rod inside, wedged to the point where I don't know where he stops and I begin. I can't move, stunned by the perfection of our coupling.

"This, Gillian…"

He slides his cock out of me, dragging the wide crown along swollen tissue from last night, and then slams it back so deep I cry out. Tears prick my eyes, the pleasure is so intense.

"This. Is. Mine. Your pretty pussy is *mine* now." His teeth clench, the muscles in his forearms, biceps, and neck are bulging with every thrust as he powers into me.

"Yes!" I cry out as my orgasm rips through me. I think I lose consciousness. All I can feel is movement, pleasure touching every surface of my skin, my insides, until I hear Chase's mighty roar as his release overtakes him. He grips my ass and holds me in place until his jerking comes to a blistering halt, his semen filling me so full some of it spills out between our bodies.

Limp. My body, my mind, my heart are limp and sated. Chase holds me close as we lie naked, his hands sliding up and down my back tracing endless infinity symbols. Is it a metaphor for us? Forever. Has he always known from the moment we met? I remember him drawing the symbol on my knee in the bar that first night.

It's too much.

Him. Me. Us.

It's all encompassing and far too much to consider after the mind-blowing sex we just had.

I lie there in the bliss. The sun on my skin is warm, but so is his chest. I snuggle in, sexually sated and exhausted. What happened here was monumental. It's not possible to wrap my mind around it. He essentially staked his claim in no uncertain terms, and I gave myself to him in a moment of passion. Completely, unequivocally agreed to being his.

My self-doubt creeps in to this blissful moment, and I worry about what he's going to think when he finds out I am like the women he committed to protect as Chairman of the Board of the Safe Haven Foundation. Safe Haven helped save me once upon a time, which means *he* saved me. I sigh, and he kisses the top of my head.

"Let's shower and get ready for this evening."

"About that. Chase, you spent an awful lot of money on those clothes and that dress." I look away nervously. "I can't let you spend that kind of money on me. It's not right."

"Baby, I am a very rich man. I will buy you whatever I want, whenever I want, and you will let it go."

"I know you're rich. I don't care. I'm not, and I can't afford things like that!" I cross my arms over my breasts struggling to find some modicum of decency for a serious conversation.

He unhinges my arms, leans down, and kisses the top of each globe tenderly. "Good thing you don't have to. When you're with me, I will buy you things. Lots of things. I will never buy you anything I cannot afford." His gaze holds mine. It's hard and unrelenting. "Now you will let it go."

This is not going as planned.

"Do you not like the things Dana picked out for you? I told her what I thought you would appreciate and told her your sizes." He looks concerned.

"Everything is beautiful. But I'm not used to this. I don't want you thinking I'm after your money. That's the farthest thing from the truth." I bite my lip and look deep into his eyes, hoping he can see the sincerity there.

He smiles a heart-melting smile that makes me want to hug him but I don't. He needs to know I'm not the type of woman who uses men and I'm definitely not a gold digger.

"I wouldn't care if you were poor, Chase."

He shakes his head and pulls me back on to his chest. "Gillian, I know that." He hugs me, skin to naked skin. It is lovely. "I want to give you the world. I'm not used to being around a woman who doesn't expect a damn thing. It's refreshing." He looks in my eyes and caresses the apple of my cheek with his thumb before moving my hair behind my ear. "Please, accept the things I bought for you, and know that it pleases me to give you them. They are yours for no other reason." He lifts my chin. "Okay?"

I close my eyes and nod.

"Not another word about this." His words come out harsh and unrelenting.

Not wanting to argue, I nod again.

"Now, shower?" He waggles his eyebrows suggestively. The man hasn't even slipped from my body and he's already thinking about sex again.

"Yes, shower. Nope to sex. You're going to have to wait until the evening is over!" I giggle and slip off his lap. The proof of our mating starts to trickle down my thighs.

He watches in fascination, before using his shirt to wipe up the inside of my leg and over my sex.

"I love seeing me on you and knowing I'm still inside you." He stands, grabs my nape, and pulls me into a toe-curling kiss. "Makes me wildly happy, baby," he says with that cocky grin.

I shake my head, and he leads me through the house, stark assed naked. I don't even question whether the staff will see because I don't think he'd be keen on sharing my naked body after he just spent the last hour claiming it.

CHAPTER ELEVEN

"The Houses for Humanity event tonight is being held in the historic Fairmont Hotel," Chase informs Kat and me.

His smile is huge, and I'm not the only one who can't stop looking at him. Kat is dreamily listening to every word. I can't blame her. He's that pretty.

Chase continues his history lesson. "The hotel was built in 1906 by a genius architect named Julia Morgan who, incidentally, also designed Hearst Castle. Unfortunately, right before its grand opening, the city suffered a huge earthquake, and the fires that followed took the lush hotel and destroyed it."

Kat's eyes widen and a hand goes to her mouth. "Oh, no," she says.

Chase nods. "The building was rebuilt and opened a year later to the day from when it was ruined." His voice tips with a sense of pride.

He really has a soft spot for architectural design and history. If he can get past the relationship I have with Phillip, those two would have a lot in common. Phillip is an architectural genius in his own right.

"Just like the phoenix. It rose up from the ashes and became something beautiful in the wake of disaster." I look out the window as the hotel comes into view. "Incredible."

I can appreciate the symmetry. Sometimes I feel as though I too could rise up and blossom in spite of the horrors of my past.

"I think you're incredible," Chase whispers against my hairline before kissing my cheek.

His hand is loosely holding mine on top of his thigh. One finger absently traces the symbol that's come to mean so much in such a small amount of time. Infinity.

We step out of the vehicle, and I'm taken aback at the property's beauty.

Chase leads Kat and me through the open floor plan swiftly. Obviously, this is not his first time here. His hand clasps mine, and I smile. In his tux, he's definitely a debonair feast for the eyes.

"Have I told you how stunning you look tonight?" He nudges my side and kisses the ball of my shoulder.

"Only a couple times already." I grin.

"That dress suits you." He squeezes my hand

He should like it. He paid for it.

Kat makes a point of looking anywhere but at the two of us as we continue through the catacomb of meeting and conference spaces. I slide my free hand down the deep eggplant satin dress and straighten any potential wrinkles. The dress is beautiful in its simplicity. The bodice hugs my chest in a corset style, flowing up into a fanned section where my breasts are tamed but the white flesh still spills over the confines just enough to entice. It seems to be working, because Chase can't stop sneaking peeks. He ogles me whenever he doesn't think I'm paying attention.

The satin slides along the rest of my curves, detailing my hourglass figure, and comes to a trumpet shape at the knee. The gown trails behind me a couple feet where it hits the floor. I feel exquisite, like a princess walking alongside her prince.

Kat follows us, quietly taking in her surroundings. She's lovely and bright in her sienna-colored gown. It has an enticing slit in the full billowing skirt that reaches all the way to the hip, exposing one of her long sexy legs. Crystals line the opening in bursts of sparkles. The light bouncing off the gems make it seem as though her dress is actually lit. The ruched fabric sweeps up her waist in swaths of oranges, reds, and copper before it goes into a halter top. Her hair is swept up in golden waves, complementing the dress perfectly. When we arrived to pick her up, she oohed and ahed over my dress, immediately trying to look inside to check the seams, how it hooked, and the boning systems in the corset. Chase didn't appreciate her familiarity with my body but watched with a grim set to his lips while she went through the process in the limo.

She gave her approval but stated that if I was going to hobnob with the elite, she'd be making me some dresses in the future. Knowing that would help her career made it okay to accept those gifts. That's how women bartered. I'd wear a dress she made and tell everyone who designed it, where I got it, and how they could get one. She'd pay for the material and use her own time. Then I wouldn't have to wear dresses Chase paid for. It would make me feel more independent and less like I was using him for what he could buy me. As it was, I'd already wondered whether I'd lost my pride somewhere under Chase's bed last night along with the dozen orgasms he spilled from me.

I trail my hand along Kat's arm. She smiles nervously.

I'm not sure if the anxiety is about meeting Carson or in anticipation of meeting "the Chloe Davis," the new, hot young designer taking Europe by storm with her distinctive fashion designs and eye for detail. My money is on the latter.

We approach an open space where several hundred people are milling about, chatting and laughing. Women and men stand, sipping from champagne flutes and eating tiny noshes from small golden plates at high tables. I can see Carson's blond head bobbing as he makes his way through the crowd.

His eyes scan Chase, quickly assess me, and then settle on Kat. A huge smile breaks across his face. It's as priceless as someone who is expecting a Ford Sedan but is gifted with a Ferrari. He eagerly grasps Kat's hand.

"You must be Kathleen." He kisses her fingers.

A light flush spreads along her cheeks. I squeeze Chase's hand and he grins.

Kat smiles shyly. "Carson, I presume. It's a pleasure to meet you."

"The pleasure is truly mine." Carson's gaze scales Kat from head to toe.

I can tell he likes what he sees, especially when she shifts her dress and one long toned leg makes an appearance.

Carson visibly gulps. "Would you join me for a drink?"

"Would love to." She grips her purse and follows him into the crowd. She turns and fans her face and mouths "Hot!" before giving us a sexy wave.

I giggle and wave back.

"Well, that was easy," I say to Chase.

"Yes, yes, it was." He shakes his head and grins.

We spend the next hour meeting San Francisco's elite,

including the Governor of California and the Democratic State Senators. Chase is in his element. He poses for photos with government officials, shares best business practices with other major moguls, and even spends a great deal of time explaining his city rooftop greenhouse plans. Turns out he has a division of his company devoted to designing green alternatives for big businesses to cut back on emissions, smog, as well as solar options for energy conservation. Not only is my man philanthropic, but also he's certifiably green. Such a dichotomy to the shrewd businessman everyone makes him out to be.

My man. Just because he called me "his woman" and had a Neanderthal reaction during our rooftop tryst after finding out about my history with Phillip doesn't mean he truly meant it in his heart of hearts. People say a lot of things when they are swept away by the moment. It wouldn't be right to give it more credence than that.

As I daydream by his side, my hair is swept to the side. His lips touch my shoulder, sending threads of pleasure to ripple along the open expanse of skin. He trails baby soft kisses along my neck to my ear. Before I can respond, a camera flash blinds me.

"Back off," Chase growls at a smiling man holding a large camera.

Jack appears from out of nowhere and drags the man away with a grip on the photographer's bicep. I can see Jack's hand turn bright white with the effort to keep a hold of the guy.

"God, I get so tired of paparazzi. Who let him in?" Chase snarls.

I lay a calming hand on his neck and force him to look

into my eyes. "Shall we go in and find our table?" I suggest.

He watches my face, adjusts his shoulders, and then nods curtly. Slowly he inhales and exhales before kissing me lightly. It's not a deep kiss, but what it lacks in intensity is made up for in sweetness and sincerity.

"You're good for me," he says, tension easing from his stiff shoulders as I massage the cords of tight muscle. "Come. Time for you to meet my mother."

That trickle of panic I had earlier about my relationship with Chase starts building, the seeds of doubt swirling like acid in my gut all over again. I've never actually met any of my ex-boyfriend's mothers. Phillip's mother was quite possibly the closest thing to June Cleaver a woman could get, but since Phillip and I never were officially an item, she doesn't count.

We enter The Gold Ballroom. The walls are gold with high arching marble stone accents. The tables are square and seat eight. I've never attended an event where the ballroom tables were square. Each table is adorned with a sateen gold cloth. Fine china in every size is already set at each place setting. In the middle of the table, a tall hurricane candle holder with gnarled twigs and white cherry blossoms spans the length of the glass. Hovering on the top of the hurricane is a tall candle encased in diamond-like jewels. The candlelight bounces off the glass and cut edges of stone to create a shattered halo around each table. The room is magnificent. Lush, posh, expensive.

Chase leads us through throngs of people to the very front of the room. We are the first ones to arrive at our table. A long golden filigree stand holds the number 1 on an ornately designed card. Under the 1, the name "Davis" is scrawled in cursive. This place pays a great deal of attention to the small finer touches and details. Something I should consider for Safe Haven events. At the front of the room is a stage with a large screen showing a picture of a house with a banner that says "Houses for Humanity—Welcomes You Home" across the front porch.

"Is that what you do with this charity?" I ask Chase.

He looks at the image. "That's one of our projects."

"What do you mean, your projects?"

"That's one of the homes I paid for. It's one of twenty-five that I funded after Hurricane Katrina hit New Orleans. It was a four million dollar project but well worth every penny." He smiles.

I am flabbergasted. Without thinking, I grip his tuxedo lapels and haul his lips against mine. He returns the kiss, delving his tongue deep. He tastes of champagne and man. Two of my very favorite flavors. When we both lack oxygen, he pulls away.

"What was that for?" His forehead leans against mine, his breath fanning my face in little bursts. His scent swirls around me in a halo of woodsy fruity goodness.

I inhale deeply. "Mmm, for being you," I answer, surprised by the deep honesty and public display of affection. I feel eyes on us, like that feeling when you know someone is watching you. Shyly, I take a peek around. We have an audience. I feel the rush of heat pinking my cheeks. All of our spectators are smiling except one, an older woman sitting in a wheelchair not ten feet from the table. She has dark brown hair with a two-inch thick band of gray swooped into an up-do. Her deep red lips are a tight grimace. Cool blue eyes squint and clearly express her distaste for what she just witnessed.

"Are you quite finished?" the woman asks in a clipped tone.

Chase smiles. "Mother," he says sweetly.

Please no. This cannot be *her*. She looks crabby, pompous, and downright mean. Maria's always telling me to watch out for the crotchety old broads because they are "*loco en la cabeza,*" meaning "crazy in the head." I smooth out my dress and wipe my suddenly clammy palms over my hips.

Chase holds out his hands and walks to the woman, leans down, and kisses the side of her cheek. She smiles warmly as he puts his hand on her shoulder. She clasps it tightly while her blue eyes turn glacial. She stares at me as if she can see right through me. She knows I'm a fraud. Most definitely not someone of her pedigree. Her shoulders are ramrod straight, her nose is stuck in the air, and she looks like she smells something raunchy. She apparently doesn't like me, and I haven't the slightest idea why.

"Mother, I want you to meet Gillian Callahan."

I walk over to her and hold out my hand. "Mrs. Davis, it's lovely to meet you."

She clasps my hand weakly. "I'm sure it is, and it's *Ms.* Davis." Her words catch on the Z sound. "Mrs. Davis was my mother," she continues.

Okay, so it's going to be like that.

Chase gestures for his mother to sit at the table. Her attendant wheels her into position. Finally Kat and Carson appear like a huge white flag waving in the wind, beckoning me, saving me from going into battle.

Close behind Carson is another large male. He stands over six feet tall but is not quite as tall as Chase or Carson.

His hair is dishwater blond. He wears an impeccably fitting tux that pulls into a nice V, emphasizing his broad chest and narrow waist. He is extremely handsome, though I prefer my dark-haired, philanthropic, green Superman. The man with dark chocolate eyes strides to the table, waving and kissing ladies' hands along the way. He stares down Chase with a hint of smugness. Chase settles his arm around my waist, and the man does a double take. He stops in front of me, a sly grin plastered on his chiseled face. I dislike him as quickly as Chase's mother disliked me.

Without looking at Chase, he grabs my hand and brings it to his dry lips. I have to try hard not to revolt, remembering to keep my cool.

"Chase, who is this lovely redheaded siren?"

Chase all but hauls me from the man's grasp. Inwardly I'm clapping. Outwardly I'm silent, deadly so.

"Her name is Gillian. Keep your hands off her, Cooper." Chase digs his fingers into my hip possessively.

The man laughs at Chase's alpha response, tipping his head back to give a full belly guffaw.

"I see you went back to the familiar, though I think this one takes the cake, buddy." Cooper slowly takes me in from head to toe and back again.

I feel his gaze as if his smarmy hands are trailing along my form. It takes everything I have not to cringe.

"Damn fine, and a redhead to boot. Need me to make sure you don't ruin your life again?"

Chase stiffens next to me. The tension pours off him like a waterfall. Niagara Falls comes to mind.

"You bastard." Chase pulls me behind him.

Carson moves between the two men, firmly separating

them. We've acquired quite a crowd of onlookers during their little tête-à-tête.

I grip Chase's arms from behind to remind him of my presence and lean my head between his shoulder blades. "Baby, it's okay," I whisper so quietly I'm not sure he can hear.

He turns and slides his hands along my bare arms. I see hurt and frustration in his eyes. He's seething, but I haven't the slightest idea why. After a couple deep breaths, he guides me with a hand at my lower back to the table, and we both sit.

"I think it's time for you to take your seat, Coop." Carson gestures at a seat next to Chase's mother.

There are two empty chairs between the men, and I'm not sure that's enough. I'm not sure the state of Texas being between these two would be enough to assuage the anger simmering under the surface. Chase is barely keeping his cool. As Cooper adjusts his tie and cracks his neck, showing he's unfazed by the little debacle they shared, Chase is on an entirely different plane. His fingers grip the back of my chair, white with strain. The other hand is high on my thigh, rubbing the satin expanse back and forth as if the movement soothes *him,* not me.

I sit across from Chase's mother with Kat next to me and Carson next to her. I watch the woman and silently vow to do my best to woo his mother and avoid any conversation with Cooper.

A leggy blonde with a pep in her step rushes through the crowd. She makes it to our table as a man in a tux taps on the microphone at the lone podium. Her dress is made of gold sequins and black silk. It's fitted to her long, curvy body like a second skin. The sequins are tailored around the lower half of her body in the shape of a high-waisted miniskirt. It's short in the front and draped with black silk flowing down the back into a train. The same black silk crisscrosses over each breast in a big X across her chest. It's a design I've never seen before. Kat looks at the gown and then the woman as if she's the Queen of Pop, Madonna herself. The stunning blonde slides into the seat next to Chase and gives him a big hug. Instantly I feel the sting of jealousy roar through my veins and heat my blood.

"Chase! I've missed you, cuz!" She kisses him on each cheek.

I roll my eyes and mentally bitch-slap myself. I'm an idiot.

"And who is this lovely woman next to you?"

His cousin is the designer Kat's been itching to meet. Her honey-colored eyes are soft and alight with happiness as if her whole face is lit with a smile. She is as beautiful as the aura surrounding her.

"This is my significant other, Gillian Callahan."

Her eyes widen. Seems everyone is surprised by my presence this evening. No more so than I am. Apparently Chase has taken us from merely dating to in a full-blown relationship in one weekend.

"Gillian, this is my baby cousin, Chloe Davis." He obviously has a great affection for the young woman, based on his ease and happiness at seeing her. The issue with Cooper seems to be overshadowed by her arrival.

"Hello, Chloe. You can call me Gigi. Everyone does. I've heard such wonderful things about you," I tell her.

"I wish I could say the same about you." Chloe eyes

Chase. "Looks like my cuz here has some explaining to do!" She jabs his shoulder.

"Ouch!" Chase mockingly rubs his bicep and most of the table laughs. His mother ignores all of us, looking out over the sea of tables, waving across the room now and again.

Chase introduces Kat, and she nearly swoons.

"I'm in love with you," Kat says, having a completely foot-in-your-mouth fan girl moment. I put my hand over my mouth to hold back my chuckle. Chloe's eyebrows rise as Kat cringes, shaking her head.

"I mean, I mean I'm in love with your work!" Kat clarifies.

Chloe laughs. Poor Kat slumps in her seat and looks away, her cheeks turning crimson. Carson puts a hand to the back of her neck, giving it a comforting squeeze, which I find utterly fascinating.

Chloe is sweet and throws out a life preserver. "I didn't realize anyone in the States has even heard of me!"

Kat instantly pops out of her slump, smiling and clasping her hand under her chin. "Are you kidding? I have pictures of your work pulled out of *Italian Vogue* and *Bazaar.* I even put them in a binder I can flip through when I need ideas for costumes!" Kat practically jumps with excitement.

Chloe's eyes widen. "Really? That's so cool! Where do you work?"

"At the San Francisco Theatre. I'm the head costume designer for the entire show." Kat beams with pride. She has worked her way up the ranks and does beautiful work. She slaves over each costume but the proof is in the pudding. Her work is impeccable.

Chloe pays close attention while Kat explains the

finer details of the show. "Wow, I'd love to design costumes someday. Sounds very couture and fun!"

Kat nods excitedly.

"Hey, why don't you and Gigi come to my private showroom sometime? I have a space in the Davis building. Fortieth floor along with a couple other designers. I'd love to get your opinion on my new line showing next spring."

Kat nudges me and whispers, "Oh. My. God." Then she composes herself by straightening her back and tipping her head to the side pushing a lock of hair behind her ear like she isn't completely dying with excitement. "That would be cool. Right, Gigi?" She plows her elbow into my bicep.

"Right!" I say with fervor and a giggle, grasping my bruised arm. "We'd love to come."

Chase pulls me into his side and nuzzles against my neck.

"You are too sweet. I could eat you for breakfast," he whispers against my ear. "Mmm." He bites down on the skin lightly. "I think will."

"You mean instead of your cookies?" I grin and sip my champagne.

He chuckles and tightens his hold. "Possibly with my cookies." With one last nibble, he breaks away and chats with his cousin.

The lights dim, and a dashingly debonair man strides through the crowd and pulls out the lone chair next to Chase's mother and Chloe. He leans down and kisses Chase's mother's cheek before looking around the table, his salt-and-pepper hair giving a hint to his age but not distracting from his good looks. He definitely has the Davis genes. He waves at Chase and then stops when Chase puts his arm around my shoulders. The man's eyes catch mine as he watches us with great interest.

"My Uncle Charles, the man who raised me," he says.

I nod as Chase kisses my bare shoulder. His uncle smiles coyly, and I return the smile.

His mother tsk-tsks between her teeth, and then focuses her attention on the stage. From the podium, the emcee asks everyone to get settled. The waiters deliver food in a flurry of activity as we listen to stories of people throughout the nation and the world who lost their homes over the past year. The presenter talks about the work the charity has accomplished because of generous donors, such as the individuals in the crowd. A slideshow is presented.

Toward the end of the presentation, the announcer recognizes one special person. "This man has not only given of himself by donating his company's architectural designs, housing plans, and services, but has personally donated millions to the cause. That is why we would like to recognize Chase Davis as Humanitarian of the Year! Chase, please come receive your award!"

Chase's head pops back, a shocked expression on his face. He's surprised. I stand and clap with everyone else in the room. He scans the room and opens his mouth before he licks his lips and looks down. He finally looks up and pulls me into a tight hug. "I had no idea," he whispers against my ear.

The room erupts in applause, and a spotlight shines over our table. Chase walks to the stage and up the steps. The big LCD screen behind him displays a huge picture of Chase in a hard hat, a "Houses for Humanity" T-shirt across his broad chest, and distressed jeans slung low on his hips.

He is standing in front of a dilapidated house, wearing a tool belt. He has a sledgehammer over one shoulder. He looks perfectly edible.

The crowd calms as Chase accepts his award.

"Thank you for this award. Honestly, I had no idea when I came here tonight that I would be receiving the Humanitarian of the Year Award." He holds up the crystal award. "I really don't know if I deserve it, for I believe that everyone has the basic human right to a warm place to live, a place to hang their hat after an honest day's work, and something they can call home."

The room roars in applause.

"Thank you, I'll treasure it always. Now, everyone, open up your checkbooks, because now's the time we give back!"

The emcee returns to the podium as Chase makes his way off the stage. "I couldn't agree with Mr. Davis more."

He continues his speech, but my eyes are planted on the man with the shy smile and an award. Chase makes his way back to the table after several handshakes and slaps on the back. I'm still standing, having not been able to sit the moment his name was called over the loud speaker. His gaze meets mine, and it's filled with happiness and a hunger I recognize deep within because it matches my own need. Chase pulls me to him, slamming our chests together, before he grips me by the waist and spins me in a circle as he kisses my neck.

"Humanitarian of the Year! Such an honor, baby," I whisper to him.

He squeezes me and then sets me down.

"Way to go, cuz." Chloe stands and hugs Chase.

Cooper actually claps Chase on the back.

"Congratulations."

Chase smiles and nods. Their animosity toward one another seems to be on hold for the time being.

"Good show, young man." Charles Davis shakes Chase's hand.

With a huge smile in place, Chase makes his way to his mother. He brings his award down to her face and she has tears in her eyes.

"I'm proud of you, my darling."

He hugs her and kisses her on the cheek. She pats his hair like a mother would a small child she adores. She's not so bad. She obviously loves her son a great deal, and he's never said a cross word about her. It seems she has an issue only with me. I'll have to ask Chase his opinion, but not tonight. Tonight we celebrate his achievement! Chase is congratulated by Kat and Carson, who are discreetly holding hands under the table, much to my excitement. Chase may have got Humanitarian of the Year, but this girl is about to score BFF of the year for this hookup. I can barely contain my need to text Maria and Bree with the juicy details of my awesome love match.

After what seems like eternity and several rounds of food, the silent auction winners are announced and a local band starts playing current radio favorites.

A Maroon 5 song is first on their set list and the floor fills quickly with couples swaying to the beat.

Carson grabs Kat's hand, dragging her to the dance floor. They seem to really enjoy each other's company, and Kat has altogether forgotten her hero worship of Chloe Davis. She's more smitten with a certain male Davis at the moment.

"Would you like to dance, Gillian?"

I nod as Chase takes my hand and leads me to the dance floor.

We move and sway to the Maroon 5 song about a woman being stuck on his body like a tattoo. I shimmy my hips left and right rounding out with a little booty tip.

Chase brings his hands over to my hips. "Damn, you're sexy!"

I laugh and calm the desire to bust out like I do when I'm out with my girls. Maria has taught all of us some serious dance moves, and when the four of us hit the floor, we drop it like it's hot. Chase twirls me and brings me back to his hard body. He's actually a good dancer, and I love being pulled against his form every so often. His hands slide up and down my back and grip my hips but never stray inappropriately.

I, on the other hand, am having a trying time keeping my hands off my sexy Superman. As the music sways, so do my inhibitions, which have me sliding my hands into his suit coat and down towards his tight ass. Before I can get to the prize, he grasps my hands and twirls me with a flick of his wrist. I pout and he winks.

We dance through two more songs and make our way to one of the cash bars in the corner of the room. Chase orders me a glass of white wine and a gin and tonic for himself. We sip our drinks and meet with the others from our table. Cooper is nowhere in sight. For that I am relieved. I don't know what's between the two of them, but Chase is in a great mood now and I'd like to keep him that way.

"Hey, Gigi! I just received a text from Ria. She says Tom has six extra tickets to the baseball game tomorrow and wants us all to come! Apparently some guys at work couldn't go. Carson said he's game. How about the two of you?" Kat says excitedly.

Chase looks at Carson. He grins and bashfully looks down at his shoes and away. He likes Kat! This is awesome.

Chase slides his fingers to my nape and nuzzles my chin. "Would you like to go, Gillian?"

"Yeah, I would. Sounds like fun."

"Well, then, we'll go to the game. My company owns a box at the stadium. We could sit in air conditioning. I could have it catered," he suggests.

My smile fades and I look away. He sees my discomfort immediately.

"What is it?" he asks.

"Nothing. Whatever you want," I say, not wanting to force anything. I know he's trying to be nice and helpful.

Chase lifts my chin and looks into my eyes. "What is it? I won't ask again," he uses his stern voice.

"If Tom is offering tickets, we should just accept them gracefully. Maybe he wants to impress the woman he's courting by taking her best friends to the game. I wouldn't want to rain on his parade."

"Damn, dude, she told you. Gigi, I like a girl who can speak her mind!" Carson laughs with uncontained glee. "When was the last time a woman told you like it is, Chase?"

"Never," he says flatly. He kisses me briefly. "You're honest. I like that. We'll go with your friends and sit in the seats he has purchased."

"I'll text Ria," Kat says.

"I'll text Phillip," I say.

"Excuse me? Why are you inviting Phillip to a couple's

event?" Chase interrupts.

There's that tone in his voice again, the one that I'm beginning to dislike immensely.

"We are conspiring to set Bree up with Phillip. She admitted at dinner the other night that she has a crush on him. This will be a perfect time to play matchmaker!" I flutter my lashes for effect.

Chase relaxes. "Bree is the one I've yet to meet. The yoga instructor?" I nod. "Sounds like an excellent idea."

Of course he's happy I am setting Phillip up with another woman. I do love that he's jealous and possessive over me though. Every girl needs a little of that to make her feel desirable. As long as he keeps it to a minimum, we'll be just fine.

We finish the evening sliding into Chase's limo. The drinks have been flowing in copious amounts, and we are all feeling the effects of the alcohol. First stop, we drop off Kat. I'm surprised when Carson gets out of the car with her.

"Would you like me to send Jack to take you home later?" Chase offers.

Kat snuggles into Carson's chest and whispers something in his ear. "Uh...nope. Won't need it. She'll take me home when we've sobered up. Get out of here. Go celebrate with your woman, Mr. Hunk of the Year. I mean...what did you win again?" He shakes his head.

"Hunk of the Year. You're exactly right." Chase laughs. "Kathleen, please don't drive him home too soon." He hands her a card through the window. "This is my business card with my cell phone. Please call if you need anything or would like to have Jack pick him up."

She takes the card. "I don't plan on taking him anywhere

anytime soon...if at all," she admits.

Carson gropes her ass and kisses her neck sloppily. I watch through the window in utter shock, leaning heavily on Chase as they make a spectacle of themselves.

"I can't wait to get you naked," is the last thing I hear Carson say before Jack maneuvers the stretched limo out onto the streets.

"Holy shit, did you see that? They are totally going to sleep together tonight!" I exclaim.

Chase's eyes sparkle, and he pulls me onto his lap. "He told me he was going to ride that mare until morning. Make her so bowlegged she wouldn't be able to walk straight tomorrow!" He laughs.

I snort and giggle with him. "What is he? A modern-day cowboy?"

Chase shrugs. "I guess. He's always enjoyed the westerns. He actually does have a farm outside of the city where he has a barn and several horses. Says it's the closest thing to the country he can do without moving to Texas."

"I like him. He's a good guy," I confide.

"He is. And he'll treat Kathleen like a princess...well, after he's done fucking her silly. That boy does like to fuck." Chase's inebriated state is making him a little more mouthy than usual.

"Speaking of fucking..." I pull up my skirt and slide to the floor.

"What are you doing?" Chase asks as I fumble with his belt buckle. "Oh shit, baby! Here?"

Surprising him is becoming a new fetish of mine. Besides, he needs to let loose more often. I grin evilly. I haven't had a chance to become close and personal friends with his dick, and right now, nothing short of a car accident could keep me from sucking him off.

I unzip his pants, and Chase looks down at me through half-closed lids. I grip his pants and underwear and slide them down to his ankles. His cock is free and comes alive as I pump it a couple times in greeting. His head drops back to the headrest and he licks those soft lips. He has a beautiful cock. It's long, very thick, and perfectly pink. Overall the largest out of any of my previous lovers, and it's prettier too. It's perfectly straight, standing out proud, anxiously awaiting my attention. I slowly drag my lips and chin along the length, becoming familiar with his scent. The musky smell invades my senses, making my mouth water. I slide my fingers through the dark thatch of curls at the base and grip his length, bringing my lips to the large crown. Chase's gaze finds mine as I dart my tongue out to lick the tip. He bites his lips and thrusts his hips as I bring my entire mouth over the tip swirling my tongue around the head.

"God, baby, so good," Chase says breathlessly, eyes never leaving mine.

His words spur me on, and I take him deeper into my mouth, dragging my lips against his length and back, ending at the crown. I tickle the slit at the top with my tongue, forcing him to jerk up into my mouth with a small thrust. Pre-cum leaks out the slit on top, coating my tongue with its salty goodness. Shivers of lust slip down my spine and wet my panties as I imagine the taste of his release on my tongue. I lick the entire length, sliding my tongue up and down him, lathering every inch of his beautiful cock with my saliva. I pull him deep into my mouth until the wide head bumps against the back of my throat. I relax my jaw and swallow around him, breathing through my nose. A deep moan pushes past his lips, and I can feel the muscles of his thighs tighten. He inhales, and I push him down the back of my throat taking him deep into my body. Then I hum and moan around his cock, the muscles of my throat constricting around the crown.

"Holy Fuck, so deep, baby, never before," he whispers.

I start to move in earnest, taking him down my throat and sucking tightly on my way up. His fingertips lightly caress my hairline as I slide up and down his length. My gag reflex is not strong, and I'm able to relax enough to bring him so deep my nose is tickled by his pubic hair. I take a slow breath in through my nose, and when he's as deep into my throat as I can take him, I swallow. His hips shoot up at the intense pressure, sliding farther into me.

"Shit, I'm going to come!"

He tries to pull away, but I double my efforts and suck and lick him until he's begging for release. He threads his hands into my hair and gently holds my head, fingers wound through my hair as he fucks my mouth. I'm wildly sucking his cock as he thrusts once, twice until his entire body tenses, his ass lifting off the leather seat to thrust deep. He groans loud as his release jets into my mouth and down the back of my throat. He's moaning my name as I suck harder, using my hand at the base to prolong his pleasure. His taste is heavenly. Thick and tangy. I happily swallow every last drop. It's a dish best served hot, and I'm one hungry lady.

When I lift my head, Chase is leaning against the headrest of the leather seats, pants down around his ankles, wet penis still semi-erect but losing its battle with rigidity. His mouth is open, and he's sucking in large gulps of air.

I smile with pride and cuddle up to his side caressing the soft skin of his thigh, scratching my nails through the light dusting of leg hair.

He turns his head and looks at me, stunned. "I've never been deep throated before. You are a goddess!" he says, wonder dripping from his tone.

I laugh. "No, I just don't really have that much of a gag reflex," I admit.

"You're still a goddess, and I'm one lucky bastard," he says and kisses me.

We take turns leading the kiss all the way back to his penthouse.

Fumbling around, the two of us make our way through the building and up the fifty flights into his home. We're both dead on our feet. He unzips my dress and turns around to grab his pajamas. He tosses one of his white T-shirts my way, and I remove my bra and throw the shirt on over my panties. He pulls back the covers and hops in. I slide in and cuddle into his chest. I kiss the space covering his heart.

"Thank you for tonight." He's silent and unmoving from my spot on his chest.

I think for a moment that he's fallen asleep, but as I look up, I find he's watching me. "I'm really proud to be with the Humanitarian of the Year."

He hugs me and kisses me softly on the lips. His eyes reach mine. "No, I'm the lucky one, to be here with you."

I smile and snuggle back down to his chest. I place my ear directly over his heart and fall asleep to the sound of his heart beating.

CHAPTER TWELVE

"Wake up, beautiful. It's game day!" Chase slides his hand along my back tickling my spine. "Your phone has been beeping like crazy for the past hour. I think you should check it."

I open my eyes and stretch tired limbs. Game day. Oh! This is going to be so much fun.

I'm bringing my significant other to hang out with all of my best friends. *Significant other.* Hmm, it's going to take some getting used to. Chase is standing in a towel, using another towel on his wet hair. I look my fill and watch him walk across the room. The man is a hunk. Carson's drunken words come back to me. "Hunk of the Year." I laugh to myself.

Chase stops, turns that gorgeous bottom, and hangs the towel around his neck. His golden chest is like a beacon calling me home as I crawl over to him. He's just too delicious to avoid.

"What's so funny?"

"I was just thinking about how right Carson was last night." I sit on my knees and place my hands on his big chest, fingers spread out in the shape of a star. His pecs are so square my entire hand fanned out still fits within the cut.

He draws his brows together.

"You are the Hunk of the Year." I kiss his right pec.

He laughs and then moans as I kiss his nipple and swirl my tongue around the small rubbery flesh. His nipples are as sensitive as mine, and I take great pleasure in knowing that I can make him crazy by licking and kissing them.

"No," he warns.

But I don't stop.

"You have to get ready."

He cradles my head as I lap at the little piece of skin, flicking it with my tongue lightly.

Chase groans and the towel at his hips starts to shift as his cock hardens. "I took the liberty of checking your texts. Maria said we have to be at the park at eleven a.m. and pick up our tickets at will call. It's close to ten now." He pushes me away by the shoulders.

I pout. "You checked my texts?"

"Yeah, the damn thing was ringing off the hook and beeping nonstop. I knew your friends were trying to get in touch with you, but I wanted to let you sleep." He walks to the closet.

The untrusting tinge of my subconscious flares at the blatant disregard for my privacy. Still, I don't really feel angry, but he did access my private information without asking. "I'd prefer if you wake me before checking my phone," I say toward the closet.

He reenters, wearing a pair of distressed dark blue jeans and a tight black T-shirt. The shirt pulls enticingly against his taut chest. Yum!

With a grace I've not known with other men, he approaches me and cups my cheek. "I'll try not to invade your personal space, but I'd rather you not hide anything from me."

I roll my eyes and remove myself from his grasp. He's already laid out clothing for me on the chair opposite the bed. Of course he picked the crazy expensive skinny jeans from Gucci and a three-quarter-sleeve flowing blouse from Chanel. Prada knee-high flat boots are sitting on the floor next to the outfit. They are a buttery tan and truly one of the most beautiful pair of boots I've ever laid eyes on. I find the clean bra and panty set he laid on the dresser and quickly get dressed.

It irks me that he's taken control yet again. If I allow him too much control of these small things, will he start controlling every area of my life the same way Justin did? By the time I finally escaped him, I had nothing. Few friends, no family, and nothing to call my own. I need time to think about how to best handle these concerns with Chase without sounding bitchy or ungrateful.

But not today! It is game day, and there's matchmaking to be done. With so little time left to get ready, a ponytail will have to do. I add a touch of makeup and am ready to hit the road in thirty minutes.

Chase has coffee in a to-go thermos and hands me something foil wrapped.

"Bentley takes Sundays off. I made us some bacon, egg, and cheese sandwiches for the road."

He cooked for me? A sexy, philanthropic, green Humanitarian of the Year cooked me breakfast? I'm so screwed. There is no way I'm not going to fall, spill my heart all over this man, and lose it all again.

When did he even have time to do this? Did he not sleep? After last night, I was gone to the world and could still use a couple more hours. "You made these?"

"Did you think I couldn't cook?" He brings his hand to his chest, pretending to be wounded.

"I would have bet good money that you couldn't cook and never spent any time in a kitchen." I smile and shake my head. He's pulled one over on me and added to the huge list of amazing reasons why I'm infatuated with him.

He pulls me in for a hug and leans his forehead against mine. "There's a lot you don't know about me. But we have plenty of time." He pecks my lips in a small kiss.

He's right, so I just nod as he continues, "I love to cook, and I reserve it for Sunday because I don't have the time to do it as much as I'd like."

"I love to cook too. Maybe we should make a meal together this evening?" I suggest.

His smile turns into a frown. "Can't. After the game, I have to head down to Los Angeles to finalize a deal first thing in the morning. I'm taking the nine p.m. flight out." He kisses me softly. "But we have today and next weekend to plan a cooking date. How does that sound?"

Amazing. Fantastic. Wonderful. I say none of those things, still stuck on the fact that this man wants to see me next weekend. That's a whole five days away, and he's planning to see me. Something inside me bursts with a giddiness I haven't felt in a long while.

"Heavenly," I agree. That will give me time to consider the control Chase has had over me this weekend and how easily I relinquished it. Maybe I can come up with a plan for safeguarding myself.

Arriving at eleven a.m. on the dot, we make our way to the will call booth. Chase is irritated that we aren't early.

He believes you should never keep someone waiting. That mentality will give him a heart attack by forty, but at least he's considerate. It's going to be my job to teach him to slow down and enjoy the things around him. If he doesn't, he's going to miss out on something wonderful.

Our seats are dead center of the stands and the second section up from the field, directly behind the batter.

"If we were in my box, we'd have a full view of everything," Chase whispers in my ear.

I elbow him. All of my friends are already sitting, talking. Tom and Maria are farthest from us, and then Bree and Phillip, and then Kat and Carson. Tom stands and makes his way over.

He's tall and very broad. Much larger than Chase, which would normally intimidate me, but since he's a cop and he saved Maria all those years ago, I have the opposite feeling in his presence. Tom's head is completely void of hair. He must shave it regularly to get the cut so close to his skull. He has a Giants jersey on and tight jeans. He is the epitome of a San Francisco detective. The man exudes authority but has the kindest green eyes, though they're currently hidden behind sunglasses.

He stretches his hand out to Chase. "Good to meet you. Chase, is it?"

Chase grips his hand. "Yes. Tom, right?"

Tom nods. "That's me."

"Hey, these are great seats, thank you for the invite."

Chase is playing nice, and I love him for it. *Love? No… well, maybe? Too soon!*

"It's no problem, man. Have a seat next to your bro." Tom gestures to the two open seats next to Carson.

Bree jumps up and makes her way through our friends. Chase takes in all that is Bree. She's stunning every day, but today she's a knockout. Her long blond hair flows freely in the wind. Her tan body shimmers in the sunlight against a baby blue tank that matches her eyes. A few inches of her belly is visible, showing a pretty flower dangling from her belly button. Her extremely low-rise jeans fit her toned curves to perfection. Gorgeous.

"I told you my friends were beautiful," I whisper to Chase.

"You weren't kidding." He grins.

I punch his shoulder. Bree pulls me into a big hug. Then she does the same to Chase. He's taken aback.

"I'm Bree, Gigi's best friend."

"All three of you are her best friends, right?" he questions.

"Yeah, but she likes me best!" Bree laughs.

It starts raining popcorn over the blond beauty, and she giggles prettily and makes it back to her seat.

"Shut up, Bree! You know she loves me more," Ria yells.

Kat is laughing but not commenting. She's obviously busy with Carson. He has his hand high on her thigh and his other arm around her shoulders.

"You two look cozy," I tell them.

Kat turns bright red, and Carson grins like the cat who ate the canary.

"*Cara bonita!* You look hot!" Maria announces as I shimmy into my seat.

Both Phillip and Chase say, "Yeah, she does."

Chase whips his head to glare at Phillip. I push Chase toward his seat. I can feel the tension in him after hearing

Phillip's comment. I decide I have to assuage his fury and deflect the attention away from me.

"Hey, Phil, doesn't Bree look hot?" I ask.

Bree flicks her hair and looks irritated at me, but then smiles and leans back against her chair next to Phil.

"She always does!" he says immediately and then blatantly checks her out. "You really do," Phil adds quietly to Bree.

Her gaze jerks to his and she smiles. Chase relaxes. Now for the next step.

"Hey, Gigi," Phil calls.

Before I respond, I pull Chase's face towards mine and plant a kiss on his lips. He deepens the kiss, putting his hand in my hair at the nape of my neck and pressing into me. When I pull away, he's smiling that deadly sexy smile.

"Oh come on," Phillip scolds.

Without moving my face from Chase's, I answer Phillip. "Yeah, what's up?" I snuggle my forehead against Chase, making a scene with my public display of affection.

The girls are smart enough to know what I'm doing. When I pull away, Maria is shaking her head in disapproval, but a hint of a smile tips at the corners of her mouth. Bree is smiling like a kid on Christmas morning, her hands clasped and close to her heart. Kat must have not gotten the memo because she isn't paying attention at all, preferring to nibble on Carson's neck. Phillip is positively fuming.

"Hey, Phil, let's get some beers for everyone," I suggest. I need to set my best friend straight and now.

Chase stands. "I'm coming with you," he says firmly.

I put my hand on his chest. "No, you're not. Trust me." I search his eyes, telling him that I need this time. "But I could use some money?" I hold out my hand.

"Of course, yes." He pulls out his wallet lightning fast.

I wink at Bree as she watches the display. He places a handful of twenties in my hand, well beyond what I need for beers, but I'm not going to complain. I know asking him for money in front of my friends was the exact thing to do. It gives him back that sense of ownership, that he can provide for my needs.

"Get anything you want, and buy a beer for everyone." He kisses me quickly and then sits back down. The smile on his face is priceless.

I look at Maria, and she rolls her eyes. Kat makes the "perfect" symbol with her fingers as Phillip pushes his way through the group.

"Ready then?" he asks in a huff.

We make our way over to the concession stand, and I twirl and put my finger to his chest. "What the hell is wrong with you?" I am done allowing his macho bullshit to go any further.

He backs up a step. "Me! What about you, sucking face in public with a man you've only known for what, half a second?"

"I've known him for almost two weeks now, and we're seeing each other, okay? I'm really happy with Chase. What's your deal?" I point at his chest harder than I need to.

"Stop that! It hurts." He pulls my hand away from his chest. "I don't know. Maybe I'm just tired of you getting with men who aren't worthy of you, that's all." He looks down at his shoes.

"And do you think *you're* worthy of me?"

His eyes shoot up to mine. A stricken look mars his

handsome face. "No, Gigi, it's not that. I love you, but..."

I groan and take a deep breath. "Phil, I know. I love you too, but it's more like a brother."

He nods and releases a breath he must have been holding. He brings his hand to the back of his neck and rubs it, clearly uncomfortable with this conversation. "Yes, exactly."

"So stop this weirdness with Chase. If it's not jealousy, what is it? I really like him, and I don't want you messing this up for me." I grip his hand and squeeze it.

He searches my eyes and squeezes my hand tightly. "You're falling for him, aren't you?"

Instead of answering, I look into the distance, needing those extra precious seconds. I can't lie to Phil, and I haven't really had the time to give my feelings enough thought.

"Gigi, I haven't seen you like this since Justin," he continues.

Just hearing his name gives me the chills.

Phil pulls me into a tight hug. "I'm sorry. I don't mean to bring him up. It's just I can see it in your eyes when you look at him, Gigi. I just want you to be careful with that beautiful heart of yours."

I nod into his chest and hug him tighter.

"I'll never forget what that asshole did to you and after losing Angie, it's just, I can't see someone I love get hurt again."

A part of me wants to do a fist pump. I knew it wasn't jealousy! Chase had my mind twisted with his possessive brooding behavior. I hug Phil tight and rest my chin on his sternum to look up at him. His eyes have lost the irritation, and I'm certain mine have too. All is right with the world again.

"Let's get that beer. Wouldn't want Mr. Macho to wonder where you are."

"Oh, shut up." I punch him in the arm. "Seriously though, you're going to make an effort with him, right?" I give him my best pout, complete with lip puffed out and sad puppy dog eyes.

He takes a breath and pulls me to his side while walking to the line. "If you're into him, I'll make an effort. Okay?"

"Promise?" I smile wide and shift from foot to foot practically bouncing in place.

"Yes! Such a pain in my ass," he finishes with a nudge to my shoulder.

We wait to place our order, and I have a moment to broach the subject of Bree. Since Angela died two years ago, I haven't seen Phil so much as ask a girl out on a date. He had that one-night stand last year when we were out and completely drunk on our asses. A little miss hot pants at the bar had her eyes on him all night and took advantage. I let it happen, knowing he needed a night of freedom. I even picked up Anabelle from the babysitter and took her home with me. The guilt he felt the next day broke my heart. He felt like he betrayed his dead wife and spent the following months in therapy. That was the last time I tried to fix him up. Until now. I want him to get over his guilt and appreciate life again. I know Angela would want that too.

"So what do you think of Bree?" I ask nonchalantly.

"She's pretty and fun. I like her. She's a great gal."

"Great, so would you consider dating her?" I ask.

"She wouldn't go for a guy like me," he says solemnly.

I was afraid he'd say that. I hum and shrug my shoulders.

"She thinks you're hot."

He physically turns me toward him and stares into my eyes. "Really? She said that?"

Nodding, I smile. "You should ask her out sometime. Alone. Not with the group." I leave it at that and walk away, carrying the four bottles of beer, two in each hand.

He laughs and follows behind me, his wheels probably turning already. We've all been out before over the years, but the two of them were never in a position to consider the other in that way. Bree usually was dating some fruit loop, and Phil was usually avoiding anything remotely related to intimacy and women. Now I can see he's thinking about it. I can only hope he'll man up but knowing Phillip, he won't. I may have to force it a little. When I maneuver down the stairs back to our section, Chase stands and grabs two of the beers. He passes them to Maria and Tom.

"Hey, thanks, man," Tom says and takes a pull from the bottle.

"Thanks for the tickets!" Chase tips the beer bottle in a man-type move only men understand.

Now that everyone has a beer, we settle in to watch the game. Every so often Maria, Tom, Carson, and Chase yell at a call they don't agree with. Chase is really getting into this. When the Giants score, everyone celebrates with a round of high fives.

Chase puts his hand on my thigh. I put my arm around his broad shoulders and lean against him as I watch my friends. Tom is holding Maria's hand. They are chatting about the game. I can tell that he appreciates her. He tilts his head to listen to her, and they laugh at the same things. It's hysterical when they both act as if they are dying when a play doesn't go the way they want. It's amazing how quickly she went from knowing nothing about baseball to being intent on every play.

Kat and Carson are completely in their own world. She's crossed her legs towards his and has half turned toward him. They whisper back and forth. Every so often he looks out at the game, but Kat is holding most of his attention. He sneaks little pecks of her lips and shoulder. They've been holding hands since we arrived and really haven't paid much attention to anyone other than one another. It's lovely to finally see her so happy.

I peek at Bree and Phillip. Since our conversation, he's making a concerted effort to talk to her. Go, Phil! I can see her playing with her hair, making a point to touch him every chance she gets throughout their conversation. A smack of the arm here, a grip of his thigh there. Bree's in full flirt mode. She's got her eyes set on Phillip, and she's pulling out all the stops. They could make a great couple, and I know Bree would be an amazing stepmother to Anabelle. He really needs a woman in his life other than me. It seems as though Phillip is enjoying the conversation too. He's pulling the shy guy move with her. When she says something funny he looks down, shakes his head, and then looks up at her through his lashes. Nice!

Chase tips his head to mine. "Enjoying the game, baby?" he asks and cocks his head to the side.

Damn, he's good-looking. His hair is windblown a bit, and he's smiling in a way that would bring any woman to her knees.

"Very much." I smile.

He turns back to the game. I nuzzle his neck, taking

in his scent. That woodsy scent mixed with citrus is my undoing. Warmth spreads through my body making every subtle touch of his seem like more.

"Will you take me back to my place after the game?" I massage his shoulders with one hand.

"You're welcome to stay at my place," he offers.

"I have work tomorrow, and you have a flight to LA," I remind him.

A scowl appears on his face. "I'll take you home."

I lean toward his ear. "All I can think about is getting you home and into my bed." Chase is making me bold sexually, not as afraid to ask for what I want. It's a foreign feeling, but exhilarating and freeing at the same time.

Chase's hand slides farther up my thigh. He strokes my center. I can barely feel it through my jeans, but it's there and I push toward it.

"I'm ready when you are," he says seriously.

I kiss his neck. "Later." I grab his hand and squeeze.

"That's a promise." He finishes his beer in one shot.

We spend the rest of the day laughing and cheering. All eight of us mostly paying attention to the game. At the last inning, the bases are loaded. The pitcher throws, and the batter hits a grand slam. The crowd goes completely ballistic! I had no idea what was happening when all four men on the field made their victory lap around the bases, each one hitting home base.

Everyone around us, including my group, jumps up, screaming and cheering for the Giants. The game announcer announces the Giants won the game! The crowd is at a constant roar, going completely wild! One by one, every man grabs his lady. Tom pulls Maria into a frenzied kiss. He lifts her off her feet and spins her in a tight circle. Carson grips Kat's hand and pulls her into his lap and lays one on her. I even see Bree hop up and down, cheering before she turns, grabs Phillip, and exclaims, "What the hell!" and lays her lips over his. He yanks her trim body against him, and they are gone, lost in a moment.

"Come here, baby." Chase pulls my face to his with both hands, cupping my cheeks.

I sigh into his kiss as he plunges his tongue into my mouth. I give as good as he's giving, swirling my tongue around his and nipping at his bottom lip. He tugs at my top one before tilting my head to the side while sliding a hand down my body to cup my ass, plastering me against the hard ridges of his sculpted body and growing need.

We're lost in the kiss, forgetting where we are, who's with us, the fact that we're in the middle of a stadium with my best friends in the world around us.

"Get a room!" Maria yells from behind us.

I pull away from Chase, breathless. God I want him, right now. "Shut up, Ria!" I holler over my shoulder.

Chase smiles and pulls me against him, hugging me. "You ready, baby?" he asks.

"Are we getting some dinner?" Bree asks. She bounces from foot to foot, obviously excited. Probably from her impromptu mega-kiss with Phil.

"Chase has to fly to LA tonight. He's going to take me home first." I wiggle my eyebrows so she gets the hint.

She looks disappointed but moves to her next victim. "What about you?" she asks Kat.

"Busy." Kat grins up at Carson.

He nods.

"We're *very* busy." She doesn't take her gaze away from the blond hunk holding her.

Bree pouts prettily. "What about you, Ria?"

I'm starting to feel bad for the girl. "Don't even ask, *Hermosa*! I'll be taking advantage of this man," she says honestly pointing her thumb at Tom.

His ears tinge bright red, but he laughs and brings his huge arms around her in an embrace. She snuggles against him, happy as a clam.

"Can't take advantage of the willing," he says.

We all laugh.

Bree's bottom lip sticks out even farther. She's clearly disappointed.

"I'll have dinner with you," Phillip says.

Her eyes widen. "Really? That would be fantastic!" I look knowingly at Kat and Maria. Phillip actually made the first move. I'm impressed and will make a point to tell him so privately.

Phillip clears his throat, his confidence seeming to have come back. "I know this really great little sushi place downtown if you're interested."

"I love sushi!" she exclaims.

"Sick! Can't you take her somewhere nice, Phil? You want to feed my friend bottom dwellers?" I shake my head in disgust.

Chase laughs and pulls me against him.

"You're a freak, Gigi!" Bree laughs. "Seafood is amazing and so good for you."

I crinkle my nose. "If you want to eat the cockroaches of the sea, far be it from me to stand in your way." I slide my arms up and down Chase's tan forearms. I love being encased in his arms. Makes me feel so at ease. Safe.

Bree sighs and puts her hand to her forehead.

Chase whispers close to my ear, "Time's wasting."

"Time to go!" I tell my friends immediately.

I hug each one and thank Tom for his generosity, telling him we had a great time. Chase shakes hands with each male and accepts a hug from every one of my girlfriends. His face is impassive as he accepts each hug but doesn't exactly return it, mostly doing the perfunctory tap on their backs. Interesting.

The group makes its way to the entrance. I happily swing Chase's hand. "This has been the best weekend ever," I tell him.

"Ever?" His face twists into one of surprise.

I think about it a couple minutes. "Yeah, ever. I've never been quite this happy."

"Oh, baby, I'm about to make you a whole lot happier," he growls and paws at my curves, sending ribbons of lust to swell and ache between my thighs.

The limo pulls up, and my friends gawk and stare as Chase ushers me in.

"You suck!" Maria bellows as she sees the plush ride. They're going to be stuck in parking hell trying to weave their way out of this mess. This particular stadium is known for the hellacious exiting process.

"You're just jealous! *Besos!*" I yell through the window and wave.

I hear a round of "*Besos*" from each of my soul sisters. I love my friends. I love my life. And in thirty minutes, I'll be making love to an incredibly hot, sexy Superman. I'm starting to believe fairytales do exist.

"Why do you say 'kisses' to your girlfriends?" Chase asks as he kisses each one of my knuckles, ramping up my desire for him.

"We always have. Ria started it years ago. It's our way to say that we love one another without being commercial. If you spell it out, B-E-S-O-S, to us, stands for Bound Eternally Sisters of Souls."

Chase pulls on my ponytail holder, and my hair falls around my shoulders. He massages the nape of my neck, scratching his fingers up along my scalp. I lean back and moan, never wanting it to stop.

"What about the tattoo?" Chase asks while kissing along my neck.

On my left wrist is a vibrant Celtic trinity symbol. It's the only tattoo I have and the only one I could ever imagine having. When you've had a past like mine, marking the body in any way permanently has to mean something. For the three women I adore more than life itself, it means so much.

"The Celtic trinity." I trace a finger along the blue-and-black design. It's about the size of a quarter. It's a rich indigo blue with deep sweeping black outlines around the three petal-like shapes. They all come together and are surrounded by the circle of protection. "It means a lot of things to people. Body, mind, soul, Father, Son, Holy Spirit..."

"And what does it mean to you and your friends? I noticed all four of you have the design, at least I suspect as much. I saw it on Maria's shoulder blade the other day and on Bree's foot today."

"Kat's is on her hip, and no, you're never seeing that one!" I warn and narrow my eyes in mock anger.

"Don't care to. I mean, your friends are all stunning beauties, but I prefer a hot, curvy redhead any day of the week." He bites down on the spot where my shoulder and neck meet.

I gasp and lean my neck over to the side.

"So what does the tattoo mean to you?"

"Oh, um…"

Chase continues kissing and licking the side of my neck, distracting me.

"Body, mind, and soul are important to all four of us, but for me personally, it represents the past, the present, and the future. They will always be a part of my past, my present, and my future."

Chase hums along my neck and twirls my hair. "You have gorgeous red hair, Gillian," he whispers against my ear.

She's a redhead. The phrase jars my memory. "Speaking of my hair, why does your family seem taken by my hair color? Carson said something about it. Cooper did, too, at dinner last night."

Chase tenses and halts his kisses. "It's nothing." He kisses me again.

Oh, it's definitely something. A something he doesn't want to talk about. I want to press for information, but his tongue is running down my neck. His hand comes to my breast and squeezes it through the thin fabric. I groan and cup his cheek to bring his lips to mine. I pull myself onto his lap and grind into his erection as we kiss languidly, losing ourselves in our passion for one another.

Chase slides his hands under my top to cup each breast. I tilt my head and delve deep into his mouth, staking my own claim on him. His fingers find their way under the cups of my bra to pluck and pull at each throbbing peak. I slide my tongue along his jaw and nibble and bite my way over his five o'clock shadow. I lick the scruffy surface until I make my way up to his earlobe and swirl around the taut skin, nibbling lightly. He lifts his hips against mine, and I take advantage, grinding into his erection harder.

"God, I want you," he says through gritted teeth, nostrils flaring.

If I didn't know he was insane with lust, I'd think he was angry, ready to go into battle.

"Then take me," I challenge.

As the words leave my mouth, the limo stops. We've arrived at my building. I refrain from doing a fist pump into the air.

Chase doesn't wait for Jack to open the door. He's out of the car, pulling me behind him towards my apartment. "Jack, bring her clothing to her apartment. Come back in an hour and a half." Chase practically pushes me through the doors of my building.

"That will be cutting it close, sir," Jack warns.

"We'll make it. An hour and a half."

"Chase, if you have to go, we can wait—"

"Not an option." He cuts me off and forges ahead. "I'm going to be gone two days. I'm taking you to bed."

He is a man on a mission and I love it. A giddiness fills my chest as I skip alongside him.

"Yes, sir!" I salute and he rolls his eyes.

"Just open the damn door, Gillian, or I'll fuck you in the hallway."

I'm trying to pull my keys out of my purse, but his hands all over me make me clumsy. He cups my breasts and bites my neck as I lose connection with the lock.

"You're taking too long," he warns, pressing his dick against the seam of my ass through my jeans. He digs his erection against me wickedly setting off a firebomb of heat.

"Shit!" I drop the keys without unlocking the door.

He grabs them, pulls me against the door, and kisses me ravenously. He presses me into the doorframe while he fiddles with the door. He pushes against me, and the door opens. We tumble in and catch our footing before falling to the floor in a heap. Chase is already pulling his T-shirt over his head. He drops it to the floor, and I lick my lips when I see his golden bare chest. I walk backwards toward my room, watching him as his eyes fire and turn dark.

I pull the designer blouse over my head and drop it to the floor as well. His shoes go, one foot and then the other, as we slowly walk. I mimic him, raising the stakes by unbuttoning my jeans and sliding down the zipper. His eyebrow goes up, and he pulls on his buttons and stops advancing to pull his jeans completely off. His black boxer briefs mold to his form like a second skin. I follow his lead and do the same until I'm standing before him in a pale pink bra and matching panties he purchased. He scans my body and bites his lip.

"Money well spent. I'm going to get you a store full of satin and lace so I can go through my days knowing my woman is wearing those sexy things for me." He points to his chest. His gaze traces over my curves almost like a caress. "Baby, I can't wait to be buried deep inside you," he says just before lunging like a cougar capturing its prey.

He grips my waist and presses his body against mine. Warm male skin. My mouth waters, and I groan, sliding my hands down his rib cage and up his abdomen, feeling his muscles bunch and tighten under my touch.

"Where's your room?" He trails his fingers over the top of my lace panties.

"Just behind me, straight back at the end of the hall."

He grips my ass and pulls me up. My legs immediately go around his waist. For a moment, I remember him taking me up against the wall in his dining room the other night. I tighten my legs around his waist. He walks us to my room and sets me on the queen-sized bed. My bright white comforter is cool against my heated skin. His lips find mine, and we kiss for what feels like hours but is probably only minutes.

He slides his fingers into the sides of my panties and slowly drags them down my legs. I lean up and unclasp my bra and throw it towards the bench at the end of the bed. He stands and pulls down his underwear. His cock juts straight out, thick and proud. I wrap a hand around it, relishing how hard it is. Knowing I did that to Chase, making the master of his universe lose a bit of his control, makes me weak and needy. I lean forward and lick the moisture on the tip. I swirl my tongue around the large crown and draw him deep into my mouth. He thrusts his hips forward, and I willingly take him in deeper. It's actually easier to take him down my throat when he's standing. I take a huge breath and pull his hips, sliding his cock deep into the walls of my throat.

"Fuck!" he cries and pulls out, his body shaking with the effort not to come so quickly.

I grin and wipe my lips with my thumb before he kisses me.

"Oh, you saucy little vixen. You are going to get it."

"In a good way, I hope." My voice is gravelly and rough from taking him so deep. It's a perfect sex voice.

"You have no idea." He presses me down and drags his tongue down to each breast. He takes one pink tip into his wet heat, and I press it farther into his face, twining my fingers into his hair gripping the scalp. He smiles against my breast and draws the bud with his teeth, biting down on the tender flesh.

Spikes of pleasure tear from each peak through my chest and down to my center where my sex moistens and softens, readying to mate. "Oh, yes, Chase!" I thrash about as he continues pulling, biting, and pinching each tip until I'm trembling under him in ecstasy. "Please."

The begging does it. Chase can't deny me when I beg for his cock. "You want me to fuck you?" He presses two fingers deep into my core. He hooks them up and rubs his thumb around my clit.

I arch into his hand and gyrate my hips with his movements. The pleasure consumes every facet of my being. With each drag of his fingers along that bundle within me, I jerk and shake. He brings me close to tears, lost in his control over me.

"Yes, Chase, fuck me...please!" I scream.

He removes his fingers, and I almost cry from the loss. He presses my thighs wide and centers himself. He pushes the tip in and teases me with it.

"Again," he demands.

I try to use my legs to pull him into me, but he's holding them fast against the bed, splitting me open physically and emotionally. "Please, Chase...baby," I beg again, my head thrashing from side to side as he twirls a finger around my clit. It's not enough. I need him. All of him.

"God, Gillian, you're so beautiful, spread open like this, begging for me to take you." He grips my knees and presses them up and back, opening me farther.

I'm completely vulnerable to him, and he has total control. He pulls the tip of his cock out, and before I can protest, slams into me to the hilt.

"Chase!" I scream until my throat is raw.

He pulls out and pounds back into me again. He starts a hammering, forceful rhythm that picks me up and tosses me head first into my release. I'm lost in the sensation. Every press and pull of his thick cock drags against that magical spot within me, and I start to spiral and throb with the pressure of my second build up. Chase picks up the pace, bringing his face down to mine for a hot, deep kiss. The new angle presses him another inch deeper, knocking against my womb. He groans into my mouth and bites my bottom lip. His cock bottoms out as he pushes against my knees, forcing every last millimeter of his length to wedge farther into my sex. I feel full, stretched to capacity.

"Want you sore when I'm gone, baby." He continues the fierce strokes and adds a twist of his hips, grinding against my aching clit with each thrust of his pelvic bone.

I cry out as he brings his hands under my ass to cup each cheek, using his full strength to pull me against his cock at the same time jackknifing into me. I explode. My orgasm sweeps over me in a tidal wave of heat and light.

As the waves of my orgasm crash over me, he pulls out and flips me over. He tilts my hips up, and he enters me hard, without apology, as if he owns me. Right now, he so does.

"Yes," I scream as my sex squeezes and milks his dick.

Chase pounds in to me quickly, building the ecstasy again.

"Fuck, you're so tight! And your ass. Goddamn, I love fucking you, watching my cock spear into your cunt. Baby…I'll never get enough of you."

More than anything, I hope he means it. He pounds into me, and I push against his thrusts, allowing him to fuck me harder. It hurts in the best possible way, like a deep tissue massage only on the inside. You know it's going to hurt the next day, but the release is worth it. Chase digs his fingers into my hips so tightly, I'm almost in pain, and I don't care. He pummels me over and over, and I can feel him tightening, his thrusts becoming more erratic.

"Want you with me," he says through clenched teeth.

He leans and reaches around. He finds my clit and he pinches and presses hard on the sensitive moist skin there, sending me into another blinding orgasm. He thrusts deep, holding me roughly against his pelvis as his release shoots hotly within my core, our bodies melting into one another. After a few last jerks of his hips, he collapses on top of me, pressing me into the mattress. His weight is wonderful and welcome, like being covered in my very own Chase blanket. All too soon, he rolls to the side, pulling me against his sweat-dampened chest. We both pant and try to calm our overheated bodies.

"It's never been like that with another woman, Gillian," Chase says softly, staring at the ceiling.

"For me either." I turn over and face him. "I just I want you so much." I stretch each tingling muscle, pointing and flexing my toes and fingers. The space between my legs is definitely sore and well used. I've got no complaints. I'll endure that discomfort gladly.

We lie for quite some time with Chase caressing my arms, swirling his fingers around a breast but avoiding the overly sensitive tips. I grin, thinking how much his mouth lovingly abused each tip in turn only an hour or ago.

Chase sighs and kisses each breast and then lays his chin on my chest. "I have to go, baby."

I frown and puff out my lips. He grins and kisses away my pout.

"I know. I don't want you to." With a sigh, I sit up and find my bra and panties. I pull them on and grab a pair of yoga pants and a tank top from my drawer.

Chase finds his trail of clothing and dresses quickly. Someone knocks on the front door. "That would be Jack."

I nod and walk him to the door. He opens it and gestures for Jack to wait in the car. He pulls me into a hug and a long kiss. It's not a goodbye kiss. It's a "wait for me" kiss. I give it my all, trying to express without words everything that's soaring through my mind and heart.

"Gillian, today was…great. The weekend." He shakes his head and tugs me to him. He leans his head into the crook of my neck and inhales deeply. "I haven't had that much fun in a long time."

I believe him. The man I met a couple weeks ago seemed a lot more reserved and conservative. This Chase, *my* Chase, is those things and so much more.

I smile my best hundred-watt smile and hug him tightly. "I'm so glad you like my family!"

"I do. Very much, but not as much as I like you." He lifts my chin and kisses me softly. "I'll be back Tuesday evening. Can I take you out for dinner Wednesday?"

"I'd like that."

He turns to leave, and my chest hurts.

"Chase?"

He turns and cocks his head to the side, waiting.

"Um, I'll miss you," I admit.

The smile that adorns his face is hypnotizing. "I'll miss you too, baby." His tone is laced with sex and possibly something more. He winks.

I shut the door and lean against it, closing my eyes. "I'm falling for you, Chase," I whisper.

CHAPTER THIRTEEN

A text from Chase first thing Tuesday morning makes me giddy.

To: Gillian Callahan

From: Chase Davis

Business is booming. Will be in LA until Wednesday afternoon. Dinner at 7:00 p.m. my place.

Even in text messages, he's bossy, but I know it's just his way. He has full control over his life and everyone around him. Not having full control over me and our relationship throws him off balance. Until now, I've never felt in control of anything in my life. I spent years being controlled by a man I thought loved me and even more years trying to heal from it.

Before I can respond to Chase's text, Taye calls me into his office. His tone is not the laid-back, easygoing one I'm used to. It's more the stressed-out and upset variety.

"Sit down, Gillian. We're waiting for Ms. Peterson to arrive."

I'm sure my mouth just hit the floor. Ms. Peterson is the Director of Human Resources, and based on his tone and stiff spine, something bad has happened. I scramble to think what I could have done to upset him. Enough that the

Director of HR is warranted.

"What's this about?" I ask Taye.

"I've been asked not to discuss the situation until Ms. Peterson arrives," he says tersely.

He doesn't look at me, and he's really tense. His jaw is clenched, and sweat beads on his forehead. He makes a point shuffling papers around his desk as if he doesn't know what to do with his hands. But what is really unsettling is that he still hasn't looked at me. Something is wrong, really wrong. I rack my brain. What could have brought this on? Why does the Director of Human Resources want to meet with me? I draw a complete blank.

Ms. Peterson enters Taye's office briskly and takes a seat across the small table from me. Her blond bob accentuates her face, but her blue eyes are cold and unfeeling. She wears a deep red power suit with a white silk blouse. Tiny pearl buttons run down the center. The woman is quite pretty. She'd be beautiful if she smiled every so often.

"Ms. Callahan, some troubling information has been brought to our attention. I felt it was in the best interest of the foundation to bring it to light promptly." Her eyes burn into mine.

I clasp my hands in my lap, worrying my fingers together nervously.

She pulls out a newspaper and opens it to a section in the center and sets it on the table. A picture of Chase and me, taken at the charity event this past weekend, half fills the page. Above it, the caption reads, "Billionaire Chase Davis, a Bachelor No More?" In the image, Chase is clearly kissing my neck as I lean against him. His hand is around my waist, affectionately holding me to him. My eyes are closed, and

I'm smiling. It's a candid shot some photographer snapped. Probably the one that Jack threw out that evening. I can't look away from the picture. It's one of those images of you and your mate looking so happy you'd want to frame and treasure always. Seeing it splashed across the San Francisco Chronicle is obviously a problem.

"That is you, Ms. Callahan, is it not?" Her tone is harsh.

I look at Taye, and he's staring off into the distance. His hands are clasped tightly. He's uncomfortable with this meeting and definitely angry. I'm not sure if it's at me or on my behalf. I hope the latter.

I nod at Ms. Peterson, not knowing what to say. Then she drops the bomb.

"This behavior is unacceptable for a foundation employee."

As if my head weren't connected to my neck, it slams backward, my mouth opening and closing ready to verbally battle. Before I can say anything in my defense, she continues.

"Mr. Davis is Chairman of our Board and the foundation's largest donor. His donation each year pays all of our payroll and overhead." Her beauty is suddenly diminished by the putrid pinched look she's giving me and the accusation in her voice.

"I'm sorry, Ms. Peterson. Where are you going with this?" I ask.

"Are you in a relationship with Mr. Davis?" she asks bluntly. Her mouth pulls together in a sneer, and her jaw clenches.

"I don't know how that's any of your business, but yes, we are seeing each other." I'm not ashamed of my relationship with him, and I have no reason to be. It's not conventional to date someone on the board, but he's a volunteer, not an employee. I do not believe this falls under any fraternization policies. Come to think of it, there are plenty of employees dating one another. I'm not sure how this is a problem.

"I'm going to make this very clear, Ms. Callahan. This relationship does not look good for the foundation. It's ethically inappropriate." She adjusts her hair and folds the newspaper. "This relationship puts the foundation in a negative light. We cannot have members of the staff dating members of our board."

"What are you saying?" The question is meant to sound confident, but it comes out weak and breathy.

"You have a decision to make." Her face twists into a grimace, and she holds up her hand displaying three fingers. "One, you break off your relationship with Mr. Davis." She pulls that finger down. "Two, you continue your relationship, and he'll have to step down as Chairman of the Board." Another finger falls.

At that moment, everything around me starts to sway and shake. My world as I know it is crumbling like a wall on the edge of a cliff that's just been hit by an earthquake. Each piece slipping off the ledge and falling into the ocean's murky depths. I'm certain my face has gone pale and probably looks frightened or shocked. All of which I'm feeling in spades. Tears prick the edges of my vision, but I don't let them fall. Ms. Peterson's grin holds an evil curl as she puts more nails into the coffin of my life and career.

"Or, three, you quit or be relieved of your position with the foundation. Your choice."

I dab the corner of my eye with a finger.

"I'm going to ask you to leave for the rest of the week

and return on Friday with your decision. You're being suspended with pay for three days. This should give you ample time to determine what's best for you. We are doing what's best for the foundation."

Ms. Peterson seals my fate by standing and turning to Taye. "Mr. Jefferson, is there anything you'd like to add?"

He shakes his head. "No, Ms. Peterson, I believe you've covered it. Thank you."

She nods and walks out of the room, a pep in her step. The entire conversation took less than fifteen minutes. Her heels dig into the carpet as she stomps away in her pristine red suit.

And that is that. She didn't say one kind word about my work, just that I was damaging the foundation by having a relationship with Chase. Everything I've worked for, two years of my life have just been tarnished, damaged yet again by my choice in men.

I shake my head and reach the door. "I guess I'll get my things."

"Gigi, wait," Taye says.

"Oh, now it's Gigi, huh? Not Miss Callahan? Taye, you didn't stick up for me when she was gutting me. All the work I've put in, everything, it counts for nothing." The tears fall, and I wipe them away and leave his office. I storm to my desk, grab my purse, and practically run out of the building.

I cannot believe this is happening. I knew once I found out Chase was the Chairman of the Board that dating him could be a slight problem, but I never thought I would be faced with an ultimatum. Chase or the Foundation? The one place that helped me when I was broken, when I had nothing, when I could have died.

What the hell am I going to tell Chase? Nothing. I can't tell him anything. It's obvious I won't be able to have dinner with him tomorrow. Now I have to figure out what to do. Fresh tears roll down my face, and my whole body heats. Slight tremors spiral through my limbs, and I hit the gas on my Honda Civic, racing to my apartment.

I burst through the door, racked with heaving sobs before I ever make it to the couch.

Maria is there, and when she sees my face, she jumps off of the kitchen barstool, ending whatever call she was on with a quick, "Shit! I gotta go!" She's to me in an instant. "Gigi, what's wrong? Are you hurt?"

I shake my head, but I can't stop crying and heaving. The pain is so fierce I ball my hands into fists and press them to my eye sockets to stop the waterworks.

"*Me estás asustando!*" She shakes me. "You're scaring me, Gigi! Speak, *hablar!*"

I take deep breaths, willing my emotions to settle so I can spare my friend her anguish over seeing me like this. "Work found out about Chase and me," I barely get out as the tears stream down my face.

She wipes them away and holds my cheeks.

"And?" Her eyes show her concern.

"And… And they said that either Chase and I have to break it off or he has to step down from the board." She hands me a tissue, and I dab at my tears. "Or I have to quit or they'll fire me!" I sob.

"*Qué mierda!* That's crazy, Gigi! *Lo siento mucho*, I'm sorry, *cara bonita!* Please don't cry. It will be okay." She pets my hair and hands me another tissue.

"But it won't!" I say with misery. "Either I lose my job, a job that I love and worked so hard for, or I lose Chase. The man of my dreams!" I cry harder.

"When do you have to tell them your answer?" She helps me up from my crumpled position on the floor to sit with me on the couch.

I blow my nose loudly into the tissue and grab another. "Friday, first thing."

"Talk to Chase. He'll know what to do," she suggests.

Not an option. I know I can't do that. I shake my head. If I tell him, he could break up with me and that will beyond hurt. It will gut me. Already I've invested too much of my heart in this thing between us. I haven't wanted to be with a man the way I want to be with him in longer than I can remember. It's as if I'd forgotten what it truly was to be excited about a man. To look forward to every moment I'm with him. To want him and know he wants me. God, what am I going to do?

"I'm going to take a shower and go to bed. I need to think this through." I take a deep calming breath, push off the couch, and start walking down the hallway.

"Okay, *cara bonita*, but I think you should talk to him This involves him too."

I don't need to be reminded. The heavy ache and crushing anxiety burning my heart is enough. The thought that he could lose his position on the board of the foundation, the one he founded, breaks my heart, shattering it into a million tiny shards. And I could never ask him to pick me over what he's built. The question plaguing me now is whether I could quit or let myself be fired from the one place that made me feel whole again. The organization that pulled me out of hell, gave me a fresh start. I owe the foundation so much more than harming their good name with a tawdry love affair. Ms. Peterson is right. I made a horrible decision to get involved with Chase, and now I'm going to reap what I've sown.

Taking a scalding hot shower, I try to numb the pain. It doesn't help. Punishing the canvas doesn't change the picture, it just distorts the view. After my shower, I fall into bed, still cursing for allowing myself to get involved with Chase. God, but he's everything I could want in a man. He's strong, drop-dead gorgeous, takes care of himself financially, a god in the bedroom and he seems to like *me*. To see the *real me*. Not just redheaded, pasty white Gillian who works at a nonprofit and lives in a shoebox with her wild roommate.

Maybe this is a sign. Maybe this is the universe's way of telling me that we weren't meant to be. The tears slip down my cheeks again, wetting my pillow.

I hear a tap at my bedroom door. "Gigi, your cell phone rang while you were in the shower, and then you received a text from Chase."

Of course I did. I sigh loudly and stick my hand into the air. She hands it to me and sits on the side of the bed, petting my hip in a soothing rhythm.

"Will you be okay? I have rehearsal, but I can totally blow it off if you need me?" she offers.

"Ria, your show is in less than two weeks. You know you can't do that. Now go. I've got my big girl panties on. I'll be fine."

She squeezes my hip one last time and leaves. I stare down at the screen. One missed call from Chase and one text message from him.

To: Gillian Callahan
From: Chase Davis
I tried calling. Call me.

I sigh. There is no way in hell I'm going to call him tonight. I can't deal with myself let alone an inquisition. I text him instead.

To: Chase Davis
From: Gillian Callahan
Going to bed early. Can't do dinner tomorrow. Another time maybe.

Okay, that should do it. One step at a time. To hear his voice, just capture even one small "baby" from his lips would soothe this hole in the pit of my being. I have to be strong, if not for me, for him. He didn't sign on for this. I'm not going to allow a two-week-long relationship to ruin what he's worked so hard for. His text message is immediate.

To: Gillian Callahan
From: Chase Davis
What's wrong?

A sound between a laugh and a sob spills from my lips as I trace the letters. The man can read minds through a text. Strong. Be strong. Ignore it. Let it go. Don't make the situation any worse. After twenty minutes, my phone rings again. It's him. I don't pick it up. Instead I turn it off. I don't want to hear him call again. It's like a knife through the heart. I pull the covers over my head and fall into a fitful sleep.

Morning doesn't bring any new conclusions other than

the fact that I'm still miserable. I grab my phone and turn it on. It loads, and I hear a litany of pings. I scroll through the notifications. Chase called again and left a voice mail message. Two texts from Kat. Another text from Chase. A text from Ria and a text from Bree. Holy hell, last night was chock full of activity. I start reading Kathleen's texts first.

To: Gillian Callahan
From: Kathleen Bennett
I'm here at Chloe's showroom. Where are you?

Regret slams into me. Shit! I totally forgot. With the horrible morning, I wallowed in my own self-pity all day and forgot that I was supposed to meet Kat at Chloe's designer showroom. Kat is going to be livid. I check her next message.

To: Gillian Callahan
From: Kathleen Bennett
I can't believe you no-showed on me! Are you okay? What's going on? You're so lucky I love you. Chloe is amazing. I'm on Cloud 9. Call me ASAP. Besos.

At least someone had a good day. I skip down to Chase's text message.

To: Gillian Callahan
From: Chase Davis
Chloe said you didn't show up at her showroom but Kathleen did. I'm worried. Call me whenever you get this.

Hold strong, Gigi. No way in hell I'm calling him. I'm sticking to my guns on this one. I need time to sort this all out. I will, however, call Chloe and apologize for no-showing. That was just plain rude. I'll also have to do damage control with Kat. One thing my girls and I don't do is blow one another off without an explanation. I'm sure she got hold of Maria and found out that I was fine, otherwise I would have had a pissed-off friend at my door late last night. The next text is Bree.

To: Gillian Callahan

From: Bree Simmons

Thank you for the hook up with Phillip. We had a great time on Sunday. He's taking me out this weekend! Woot woot! Oh and your ass is going to need its own zip code if you don't get it to class soon. Besos

I laugh out loud. *Oh, Bree, you're just what I need right now.* I'm definitely going to attend class tonight. The mental relief and peace yoga provides is exactly what I need. For me, yoga has always been a form of moving meditation. I quickly text her that I'll be there tonight for class. Kat is next. I call her and get her voice mail. Score! I leave her a detailed message telling her a little about what happened yesterday and that I was in no mood to see Chase's family. An apology coupled with kiss noises is the icing on that apology. She'll forgive me. Soul sisters don't hold grudges and the unwritten rule book states when one sister is flipping out, the others have to accept that the current sister may be out of her mind and not to take offense.

Ria's text was just to see if I was okay, but I slept through it. She knew where I was when she came home, and I was asleep in the same position she left me in hours before.

I walk around my empty apartment. It's Wednesday morning and I'm not at work. I'm not sick, though I feel as though I could toss my cookies at any moment. I decide to hit the gym. A nice long run on the treadmill will help clear my head.

A couple hours of cardio later, I'm still no closer to figuring out what to do about work and Chase. After eating a quick lunch, I decide to hit the yoga studio early in the evening. No reason to wait around doing nothing at home.

I arrive at I Am Yoga, and the five o'clock class is just getting settled on their mats. Bree sees me and looks up at the clock, back at me, and frowns. She walks over and gives me a hug.

"Hey, everything okay?" Concern fills her gaze.

I shake my head and take a deep breath.

"Are you sure you want to be here right now?" She holds my hand and squeezes.

"I need to be somewhere right now," I say.

She nods. "Well, it looks to me like you need to center your Heart Chakra. The Heart Chakra is your heart's power station. It connects you to your emotions. It is the center that allows you to love and give unconditionally. The heart governs your relationships. It is the energy center that integrates one's physical reality to one's spiritual connection." She smiles and continues. "Are you having trouble with Chase?"

"Sort of. It's hard to explain right now." I gesture to the room of individuals sitting quietly waiting for class to start.

"Okay, but we will discuss this after class." She quirks a brow, leaving no room for argument. "Now, get ready to fill that chakra full of love again!" She smiles and saunters to the head of the class. She has a raised step where her mat sits and situates herself into the lotus position. There's track lighting above her shining on her form. She practically glows with her shiny blond hair reflecting the light. You can almost feel the ephemeral Zenful vibes she exudes.

Behind her is an entire wall of mirrors so that patrons can see their positions and adjust accordingly. The lights in the large open room are dimmed, and candles are lit throughout each corner of the room. She has Middle Eastern music softly pumping through the surround sound. It's just loud enough to have something to focus on when you're holding a position. The room smells like Valor, an essential oil that Bree burns in the corner of the room to help heighten the senses. It's meant to help people calm and find their own personal center. Along the back wall are a total of five six-foot-tall and several feet wide brushed metal symbols. The one in the middle represents the "Om" symbol. The only reason I know that is because Bree has it tattooed on her wrist in the same position I have my trinity. The other four are pictorial symbols of the words "Mind, Body, Soul, and Happiness."

I set my mat down and start to breathe deeply. I feel myself starting to dissolve into my headspace, otherwise known as my happy place. Nothing can hurt me here. Everything is calm and peaceful, and there are no worries to be had. I focus my full attention on the sound of Bree's melodic voice bringing us into one asana or pose after another. My body reacts naturally to the instructions, seamlessly moving from position to position without problem. When my mind tries to muddy my happy place, I just breathe deep and focus on my breath and the pose I'm in. All thoughts are drowned out by the pure essence of the experience.

After Bree brings us out of what she refers to as "deep

relaxation" or Shavasana in Sanskrit, I give her the lowdown. She is saddened by what I had to go through and wishes me luck finding my answers. Like Maria, she also encourages me to talk to Chase about it. I assure her I'll think about it and touch base with her in a couple days. She hugs me tightly, and then I am on my way home. My mind and body feel lighter, more relaxed, but my heart still hurts.

I still haven't come to any conclusions as I walk to my building. I enter the hallway and stop dead in my tracks. A large ominous man in a dark suit is leaning against my doorframe, obviously waiting for me. His face is stoic and unmoving but no less beautiful. *Chase.* I close my eyes, take a deep breath, and walk toward him.

He doesn't wait until I get to the door. In three strides, he's looming over me. He grips my biceps and hauls me into a fierce kiss, moving to cup each cheek with his hands. I'm completely taken by surprise, his response not at all what I expected. Anger, yelling—those are emotions I expect, not bone-crushing lust. His lips fuse with mine as his tongue demands entry. I give in to him instantly, starved for his mouth, his taste, his everything. I melt into him, gripping and clawing at his neck and back to get closer, go deeper. He holds my head tightly, turning my face to the side, always inserting control. I am at his mercy, and right now I bend to his will, kissing him with a ferocity I hadn't realized I had in me. Eventually he pulls his mouth away. His forehead presses to mine as we both pant and gulp for air.

"What the fuck is wrong, Gillian?" He's fuming.

I don't blame him.

"You ignore my calls, my texts, ditch me and my family?" His voice is scathing, ripping into my soul with each exhalation. Chase groans, pressing our bodies together. He barely contains his emotions. Physically, his back is ramrod straight. Muscles strained along the taut skin of his tight back. He holds his neck stiff as a board with a clenched jaw and that ever present twitching muscle.

"I know. I'm sorry," I say miserably. Tears stream down my face. He pulls away and sees the misery in my eyes. He searches my face and kisses my tears away.

"Baby, tell me. I'll fix it. Whatever it is, just tell me." His anger is completely replaced with concern, and I want to fall into his arms and cry until I can't cry anymore. The situation feels so hopeless.

I nod. "Let's go inside. I'll tell you everything." I know now that it was stupid of me to even think I could manage such a harrowing decision on my own. It's not fair of me to keep him in the dark when the outcome directly affects his role on the board or our relationship as it stands now.

Over the course of the next hour I explain in great detail what occurred yesterday morning, not leaving anything out. He paces the floor in front of me while I sit on the couch, hunched. My arms hold my knees to my chest in a protective ball.

"So I didn't know what to do. I still don't." I sound like a whiny loser.

"That bitch! She will regret this," he says out loud. His jaw is set, teeth clenched, and his fists are at his side as he wears a path in my carpet with his pacing.

"What? Who are you talking about?" I ask dumbfounded.

"Peterson. She's pulling this shit because she found out that we're together," he says.

"That's exactly what I just told you."

I'm still confused when he stops and removes his jacket, folding it and setting it on the arm of the couch. His tie follows and he unhooks a couple of buttons at his collar. He takes a deep breath and adjusts his shoulders back and down.

Chase looks at me, not really wanting to continue. I plead with him with my eyes to be open to me the same way I have been with him.

He sighs. "Gillian, she has made several advancements towards me, none too subtly. I've turned her down each time."

It finally dawns on me what he's saying. "Are you telling me she's doing this to us because she's jealous? That it has nothing to do with the foundation being defamed or unethical business practices?" I'm completely stunned by his admission.

He smiles at me and points to his nose. "Exactly, my sweet. Obviously, it's not ideal for a board member to date a staff member, but it's not the end of the world. Not something she can use against you or threaten your job with. I'll handle it," he says with finality.

"Chase, what do you plan on doing?" I ask, scared of his answer. "Please don't tell me you're going to step down as chairman of the board. I couldn't handle that." The fear creaks up my spine as I stare at his disheveled appearance, from his wrinkled shirt to his finger-combed unruly hair. I put him through hell the last couple nights and for what? I should have gone to him at the very beginning.

He goes to his knees and places his hands on mine. "Baby, no. Just…" He takes a deep breath. "Trust me to handle this."

I stare deeply into his eyes, trying to figure out my

mercurial man.

"You are not going to lose your job. I am not stepping down from my position, and we are not ending our relationship." He says in a calming tone. "Unless, of course, that's what you want?"

"No, God, no. That's the last thing I want."

Chase visibly relaxes. He pulls my legs off the couch, separates my knees, and settles his large frame between them. He hugs me tight, leaving no room between us. I lean my head on his shoulder, taking in his scent. His wood-and-fruit scent cling to his clothes, soothing and enchanting. The man smells so good, every nerve ending in my body tingles. Finally I'm able to relax. The last two days drained me, and feeling his arms hold me tight makes me realize I should have never tried to figure this out on my own. Lesson learned. I squeeze him tighter to my body. His hand sweeps through my hair. I close my eyes and allow him to just touch me.

"I need to be with you tonight," he whispers in my ear. His tone is thick with emotion.

My eyes must answer for him because he lifts me off the couch, and I wrap my legs around his waist. I think the alpha caveman in him likes carrying me to bed. While he walks to my room, he pulls out his phone and hits one button. The other arm rests securely under my bottom.

"I'll be staying at Gillian's," he says into the phone. "Pick me up seven a.m. with a fresh change of clothing. Tell Dana to secure a meeting with David as early as possible first thing in the morning." He hangs up without saying goodbye.

His take-charge voice and tone sends shivers of

excitement through my body, making the space between my thighs soften and moisten.

He sets me on the bed and slowly removes my clothing. He grazes my ribs, down my sides, circles the flesh at my hips in a worshiping manner.

"I'd like to take a shower." He frowns for a moment. "Join me?" And there's the smile.

We take a nice long shower, making sure to wash every nook and cranny. Chase leads me to bed and spends the next couple hours making love to me. It isn't the heated, rushed, "can't wait to slake the lust" type of sex we've had before. He spends his time pleasuring me, bringing me to release several times over the course of our lovemaking. He's relentless in his efforts. It's as if he's ensuring his position in my life, in my heart…within my body, deep into my soul.

I'm about to fall asleep, my head flat against his chest, his hands smoothing up and down my naked back in a loving caress, when he takes a deep cleansing breath.

"Don't ever hide from me again. From this." His tone is thick and unyielding.

Lifting my face, I lean on his chest and stare into his eyes. I don't expect such intensity. His gaze is unguarded, soulful. "I won't. I promise," I whisper in the dark and kiss him softly before snuggling back into position on his bare chest. I know the promise I made is unending. We're in this together. If we're going to be together, I'm going to have to be honest with him in all things, at all times. I just hope he can handle knowing all of me, including my past.

CHAPTER FOURTEEN

Thursday morning I awake alone. Chase held me through the night but left before I woke. The alarm clock reads eight a.m. I can't believe I slept through him leaving. The guilt and fear of the last couple days hits me like a sledgehammer. He's going to meet with the Chief Executive Officer of the Safe Haven Foundation, David Hawthorne, today. I cringe and realize there's nothing I can do but wait to hear from him. I can't imagine what he's going to say or do or how he's going to change Ms. Peterson's ultimatum.

I walk into the kitchen and see a full pot of coffee made. It's official. The man is a keeper. Chuckling, I pour myself a cup and pull out my vanilla creamer. I pour a heavy dose in my cup. It's not my beloved vanilla latte, but it's as close as I can get at home. I notice a note by the phone on the counter.

Babycakes.

I roll my eyes. I haven't decided if I'm going to accept this new term of endearment he's testing. I'll probably force him to cut it from his vocabulary someday. Right now, it sounds lovely as I imagine it rolling off the man's tongue when his tone is low and sexy. Yeah, maybe I'm okay with it. I continue reading.

Last night was…memorable. Don't worry about today. I will

take care of the problem.

CD

Not exactly a love note, but it's definitely Chase. I decide I can't wait around all day and do nothing. First order of business will be to text the girls and catch up with Phil. Instead of sending individual texts, I take the lazy man's route and mass text all three of them.

To: Maria De La Torre, Bree Simmons, Kathleen Bennett

From: Gillian Callahan

Thank you all for your advice. Chase and I talked. He's taking care of it. Whatever that means. Stay tuned. Love you all. Besos.

That should stave off the wolves for the time being. I know they're all worried about me. They'll be relieved Chase and I worked it out. My phone pings and I look down at the display. Maria has responded.

To: Gillian Callahan, Bree Simmons, Kathleen Bennett

From: Maria De La Torre

You talked? Mentiroso! Talking isn't what kept me up all night! Perra, pull your headboard away from the wall! Te amo, Besos!

I laugh out loud! *Perra*? Oh yeah, bitch or slut in Spanish. I snort as I gulp my coffee. Mmm, so good. I distinctly recall a couple times last night where the headboard may have banged against the wall. My cheeks flame. As I set the phone down, another loud ping makes me pick it back up.

To: Gillian Callahan, Kathleen Bennett, Maria De La Torre

From: Bree Simmons

I'm so glad you made up. Sounds like you gave the ol' mattress a workout. 'Bout time! Send that luck my way for my date this weekend with Phillip!

Bree's message makes me gag a little. It's like hearing about your brother having sex. Then it dawns on me that I haven't even talked to Phillip about his rendezvous with Bree this past weekend. I'm a crummy best friend. I dial his number, knowing he's at work but hoping he can take a quick break. He answers on the first ring.

"Hey you, what's up?"

I smile. He truly has been the only man who's been there for me throughout the years and hasn't hurt me. I hope against all hope that Chase turns out to be just as good, with the added benefits. I cross my legs and am instantly reminded of the many benefits I experienced last night.

"Do you have a few minutes?" I ask.

"Sure, I was heading to get a new cup of coffee anyway. What's going on, beautiful?"

Each and every time I see Phillip, I'm happier. He's just one of those people who gives you a sense of familiarity and peace. A calming nature. Over the next few minutes, I give him the abridged version of the past couple of days.

"I knew you were playing with fire, dating the boss, Gigi," he reminds me.

Leave it to a man to rub it in my face.

"Are you seriously playing the I-told-you-so card?" We laugh at my question.

"No, no, I'm not. It was just a risky move. So what's going to happen now?"

His concern is genuine, and I can tell he's worried. He knows how much this job means to me.

"I'm supposed to give them my answer tomorrow, but Chase is meeting the CEO today. He assured me he'd take care of it. I don't know what that means though. It's driving me crazy." I sigh into the phone and plop my head back on the couch. "So tell me, how was your date with Bree on Sunday?"

He laughs. "I see the real reason for your call. You're fishing. She didn't put you up to this did she?" he asks nervously.

"No, but I wouldn't tell you anyway." I laugh. "So how was it?"

After a pause, he says, "It was… It was wonderful, Gigi. She's wonderful, and beautiful, and funny, and—"

"Okay, okay, I get it." I cut him off. "She's wonderful." I hold the phone closer to my ear to hear his happiness. I would like nothing more than to reach through the phone and hug him, but that will have to wait until I see him in person. "She said you asked her out this weekend." I allow him to fill in the rest. I want to hear his excitement.

"I did. I'm taking her to dinner and then to see a local jazz band. Do you think that's a good idea? Shit, maybe she'd like a fancy dinner and a show or a play?" I can tell he's starting to worry. "Gigi, it's been a long time since I've dated. Nothing since Angela." He releases a long breath of air.

"Phil, it's okay. Bree is really chill. She will love a nice dinner and a cool jazz band. She's into you. It's going to be fine. Have a good time and don't over think it." It's the best advice I can give him, or myself for that matter.

"I am excited. She's incredibly hot, and her body is smokin' hot," he says, sounding like a player.

"And the male chauvinist pig comes out. Was wondering when her attributes would make you stupid."

He laughs out loud and I join him.

"Though, I agree with you. She's got a pretty rockin' body!" My phone beeps, signaling another call. "Okay, Phil, I want a full report on Sunday! I gotta go. I have another call." We both hang up and I hit the "switch" button.

"Hello?" I answer.

"Miss Callahan, this is Dana, Mr. Davis's personal assistant."

"Hello, Dana. I forgot to thank you for the clothes! They were incredible by the way. Though I would have been fine with clothes from Target," I tell her happily.

"You're welcome. I'll keep Target in mind, though I don't think Mr. Davis would approve," she warns. "Mr. Davis is sending Jack to pick you up in an hour. That's the reason I called. He wants you to be ready for a meeting with the CEO at Safe Haven at eleven a.m."

I lose my voice, suddenly overtaken by fear. "Did he say why?" I croak, a new bout of anxiety slithering along my subconscious.

"I'm sorry. He didn't."

"Okay, thank you, Dana. I'll be ready." I sigh loudly and press my fingers to my temples trying to relieve the tension that just cropped up.

"Gillian? May I call you Gillian?" she asks.

"You can call me Gigi, if you'd like. Everyone does."

"Gigi, I just wanted to say..." Her voice softens, becoming gentler somehow. "I just wanted to tell you that

Chase has been really happy these past three weeks. I know that's because of you. And well, I just—" She takes a breath and quickly says, "I wanted to say thank you."

I did not expect that. My throat clogs with an emotional lump. "He makes me happy too, Dana. Thanks again for the clothing. You have impeccable taste."

"The car will pick you up at ten thirty a.m. Miss Callahan, please be ready. Chase hates tardiness." She returns to her official duties. She's comfortable speaking frankly with me about her boss's happiness, but reverts back to professional etiquette.

Right then and there I decide I'm going to make an effort to getting to know his personal assistant. She seems genuinely happy that Chase has been in a better mood. In girl terms, her making a point to tell me would make her trustworthy, but I've been burned too many times by wicked women who claim to be my friends to open my heart and give her even temporary BFF status.

I remove Dana from my mind and choose a sharp dark charcoal gray suit. I pair it with a lavender button-up dress shirt. A chunky silver necklace and silver hoops tame the fierce look. I pull out my favorite pair of gray suede four-inch heels. Simple but sexy. The entire situation has me not knowing what to expect. It's not often that I meet with Mr. Hawthorne and never because I've done something unfavorable. Is he going to fire me? Shit! I'm going to be fired and have to clear out my desk before the weekend.

No, Chase said he'd deal with *it,* and I have to trust him. Believe in him. I just don't have a clue what the hell *it* means for me and my role at Safe Haven.

I grab my purse and check my appearance in the mirror

by the door. My hair is pinned back into a neat bun with bangs sweeping across my forehead. It will have to do. I brush on a simple peachy lip gloss and head to the front of the building.

Jack is there waiting for me. He opens the car door as I walk toward him.

"Morning, Jack."

"Good morning, Miss Callahan," he says and smiles.

Wow! The linebacker actually smiled at me. Maybe I'm breaking down his defenses after all. Then again, maybe he got laid last night. I can't be positive that his niceties are a direct result of my presence.

In twenty minutes, we're in front of the Safe Haven Foundation. I take a deep breath and exit the car, taking Jack's hand. "Thank you. Wish me luck."

"You won't need it," Jack says with confidence.

I furrow my eyebrows at him but walk confidently toward reception.

Once I enter the building, the receptionist immediately whisks me to Mr. Hawthorne's office. As I near the large double doors to his office, I distinctly hear laughing from the other side.

The receptionist knocks and pops her head in. "Miss Callahan is here to see you," she says.

"Send her in. Thank you."

She opens the door wide, and I walk in. Sitting at a large oak desk is the foundation leader, Mr. David Hawthorne. He's a middle-aged man, tall, thin, and tanned. I hear from the rumor mill that he golfs regularly with board members, vendors, business affiliates, and the like, which is probably where that tanned skin was earned. The word is that as

CEO, he's fair and a solid leader. Short brown hair caps his head, and a beard dots a square jaw. He's not unattractive, but he isn't a heartbreaker either. He's nice looking and smiles when I enter.

"Thank you for coming, Miss Callahan. I believe you've met our board chairman, Mr. Davis."

I turn to my left and realize Chase is sitting on a brown leather couch at the back of the room. He grins at my surprise, taking in my body from head to toe and back again. I warm and close my eyes to compose myself.

"Good morning, Gillian." He smiles and gestures to the seat next to him.

I walk over and take the seat offered next to him, leaving plenty of space between our bodies. I cross my feet at the ankles and sit straight and tall, waiting for Mr. Hawthorne to address me. If I'm going to lose my job, I'm going to do it with dignity, though I don't know why he'd need Chase here to witness it.

Mr. Hawthorne comes around his desk and takes a seat across from us. We're separated by a glass coffee table with magazines splayed across it in a crescent. "Miss Callahan, Chase brought my attention to an issue that came about earlier this week."

I nod but stay silent.

"I understand that our director of HR, Ms. Peterson, notified you that the foundation was aware of your personal relationship with Mr. Davis."

"Yes, sir. She did."

"As I understand it, you were given an ultimatum to either end your personal relationship with Mr. Davis, quit your job, or you'd be let go. Is that correct?" he asks.

Here it comes. He's going to fire me. I stiffen further and my eyes fill with unshed tears, but I hold them back. Chase sees my discomfort and grabs my hand, holding it close to him. I don't look at him but appreciate the small gesture.

"It is." The words come out as a whisper.

"After speaking with Mr. Davis this morning, I've done some digging, met with Mr. Jefferson, looked into your campaign results, your charitable giving ROI over the past two years, and am honestly amazed that this wasn't brought to my attention sooner. You are an incredible asset to the foundation."

Asset is a good thing, my subconscious reminds me. That's the opposite of deficit or defaming or negative.

"I can assure you, your position at Safe Haven Foundation is stable. As a matter of fact, I want to promote you to Associate Director of Contributions." He smiles widely.

Chase squeezes my hand.

I open my mouth in shock. I'm having trouble making sense of what he just told me. A moment ago, I was sure I was going to be fired, and now I'm being promoted?

"Ms. Peterson has been relieved of her duties. Threatening staff for personal relationships is not how I run my ship. Your relationship with Mr. Davis might be seen as preferential treatment, and some may question your promotion, but you'll handle that in a professional manner, I'm sure, and impress naysayers with your work."

I nod like a bobblehead sitting on the dashboard of a Pinto.

"Thank you, Mr. Hawthorne. I hadn't expected our

meeting to go this way. I will work hard to grow the department and increase our charitable revenue to the best of my ability."

"I'm confident you will. Please take the rest of the week off as a bit of a thanks for handling this misstep with grace," he finishes. "I look forward to working more with you in the future now that I've discovered your abilities."

"I can't thank you enough, Mr. Hawthorne."

I'm reeling from what he's told me. He fired Ms. Peterson? He's promoting me? This is far too much information to process.

"See you on the course next month?" Chase stands.

"You know it." Hawthorne grins and claps Chase on the back. "Give me an opportunity to win some of my money back!"

"Not a chance, Dave." Chase grins and shakes Hawthorne's hand.

Chase and I make our way out of the building. Jack is there with the car door open. I slip in and sit in silence, completely stunned.

Chase grabs my hand and brings it to his lips. "I told you I'd take care of the problem."

My heart sinks. He has a smug, egotistical look on his beautiful face.

"What did you tell him?" I ask.

"I told him about our relationship, what that hag Peterson did to you. I told him I wouldn't stand for it. No woman of mine is going to be given an ultimatum to choose between me and her job."

I look at him, shaking my head. He doesn't notice that every word he speaks is putting nail after nail into the coffin of our relationship.

"I threatened to walk and take my money with me." He smiles from ear to ear.

The tears I was holding back fall down my cheeks. "Stop the car, Jack," I say loud enough for Jack to hear.

Chase looks at me, and Jack peers at me through the review mirror but doesn't stop.

My insides heat to boiling, fueled by my anger. "Stop the fucking car now!" I scream and slam my fist on the leather, ensuring I've gotten Jack's notice. Traitorous tears run down my face, and I wipe them with the sleeve of my suit jacket. Screw it! I'll get the damn thing dry-cleaned.

"Gillian, what the fuck?" Chase says angrily.

Jack finally pulls to the curb, and I bolt from the car. I have no idea where I'm headed, but I stomp off down the busy San Francisco street on a mission with no destination.

Chase's footfalls slam against the concrete as he tries to catch me. "Gillian, stop now!" he yells forcefully.

I don't care. He can't control me. I'm not his property. No one owns me. I walk as fast as my four-inch heels will take me. As I'm about to round a corner, I hear the one phrase that stops me in my tracks.

"You promised you wouldn't run!" he yells.

I close my eyes, count to three, and turn around. "I cannot believe you did that to me," I say through my teeth.

"What the hell are you talking about? I just saved your ass from losing your job!"

He doesn't understand, so I'm going to spell it out for him. "No, you did the same thing they did to me. You gave them an ultimatum." I put my hands up to my forehead, wishing away the anger, the frustration, the heartache. "Take care of the little woman, or I walk with all my money! You knew he would cave and do whatever you wanted!" I can barely contain the helplessness controlling my emotions.

"I don't understand the problem. You didn't want to lose your job. I didn't want to lose you. Problem solved and you got a promotion." He brings his hand to my cheek, to swipe his thumb along the skin.

Like lightening striking, I slap his hand away. He steps back and away as if burned.

"I didn't earn the promotion. Oh, wait, but I did… On. My. Fucking. Back!" I roar loud enough for passersby to take a wide circle around our bodies.

He stares at me, clearly clueless as to why I'm angry.

"God damn it, Chase! I can't talk to you right now. I am so disappointed I can hardly breathe." I hiccup and hold back the sob that wants to tear through me. "Leave me alone." I turn and start walking again.

I see a cab ten feet away, and I rush to it and jump in. I give the cab driver the address and try Bree's yoga method of taking deep calming breaths. In one nostril, out the other then reverse it. It starts to work. Numbness settles over me instead. The cab driver makes it to my destination. I get out and enter the brick building.

Dodging people in varying costumes, I make my way to the back of the theatre. Everyone has seen me before and knows I'm stopping in to see Kat or Maria. I head to the very back where Kat's design closet is. It's actually a large room, but it's filled with costume upon costume, making you feel like you're in a big closet.

Apparently the gods have given me a respite because Kat comes into view. She's down on her knees, tailoring an outfit. Inside the outfit is Maria. I offer thanks to the almighty and enter so I can be seen. They look up and can tell something's wrong. It's not their first day being my soul sisters.

Kat looks down at her watch. "Would you look at that? Lunchtime. Ria? You hungry?"

Maria stares at my solemn face. "Famished. Gigi?"

"Starving," I whisper, my voice chock-full of unshed tears, a few octaves lower than normal.

Kat messes with her cell phone while Maria removes the shredded outfit. It's some type of "hell hath no fury like a woman scorned" number, and Maria is covered in swaths of deep red fabric that look like they've been stretched and ripped by a cat's claws.

"Bree will meet us at our favorite place. She doesn't have another class until this evening," Kat says.

"I love you guys," I say so seriously they both look up.

"We know, Gigi. *Te amo.* Now let's go and deal with this shit."

Ria's riled. This is the second time in as many days I've been in hysterics, and both of them involve Chase. Her useless men theory has some serious merit.

★ ★ ★ ★

We arrive at the little hole in the wall Irish pub. It's relatively quiet since it's after the lunch rush. The tables are all made of stones with Celtic symbols prominently encased in the center. The table we always try to sit at has a huge trinity symbol with a circle of protection around it just like our tattoos. Our little group has adopted that single symbol to represent our undying bond and sisterhood. The Celtic trinity can mean different things. It can represent the body, mind, and soul, but in religious circles it represents the Father, Son, and Holy Spirit. For us, it represents our past, our present, and our future. We will always have a past, our present will consistently be linked to one another, and our future is limitless as long as we have each other.

Bree has arrived and ordered four Poor Man stouts, a mixture of Guinness and hard raspberry or apple cider. Since our drinks are dark chocolate in color on bottom and bubbly pink on top, I assume it's the raspberry cider.

I slide in next to her.

She grabs my face, searches my eyes, and presses her forehead to mine. "Gigi, boys that make girls cry suck!"

I nod against her forehead.

She kisses my cheeks and wipes my tears. "You've been mad at men before, had shitty men hurt you before, and you have never cried like this," she continues.

"You're in love with him, aren't you?" Kat says, as if she just asked something as simple as "How was your day?"

I look into each of their eyes. Brown, blue, and gray, the colors that help breathe life into my world. I can lie to myself over and over, saying the feelings aren't there, that they don't matter. I am incapable of lying to them.

In a horrible moment of honesty and bubbling anger, I answer on a screech, "I do, damn it!" I groan and grip my pint glass so hard I wish it would break. "I don't want to, but I do!" I press two fingers from each hand into my temples, but the pain doesn't go away. It's still there. He's still there, his sad face broken and apologetic as I screamed at him on the street…still there taunting me.

"Why don't you want to, honey?" Bree asks. "You haven't been in love in a long time. Is it because that big meanie makes you cry? I'll kick the good-looking bastard's ass from here to next week if you'd like!" She'd do it too. She will open up a can of whoop ass on him, and he will be powerless to stop the tiny firecracker.

"That's exactly why she doesn't want to be in *amor* with him, Bree," Ria responds for me. "The last man she loved hurt her…*muy mal*, really bad." Her Spanish accent comes out when she's emotional.

She knows exactly how I feel. I know it's how she feels with Tom.

"It gets worse, guys. He gave the CEO of the foundation an ultimatum. Fix the situation with me, or he walks as chairman…along with his forty million dollar annual donation. That money pays half of our operating costs." I take a huge gulp of my Poor Man and let the frothy drink soothe frayed nerves.

"Whoa. He did that?" Kat says, mouth agape, eyes wide.

"It gets worse. The HR director was fired, and I was promoted to associate director of contributions." I sneer and take a slug of my drink.

"Am I missing something, Gigi? That sounds pretty fucking fantastic. Congratulations!" says Bree.

"I didn't get the promotion because I deserved it. I got it because of Chase's influence. He even said something to the effect, 'no woman of mine is going to be given ultimatums and be told to choose between me and her job,' blah, blah, blah," I say, using my best impression of a male voice.

"Wow, he's in love with you."

I twist my head toward Kat and shake off what she just

said. "Excuse me, Kat. Where the hell did you get he's in love with me?"' I take a breath and groan. "I basically got a promotion because I'm fucking the boss like a common whore!"

"*Jesús Cristo, cara bonita!* That's such bullshit. You deserved that promotion. You've been bringing them tons of *dinero* over the past two years!" Maria exclaims.

"But the timing is no coincidence. The boss did it to get into Chase's good graces." I slump, my shoulders sagging low. I feel weighted to my seat. The heaviness of what happened with Chase, of how we fought, is crippling.

"So what if he did. You still deserve it. You get the chance to prove it to everyone, including yourself and Chase!" Bree argues.

I go several more rounds of "woe is Gillian" and come to the conclusion that I'm going to have to talk to Chase. My cell phone pings, and I pull it out of my purse. It's Chase. I'm a little surprised it took him this long to contact me.

To: Gillian Callahan

From: Chase Davis

I'm sorry. I still don't know what happened. Please come to the penthouse so we can discuss this. I'm lost without you.

That's the closest thing to an "I love you" I'm going to get right now. I don't even know if I want him to profess his undying love for me yet. It's only been a few weeks. The butterflies in my stomach and ache in my heart can only be mended by an egotistical, wealthy, over protective, controlling, breathtakingly good-looking bastard. And he's all mine.

I kiss and hug each friend as if it's the last time I will see her. I don't know where I would be if I didn't have them to walk me away from life's ledges.

We share a round of "*besos*," and I go hail a taxi. The driver asks me where to.

There's only one place I need to be right now. "Davis Industries, please."

CHAPTER FIFTEEN

The taxicab pulls up to the building, and I run to the bank of elevators. Jack is sitting on a bench next to them. He stands when I push the button.

"He's expecting you," he says with contempt.

"He made you sit out here and wait, didn't he?" I already know the answer based on the permanent scowl he's sporting.

"You don't have access to the penthouse. We're going to rectify that situation now." He's clearly irritated. He pulls a small black box from his pocket. It has a LED screen with an outline of a thumbprint on it. "Place your right thumb on the panel here." He points.

I do as he asks, and the screen scans my thumb. He pulls it back, slides out a tiny keyboard, and enters Gillian Callahan next to the imprint. "As requested by Mr. Davis, you now have unfettered access to the penthouse."

"So I can come and go as I please?"

"Yes, you may. Please consider the fact that he is entrusting you with access to his private quarters. If you bring anyone with you, I must be privy to the information in advance so I can run appropriate background checks." His tone is flat and unwelcoming.

"Seriously?"

He nods.

"Did you run a background check on me?"

"Of course," he says, as though I'd asked him something as simple as if the sky was blue, not whether or not he'd violated my personal life and private information.

"May I see it?"

He shakes his head. "That information was obtained by Mr. Davis. If you want to see yours or anyone involved with you, you'll have to ask him directly."

"Excuse me? What do you mean by anyone involved with me?" He can see that I'm less than impressed and getting agitated. I've got a hand on my hip and the sucker is cocked, ready for battle.

"Mr. Davis has background checks done on anyone he comes into regular contact with. We've done them on a Ms. De La Torre, Ms. Bennett, Ms. Simmons, Mr. Redding, Mr. Parks, and a few others."

I close my eyes and breathe deep, trying to understand without reacting why he would invade my privacy and the privacy of my friends.

"There are plenty of people who would be thrilled if Mr. Davis were seriously damaged, hurt, maimed, or dead. As his security advisor, I insist on background checks for all parties he comes into contact with."

The words "maimed or dead" ring loudly in my ears, lessening the initial shock. He does have a point. Being filthy rich comes with disadvantages. "Is that all, Jack?" I blow my bangs out of my eyes. I'm eager to see Chase. I need to clear the air with him.

"No," he says as his eyes turn hard.

The hairs on the back of my neck stand at attention at

that frosty gaze.

"That stunt you pulled today on the street was childish and immature." His tone is scathing.

"Frankly, Jack, that's none of your business." I say it with confidence despite knowing he's right. It was a bit juvenile.

"Everything involving Mr. Davis is my business. I've been there for him since he was seven years old. I have no intention of allowing anyone to hurt him again." He sounds like an overprotective father.

"You're not his father. You're his bodyguard. He pays you to be there." I can see that my statement hits home.

"No, I'm not. His father was the devil." He leaves it at that. "I hope you're the real deal, Ms. Callahan, because it's been a very long time since he's allowed a woman anywhere near his home, let alone his heart. Don't make him regret it."

"I don't intend to. Now if you will excuse me." I enter the elevator, and the doors shut with him staring me down. I put my right thumb into the LED box, and the red light scans my thumb. Once scanned, the light turns green and the elevator rises to the penthouse. Modern technology… incredible.

Jack is a mystery—one I can't for the life of me figure out. One minute he's tough as nails and just as pointy. The next he's fatherly and protective. As I mull over the conversation with Chase's linebacker, my stomach drops. I really don't know what to expect from Chase now. I left him in the dust after he did what he thought was right. After I promised him in the safety of his arms just last night that I wouldn't run again. I wish he didn't use his influence to devalue the hard work that I've put into my career and the time I've spent at the Safe Haven Foundation. I owe them so much. I've worked damn hard to prove myself. But I also don't want this to ruin what we have together.

The elevator doors open, and I exit. I'm still wearing the same clothing I had on for the meeting today. I skim my hands down my skirt. Rumpled clothing and puffy eyes are what's available this evening. If there's a stitch of makeup left, it has to be smudged. I probably look like I've tied one on. I'm surprised to find his door unlocked. I enter and look around. Music is playing in the distance, and I walk toward it.

In the main living room, a fire is roaring, and I see Chase sitting with his back to me on the plush sectional. He's sipping a glass of wine, listening to the music on surround sound. Christina Perri's haunting voice sings "The Lonely," and tears well up. The song brings painful memories to mind. I played that exact song so many times after Justin beat me, trying to figure out why I couldn't escape. Why love was so brutal when really, it wasn't love at all. It kills me knowing that Chase is feeling that way because of me.

No more. I can't take it. Sadness overwhelms me. I enter the room, making my way to the couch. He looks up over his glass of wine. His face is tortured, and seeing it destroys me. His eyes are hooded but a tiny spark lights those glassy blues as they land on me.

"You're not alone," I whisper.

He picks up the remote and turns the music off with the push of a button. He sets down his wineglass.

"Aren't I?" His face is stoic and pale, void of emotion.

I shake my head. Walking over to him, I stop between his outstretched legs. He grips my hips fiercely and brings his head to rest against my stomach. He nuzzles me in silence. The need to purge this ache welling deep inside is unbearable.

"I'm in love with you." It comes out a whisper but he hears it.

Chase's grip intensifies. I'm scared shitless, and I can't back away or hide from my feelings any longer. If he doesn't feel the same, I'll move on. I won't like it. It will hurt like hell, but at least I'll know I said it and meant it.

Those hands of his tighten until it almost hurts before he looks up at me, his eyes searching my face, his gaze open and broken at the same time. I can barely breathe with the honest fear and heartbreak staring back at me. It's almost too much to bear.

He assesses me. I can practically feel him trying to discern the truth of my statement. "Say it again." His voice sounds rough, as if his esophagus was rubbed with sandpaper. Thick and gritty.

"I'm in love with you, Chase." The words spill out as if in prayer.

He closes his eyes and pushes my shirt up. His eager mouth plants soft kisses all over the bare flesh before trailing kiss after kiss up my torso over my shirt until he's standing in front of me, eyes piercing my soul.

"Again," he whispers against my lips.

"I love you, Ch—"

Before I can say his name, his lips are on mine, devouring me. He cups my cheeks, holding me to him. His kiss is long and deep. I'm not sure who's leading who, and it doesn't matter. He turns my head, delving in, sliding his tongue in, tasting, drinking, sipping from my mouth as if it's the last time. It's not. Never will be again. I'm lost to him and will take whatever he can give me.

He pulls away and then smashes our chests together in a harsh embrace, one that you give someone you never plan to let go. I close my eyes and relish the beauty of being his. Warm and safe.

"I was so afraid you were done with me," he says against my ear.

I shake my head and kiss the side of his neck, reaffirming the connection to this man, my man.

"Where do we go from here, baby?"

"That depends on whether or not you feel the same about me." My confidence wanes. I need to know I mean as much to him as he does to me. It's the only way we can move forward.

"Are you kidding?" He searches my eyes. His mouth twists in surprise. "You don't know, do you?"

"Know what?" My chest constricts, and I'm uncertain what he'll say next.

"I knew you were the one when the hospital called me in Chicago. Everything went utterly black when they told me you'd been attacked. I was crazy with worry. I had only known you a short time, but that phone call wrecked me." His face contorts as he tells me his experience.

I understand the feeling.

"God, Gillian, I'd do anything for you. Saying 'I love you' doesn't seem like enough to quantify what I feel for you." The smile across my face is so big it hurts my cheeks.

"Say it anyway," I urge.

He caresses my cheeks and kisses me softly. He pulls back, and his glorious blue stare owns mine. "Gillian Callahan, I love you. So much it scares the hell out of me."

Tears fill my eyes as he kisses each cheek.

"Please, please stop running from this. This is new for me. I know I won't always make the best decisions when it comes to you. You bring out the control freak in me. I want you safe. I want to protect you and provide for you. I want to give you everything your heart desires."

Placing two fingers over his lips, I open my heart and let the truth fly free. "I only want you."

His eyes close as he kisses my fingers. He leads me to his bedroom, his hand clasping mine. "We will discuss this further, but right now, all I can focus on is my need to feel you and bury myself so deep inside the woman I love, you won't know where you begin and I end."

It's not poetry, but it's real. It's Chase. I couldn't agree with him more.

★ ★ ★ ★

It's late and Chase is caressing my bare arm while spooning me from behind. "Who's Justin Durham?"

My entire body tenses. Alarm bells ring loudly in the quiet room. "How do you know about Justin?" The mention of his name sends a pickax to my gut.

"You have a restraining order against him. It came up when Jack did your background check. There were several different police reports against him with charges ultimately dropped. They all related to domestic violence."

Oh God in heaven. He knows.

He traces a scar on my hip. It's four inches long. The puckered skin is a physical reminder of something I'd prefer to forget.

"Justin was one of my ex-boyfriends."

"Why do you have a restraining order against him?" His fingers continue to soothe, a direct contrast to the swirling shame and fear spiraling through my mind.

"You really don't want to hear about this, especially now. It's not a conversation to have after a night of incredible lovemaking—with emphasis on the love part." I grin. He hugs me and places sweet kisses on my bare shoulder. It's become one of his favorite places to kiss me.

"Tell me," he urges.

I know he won't let it go, and the more I hide it and try to make it go away, the more those skeletons get brought to the surface. It's time I bring them out in the light myself, without the halo of doom. I'm stronger now. It's been years. Even if it still affects me, I can't let it take residence in my thoughts and dredge up old wounds. I think for a few moments as Chase snuggles into my side.

"Nothing you can tell me is going to make me love you less, Gillian."

I carry a great deal of baggage when it comes to Justin. He may regret that comment. I'm at war with the fact that to have an honest relationship, I'm going to have to share this part of me. It's an unfortunate part of my past, but it defines who I am today, how I deal with relationships, how I respond to him, even now, years later. Chase deserves to be privy to the things that trigger pain.

"Who is he?" he asks again.

"He was a mistake." I grip his hand and rub my head into his chest. I need the connection if I'm going to make it through this. "I met him when I was eighteen. He was five years older. I felt so mature, shacking up with a man a few years my senior."

Chase laughs. That's exactly what I've done again. I'm twenty-four and he's almost thirty.

"Guess it's a pattern with me." I grin.

"Continue." He kisses my shoulder.

"In the beginning, Justin was everything I thought I wanted in a man. Handsome. Smart. Strong. We moved in together within a few months of dating when I started college. My grades in high school were stellar, and I was lucky to secure a full scholarship to Sacramento State. So I went to school, and he paid the bills."

"As he should have."

It takes extreme effort not to roll my eyes, knowing there is no chance in hell I'm ever going to pay a tab or buy myself anything in this man's presence. He's old-fashioned in that way. I ruffle his hair and peck his lips.

"Don't stop on my account. I want to know everything there is to know about you."

I sit up and pull the sheet over my naked chest. "Chase, you see me as this strong, independent woman because that's what I've wanted you to see." The tears well again. He'll think I'm weak. I don't want to be that woman again, and I don't want him knowing her. Regardless, it's important I get it over with. He needs to know the truth. "Justin spent years beating me to a bloody pulp. Worse…I allowed it!"

His eyes go wide, his nostrils flare, and that sexy jaw clenches. "He put his hands on you?" He sounds calm but intense, holding back whatever reply he wants to make.

In that moment, I am immensely thankful.

With a heavy heart and a deep sigh, I admit what Justin did to me. "Chase, he beat me so often it became the norm.

Broken bones, bruised ribs, black eyes. Those were regular occurrences in my world. The scar you've been tracing on my hip. That was from being thrown through a glass coffee table."

He recoils in disgust.

"At the time, I believed I deserved every beating. He made sure I believed it."

Chase's hands ball into fists, and he presses them into his eye sockets. This is upsetting him, but I have to finish. Rip the Band-Aid off fast.

"For years it was really bad. But it was nothing compared to the last time." I take a deep breath and he twines our fingers together. I close my eyes and continue.

"One night, he thought I was cheating on him. He always thought I was cheating on him..." I take a deep breath. "But this time was different. I..." Tears stream down my cheeks.

Chase cups my cheeks and swipes away my tears with his thumbs. I feel his tenderness, his strength, his love.

"Baby, it's okay. Tell me everything. I need to know," he says softly.

I clutch his hands in my lap, holding them so tight my knuckles have turned white.

"I told him I was pregnant."

Chase gasps. His eyes are the size of two full moons.

"He didn't believe it was his. We always used condoms, but there was this one time he was drunk and didn't. It was after a particularly rough beating. I barely recalled him having sex with me. I was in so much pain. I let him do his business. At least when he was getting off, he wasn't hitting me."

Chase cringes. "Jesus Christ, Gillian…" He clings to my hips, his touch grounding.

I continue. If I don't get this out now, I never will. "He said the baby wasn't his. He called me a whore." I shrug as the tears fall and wet Chase's forearms as he holds my hips. He brings his forehead to mine. It's the strength I need. "He always called me a whore."

Chase physically shakes but doesn't say anything.

"He beat me within an inch of my life that night. He kicked my stomach over and over, strangled me, and slammed my head repeatedly into the wood floor. I passed out. He probably thought I was dead, because he left me lying on the ground in a pool of my own blood. When I came to, he was gone.

"It took a while, but I crawled to a phone and dialed Safe Haven. I had programmed it on the speed dial. It's all I could think of in my haze. That one button was my entire focus. The cops had been called so many times over the years, I honestly thought it was possible I'd die before they arrived." Chase trails his hands up and down my biceps in a whisper-light fashion.

"Safe Haven sent one of their trauma volunteers to help."

He doesn't seem surprised by that bit of information, probably because he had a hand in making that part of the protocol.

"It was a husband and wife team. The man carried me to the car. I could barely walk after so many kicks to the ribs and stomach. The wife grabbed clothes to last me a couple weeks and all the cash I had stashed around the house when Justin wasn't paying attention. Then they stayed at the hospital with me and held my hand while the doctors set my bones and stitched my wounds." Without realizing it, I had started rocking back and forth.

Chase stops the movement, pulls me out of my protective ball, and wraps my limbs around him, setting me in his lap like a Gillian blanket. He hugs me to him, surrounding me with his warmth.

I set my head on his shoulder and keep going. "Then I was told that I miscarried the baby." The tears drip down his bare back. Eventually I wipe the tears with my arm. "After I was patched up, they took me to one of Safe Haven's shelters. They took me in, gave me a room, and the counselors helped me get my mind straight. I grieved for my loss, and they helped me realize what Justin did to me was wrong. They showed me I was worth more than that. That's where I met Maria. She was a victim too."

Chase's eyes are closed when I pull my face away from the solace I seem to always find in the crook of his neck. He takes a deep breath.

"Gillian, God..." He pulls me into a fierce embrace, holding me against his chest. "You will never be hurt again. I'm so sorry you had to endure all that pain."

"I'm okay now. I don't want your pity, but you need to know what and who I am. Trusting men with my heart has only hurt me. My only defense is to run."

I see my words feathering over his features as he takes them in and dissects them. His eyebrows draw together, and then that sexy grin I've come to adore slips across his mouth.

"I'm an excellent runner myself. I'll catch you and bring you home. To me. To this. To us."

No man has ever made me feel so secure. Loved. I kiss

him lightly. "Promise?"

"Yes, I promise." He smiles wide.

"That's why Safe Haven means so much to me. It's not just a job. They saved my life. In effect, your foundation is the reason I'm still here. I owe them, and you, so much."

"Gillian, I understand what you're saying, but I'm not sorry I intervened today. That woman was sabotaging you because of me. She didn't deserve to keep her job. You, on the other hand, did—as well as the promotion, Gillian. The money you've brought the foundation over the past two years has been double what the whole contributions department has brought in the last five years."

I let out a huff. "About that. I talked to the girls and came to a conclusion."

He raises an eyebrow.

"Regardless of what happened or how it is perceived, I'm just going to prove to myself, and everyone else, that I'm right for the position. Anyone who sees it otherwise is wrong."

He grins, pulls me back into a hug, and kisses me. "That sounds like an excellent idea."

So now that we've had a show and tell about my past and solved today's debacle, I want to know more about him. *His father was the devil.* I hear Jack's words in my head. "Tell me about your father. You've never told me why you lived with your uncle when you were a child?"

Chase leans back on the bed. "Gillian, you just revealed a lot. I don't know that tonight is the night for me to share that sordid tale."

"No hiding and no running, remember? It's just me and you."

"My story is similar to yours," he begins, leaning back against the headboard. "My mother was battered by my biological father. Except, she didn't get away." He looks off to the side, stuck in a distant memory.

"What happened?" I try not to push too hard.

"My father had a bad habit of mixing copious amounts of alcohol with methamphetamines. They made him psychotic. He was already evil, but on drugs and alcohol he would hallucinate, talk to people who weren't there." His lips twist into a scowl. "And he had a burning desire to beat the shit out of anything that entered his path. Namely me, and my mom."

I pet his arm, wanting to sooth him as he did me. Be there for him as he rehashes his own tortured past.

"I remember the night everything went to hell. It was my seventh birthday, and he'd just lost his job. He came home and dragged me by the ear through the house. I screamed, and Mom ran out of the kitchen. She was baking my birthday cake and had a butcher knife in her hand." He takes a deep breath and his voice becomes deeper. His eyes fill with unshed tears.

"She begged him not to hurt me, told him it was my birthday. He backhanded me and pushed me at my mother. She dropped the knife." His voice shakes, but he continues, "He came to Mom and punched her so hard she fell back. Blood sprayed from her broken nose all over me. I fell with her, and my hand made contact with the handle of the knife."

I sit perfectly still, tears running in rivulets down my cheeks.

"I was so fucking stupid. I thought I could stop him

from hurting her. I grabbed the knife and stabbed him in the thigh. It didn't go deep, barely made a wound at all. But it enraged him. He threatened to kill me. He held the knife to my neck. Mom jumped between us and turned to push me down the hallway. I heard her blood-curdling scream after I caught my balance. He had stabbed her in her lower back. She fell to the ground, and he pulled the knife out. I can still remember the sound it made as it retreated from her body. The slurping noise haunts me." He takes a deep breath, and his voice cracks. "He kept stabbing her, over and over like a sick horror movie. I kept thinking, 'This isn't real. This is pretend.' But it was real."

At that point Chase starts crying, clutching at me as the memory of that day rips through him. I pull him to me and rock him back and forth, kissing his temples, forehead, lips.

"There was blood everywhere, Gillian, fucking everywhere. He kept stabbing my mom while she screamed. I just stood there, helpless. She yelled for me to run and get help, and I flew to my room, locked the door, and went through the window. Just as I was out the window, I could hear my father. He had kicked in the door and was yelling at me through the window."

"How did she survive?"

He sniffs and wipes his eyes with his hands. "The neighbors called the cops. He left my mom there for dead, but the paramedics got there and she made it. Survived against all odds. Thirty-seven stab wounds, and she's still here. It was a miracle. After the attack, she spent a year in a coma, and another year in therapy. In the end, she never walked again."

"And your father?" I ask while sweeping his chocolate

hair off his brow and around his ears. Mostly just to touch him, which I know he likes.

"He was picked up at a local bar. The bartender called the cops when he entered covered in blood. The bastard had the audacity to sit down and ask for a drink. Bartender kept him there until the police arrived. He's in Joliet Correctional Center in Illinois for two counts of attempted murder."

"Chase, I had no idea. That didn't come up when I was Googling you."

"It wouldn't. My name has always been Davis, but I was born with the hyphenated father and mother's names. James-Davis. My uncle changed it back to just Davis and spent a lot of money ensuring that both names stayed out of the papers. Since I was a minor, the records were locked. It would be quite the scandal if it came out now."

I loop a leg over his and mimic the position he had held me in during my story. He lies back, and I follow him down, covering him like a blanket once more with my head on my spot, directly over his chest and his heart. He slides his hands enticingly over my bare back. Story time is over. It gutted us both, leaving us raw and emotional. Tonight we let the ugly out. Our pasts are behind us, our love between us. I kiss his chest over his heart. *Mine*

"Thank you," I whisper, lips against his chest.

He tunnels his hands into my hair and urges my face to his for a sweet, deep kiss. A kiss of rebirth, of the gift of knowledge that we both survived and came out on top, against all odds. Just like our relationship.

"For what?" he asks.

"For listening. For not judging me. For trusting me with your past and allowing me to be part of your future." I search his gaze and his eyes shine in the dim light.

We lie, holding one another, until we both fall asleep, completely spent from baring our souls, content in the knowledge that tomorrow will be brighter because we're together.

CHAPTER SIXTEEN

The next few weeks provide a whirlwind of activity. Chase and I alternate between each other's homes most nights. It constantly surprises me that a man so used to luxury willingly stays in my cramped apartment, sharing space with my wacky roommate. He even seems unbothered by the frequent bouts of marathon sex between Maria and Tom on some of our shared evenings. Maria and I did try to schedule our overnight stays at our boyfriends' houses so that we would each have a bit of privacy, but more than a couple times a week that didn't work out. Most of the time it was because Chase's schedule was sporadic. Everyone, including me, seems to want a piece of him.

Since the night where we uncovered our demons, we've been inseparable. At least as much as possible considering he often travels or has meetings well into the evenings. We haven't said the "L" word to one another again after that deeply emotional night of baring our pasts. I think we were both afraid to break the spell. Somehow we accepted each other's pasts as just that—our pasts. We chose not to let it taint the relationship we've built.

I am up to my eyeballs in alligators at work, dead set on proving that I deserve my new title and promotion. I have regular meetings with Mr. Hawthorne and Taye about upcoming fundraising initiatives and events we are working on. This weekend, I am going on my very first major giving donor prospect visit with Taye. He's going to teach me the fine art of asking a wealthy donor to give tens of thousands of dollars to the foundation. In equal parts, I am excited and terrified.

The only problem I have now is telling my very overprotective boyfriend that I am going to be gone for a few days without him and meeting privately with a rich stranger. Both of which he'll balk at. In a normal relationship, this shouldn't be a problem, but Chase and I are anything but normal. It's not as if he doesn't go on plenty of business trips alone. I don't bat an eyelash when he jets off to put out some fire at one of his companies across the nation, or the globe for that matter. Sure, I miss him terribly when he is gone, but didn't some philosophical genius say that absence makes the heart grow fonder? I believe it to be true, because when Chase is gone, I think about him incessantly. So much so that the girls all know when he is out of town based on my depressive sulking and lack of interest in going out with them. They understand that I am in deep with Chase and tease me like crazy over it.

It takes some time to get up my nerve, but I finally I come to the conclusion that the best way to handle this trip is to *not* make a big deal about it. I am going to New York with Taye whether Chase approves or not. I'll just shoot him a quick text and be done with it.

To: Chase Davis

From: Gillian Callahan

I'm going out of town on a donor visit Thursday through Sunday with Taye. Excited! I've never been to New York City.

I reread the text. Sounds straightforward, to the point. There's nothing special about it or any hidden meaning. I click send and turn to my computer to crunch some numbers. Ever since the promotion a few weeks ago, I've been thrown into the world of budgeting and forecasting. At first it was a daunting world I wasn't familiar with, but I've found that I'm actually pretty good at it. I'm able to see the areas where we can grow our donor dollars as well as the areas of concern that need more attention. My cell phone pings.

To: Gillian Callahan
From: Chase Davis
I'd prefer you didn't go alone.

If I'm honest with myself, I had an inkling that he wouldn't be thrilled about me heading out of town, but I won't be alone.

To: Chase Davis
From: Gillian Callahan
I won't be alone. I'll be with Taye.

I send the text and start reviewing my numbers again. I'm disrupted by the ping from my cell phone once more. I roll my eyes and look down at the display.

To: Gillian Callahan
From: Chase Davis
That doesn't make me feel better. I'll schedule one of my jets for the three of us. End of discussion.

End of discussion? Is he psychotic? He knows that's

going to piss me off. I'm not a wallflower. I can handle myself. Though I can't say I wouldn't mind being in the city that never sleeps with my sexy man. My mind flitters back to this morning, his long, thick cock hammering into me, the hot water from the shower sluicing down my back adding to the fire raging within our melding bodies. His mouth covered mine and his tongue entered me hard and fast in the same mating dance our lower bodies were in. I shake off the thoughts and squeeze my thighs together, relieving some of the pressure. The desire I get just thinking about our lovemaking makes me completely stupid. I fire back a text as fast as my fingers can type.

To: Chase Davis
From: Gillian Callahan
I don't need a chaperone. I am a big girl. I can handle myself.

I wait for his return text. Doesn't he have a job running an empire?

To: Gillian Callahan
From: Chase Davis

I won't sleep knowing you're in NYC without me. I'm coming with you. I own an apartment there. We'll have dinner with my cousin.

That's right! His cousin Craig lives in New York. I haven't met him yet. Of course he knows that the desire to meet his family would sway me and seal the deal. *Sneaky bastard.*

To: Chase Davis
From: Gillian Callahan

Fine.

No kissy faces, no XOXO. Responding flippantly is all I can manage. As upset as it makes me that he's hovering over me like a helicopter mom over her five-year-old, I do love spending time with him. The prospect of seeing his apartment in New York City is exhilarating as well. Funny, he never mentioned it before. I remember him mentioning a home in Chicago and of course the penthouse in San Francisco. Makes me wonder how many homes he has. I'll have to ask him about it later. He doesn't text me again, and for that I'm grateful. He's probably gloating about winning, this time at least.

After a brutal day of staring at numbers and spreadsheet after spreadsheet, I need a drink. Entering the apartment, I stumble on Maria and Tom making out on the couch. His hand is under her shirt, rhythmically squeezing her large breast. Her hand is shoved deep into his underwear, fondling his manhood. I stare in shock, mouth wide open in awe. Ribbons of excitement tingle along my skin. The scene before me is so fucking hot. Her tongue is delving into his mouth while her hips gyrate against his groin. Makes me wish I went to Chase's apartment instead of coming home. I could be riding my own man right now. Probably not. He mentioned something about working late.

I try to quietly sneak to my room to give them privacy when my briefcase catches on the wall and drags against the stucco. *Dammit!* I turn slowly and the couple has righted themselves. Both are gasping for air. Maria crosses her legs sweetly.

"Gigi, didn't expect you to come home tonight," she

says through gasps of air.

A smile slips over my features. "Obviously." I grin wickedly.

She looks at me with a satisfied glint in her eye. She's not at all embarrassed by her sexual display. She's very comfortable with her sexuality and doesn't apologize for it. Tom, on the other hand, has turned beet red, his hand covering a very impressive erection.

"I'll just be a minute. I need a glass of wine," I tell her while walking down the hallway.

Purposely, I take longer than usual putting my things away and changing into yoga pants and a tank top. When I walk back into the living room, I hear laughter coming from the kitchen. Making my way around the island, I plant my bum on one of our barstools. Maria is opening my favorite white wine. Tom is standing behind Maria, gripping her hips and kissing her neck playfully. She's smiling and wiggling her ass provocatively against him. He keeps jutting his hips back, not allowing the contact. She knows what she's doing to him. The poor guy doesn't stand a chance.

I sit and watch them be frisky with one another, my elbow on the counter and my chin in my cupped hand. Seeing Maria happy and in love is a dream come true. There was a time I wasn't sure either one of us would have a happily ever after again. She's had her own fair share of shitty men in the past. Antonio was right up there with Justin, but this one seems to be the real deal.

Eventually, I clear my throat. They both look my way, full of smiles. She saunters over, swaying her hips giving her man a show from behind.

He doesn't miss a beat, blatantly staring at her ass.

"Damn, woman, you know how to work that ass!" he says without shame.

"I know," she says saucily.

Laughing, I accept the glass she hands me.

"So *bonita*, where's Chase?" she asks.

"Working late. He'll probably come by this evening. Just then the landline rings, and Maria answers it.

"*Hola.*" She listens for a moment while Tom and I wait. "*Hola, sexy hombre de negocios.*"

I can't remember what *negocios* means. But I caught the part about saying "hello sexy man."

She continues in her native tongue. "*Estoy bien, ¿verdad?*"

I watch her intently. She's smiling that sneaky grin. *"Ella está aquí. ¿Qué tan malo es lo que quieres hablar con mi hermosa?"* she says defiantly. She said something about speaking to her girl. Then she hands the phone to me.

"It's for you," she says, smiling.

I cringe at her and she sticks out her tongue. The only person I know who can speak Spanish as well as she can is Chase.

"Hello?"

"Evening, gorgeous."

This time, I smile at his newest endearment. Kitten went the way of the wind, thank God. Wasn't fond of that one. Babycakes came and went. Baby and gorgeous seem to have stuck. I'm not complaining.

"Evening. What's up?" I ask.

"I texted you, but you didn't answer so I figured I'd call your landline. I have to jet off to Toronto this evening. One of my sky rises that's being built had a tragic accident. Apparently one of the crewman didn't secure himself to the scaffolding and fell off. He died instantly. I need to deal with the architect, the foreman, the insurance companies, pretty much everyone involved with the incident, not to mention I want to say a few words to the family."

"Oh, no, I'm so sorry to hear that. Did you know him?" I ask solemnly.

"Know who?" he asks.

I hear him shuffling papers and moving around in the background. His breath is labored like he just finished exercising. He must be pulling his things together to leave now.

"The man who died?" I ask.

"Oh, no. I employ around fifty thousand or so people, Gillian. I only personally know the heads of my companies and some of the key executives."

Wow, I guess that makes sense. Then it hits me—fifty thousand people? Holy hell, that's a lot of people counting on him and the success of his businesses. I usually joke about him running his empire, but he really does have a lot on his plate.

"Makes sense. Go, don't worry about me. I'm not leaving for New York for a couple days."

"That's why I called. One of my jets will be ready to take you and Mr. Jefferson to New York on Thursday morning. Jack will pick you up at the airport. He'll drop off Mr. Jefferson at his hotel and then he'll bring you to me." The sentence is laced with desire and want, making my heart pound and the space between my thighs moisten.

"Is that right? He'll bring me to you?" I try to put as much sex in my tone as possible.

He growls seductively. "Yes, he will bring *my woman* to

me," he emphasizes.

"Two days is a long time to wait," I warn. It's been months since we've spent a night apart. I'm not sure if I remember what it's like to sleep alone. I'm pretty sure I'm in full pout mode because Maria is in the background making the duck symbol with her hand then mouthing "*que*."

"But it will be worth the wait. And Gillian?"

"Yes, Chase," I answer, a little out of breath and squirming in my seat excited about meeting up with my lover in a new city but also aching to be in his arms.

"Don't be wearing any panties. I plan on fucking you the second you arrive."

Desire streaks down my body and settles at my center. I can't speak. Visions of exactly what he'll do to me when I see him flutter in quick pornographic images across my mind. I try to shake them off, to pay attention to his words, but am unsuccessful. God, I wish he were here now.

"Until then, gorgeous, remember the rule." His voice is gruff and strained. "Your pleasure is mine. Don't touch yourself," he warns.

I practically come from that request alone. Jesus, he knows how to play me until I'm weeping with desire.

"And what if I do? What if I can't help myself?" I ask boldly.

"I'll know, and I won't be happy." His tone is unyielding.

"I won't," I mutter quickly. I want him happy at all times, in all things.

"Goodnight, baby," he says and hangs up.

Fanning myself, I put the phone back into the receiver. Maria studies me, and I take a huge swallow of the chilled wine, hoping it will help the internal fire raging deep inside.

Two whole days without the feel of him, waking up near his warm, naked body. I sigh and mentally berate myself. What am I doing? I'm freaking myself out. I can handle this. It's two freakin' days, for crying out loud.

"What's the matter, *cara bonita*?" Maria asks.

Tom looks concerned.

"Chase has to fly out to Toronto. A crewman working on one of his buildings fell to his death today."

Maria gasps and Tom puts his hands on her shoulders. The movement does not go unnoticed. He's totally and completely in love with her. I wonder if she is in love with him. Hmmm. Looks like we need some girl time.

"I know, it's sad. He'll meet me in New York though on Thursday. So you'll have to put up with me here for a couple more days." I laugh.

"*Chica, esta es tu casa*...your home. If we want to be alone to bump uglies, we can go to his house." She points her thumb over her shoulder at Tom, who starts laughing at her unique way of referring to having sex.

"Thanks, girl. Now what's for dinner?" I ask, knowing she rarely cooks.

She looks pointedly at me. "I don't know. What is for dinner?"

Of course she looks to me. I roll my eyes.

"How about some good old-fashioned pizza?" Tom suggests. "I know the best place. I can pick it up, give you two some time to catch up," he offers.

To hell with Maria, I think I love this man! A man who knows when women need some girl time and offers food is marriage material.

"You're too good to me, *Papi*." She whirls around and

kisses him. *Papi?* I laugh at her nickname for him.

He returns the kiss and his face turns red again. It's actually quite sweet, what they have. I wonder if our friends think the same about Chase and me. We had a rocky start, but aside from the demonstrative way he tries to dig his way into my life, we're really happy. Tom goes into the other room, and I hear him ordering the pizza and riffling through the keys in the bowl at the side table. The last thing I hear is the door shutting and that's my cue to pounce.

"So, Ria, you two looked pretty cozy."

A huge smile breaks across her face. "He makes me happy and the sex, *cara bonita*, the sex is *caliente*!" she confides.

"Do you love him?" I ask, holding my breath.

She sets her hands on the counter and cocks her head to the side. She bites her lip and thinks a moment. "I think so. I don't want anyone else."

I nod in understanding.

"You know how it is, Gigi. It's hard to give my heart. He's told me he loves me though," she hedges.

"Oh. My. God! And you didn't tell me. What the hell? I'm your best friend," I chastise her. "Did you say it back?"

She shakes her head.

"Why not?"

"I don't know. I'm guess I'm just waiting for it to go bad. Eventually, he'll *joder*," she says.

"He will not fuck up! No *joder*!" I yell as convincingly as possible, but lack the Spanish flair in pronouncing my words.

"Maybe, but I'm not there yet." She pulls her long tresses up into a ponytail using the hair tie she has around her wrist.

"Okay, okay. Just don't wait too long to tell him, Ria. Don't sabotage yourself because you're afraid of being happy." I hit the nail on the head.

She nods, tears welling in her ice-blue eyes.

In two strides I'm around the island and pulling her into a tight hug. "I love how he looks at you like there's no one else in the room but you. He's in deep, sister. Don't think he's not as far gone as you are."

"You think?" Her voice comes across so small. Nothing like her typical boisterous self.

"I know." I pull her chin and stare into her eyes.

A tear slips down her cheek and I wipe it away.

"I know," I reiterate.

She nods and hugs me again.

★ ★ ★ ★

I spend the next two days getting ready for my trip. Maria and I go to Bree's studio for some hardcore yoga and meet up with Kat. We have dinner in our grubby workout clothes and catch up. Kat tells us everything is going well with Carson and that she, too, is falling in love with him. Bree lets us know that things are progressing with Phillip but more slowly than our three relationships. We set her mind at ease, assuring her that he is into her, but that single dads have more on their minds than hitting the sheets with a hot blonde. She feels better but is frustrated that they haven't taken their relationship to the next level. Maria and Kat both give her their ideas for seducing him. I stay out of it. It is like talking about getting my brother laid. It feels icky and gross. The next evening, I hit the gym one last time before my flight in the morning.

Running is just what I need to release the sexual frustration built up from a two-day dry spell. I up the incline on the treadmill, and my heart pounds along with my feet as they thump against the revolving belt. Black Eyed Peas' "Hey Mama" blares through my MP3 player as I hit the euphoric runner's high. Images of Chase running alongside me slither along my vision. His sweat slicked chest, the shower for two after we've worked our bodies to the limit, the pounding sex against the shower wall like icing on our workout cake. I sigh and up the incline one more time.

After a solid hour of pushing myself, I finally hit the stop button and jump to the sides of the machine. The endorphins run rampant through my system, and I tilt my head back and practically moan. It's the closest thing to euphoria I've felt in three days. I've gotten used to Chase pleasuring me to the point of madness each night, and it's hard to fall asleep without that release or his warm arms surrounding me. Exercise is the only option until tomorrow. I can't wait to see him.

"Gillian?" A deep voice booms from behind me.

I pull out my earphones, press stop on the Black Eyed Peas, and turn to see Daniel, my ex-boyfriend. I try my best not to cringe. It's been close to a year since we last spoke.

"Daniel, wow, it's been a while," I say and climb down off the machine.

He pulls me into a sweaty full-bodied hug. Once our chests make contact, I stiffen. The only man's sweat I want anywhere near me is Chase's, and typically, while I'm licking it off his naked chest.

"What has it been, six months?" he asks.

"Closer to a year. How are you?" I ask politely, not really wanting to talk to him. Even though he treated me like a princess, I still had to break up with him. It was awkward, and he was genuinely upset that I was breaking it off. It wasn't possible for me to get past his *you want me to fuck you like a whore* comment in the bedroom when I tried to discuss ramping up our sex life. Basically, I wanted to come, and he wasn't able to take me there. Sex with him was too nice and backed by little feeling on my part. For me to orgasm, I need to be emotionally invested, and with Danny, I just wasn't. He said he loved me often. I never uttered those words. After a less than a month with Chase, I was devoting my heart to him forever more. That ought to say something.

"Good. What are you doing after this?" he asks as we head toward the locker rooms.

"Heading home. I have an early flight to New York City tomorrow." There is no way I'm meeting up with him for a drink or anything remotely close to a date. No way, no how.

"Oh, yeah, business or pleasure?" he asks.

Internally I groan. I just want to get my purse and leave.

"A little of both. Donor visit for the foundation but I'm meeting my boyfriend," I say nonchalantly.

Daniel runs a hand through his hair and shakes his head. "You have a new boyfriend?" he says with a hint of surprise. He looks genuinely puzzled by my admission. "Who?" he asks.

I don't recognize the tone in his voice.

"Chase Davis," I say confidently. That's right, buddy, someone else did want to be with me. *The whore.* My mind reels to our last sexual encounter, where Daniel told me he wouldn't fuck me like a dog and he couldn't believe I wanted to be treated like a whore. That was the last straw for me. Even though Danny treated me like a queen, if a man thinks that fucking you from behind is raunchy, he can find someone else who likes perfect vanilla missionary position for the rest of their lives. I feel bad for the next woman he's with. He's "no orgasm Danny."

"The billionaire?" he asks in shock.

"That's the one. Hey, Danny, it's really nice seeing you, but I do have to run. I need to call Chase. I'll catch you around some time." I quickly enter the woman's locker room. I don't even wait for a good bye. The last thing I want to do is shoot the shit with my ex. I'd rather get my teeth cleaned. Besides, Chase would be absolutely livid if he knew the man so much as hugged me.

Whistling a tune to myself, I think on how I just saw Danny, a man I spent a year with, and didn't feel anything. Not even guilt for breaking up with him. It feels good to know what I want in life, and he's over six feet tall, broad shouldered, with ocean eyes and a "I'm going to fuck you till you scream" attitude. *Chase.* The mere thought of him makes my sex jump. I need him. Tomorrow cannot come soon enough.

CHAPTER SEVENTEEN

The plane roars to a stop. Taye and I spent six wonderful hours talking about everything from his crazy kids and wife, Melody, to my wild friends and their constant shenanigans. We spent only a little going over our meeting with our donor prospect, Theodore Vandegren. The seatbelt signs are off, and the captain makes his appearance.

"Ms. Callahan, so nice to see you again," he says.

"You too. Another excellent flight and perfect landing." I beam and shake the man's hand.

Taye and I make our way out of the plane, and true to Chase's word, Jack Porter is standing next to the limo, awaiting our arrival. He grabs our bags and starts for the trunk.

"Afternoon, Jack," I say over the noise from the airplanes.

"Ms. Callahan. Glad to see you arrived safely. Mr. Davis will be pleased. He's anxious for your arrival." I see a hint of a grin at the corner of his stern face.

Taye and I settle into the limo. "Must be nice having a boyfriend with such frills. Mel was shocked that we were flying in a private jet and being taken to the hotel in a limo."

I smile. Taye's truly in awe of such luxury. It still blows me away, too. "I'm not used to it either, but it comes with the man, so I deal with it." I point at Jack. "It also comes with a 24-7 linebacker," I say loud enough for Jack to hear.

Jack rolls up the privacy screen. The man ruffles my feathers more often than not. He has decided he doesn't want to like me, and it irks me. Everyone likes me. The people pleaser in me is frustrated that he's such a tough nut to crack. I'm committed to winning him over. One day, Jack Porter will be my friend, or at the very least, friendly toward me.

"That's got to get to a woman like you," Taye says knowingly.

Ever since Justin, I pride myself on being able to take care of myself. I don't need a man to take care of me, but I want Chase. And Chase is a man who needs to take care of his woman. So I deal.

"It does, but I've gotten used to it. Chase has to deal with the possibility of people wanting to hurt him. I give them a unique way to hurt him, so he's overly protective of me. Plus, after what happened on our last business trip, he's not taking any chances." I rub the scar over my eye that hasn't quite gone away. Chase says he'll have it removed permanently if it continues to bother me. He hates seeing it as much as I do. Not because it mars my looks, but because of what it stands for. Same with the jagged one on my hip. He wants it gone, but I refuse. I need the reminder of what I've survived.

"Good man. You know how I feel about you, girl. You're like my own daughter. Sounds like he knows a good woman when he sees one." He smiles and pats my knee.

Over the past couple years, I've grown attached to Taye. He truly is like the father I never had. He's kind, considerate, and genuinely cares about me and my life.

"Thanks, Taye." I look out the window as the limo comes to a halt outside a huge hotel. The bellman opens the door, and Taye gets out. "I'll see you tomorrow afternoon before our dinner. Meet in the lobby around four?"

"Sounds like a plan. I'd ask you to meet me for dinner but I'm pretty sure that boy of yours has plans for you." He shakes his head, laughs, and heads into the hotel.

Jack pulls the limo out into the busy New York City streets. I press the down button on the privacy screen. "Where we headed, Jack?"

"Park Avenue," he says flatly.

It takes everything I have not to burst out the theme song for *Green Acres.* Where else would a billionaire live? With effort, I refrain from rolling my eyes and peer out the window.

Down the entire length of the avenue is a median with lush flowers and small trees lending to its name. Despite the hustle and bustle of Manhattan, there is a Zen-like flow to the traffic. The greenery dissecting through the cars going in opposite direction is lovely in its yin and yang quality of movement. I'm taken out of my reverie by the ping from my cell phone. I can't believe that man. He's so anxious! I look down at the display and frown at the unknown number.

To: Gillian Callahan

From: Unknown

Don't be gone long. I'm waiting.

That's strange. I click on the "Unknown" name and not even a number pops up. Who's waiting for me? I wonder if one of the girls got a new phone. I decide to respond quickly.

To: Unknown
From: Gillian Callahan

Who is this?

That should help me figure out the mystery caller. The phone pings, and I look down. The hair on my neck stands on end and my stomach twists.

To: Gillian Callahan
From: Unknown

All will be revealed when we're alone.

Chase has got to be messing with me, pranking me. It has been three days since I felt his embrace. I shake off the weird vibe, sure it's nothing. Probably a wrong number. No need to get worked up over nothing. Besides, I'm about to see Chase. Excitement swells and lies heavily between my thighs. When Jack stops the car, I hop out before he can open the door. He frowns and proceeds to grab my bags.

"You may go on in. Use the elevator." He gestures to where the doorman is holding open the door.

The doorman tips his hat as I walk through. My legs feel weak with anticipation.

"Which floor?" I ask Jack over my shoulder, too excited to completely stop and wait for him. I turn when he doesn't respond.

Jack looks at me with disdain. "The penthouse, Ms. Callahan. Use your thumb. It's the same drill as back home."

I scowl and pop my hands on both hips. Dramatic effect

is necessary to get this point across. "You needn't be such a jerk about it!"

His eyebrows go up, and the doorman chokes back a laugh. Him I like. I smile at him and saunter into the elevator.

I put my thumb on the screen and wait for the scan to finish and the green light to beep. Every time, it's still incredibly cool, and it works even three thousand miles away! The doors close, and the elevator starts its ascent to the top floor. I have to figure out a way to win Jack over. This tension between us is thick as Texas toast and not as yummy.

I adjust my skirt, making sure everything is in place. With Chase in mind, I chose a simple black A-line skirt that flows out at the knee. I've paired it with a silk cream-colored buttoned sleeveless blouse. I take off my fitted chocolate-colored blazer and hang it over my arm. I'm feverish with anticipation of seeing Chase. My hair is pulled up into a chignon, held there with one long dainty clip through the center of the swirl. I look down at my feet and thank the shoe gods for these sky-high sexy strappy heels. They are going to make Chase weak at the knees. My toes are painted a perfect pale pink. A trip to the salon yesterday made sure my entire body was buffed, exfoliated, and waxed. I wanted to be sure there are no rough edges, only soft, smooth planes. I can't wait to rub them along every ridged surface of my man's body.

The elevator doors open, and I lose the ability to breathe. He's there waiting for me. The man who has taken over every fantasy and dream for the last three nights. He leans against the opposite wall, arms folded, dress shirt pulling at his muscular arms. His dress slacks are navy and hang low on his delectable hips. He's not wearing a tie, and the first three buttons are open, giving me a hint of his beautiful chest. I look into his eyes. They are smoldering, no longer ocean blue but a smoky gray.

With as much grace and elegance as I can muster, I saunter over to him slowly and drop my purse and jacket to the ground. I stop a foot in front of him, close enough to feel the heat radiating off his much larger frame. Even when I'm in four-inch heels, Chase towers over me. I take a deep breath, and his sandalwood and citrus scent assails my senses, filling me with incredible want and need. I lick my lips slowly, and it's over. He moves lightning fast. Strong hands grip my waist and haul me against him. His hands slide up my back and around my neck. Chase's lips assault mine in a fiery ball of desire, his slippery tongue invading my mouth. His taste beckons me, surrounds me, and holds me to him. It is like being enveloped in a hot bath. I'm lost in the sensation.

He pulls his lips from mine and drags them along my neck. "Jesus, baby, I missed you."

His breath is hot against my earlobe sending the little hairs on the back of my neck to stand up with excitement. Sharp teeth clamp on the tender flesh at my pulse point, eliciting a tremor that goes straight to my core.

I can't speak. I can't think. I can only feel as his tongue slides along my clavicle, making me lose all train of thought. The buttons on my blouse are magically undone, and his large hands squeeze and test the weight of my breasts. They swell, my nipples pebble, engorged with the need to be touched. His fingers make quick work of the front clasp of my bra, and his mouth engulfs an aching peak. Closing my eyes, I'm assaulted by his hot, feral desire and pure want. It zips through my body like lightning.

"God, Chase," I moan, mentally congratulating myself for having the foresight to wear a front-opening bra.

He clamps his teeth down on the tender flesh, and I cry out in pure ecstasy. My fingers weave into his hair, and I arch my breast into his mouth harder. He growls his appreciation, ravenously taking the offering.

In two quick moves, he reverses our positions. My back is now against the wall, and his solid flesh presses hard against mine. I deftly undo the remaining buttons on his dress shirt and scrape my nails along the open expanse of golden male skin. Two hands slide up my skirt and fasten against my bare bottom.

"Oh, good girl, you take direction so well." He grips my bare ass and hauls me higher against the wall, as he presses his turgid length against my center in the perfect position. "You deserve to be rewarded," he says against my open mouth. He grinds his erection against my bare sex.

It ignites a fire in me so deep I clench my legs tightly around his waist and lick into his mouth, sealing our lips in a searing kiss.

I pull away roughly from his swollen lips. "Fuck me, Chase. I can't wait another minute."

He grinds his ridged cock against me again, making me spiral out of control with lust. I squeeze his waist with the power of my thigh muscles and tip my pelvis against his erection, trying for more pressure. For more of anything to relieve the torturous ache three days bereft of Chase can do to a woman. My heels dig into the tender flesh of his lower back, and he groans.

"Baby, I love it when you beg me to fill you." He holds me up with one hand and unbuttons his pants. They slide down his legs and his engorged cock is free. He cups my bottom. In one swift move, he's tilted his pelvis and pulled my hips down on his cock, embedding himself, stretching the walls of my pussy wide, plundering so deep my head slams back against the wall.

"Ahhh, God, Chase," I scream in sweet relief. I can't even remember what life was like before feeling this full, this complete.

The elevator pings, and we both stop moving. The hair on my neck stands in the scary way when you know someone is watching you. Our breaths sound overly loud as we pant in the quiet space. I hide my face in the crook of Chase's neck—my haven, the place I go to find solace.

Chase turns his head toward the intruder.

"Guess I should have waited a little longer to come up," Jack says. He opens the door next to us and disappears quickly.

Chase laughs and picks up right where he left off, pulling his hips back and slamming into me.

Before I can comprehend that Jack just caught Chase balls deep inside me, his hips move faster. With strong thrusts, he presses me into the wall, my back grating along the smooth edge. Twinges of pain slip along the surface but die out instantly with another delicious move of his hips into my center. Every thrust makes me forget that we were just caught in a compromising position, and I give into the passion between us. It's been too long since we were together. Three days feels like three years when a sex god like Chase Davis is fucking you.

Chase captures my lips. Our tongues tango, our lips nip at one another, and our teeth bite and graze on warm flesh. He picks up his rhythm, pounding into me. I welcome each push of his hips with a tilt of my own, allowing each thrust to penetrate against my tender bundle of nerves. He grinds and presses into me so deep and with so much force, it's like he's physically squeezing and pulling my release from me by sheer will alone. My body goes tight, a top wound too tight and ready to spin. One more crush of his pelvis against my clit and I cry out, screaming a litany of expletives in my pleasure. He continues to batter me roughly, pressing so hard it's as if he's reaching into my soul.

"Again, baby, give it to me again," he whispers in my ear. His teeth clench down on my shoulder.

And just when I think I can't possibly feel the pleasure again so quickly, he shifts me higher, and the new position presses his thick cock perfectly against that miracle spot within my core. I arch into it greedily, practically climbing up his body, bouncing on him like a pogo stick, using his shoulders for leverage. He fucks me so hard the texture of the wall behind us abrades my skin. Only instead of hurting, the tiny sparks of pain push me further into the abyss.

"That's right, baby. I want it. You come for me, only me," he urges with a particular deep stroke that crushes my clit between our bodies.

My mind is thick with lust. I forget everything but being with him and receiving the pleasure he gives me. My entire body is aflame. I can do nothing but obey his command.

He jackhammers into me. I hear the wet noise of our bodies coming together and pulling apart with each penetration and twist of his hips. Finally, he shows me mercy, slipping a hand between us and pressing my clit with the pad of his thumb in tight dizzying circles. I go crazy and practically squeeze the life out of him with the strength of my thighs. He bites my lips, capturing my attention. My eyes meet his in a silent command. I come so hard I lose all sense of hearing. Chase's mouth moves, but I can't hear anything. I just see his beautiful eyes as they swirl with feral hunger. My body and mind focus on the apex between my thighs where his length is ramming into me, over and over as his fingers spin me into sweet oblivion. The second orgasm rolls into a third. He's relentless. I'm completely limp as he tortures me with his pounding cock, twirling fingers, and blessed mouth.

I scream when he sinks his teeth into my shoulder. I regain awareness the moment Chase loses it. His body strung as tight as a drum, muscles flex and ripple as he releases his essence into me, holding my hips in a bruising grip. I can feel every tingle, every twinge of his cock as he muffles his cry into the crook of my neck. Beautiful oblivion. God, I love him.

Once we catch our breath, I unwind my legs from his waist. He kisses me with such passion that I want to scale his body and ride him again, but I'm exhausted. He stares deep into my eyes as he holds my shoulders and cups my neck. He lays his forehead against mine.

"Too many days without you. I don't like it."

"I missed you too, big guy," I tell him and kiss his nose.

He grins from ear to ear. "Come on, I have dinner being made for us by a world renowned chef." He pulls his pants up and in place. "We have time to take a shower, and you can put on something more comfortable."

"What's more comfortable than this?" I ask, knowing the answer but enjoying playing with him.

"I was thinking a saucy little number I left waiting on the bed would be perfect for this evening," he retorts.

"I highly doubt the lingerie you had Dana buy me is ideal for eating a world renowned chef's meal," I counter.

"I actually picked out the piece and bought it for you myself when I was in Toronto," he tells me. "It comes with a perfectly appropriate robe, and I'd like you to wear it."

I grip his arm and rub my head against his shoulder. "Anything for you, baby," I whisper and kiss his neck.

He holds open the door and we enter arm in arm.

We walk through the spacious apartment. It is completely different from his home in San Francisco. This one is much colder. The floors are white marble. Every wall except one is stark white with black-and-white photos hanging throughout the space. The accent wall is a bright color. The wall closest is a royal blue with an image hanging dead center. A canary-yellow wall off in the distance has photographs of random objects—the wheel of a car, the front of a train, the window of a plane. This place is not at all like the Chase I know and love. His home in San Francisco is filled with books and trinkets from his travels and feels warm and inviting. This seems like a museum.

"Did you design this house?"

"A friend of mine did. I hate it actually, but I didn't have the heart to change it. I don't want to hurt his feelings," he admits dryly.

I knew the man had a heart, but he takes friendly consideration a little too far. Instead of raining on his parade,

I figure it's probably best to leave it alone and follow him to his room.

We take a long, hot shower, reacquainting ourselves with each other's bodies now that the initial need has been slaked. I inspect the black lingerie Chase picked out for me. It's beautiful and very tasteful. A lacy spaghetti-strapped camisole with high-cut matching lace shorts. The satin robe that goes with it is floor length and covers me from shoulders to ankles. I quickly put the lingerie on, and it fits like a glove. He has an uncanny ability to size me.

Once I'm dressed, I brush the tangles from my wet hair. Chase comes up behind me and wraps his arms around my waist, hugging me. He inhales against the crook of my neck and layers the skin with tiny kisses.

"You always smell and feel so good."

"Thank you. Now about that dinner? I'm starving." I puff out my bottom lip and turn in a circle, clasping him around the waist. He's wearing pajama pants that look suspiciously similar to the ensemble he laid out for me. Chase nibbles on my lip before pulling away.

"After you, my sweet."

He gestures for me to lead the way even though I'm not at all certain where we're going. *My sweet?* Another new one. I smile. Eventually he takes the lead, clasping my hand and bringing me to a dining room. Another boring white room with black-and-white images of objects gracing the walls. Only these images are worse. An old-fashioned milk jug, a fruit bowl, and a picture of mismatched place setting. Chase really needs to have a chat with that designer.

The chef he hired definitely earns his status as being world renowned. Every bite is better than the last, and I feel as though I could die a happy woman now that I've consumed an incredible meal and been thoroughly pleased by my man.

"Who are you prospecting tomorrow?" Chase asks around a bite of fresh bread.

I sip my wine and hold it on my tongue for a moment, appreciating the thick berry notes. "Theodore Vandegren."

He narrows his eye.

"Taye has a friend of a friend of a friend who got us the meeting," I say, unable to hide my excitement over my first donor visit.

"You're not meeting with Theo, Gillian," Chase says stiffly.

Alarm bells flare, and I lift an eyebrow, waiting for him to rephrase his command. He doesn't.

"What do you mean I'm not meeting with him? Do you know him?"

He nods. "Theo is a business associate. He probably agreed to the meeting because he knows I'm the chairman, and it's my foundation."

"So what's the problem? Taye says he's incredibly wealthy and gives to a lot of charities. We'd be lucky to secure him as a major donor, Chase." I place a hand over his arm to remind him of the reason I'm meeting with this man.

"Theo is a player. He will get one look at you and make every effort to woo you and get into your pants. I won't have it." He takes a sip of wine and puts down his fork. It clangs loudly against his plate. He turns toward me, arms crossed over his chest.

I lick my lips and take a deep breath. I've learned a

thing or two about Chase over the past few months. When he feels threatened by a man who he believes may have interest in me, he gets extremely unreasonable. I've given him no indication that I would ever want anyone else, but something inside him drives this jealousy. Eventually I have to get to the bottom of it. For now, I need to remind him of his place.

"You don't get to decide who I see professionally. You're my boyfriend, not my boss. You agreed to not get involved in my job any more than you already have," I remind him, trying to be reasonable.

He takes a deep breath through his nose, and that sexy jaw, the one that delectably abraded my skin just an hour ago, becomes hard.

"Remember, if this is going to work between us, you're going to let me do my job. There are things you can't protect me from."

"The hell there are!" he says, angrily. "That man will do everything in his power to fuck you. I know his tastes well, Gillian. I used to have them."

I grip his arm, forcing him to unwind from his defensive position with them crossed over his chest. I put his hand in both of mine. His thumb instantly traces his favorite pattern over the top of my hand. That's it. My lovable Chase is coming around. Touching me always helps. I grin internally, not wanting him to know I have my own way to secretly soothe him.

"I'll be there with Taye. I have to learn, and the foundation is paying me to be here. Now, I'd prefer we not discuss this further and enjoy the rest of our evening."

Chase grips my hand. "Fine, but Jack will take you and

wait outside the restaurant until it's time for you to leave and bring you back to me." His tone is back to being demanding and unrelenting. It's the best compromise I'm going to get and the only way to salvage the evening.

"Deal." I smile.

He takes a deep cleansing breath, irritation twisting his features. "How's your food?"

I can tell that it took every bit of control he had to control his response. It makes me ridiculously happy to know that I'm getting through to him. He's finally starting to trust our place in each other's lives and realize that I'm not going anywhere. I haven't run since the day I was granted my promotion. And now, there's nothing that could ever make me run from him.

★ ★ ★ ★

I shake Theodore Vandegren's hand. It's clammy and instantly gives me the creeps. He's tall, thin, and very handsome. Nothing like my personal Superman, but drool-worthy to the right woman. His smile is charming, and I see why Chase would be worried. This man oozes sex from the white suit to his bedroom eyes. Even his blond hair is tousled in layers.

He roams my body with his gaze from tip to toe and back again, landing on my breasts. They stay there much longer than is appropriate. The black cocktail dress I wore is the least revealing of the items I brought with me. Chase rummaged through all of my clothes and insisted on it, right after making a call to Dana about ordering me a new wardrobe to be added to the New York apartment. The dress falls delicately to the knee, covers most of my bosom, leaving only a small swath of skin to feast on. However, it still hugs my curves in a way that makes me feel young, sexy, and professional.

Throughout dinner, Theodore stares at me, blatantly disregarding Taye's presence. He's officially a world-class rich scumbag. I sit quietly, trying not to give the impression I'm interested in anything more than his donation.

"I'm a very busy man, Mr. Jefferson. Can you get to the point?" he says to Taye while looking at me.

I wish I weren't here. Chase was right. I vaguely hear Taye give his spiel and ask for the charitable donation. Theodore waves off Taye, forcing him to stop talking. "Look, Mr. Jefferson, I will give the Foundation twenty-five thousand dollars if this lovely young lady will accompany me for an after-dinner drink...alone. I'll hand the check to Ms. Callahan tonight."

Twenty-five thousand dollars for a drink? The man is bat-shit crazy, but whatever floats his boat. "Okay," I say confidently with a shrug.

Taye furrows his eyebrows, and a frown mars his face. "Gillian, are you sure? You don't have to," he says.

A drink can't hurt. There really doesn't seem to be anything nefarious about him besides being slimy and a bit forward. "I'm fine. I'll call you tomorrow," I say to Taye. "You can have Jack take you back to the hotel.

He stands and walks out of the restaurant. I can see through the window that he says something to Jack. Jack shakes his head and gets into the front seat of the limo. Taye then raises his hand for a taxi.

I watch Theodore, not knowing really what to say. The waiter brings over a bottle of wine and fills our glasses.

My cell phone pings. "Excuse me."

To: Gillian Callahan

From: Chase Davis

Why are you alone with him? Jack tells me Jefferson left, and you haven't come out to the car.

I ignore Chase's text, slip the phone back into my purse, and click the "silent mode" button before stowing it away. The man has to learn to trust me.

Twenty minutes and two cocktails later, I've listened to Theodore drone on and on about his success, his money, his Ferrari, and I couldn't be more bored. He stands, and I stand with him, ready to get back to my control freak before he blows a gasket. I can only imagine how many texts await me when I get back into the limo to check.

As we exit the hotel restaurant, Theodore grips my elbow and leads me toward the bank of elevators. I try to pull away but his grip is firm. "Come on, sweetheart. I need to give you that twenty-five thousand dollar check. While I'm writing it, you can remove your dress. Save us a little time."

"What?" I yank my arm from his clammy grasp. He thinks I'm going to bed him because he donated to our charity? The warning bells clang loud, only I wish they had gone off sooner. *Shit!* Chase was right.

"That's right. I give, you give. If you're good at giving to me, honey, I'll make sure your boss knows how convincing you are and donate more." He pulls me against his chest and grips my hip roughly. He drags his chin along my neck and bites the skin hard.

Chills race along my spine, and my chest tightens. Panic

starting to tickle the sense.

"But you need to get down on your knees first and get to work," he says smugly.

He's holding me so tight I'm certain I'll have bruises. The skin around my bicep feels pinched and swollen as I pull hard away from him, just enough that I'm able to pull my leg back and bring my knee up into his crotch. He screams and falls back, but not enough that he lets go of his hold on me. Just as he's trying to drag me toward him, a firm arm around the waist yanks me backwards. I'm catapulted back a few feet as a fist comes out of nowhere and connects with Theodore's face. He falls to the ground in a heap, shouting in pain. Blood pours from his nose, a stark contrast to his white suit.

"Stay the fuck away from my girlfriend, Theo. I'll only tell you once," Chase yells, his face red, cheeks puffed with anger. That sexy jaw is working overtime, the tic clicking away like a clock.

Momentarily, I'm stunned by his presence. I didn't even see him come up behind us. Chase's anger is palpable as he hovers over Theodore's prone form. Then I realize I'm still being held back with a firm arm around my waist. Taking a peek over my shoulder, I realize it's Jack. His arm locks around my waist and he's not moving.

Theo looks up at Chase, recognition dawning on him. His features turn arrogant as his eyebrow perks up and his lips quirk into a sly grin.

"How was I supposed to know that hot piece of ass was yours?" His voice is nasal as he pinches the bridge of his nose.

Chase lunges for him again, fingers around his neck.

"Hey, man, okay, okay. She wasn't wearing a ring or a sign around her neck that says she belongs to Chase Davis. Give me a fucking break!" He grips Chase's hands and pushes him off.

Chase heaves as Theodore backs against the wall, putting some serious distance between them.

"Never again, Theo. She's mine." In a few steps, Chase assesses me, his gaze zeroing in on the red imprint marring my arm. With reverence, he cups my chin, lifts it, and turns my head to the side. He caresses the sensitive skin where Theodore bit me.

"I'll fucking kill him," he growls.

"Baby, no," I whisper. "Take me home." I lift my arms to the beautiful face of the man I adore.

Chase clasps my hand, turns me around, and hugs me to his side as he leads us towards the exit. He has absolutely no concern for the man he left bleeding all over himself.

I'm still trying to wrap my mind around what just happened and how Chase made it to the restaurant so quickly when my knight in shining rayon forcefully pushes me into the limo. I slide in spastically. He settles me into my seat. Chase slams the door and turns to me. His eyes are black, hungry, and filled with lust.

I hear the privacy screen roll up as I scrutinize the giant bulge in his pants.

"Your underwear. Off. Now!" he demands.

I've never heard this tone from him before. His nostrils flare, and his eyes narrow, their depths an inky onyx color. Quickly I hike up my dress and shimmy out of my underwear. Excitement and fear a hazy line he's making me walk. With jerky movements, he unbuckles his belt and pulls his pants down. His cock appears fully erect and bulging. The tiny slit at the top weeps. A pearly drop sits at the crown of his massive erection. My mouth waters at the sight, and I want nothing more than to take his fullness into my mouth and taste his need. When his pants are around his ankles, he hauls me onto his lap. In one second flat he powers into me, sheathed to the hilt. I scream out, the pleasure and pain of his entry coalescing into one.

"Fuck!" he groans.

I'm not prepared for his penetration. There is no foreplay or kisses, just his carnal need to mate. After the burning sensation of his rough entry wears off, I slide up and down his length, rocking slowly. I grip him with my internal muscles and grab hold of his shoulders for leverage. He searches me with his gaze as if he's memorizing every facet of my face. Then he smashes our lips together in a brutal kiss, one hand holding my nape close. He pulls back and bites and nips down my neck.

His words are a chant against the tender skin. "I love you, I love you, I love you," he says while he bites, licks, and sucks on the skin he can reach.

There's the man I know. There's my Chase. He grips my waist, pushing me up and slamming me down on his cock in punishing thrusts. The rough pleasure of this coupling is unlike anything we've had before. Something about his need is feral, animalistic, stripping him down to want and need. All of which seem to be one thing—me.

"You're fucking mine!" he says through gritted teeth, his jaw tight. "Do you understand?" He jackknifes his hips up, going impossibly deep.

I scream out in pure ecstasy, climbing to the crest and

falling over the edge.

"Say it!" he demands with another harsh thrust.

I cry out, lost in a never-ending orgasm. "I'm yours, Chase. Always, yours." Tears prick at my eyes. "I love you, Chase. I love you," I scream as he thrusts deeper and deeper. I lean back and rest my hands on his knees behind me, changing the angle, allowing him more access to penetrate farther. He moans and presses hard into me. His fingers dig into the flesh of my hips. His cock is rock hard as it pounds into me. I can feel every steely inch of him drag along the tender inflamed tissue inside.

"Come, baby. Come again for me," he says in a tone I recognize, one as intimate as my own voice.

I come long and slow, my sex tightening in leisurely pulls against his length, tipping him over the edge with me.

Lying against his chest, I wait for the storm to pass. He caresses my back in lazy circles, but he doesn't speak.

"What just happened, Chase?" I whisper against his chest. This sexual encounter was rife with anger and possession.

"I lost control."

CHAPTER EIGHTEEN

We don't discuss what happened with Theodore-the-slimeball-Vandegren or what took place in the limo after we reach his Penthouse. Chase waves me off to bed saying he has work.

Instead of talking to me, he chooses to internalize his issues and isolate himself in his study. It hurts and makes me feel as if we're taking steps backward instead of forward. I feel alone, like a cork bobbing in a sea of disappointment. I thought we'd gotten past the bulk of our communication issues. So wrong. Every time it bubbles up, it's like a pot of water forgotten on a burning stove, left to overflow with the intense heat. I go to bed alone, exhausted over the day's events. When I awake, disappointment once more crashes over me. He left me alone. I don't even know if he slept next to me, though he did leave a note on his pillow.

Gillian,

I have to work today. Dinner tonight with Craig and his wife at 7:00. Jack will take you wherever you'd like to go today. I'll call later.

Yours,

~CD

At least he left a note. I can't help but hope the "yours" signoff means something. Last night was the first time he'd said those three little words in months. Under the circumstances, I wish he hadn't.

We also haven't discussed any of what we revealed of our pasts since that night. Do I regret telling him about my past? That I love him? No. I could never regret that. Last night when I screamed my love for him as he took me in the limo was the only other time I told him. It was such a relief. It's as if we're holding onto that night and those revelations as if they never occurred. Even the "love" part.

As I get ready for the day, I decide not to sit around waiting for Chase to get home. I call the bellman and schedule a taxi to pick me up. I walk out of the building and jump into the waiting taxi as I wave at Chase's sentinel sitting on his perch near the car.

Jack shoots me one of his patented scowls. He bounds over to the cab, but not fast enough. I promise the cab driver an extra twenty bucks if he squeals the tires as we speed off. I smile coyly as Jack puts his phone to his ear. I use my thumb and pinky to give him the symbol for making a call and mouth "call me," adding to his irritation. He seems pretty peeved. Mission accomplished. I feel vindicated and free. Now for a little "me" time. I need the space to put things into perspective.

Besides, I refuse to be chauffeured around New York by Chase's personal soldier so he can be apprised of my comings and goings.

My phone rings. I answer, saccharin sweet, "Hello darling."

"What the hell are you doing going off without Jack?" His deep voice is clipped and razor sharp. "Didn't you get my note?"

"I did."

"Why the hell are you out without protection?"

"Look, Chase, you are not my great protector—"

"Wasn't I last night?" he interrupts. "I protected you from potentially being sexually assaulted."

"Last night was"—I have trouble finding the right words—"difficult." I choose a light word, one without malice. "Today is a new day, and I'm more comfortable on my own. I will meet you back at your penthouse in plenty of time to get ready for our dinner this evening."

His voice lowers. "I'd be more comfortable with Jack—"

I'm tired of his controlling ways. He cannot leave me lying in bed, cold and alone, and expect me to just do what he says. "Chase Davis…you, mister, do not own me."

"Yet," he growls.

Shaking my head, I try to wrap my mind around what he just said. Nope. Still doesn't compute. "What?"

"I do not own you…yet," he adds with a strained tone.

I can tell he's barely holding on to his anger.

"Whatever, Chase. I'll see you later this evening." And with that, I hang up just like he does with me, never saying goodbye, just cutting him off with a dial tone. Serves him right.

I'm actually feeling quite proud of myself. He's the one who avoided me last night. I don't even know if we slept in the same bed. That thought more than anything saddens me. The last thing I need right now is to feel uncertain of my place in his life, in his bed. A day of shopping will perk me up. Shopping in New York City is exactly what every California girl dreams about. I tell the driver to head to the outlet stores. The closer I get to my retail therapy, the more I start to relax. I'm going to get a smoking hot dress for this evening and wow the socks of the temperamental Mr. Davis. Remind him of what he has so he never ever feels the need to isolate himself from me again.

★ ★ ★ ★

I feel his presence before I see him. He's sitting in the armchair across from the bed in the darkened room as I enter with today's bargain finds. His elbows rest against his knees, his face teetering on the tips of his fingers. The drapes covering the window behind him are open enough to shine a slice of light across his furrowed brow.

"I was worried," he says brusquely.

Setting my loot on the bed, I turn toward him, hands firmly planted on my hips. "I told you I'd be back in time for dinner. I keep my promises, Chase."

"Just the thought of you out in the city, not knowing where you were, that you were safe…" He cocks his head to the side.

Preparing for battle, I adjust my shoulders, not really wanting to have this battle with him before I meet his family.

"Everything was fine. I went shopping. Got a dress for tonight," I say, trying to change the topic. I riffle through my bags, looking for the outfit I plan on wearing.

"You think I don't know that? It was nothing to have your credit card traced." He is nonchalant in his admission, not even a hint of apology can be heard.

I whip my head to his side of the room, settling on him. I let go of the bags and they drop in a heap at my feet. "You what?"

"You heard me. I also paid for those items." He gestures to my purchases.

Just when I'm about to respond, he continues halting me.

Chase lifts his hands and ticks off each finger with his next announcement. "I paid off your credit cards, and I put a large sum of money into your checking account." His words are calm and evenly spaced.

However, that's not how my twisted brain interprets them. He says "paid" and my mind morphs it into "owing." He says "large sum of money" and my mind warps it into "you are my possession."

I can't breathe. My ability to speak is gone. Pretty much the only thing I'm capable of is standing still with what must be a stupefied look across my face. Again, I open my mouth and close it several times, trying to form a response, but nothing comes out. Panic swirls like liquid acid in my stomach, sending spikes of fear to hammer at my heart. I clutch my stomach and chest protectively.

"No woman of mine will go without. No woman of mine will live paycheck to paycheck." He stands abruptly and walks over to me. "No woman of mine will need to shop at thrift stores when she can have everything she ever dreamed right at her fingertips!" There's a grimace to his features, almost disgust twisting his beautiful lips.

"They were outlet stores, not thrift stores, and what the fuck?" I say.

He slides his hands around my waist. Scowling, I push away from him. He doesn't relent, holding me tighter. His magic fingers move enticingly along the fabric of my hips and up my ribs. I close my eyes in frustration and excitement, the panic transitioning into lust. I want to be pissed at him. I *am* pissed, but when his hands are on me, I turn into a pile of goo. Chase hasn't touched me since last night in the limo, and although the sex was satisfying, something happened to him. Since that moment, we've been off kilter. Proof can be found in his reaction moments ago.

He completely ignores my question, his hands burning a path along my sides up and over my swelling breasts, cupping them firmly. I gasp.

"And no woman of mine will go unprotected as long as I am around." He slips his fingers into the straps of my dress and pulls them down my shoulders. The summery dress falls in a pool of cotton around my feet.

"I'm not your woman, Chase." The words cross my lips in a breathy whisper, lacking conviction.

"No?" he asks flatly, while thumbing the erect peaks that are reaching for his attention.

He knows he's affecting me. The grin that comes across his face is confident, smug. *Handsome bastard*. My nipples bead into impossibly tight knots as he pets them, pushing tightly against the white strapless bra. Moisture pools between my legs, soaking the barely there matching G-string.

He inhales deeply and stares into my eyes, straight through to my soul. He slides his right hand along the swells of my breasts, and his fingertips caress the skin so softly in a wide infinity symbol. Chills race up my back. The movement of his fingers reminds me of a scent wafting in a breeze, gone too quickly to place the origin. I let out a ragged breath as he trails down between my breasts and along the line of my stomach. Goose bumps cover my skin, but I'm not cold. Far from it. A fire burns so hot in my belly, only one thing can put it out, and he's standing right in front of me, toying with me. He knows it too. He is intimately aware of the power he holds over me.

"You are *my* woman, and I'll prove it." He dips into my panties, and without preamble, he pushes two fingers deep inside.

I cry out and grasp onto his shoulders. A firm arm already around my waist holds me up. Never for a moment would he let me fall.

"You see how wet you are for me?"

I close my eyes. Regardless of what words come out of my mouth, my body is Judas, a traitor working for him, and he knows it too well.

"Chase," I breathe, trying to say something, anything, before I lose the battle completely. His fingers dig deeper, and he presses me back. His knee comes up onto the bed, and I'm floating down to its surface on a haze of lust. He's a puppeteer, controlling my body's responses, and I'm his willing marionette.

"I don't know why I have to repeat myself." He tangles his fingers into the side of my panties and slips them off my legs. He grips my legs and spreads them apart more roughly than I expect. He palms my thighs and drags down to my center. Slowly, just his thumbs draw apart my lower lips, exposing me fully to his gaze. He groans deeply at the sight.

He brings his head down to me and inhales. "I'll never forget your scent. I love knowing that I'm the only man who gets to experience this piece of heaven." And then he's everywhere at once. The flat of his incredible tongue laps at me in long strokes, from the tiny rosette that tingles every time he touches it with his delectable tongue to the place where I need him most.

"More," I whisper.

"I'm sorry, baby. What did you say?" He twirls his tongue in a circular motion around my engorged clit. "Because I think you said you wanted more." He delves deep into my core, stabbing in and out, his mouth fucking me where I want his cock.

"God, yes, Chase." I squeal and gyrate my hips against his face trying to get more pressure, more tongue, more of him, more, just more.

"Tell me what I want to hear, gorgeous, and I'll give you what you want," he says with extreme confidence.

I moan in answer. He's not playing fair. He knows I'm going to cave.

He spreads my cheeks wide and swirls his tongue around my anus, stabbing at the puckered hole, making me squirm with pleasure. He wets the area fully and then replaces his tongue with the soft pad of his thumb, pressing into the tight muscle as it flowers open for him.

"Has any man ever had your ass, Gillian?" he asks.

I shake my head repeatedly, lost to the dark feeling roaring through me.

He grins. "That's good, real good. I want to be the only man who has had you in every way possible."

My hands come up of their own accord and cup my breasts. Pushing the bra down, I twist and pull at the pebbled peaks. His words of ownership, the force with which he is staking his claim in a way I've only fantasized about before today, have me out of my mind with lust. Then it dawns on me, like the sun peeking out behind dark clouds. I'm choosing to let him control me, entrusting him with my body, mind, and soul.

It's my choice.

He presses harder into my most private juncture and pushes pasts the tight ring of muscle. A burning sensation scalds me from the inside out but quickly dissipates into white-hot pleasure. He pulls his thumb slowly out and presses it back in again. The feeling is intense, unusual, but so good I start to press against it, seeking deeper penetration.

"Damn, baby, you're stunning. I love fucking you. You make me so hard," he says and licks his lips.

His tongue comes back into play and twirls around my swollen clit, flicking and stabbing in perfect succession. Two fingers from his other hand push into me and hook up rubbing against the pleasure button deep within me. He's penetrating my cunt and ass as he sucks and nibbles on my clit. Full. So full I'm about to burst. I push against his fingers and thumb shamelessly as he laps and licks at my clit. His mouth clamps over the overstimulated bud and he sucks hard, pushing me into a blinding orgasm that has me screaming his name at the top of my lungs.

He's relentless in stretching out my pleasure for as long as possible, his tongue roughly continuing the torture of my clit. I twine my fingers in his hair, grip his head, and clamp my thighs around his head as my orgasm rolls from one into another unending burst of pleasure. He keeps up the pressure until he's wrung two orgasms in a row out of me, leaving me in a boneless heap, spread eagle on his mattress, my bra twisted around my waist.

His gaze is predatory as he pulls off his shirt and pants, looking down at me spread before him. "Now, tell me again that you're not my woman," he demands.

I close my eyes and accept my fate. "I can't," I say, realizing there was never any other option. From the minute I met Chase, he had me.

It dawns on me that I was daydreaming when I felt his fingertips trail along my face. His cock nudges my entrance and presses into me. He gives me one slow inch of his thick cock at a time. Almost teasing me with it. Then finally, he's seating to the hilt. All the air leaves my body in a whoosh the moment his bare chest meets mine. Heart to heart.

"God, I love you." His breath shimmers across my lips when he's imbedded fully.

Tears spill down my cheeks. I open my eyes and see the truth shining through his. I've waited months to hear him utter those words again.

Wrapping my legs around his waist, I enfold myself completely around this man I adore.

"I love you, more."

★★★★

Our lovemaking makes us twenty minutes late for dinner with his cousin Craig and his wife, Faith. Craig is tall and more distinguished looking than his siblings, though he smiles as big and as often as Carson. His wife is an elegant brunette. Her full lips stretch into a genuine grin as she offers me the seat next to her.

We fall into easy conversation with the couple, laughing a great deal throughout the meal. I really like Craig and Faith. They are new parents and spend dinner filling us with hysterical tales about their nine-month-old son, Caden.

Stories that horrify Chase and amuse the hell out of me. I've always wanted children, so I soak up every detail of their experience with their son.

Chase's phone rings throughout the entire dinner. Finally, I encourage him to take the call and settle the issue or he will continue to be distracted. He grins and kisses me on the temple as he excuses himself.

Just when he is out of earshot, Faith pounces. "So you and Chase seem pretty serious."

"Faith, really? You've met her once!" her husband admonishes. "I'm sorry, Gillian. She just can't help it. She's a matchmaker at heart."

"I just want everyone to be as happy as I am with you, babe." She bats her eyelashes and grins wickedly.

He rolls his eyes, clearly taken with his wife.

"I don't mind, really, Craig. Chase and I are enjoying our time together, and we're committed to one another," I say and look off into the distance.

Chase hovers by the bar. His hand rests on the elbow of a woman. Every so often he smiles and tips back his head in laughter. The woman turns around, and what I see floors me. She's tall with a curvy body wrapped in a formfitting blue silk dress. One delicate-looking hand pulls her long red hair over one shoulder. She looks a lot like me, as in, we could be sisters.

"What the hell is she doing here?" Craig says with a twinge of anger. "Excuse me." He stands and stomps towards Chase and the mystery woman.

"Who is that, Faith?" I never take my eyes off Chase and this woman.

He keeps touching her, clasping her elbow with one

hand and moving a piece of hair away from her face. That simple act is far too intimate to be an acquaintance. Jealousy rears its ugly head, and I push it deep down in the dark recesses of my subconscious.

Faith bites her lip and I stare at her expecting an answer. "That's Megan O'Brian." She looks at the woman with disdain, shooting daggers across the restaurant.

"And why is she important? Chase seems to know her well," I say quietly, trying to suppress the worry in my tone.

"Of course he knows her. That's Megan, *the* Megan," she emphasizes with quotes around the words "the Megan" as if that explains everything.

I shake my head and shrug my shoulders.

"His ex-fiancée, his first love…that Megan!" she clarifies.

I'm certain my skin goes white.

Faith scowls, watching the two interact. "I hate her. She almost wrecked our family." She stares at Chase, Craig, and "the Megan."

I still haven't been able to form a response, stunned by her revelation. He was going to get married? Married to her.

Faith finally tears her eyes away from the trio and focuses on me. Her face pales. "Oh, shit. You didn't know, did you?" She lowers her eyes.

Trying to appear as though hearing about Chase's engagement to another woman isn't gutting me alive, I shake my head.

Standing, I walk over to the group. Craig sees me and widens his eyes. He retreats the second I arrive, saying something about needing to get back to Faith and settling the check. Chase doesn't even look at me, his eyes still glued to the beauty before me. And she is just that, a true beauty. Her hair is a fiery red whereas mine is more a deep mahogany. Her doe eyes are a startling sky blue. Mine are the color of emeralds. She has luscious lips as pink and full as a plum rose.

She licks them surreptitiously, but I notice her game. She's overtly flirting with Chase. I tap his shoulder, and she looks at me, sizing me up from head to toe. Chase turns his head and his eyes go wide, a full deer in the headlights, kid caught with a hand in a cookie jar look, along with every other euphemism for one who has been caught red-handed.

"Um, Gillian, uh, this is Megan, um Megan O'Brian," he stammers.

The first time I have ever truly heard him at a loss for words.

I shake the woman's hand, though I'd rather punch her just for existing. "Pleased to meet you." I slide my hand around Chase's waist and snuggle in.

His hand loops around my shoulders.

"I'm sorry, Chase has never mentioned you before," I say, trying to sound nonchalant, but I'm anything but. I'm literally dying inside.

"He wouldn't have. What we had together was…" She pauses and looks deep into Chase's eyes. "It was very special," she finishes, breathless.

I can feel Chase's heartbeat pounding in his chest even though he locks me to his side. For some reason, he's still deeply affected by this woman.

"It was a long time ago," he says sternly.

She smiles coyly. "That it was," she says, biting her lips

and twiddling with her hair. "I still remember everything."

He bristles.

"Well, I'll see you at my uncle's sixtieth birthday bash next week, then?" He backs up a step and turns us sideways.

"I wouldn't miss it for the world." She flicks her hair and turns. "See you then, handsome," she says without even a nod in my direction.

Pulling away from him, I head back to the table quickly, and grab my handbag. My movements are shaky and a bit frazzled. I try to hide the overwhelming emotion as best I can.

"We'll see you next week, right, Gillian?" Faith asks. "We're flying in for your father's birthday extravaganza next weekend, right, babe?"

Craig nods.

Before I can answer Faith's question with the reply that I wasn't, in fact, invited to the birthday, nor had I heard about it before Megan mentioned it, Chase beats me to it.

"Of course she'll be by my side. Then, now, and forever," Chase answers smoothly.

I'm certain that was in effort to calm my irrational emotions. He lays a hand on my lower back, and even though it makes me feel better, I'm still seething.

Chase and I exit, a good two feet between our bodies at all times. I can hardly look at him for fear that I'll cry. We take the limo back to his penthouse in complete silence. The elephant looming over us restricts all the air in my body like a snake coiled tightly around me.

I storm into the bedroom and throw my purse on the bed. I whirl, and he's standing there, quietly watching me.

The lines in his face seem deeper, his eyes definitely

apologetic. "I'm sorry I didn't tell you about Megan," he offers.

Yeah right. "What else haven't you told me? Are you actually married? Got a couple of kids I should know about too?" The words fly from my lips on acid-soaked wings.

Chase shakes his head and frowns. "Look, Gillian, it was a long time ago. A lifetime ago."

"Back there, the way you looked at her, it was like it was yesterday. You still love her." My voice cracks.

Chase's eyes narrow, and the initial frown turns into a tight scowl. "No, I don't love her. I loved the idea of her." He pauses and takes a deep breath. "Look, all you need to know is that Megan and I are not together, and we never will be again. She hurt me too deeply." He pulls off his blazer and tosses it into the armchair. The tie follows it but slips off the chair onto the floor.

"I saw the way you looked at her. Sometimes I think that's the way you look at me." Tears fill my eyes, but I don't let them fall.

He comes over and pulls me into a tight embrace. "Gillian, I'm only going to say this once. Megan is history. She is not in my life. You are. You're the only woman I want." He looks into my eyes as the tears fall. "Do you trust me?" he asks—the most loaded question of the century.

"I want to," I say quietly. More tears stream down my cheeks.

He kisses them away. "That's good enough…for now."

Chase takes his time with my lips, kissing me so softly. It feels like a promise. For now, it is enough.

CHAPTER NINETEEN

The next week I throw myself into work and much-needed time with my girlfriends. The past few months have been life altering, wreaking havoc on emotions that I thought I buried long ago. When I cut ties with Justin, I avoided things and people that would put my thoughts and emotions into a state of flux. Unfortunately, there is no escaping Chase Davis, and, frankly, nothing could keep me from that man. He owns me in all the right ways. Even with his overbearing, possessive, demonstrative ways, I still want him. Need him. Have to have him in my life, now and hopefully forever.

Years ago when I sat in group therapy, I promised myself up and down I would never, could never, let a man control me. With Chase, there is no question. He doesn't use his power to hurt me. He never touches me in anger. Does he use me? Yes, he does. Often, and in the most pleasurable ways. He uses my body and my love for comfort and joy, not as a punching bag to get his rocks off or make himself feel manlier.

The only problem is after New York, I've conjured up all kinds of bad thoughts and scenarios as to why he couldn't possibly love me the same way I love him. It bothers me that he picks and chooses what information to share with me, never telling me how he feels. It's as if he just assumes

I know. After years of being told I was worthless, a whore, nothing but a fuck toy or the reverse, being treated like a porcelain doll leaves a girl a bit destroyed emotionally. Daily, I wish he'd tell me what it is he feels. For me. For us.

"Earth to Gigi," Bree says over her chai tea.

My three cohorts, the sisters I've never had, the best friends a girl could ever dream of having, are all staring at me.

"I'm sorry, guys. I just keep going over and over the trip in my head." I shake my head and take a sip of heaven. The vanilla latte is frothed to perfection with the exact amount of syrupy goodness needed to soothe and warm my soul.

"I'd be too, if Tommy tried to replace his ex with me." Maria drops the bomb that everyone, including me, has been thinking since my return a few days ago.

I close my eyes and take a deep breath. "I can't be Megan's substitute. We've been through so much over the past few months. I've told him I love him. He's shared those words with me. When he was saying them, I believed him." I cringe and rip at the napkin under my latte. "I can't be a replacement for 'the Bitch' can I?"

"Gigi, you're not!" Kat plays devil's advocate. "We've all seen the way he looks at you. He's told you he loves you."

Her small smile is sweet and loving. Exactly what I expect from the positive one in the group.

"Even Carson said he's never seen Chase so happy, and he's known him all of his life."

Her words make me feel the tiniest bit better. I place my hand on her arm and give it a reassuring squeeze.

"Maybe he just means happy *again*? Post-Megan," Maria counters.

My lip trembles, and I hide behind my latte. Sometimes having a best friend that has gone through the exact hell you have can work against you. That's why we have Kat and Bree to balance out our damaged experiences.

"That's not fair, Ria. It could be a coincidence that they look alike. We date men all the time that look similar. Everyone has a type. Hot redheads just happen to be Chase's," Bree says confidently and smiles sympathetically at me.

She's got a solid point.

"Thanks, guys. I appreciate your support, so much." I squeeze Bree and Kat's outstretched hands on each side of me.

Maria sits across the table, her arms crossed over one another in front of her chest. A thick scowl mars her pretty face. "Don't thank me. I still want to kick his *maravilloso* tight *culo!*" she says with venom. "His *culo* is mine! Just wait until I get me a *pieza*."

"Um, no. His *culo*, his ass, is mine, *chiquita*!" I say in mock anger.

The girls bust out in laughter at our parrying. Maria cracks a slight grin. She's pissed off at him, and once you've messed with the bull, you get the horns. Eventually she will have words with Chase, and I'm not looking forward to the aftermath of that discussion. Two hot-tempered possessive personalities duking it out. Actually it might be popcorn worthy. I could even sell tickets to the show and make a few bucks.

"Don't worry about seeing 'the Bitch' this weekend," Kat says. "Remember, I'm going to be there with Carson. I'll have your back."

Thank God! I can't imagine going to that event

knowing my doppelganger, the woman that came before me, is going to be there in all her beautiful glory. I just wish I knew what happened between them. If I did, it might help me believe that there really isn't anything between them now.

"That's true. Now I just have to find the most incredible dress. Something that will put 'the Bitch' to shame."

"Oh, hell, yeah." Bree high fives me. "Your body has been looking bangin'." She scopes out my form and nods her head.

"It's from all the banging she's been doing with Chase," Kat teases and giggles.

I throw my napkin at her. "Shut up. Like you haven't been with Carson every night since I set you up!"

"We need the details," Maria demands and cracks her neck from side to side. She looks tired, worn out. The show she's in has been kicking her butt good, although she'll never complain.

"Well, we've been having fun together." Kat's face turns red. "A lot of fun together. The man is a stallion in the bedroom. He does things to me that I…" She fans her face. "Let's just say that he is quite the multitasker. Always knows what to do with his hands while other parts of his body are busy!" She blushes crimson.

"*Fantástico*," Maria responds. Talking about sex always puts Maria in a good mood. Our little nympho.

"What about you, Bree?" Kat asks. "How's sexy Phil?"

I wait patiently for a reply. I don't really want to know the details about Bree and Phillip's sex life. but to be a good friend, I'm going to have to suck it up and deal with the icky. It's the same thing as finding out your brother is dating your best friend. Probably not the right analogy, seeing as I lost my virginity to Phillip. I banish the disgusting place my mind has gone and force myself to pay attention.

"We haven't really."

Bree stops as three wide-eyed women stare at her in shock.

"We're taking things slowly," she says.

"You haven't had sex with him?" spills from my mouth in a gush of words.

She looks around. "Shh. Jeez Louise, do you think they heard you in France?" Bree bites her lip and spins a curl of hair around her finger. Oh no, she's embarrassed. Nervous rather. "We've done everything else!"

"Is his *pene roto*?" Ria asks.

"No! His penis is not broken, Ria! We're just taking our time," Bree explains. "We've had very little alone time. I've been crazy busy at the studio, and on the days that I'm available, he has Anabelle. He doesn't want to have sex with her in the house." She crosses her arms and blows a puff of air out over her bangs.

"Oh, honey, he needs to have her grandparents watch her for the weekend so you two can have some much-needed alone time together. I'll suggest it to him," I offer.

The rest of the girls nod.

"You know, your birthday is in a couple weeks. That would be an excellent time," I say. "Also, us girls can trade off some nights here and there to give the two of you some alone time. Okay?"

Kat and Maria both nod their heads and agree to babysit. We all adore Anabelle. She truly is an angel child.

"Thanks, guys, I'd really like that." Bree looks at her

watch. "Shit! I have a class in fifteen minutes. Gotta run!" She jumps up and hugs each of us in turn. "*Besos*!"

Three rounds of "Besos!" call back to her. We each finish our coffee and head off to meet with our men. I have to buy an amazing dress and then stop at the apartment and pick up some clothes for the weekend before meeting up with Chase. I'm dreading seeing "the Bitch" again but plan to blow her and Chase away with my outfit.

My cell phone pings and I look down, realizing it's the unknown prankster again.

To: Gillian Callahan
From: Unknown
Never forget who you belong to. I won't wait much longer.

What does that even mean? Chase knows I belong to him. He's insanely possessive, but I can't imagine Chase would send weird messages to me though he can be unconventional at times. Regardless, I close the phone and head off on my mission. I don't have time for cryptic messages from strange people.

★ ★ ★ ★

I stumble into the house, holding the new dress I spent a fortune on. Chase didn't lie about putting money into my account. When I went to the ATM for some quick cash, the receipt showed that the crazy sneak put a hundred thousand dollars in my bank account. I almost threw up at the thought of that much money. My car isn't even worth ten thousand dollars, and a hundred thousand is more money than I make in a year. True to his word, he paid off all my credit cards.

So with all this newfound money I went straight to Gucci and bought a five thousand dollar dress and a seven hundred dollar pair of shoes to match. Chase will be ecstatic that I finally splurged, but the thought of spending that much money on one outfit makes me want to hurl. The end result will be worth the spend I keep reminding myself. I have to please not only Chase, but also his mother and family, and now put "The Bitch" to shame. She's not the only redhead who can turn a few heads. I'm stacked, and tonight, everyone's going to know it, especially my man.

Since our return from New York, I've only spent one evening with Chase. The girls and I devised a plan to make him miss me. The idea was to put a little space between us. I want him crazy with desire for me by the time the party rolls around.

Over the past week, I made every excuse in the book to get out of spending every night with him. We came home on Sunday evening from NYC, and by Tuesday, he insisted I stay the night with him. It was lovely. We had dinner on the rooftop garden and made love a couple times, squashing any strangeness lingering from New York and meeting my twin.

After that, I made certain that the girls needed me for random things so I couldn't be available to stay with him. Chase was not pleased. The first two days he became downright indignant. I had to be careful, because I didn't want my ruse to make him resent my soul sisters. That's the last thing I need. Instead, I promised him it would be worth the wait and to trust me. Using the "trust" word goes a long way between us.

I set the bags on the table, and Maria comes into the living room dressed in a towel, another towel wrapped around her hair. She looks like a goddess. The damn woman could be a swimsuit model with all her mocha skin, long hair, and dancer's body. I love her and hate her at the same time.

"Hey, *bonita*, some flowers arrived for you when I got home." She gestures to the kitchen table. "Looks like operation miss me is working." She shimmies her hips and points to the table.

Two dozen red long-stemmed roses stand proud and happy. I look at the flowers and cringe but force a smile. I hate roses, but it's the thought that counts.

Keep saying that to yourself, Gigi, and eventually you'll believe it.

It's the thought that counts.

I pick up the phone and dial Chase's number while I finger the card. His "Hello, sweet cheeks," melts my heart. Looks like he's got a new one to test.

"Thank you for the flowers." I smile into the receiver.

"What flowers?" he asks with a confused tone.

"The two dozen red roses that arrived while I was out today," I respond, flipping over the card.

"I'd love to take credit for sending you flowers, baby, but I wouldn't have sent roses. I know you prefer daisies over any flower."

There was nothing that could remove the smile on my face at the thought that he knows my favorite flower. "Who are they from?" His voice holds a twinge of jealousy.

"I don't know. Let me see." I feel uncertain that it wasn't him who sent them. I open the card and read it. As I stand there, dumbstruck, the card drops to the table, slowly making its descent like a leaf falling off a tree in late

October. The hair on my neck stands up and my belly turns sour.

"Gillian, who are they from?" Chase asks in my ear.

I stare at the card, not saying anything. Bone-deep fear slithers along my spine and coils around my heart squeezing.

"Gillian? What's going on?"

I can't really hear him. It's as if my ears have been hit with a burst of air so hard that everything around me sounds as if it's coming from a super loud bass drum.

I close my eyes and take a deep breath. "Um, uh," I stammer.

Chase's voice filters through the noise in my head. "Baby, read the card to me…now." His tone is forceful and clipped. When Chase gets mad, he becomes extremely direct and snappy.

Gillian,

You don't belong to him. You belong to me. I will have you. It's only a matter of time.

You're mine…bitch!

I read the card to him, and chills scream down my spine as fear takes hold. Maria comes and pulls the card from my shaking hand and reads it. Her spine stiffens. She yanks the phone from my other hand. I can hear Chase's outbursts through the phone but am unable to make sense of anything. I stand still. Fear envelopes me and stuns me cold. I shiver as I listen to Maria's conversation with Chase.

"We'll see you in twenty minutes. I won't leave her. I'm calling Tommy now," she says and hangs up with Chase.

She walks me over to the couch and sets me down. She pulls the afghan off the back and wraps it around my shoulders. "You okay?" she asks, searching my eyes.

I may have nodded or said something in reply, but I can't recall. Everything is going numb, and color and sound seem to fade in and out as I sit.

She leaves the room with her phone to her ear. "Tommy, I need you…now!" she says into the phone.

I don't hear the rest of her conversation as she enters her bedroom. The moment I realize I'm all alone in the room, fear takes over. I look around the space, my eyes scanning every surface. Maria returns a few minutes later in yoga pants and an oversized shirt that hangs off one shoulder. A tank top underneath helps cover her large chest. It's a very *Flashdance* look. She brushes out her wet hair, assessing me and tapping her foot.

"Tea?" she asks but I don't respond. She must take that as a sign of approval because for the next several minutes, I watch her move around the kitchen.

As my heart stops pounding the vast, heavy rhythm, the fear of the note accompanying those flowers starts to dissipate. I take a deep breath, trying to calm my rattled nerves. Who would send something like that? *Justin* is the only name that comes to mind. All of a sudden, an incessant banging startles me, and I grip my arms around my legs. A deep tremble coats me as I pull my legs up into my chest and cling to my calves in a protective ball.

Maria rushes to the door, and I hear Chase.

"Where is she?" he says, panicked. He practically runs into the room.

I jump up the moment I see him. His arms go around me in a tight embrace, and I rub my cheek against his solid chest. He cups my neck and holds me to him tightly. Behind him, I hear Jack and Maria speaking. She shows him the flowers and the note. He takes pictures of both, and I squeeze Chase tighter. Another knock on the door has me trembling once more.

"Baby, you're shivering," he says and leads me back to the couch.

I crawl into his lap like a child. He doesn't seem to mind, just holds me tightly, pets my hair, and caresses my back in long, soothing swipes.

Tom comes in with a police officer in uniform. I grip Chase's arms tightly. Seeing a police officer in my home reminds me of times I'd prefer to forget. Too many times a policeman or woman took my statement after I'd endured one of Justin's beatings and the neighbors called the cops. I cringe at the memory and try to find the strength I need to get through this.

Everything happens so quickly I just go through the motions. The officer takes my statement. The card is put in plastic and taken for evidence. Even though the situation isn't dire, Tom being a long time well-known and respected detective and Chase being personal friends with the Chief of Police means they aren't taking any chances.

"Did the suspect ever contact you prior to this?" the officer asks.

I shake my head.

"No," I say and stop for a moment. The weird text messages come to mind.

"What is it, baby?"

"Um, maybe. Chase, can you grab my phone?"

He furrows his eyebrows, and his jaw sets in a grim line. He pulls my phone out of my purse and hands it to me. My hands shake, but I manage to bring up the texts.

Chase grabs the phone before I can hand them to the officer and scans each one quickly. "Fuck, Gillian. There are three, and they start back over a week ago!" he says with contempt. "Why didn't you tell me about them?" He shakes his head, holding his hand into a tight fist.

He hands the phone to the officer. He reads them, taking notes.

"I didn't think they were a big deal. And I..." I swallow the lump in my throat, realizing that not mentioning them was a bad idea. "I thought they were a wrong number and forgot about them until the flowers and the one I received today. I was... I was busy. I just ignored them." I feel like a complete idiot now. Could Chase have done something sooner? It's obvious this person has a crush on me. A secret admirer perhaps? Unless it's Justin, and if that's the case, there's not much anyone can do. He will find me, and, if he does, he may do worse than beat me up. He's the only man besides Chase that has ever used the word "mine" in reference to me.

"I'm going to keep this phone. See if we can trace the texts," the officer says. "Maybe we'll get a hit, but it's likely that the perpetrator used a phone you can buy at any department store for thirty bucks and tossed it after."

Responding seems useless right now. Chase will bulldoze over anything, and I can't muster the effort to care. I'd rather be in his arms feeling safe and sound then dealing with the repercussions of some obsessed freak.

"Don't worry about your phone. I'll have a new phone delivered to the penthouse tomorrow. One that has a tracking device and a new phone number," Chase says.

"Thank you," I say quietly, choosing not to mention

anything about the additional security. If it is Justin, I'll need the extra security. "Are we done? I just want to take a shower and go to bed."

"Not here you're not. Neither of you are staying here." Chase gestures at Maria and me.

Maria balks and protests, but Tom stops her cold.

"You will stay with me," Tom says. "At least until this asshole is found."

Maria rolls her eyes and stomps into her room, complaining in Spanish. I choose not to argue with two overpossessive pissed-off males. In past experience, the combination can turn volatile. Tom follows Maria into her room, and I head to mine. Once inside, I grab the suitcase I emptied a few days ago and plop it on my bed. Chase enters and leans against the wall. His appearance is more disheveled than usual, and his hair looks like he's combed his fingers through it a time too many.

"How long am I staying with you?" I ask over my shoulder wanting to pack the right amount of clothing.

"As long as it takes…forever maybe."

He pauses when I look up, trying to gage his sincerity. This is all happening far too quickly for my taste.

"Chase," I start but am cut off by his arms around my waist and his chin nestled into the crook of my neck. I clasp my hands over his and lean back into him. I always feel so safe in his arms. But I'm not moving in with him, and he has to know that. "I'm not moving in with you because some immature lovesick puppy is choosing to mess with my head."

"We'll see," he says noncommittally.

I roll my eyes and turn to face him. I kiss him deeply

and he nips at my bottom lip playfully, lightening the heavy mood. I love him more for that.

"Thank you for coming so quickly."

"Gillian, I will always run to you, remember?" He smiles and kisses me softly again. "Now let's get your things."

He helps me pull together a good week's worth of clothing. He assures me that anything else will be taken care of. A messenger will pick up our mail each day and deliver it to both Maria and me. Our plants will be watered, and the house will be watched. If the perpetrator tries to access the home, Chase's people will know it.

★ ★ ★ ★

The next few days go by in a blur. Chase has taken overprotective to an all-time high. First thing Friday morning, I'm introduced to my very own personal bodyguard. Austin looks like Sylvester Stallone on steroids. His nose has seen better days and looks as if it's been broken a few times. His shoulders span a good three feet, and he's over six feet tall. The man couldn't be a day over thirty but has already served a decade in armed forces. Even though I fought Chase on the concept of personal protection, I do prefer Rambo over the linebacker who hates me. At least Rambo doesn't look at me with contempt and answers every question I ask with good manners saying, "Yes, ma'am and no, ma'am." His Southern drawl surprised me at first, but I find the quality endearing.

"Will you be eating lunch in today, ma'am?" he asks as we drive to the office.

"I'll be meeting my girlfriends, but I'll take a taxi," I

tell him.

"No can do, ma'am. Sorry, against orders."

"What orders?" I ask.

"Mr. Porter and Mr. Davis briefed me on the situation. You tell me what time you need to be somewhere, and I will be ready at reception. I'm not leaving the premises. I will be doing rounds the first few days, checking the area, ensuring that people can't come and go unannounced."

The information is mind-boggling and annoying. I decide it's best not to fight it. Hopefully my secret admirer or *stalker,* as Chase puts it, gets caught quickly. Honestly, the whole thing seems utterly ridiculous. I keep thinking that if it were Justin he would have already shown his cards. He was never a patient man. He took what he wanted when he wanted. Nothing would stand in his way, though a Rambo clone could definitely thwart his attempts.

"Okay, well, pick me up at eleven forty-five. I'll be meeting the girls for lunch," I tell him.

"A Ms. De La Torre, a Ms. Simmons, and a Ms. Bennett," he reads from a clipboard he set in the passenger seat.

"Those are the ones," I say and open the car door.

He jumps out, comes around, and opens it the rest of the way. He scans the area. "Ma'am, please don't get out of the car until I've assessed the location's safety. I will always open your door, not to mention my mama would take a switch to my hide if I didn't open the door for a lady, even if it wasn't my job." He smiles.

I like my Rambo more and more. He's sweet, nothing like the stuffy, stuck-up suit-wearing linebacker Jack.

Austin walks me in, and as I'm about to say goodbye, we're buzzed through the glass doors to my office. My promotion came complete with a small office about half the size of Taye's but situated right next to his.

"I can find my way." I laugh.

"Ma'am, I'd like to see where you sit, your surroundings and such so that I may commit it to memory." He's so serious. He scans the halls. Overall he looks pretty scary. Then again, Chase would only hire someone who was well trained with the proper credentials. Probably makes double my salary, too.

As I lead the way to my office, I decide to test him. "So what's my middle name?"

"Grace," he answers.

"And the middle names of my best friends?" I toy with him.

"Bree Elizabeth, Kathleen Michelle, and Ms. De La Torre doesn't have one," he rattles off without spending a moment to think about it.

"Damn, you're good," I say, shocked. The guy has done his homework.

"Thank you, ma'am," he says shyly, a bit of pink dotting his cheeks.

A Rambo lookalike who blushes. This is my life.

"So one more thing."

He nods as we continue walking toward my office.

"Would you take a bullet for me?" I ask.

"Yes. No questions asked," he says flatly.

"Seriously? Why?" I'm flabbergasted by his answer.

"My job is to protect you, and if that means taking a bullet, I will. I've done it before, and I'll do it again." We reach the door to my office.

I'm genuinely surprised by his admission. I wonder who

he took a bullet for. Was it during his time as a soldier? Was it while serving as a bodyguard for someone else? Where did he get shot? A million questions run through my mind as I open the door and stop dead in my tracks. Two dozen red roses sit dead center in the middle of my desk like a homing beacon to Hell. Austin senses my unease and pulls me behind him, his right hand going to the gun holster at his hip. I had no idea the man was even carrying a weapon. He looks around the room.

"Those shouldn't be here." I point to the roses.

He nods, pulls his phone out, presses one button, and brings it to his ear.

"Mr. Porter, we have a problem," he says. "She received more flowers, this time at work."

His lips are drawn tight and he pulls at the card. He opens it without asking. I could complain but I'm too scared and choose to let him handle it and stand utterly silent.

"She's right here. I'd rather not read this in her presence," he says into the phone.

I pull the card from his fingers lightning fast. He scowls.

"It was addressed to me. I have every right to know what it says, Austin," I snap at him.

He has the good manners to look apologetic.

Gillian,

You can't hide from me. I know where you work. I know where you live. If I don't have you soon, I'll make sure no one does.

You're mine…bitch!

I fall into my office chair and put my face into my hands. Austin reads the card to Jack over the phone.

"Yes, I understand, sir. I'll bring her to him now." He hangs up the phone. "We have to leave, now. Jack will handle the situation, but Mr. Davis wants to see you at Davis Industries now."

At this point I just nod and stand, feeling completely numb.

"Do you want to grab anything, Ms. Callahan? You won't be coming back to work for a while."

I close my eyes and take a calming breath. I gather up my laptop and grab the ten donor prospects files I was working on and a few project briefs. Everything else I can have messengered later. I'm sure Chase will call Mr. Hawthorne and explain the situation and my need to work remotely for the time being.

Austin ushers me quickly to the car and settles me in. The ride to Chase's office goes by in a blur. It's as if I'm stuck in a walking coma. Before I can grasp where I am, the elevator dings and Austin leads me down the hallway to Chase's office. I walk alongside him blindly, not saying anything. His hand is firm on my bicep as he leads me to an office I've been to a million times already. Not like I need to be escorted, but if I'm being honest, the hand holding onto me keeps me up and moving forward. I just need to see Chase. My rock. I see Dana jump up from her desk and run to the door and open it for us.

"She's here, Chase," she says as I'm guided through the doorway.

"Thank you, Dana, Mr. Campbell. That will be all," he says as he walks over to me.

I saw him this morning, but he's never looked so good. My face crumbles the closer he gets, and I lose it. The door behind me clicks, and I flinch. His arms are around me, holding me, instilling light, warmth and the much-needed safe feeling I have only in this man's embrace.

"Oh, baby, you're okay. I'm here."

The tears come hard and fast as I cry into his chest, the situation finally taking its toll. Someone wants to hurt me. Again.

"I don't know what to do." I sniff and he hands me his handkerchief. "I have no idea who this guy is or why he wants to hurt me." The tears stream down my face and Chase wipes them with both thumbs on each side of my cheek.

"You didn't do anything, baby. Don't worry, my people will handle this. You just need to lie low for a while. In the meantime, you can work in an empty office here with Mr. Campbell and Jack on point to ensure you're safe."

Rubbing my nose into his chest, I hug him tightly. When I scrape my nails along his sides, he reacts to my touch, his cock hardening. A powerful sensation rushes through my system and something deep within me snaps.

Control. I *need* control of something. I tip my head up and cover his lips with mine, kissing him deeply. I start to walk backward toward the long couches as the kiss becomes heated. Once I feel the soft leather bump against my calf, I turn around and push him into a seated position. He falls into a heap, a concerned but still sexy grin plastered across his face. I shimmy his knees apart with my hands and kneel between his spread legs. Even as his eyes assess my mood, he lets me take the lead.

"Sexy, what are you doing?" He grins. He usually only uses that particular pet name for me when we're being intimate.

"I'm taking what's mine," I say and pull his belt open,

unbutton his pants, and pull down the zipper. I rub my palm against the large cotton covered bulge and watch him close his eyes and tip his head back, groaning.

"What do you want?" he asks coyly, knowing exactly what I'm going to do. He's playing along, and I love him for it.

I slip my hands to the sides of his slacks and pull them down his hips, dragging his boxer briefs up and over his straining erection. Once I have his pants down to his ankles, I admire his cock. It's large, long, and thick enough to fill me to the brim. But not now. I have other things in mind. A pearl of liquid builds at the pretty pink crown of his cock, and I lean forward, my hands on his hips. I inhale his musky male scent and salivate. He watches me as I flick just the tip of my tongue out, capture that bead of his essence, and lick my lips on a moan.

"Jesus, all I can think about is stuffing my cock in that pretty little mouth of yours."

His words are strained and laced with sex. They rocket my desire to a boiling point.

I bring my head down and lap the entire length of his cock, enjoying the answering moan I receive for my efforts. I nibble and drag my lips across every speck of his manhood, leaving no space untouched, un-licked by my tongue. He moves his hips toward my face but doesn't pull my head down. His hands lightly entangle in my hair and lovingly caress my scalp. It's not what I want or what I need right now.

I suck his cock into my mouth as far as it will go in this position and hollow my cheeks on the way back up. His ass almost levitates off the chair to keep my lips from leaving his shaft.

"Fuck, Gillian," he says.

"I don't want nice, Chase. I want you to fuck my mouth, hard. I need it." I don't recognize my own voice.

He doesn't need to be told twice. When I bring my lips around his cock, his hand comes around the base of my neck and he pulls me against his body, his cock sliding all the way down my throat and back again. I swirl my tongue around the tip and groan as he rocks up into my throat repeatedly, barely allowing me the time to breathe before my throat is again filled with his cock.

Before I can finish him off, he pulls my head back, fingers tightly pulling my hair at the root, keeping my wet lips just off the tip of his cock. He yanks my hair and kisses me hard, devouring my mouth. "Need to fuck you," he says. "Mark you as mine."

I nod, fully understanding his need. We both have ridiculous possessive habits, and this stalker issue is bringing them to the surface ten-fold.

He stands and pulls me up. Then he leans me over the arm of the couch, roughly pushing up my skirt. I hear only his heavy breathing and the shredding of lace as he rips the sides of my panties off. Two fingers plunge deeply inside my soaked sex from behind. I scream in pleasure. He pushes his fingers deep as I push back against those searching digits. He fucks me with his fingers a few times, prepping me, and then they're gone. I mewl in protest just as the wide-knobbed head of his cock notches at my entrance and impales me in one hard thrust. His fingers grip my waist as he presses hard, the angle allowing maximum depth.

"You. Are. Mine. I. Am. Yours," Chase roars, holding my

hands behind my back to arc my body. His fingers yank at my waist, pulling me back to meet his brutal thrusts.

He fucks me harder than he has ever fucked me before. Chase is relentless in his thrusts. His balls slap against my lower lips, making my clit swell and tingle painfully. Every thrust is as if he's trying to tear me in half. He puts his thumb in his mouth, wets it, and then circles it around the tiny hole of my anus. On a deep thrust he shoves his thumb deep into my backside. I cry out as he fucks both my holes crudely. I can't see, I can't think, I can only feel every delicious inch of his cock hammering into me over and over again, bringing me to the point of no return.

"You're"—*thrust*—"my"—*thrust*—"woman!"

On the last word, he slams into me so hard my teeth rattle. We both come, screaming into the open office. His body falls over mine, and I struggle to hold us both up in my position over the arm of the couch. We take huge gulping breaths, trying to come down from our high but never wanting to leave heaven.

"Shit, baby, I don't know what came over me," he says. "Are you okay? Did I hurt you?" His voice is concerned and breaches my post-orgasmic haze.

"Do I look hurt to you?" I grin saucily and stand. "Never been better. I'm also sorry I came at you like that. I definitely didn't intend to have the reaction I did when I got here." I slip my skirt in place and walk to the bathroom across the room.

He pulls up his own pants and follows me, hovering near the door. I do my business, wondering why he's content with watching, but keep the thought to myself. He hands me a warm wet washcloth, and I remove any additional residue from our lovemaking.

"Anytime, baby." He grins wickedly. "Any time you want to take advantage of me sexually, consider it an open invitation." He laughs.

We right ourselves, and Chase informs me that he needs to settle a few things before we leave for the day. I decide to visit Phillip on the twentieth floor and catch up with him. I phone Maria, explain what happened with the second round of flowers, and that I won't be meeting them for lunch today. She says she'll notify the girls but will expect a call to touch base with them this weekend.

★ ★ ★ ★

Phillip envelopes me in a huge bear hug, and I hold on a little tighter than normal. He walks me to the cafeteria to sit and catch up over a sandwich. Halfway through the cafeteria line, he realizes that we're being followed.

"Gigi, there's a huge guy I've never seen before following us. He's been watching us ever since you met me on the twentieth floor. He took the elevator with us, and now he's standing off to the side wall watching you like a hawk. Actually, I think he's watching me more than you."

A snicker bubbles out of me when he notices my Rambo.

I wave to Austin, and he gives a chin lift but continues to scan the room, ever on guard.

"That's Austin Campbell, my own personal bodyguard, courtesy of one rich control freak boyfriend." I smile.

Phillip laughs and waves to Austin.

We sit and eat our lunch and catch up on everything.

I explain what went down in New York with "The Bitch" and then about both flower deliveries, as well as the fear that's starting to cripple me and steal my freedom. He didn't like hearing about "the Bitch" and the fact that she looks like me. He's suspicious of Chase's motives, too. He doesn't know Chase like I do, though. Even though the past few months have given him ample opportunity, the two of them really haven't clicked like I hoped they would. Won't stop me from wishing for it.

"So, Phil, what's up with you and Bree?" I decide to go straight for the belt, though not the same way I went for the belt with Chase. I grin, remembering how I took his cock deep into my throat. I cough and continue. "I can't believe you haven't slept with her yet."

His mouth drops open. "She told you?" He shuffles a hand through his hair and scratches the back of his neck.

"Are you kidding, dumbass? She told all of us that after four months you haven't taken her to bed. What's the matter? Maria thinks your dick is broken."

"God, this is so embarrassing." He shakes his head and looks down at his food. "I just… I don't know. I'm feeling gun-shy since Angela. Bree's different. She's the kind of girl you marry, not the kind of girl you love and leave."

Understanding dawns on me. "You don't want to fall for her? Do you think you'd be betraying Angela if you did?"

He nods solemnly. "Something like that, yeah," he admits. He's such an amazing man. He doesn't want to soil his dead wife's memory or the relationship they had by allowing himself to love again.

"Phil, Angela loved you and would want you to be

happy. She would want you to find love again. Bree's not trying to be Angela. She knows she could never be her, and she'd never try. She wants to love you in her way, share a relationship with you, one that's only between you and her."

"I guess. I just… I'm not ready for marriage again."

"You don't have to be. Bree's not ready either. Just have fun. Let yourself enjoy the feeling of falling in love."

He gifts me a small smile.

"And for God's sake, get a frickin' babysitter and fuck your woman already!" I say with as much raunch as I can muster.

He chokes on his soda.

I pat him hard on the back as he hacks and coughs.

"Jeez Louise, Gigi. Okay, okay!"

"Her birthday is in a couple weeks. I'll be deeply disappointed if you don't plan something spectacular for her, and I don't mean a present." I nudge him in the side with my elbow.

"All right already, Dr. Ruth. I have to go back to work." His eyes are bright and he pulls me into a Phil-style bear hug. All arms with a side dose of heavy squeezes.

"Yeah, I'm going to go to the penthouse and take a long hot bath. I love you." I kiss his cheek and give him a hug.

"Don't let 'the Bitch' get you down tomorrow at the party, Gigi. Most women pale in comparison to your beauty and brains. And if Chase needs a good ass kicking to remind him of what he has, just say the word." He enters the elevator and goes down.

I hit the button prepared to go up to the penthouse.

"Where are we going now, Ms. Callahan?" Austin asks

as I place my thumb into the LED screen to access the penthouse. It scans, and the elevator lifts.

"I'm heading to the penthouse for a long bath and a nap. You going to watch me take a bath?" I ask with a wink.

He blushes a deep red. "Um, no ma'am. I'll just check the premises and wait in the security viewing room off the entryway. If you plan to leave, you know where I'll be." He continues, "You staying home for the night, ma'am?" The elevator opens to the penthouse floor.

"Home," the word dangles on my tongue. The thought of this being my home isn't altogether unpleasant. It's downright appealing. I'm getting more used to sharing a space with Chase and rather enjoy waking up next to him each morning. Getting kissed like the dickens before he's off to work each day isn't too bad a start to a new day either.

"Yes, Austin, I do believe I'll be staying home for the night."

CHAPTER TWENTY

I add the finishing touches on my makeup and then take a long look at myself in the mirror. The Gucci black lace dress hugs my curves like a second skin. The slip dress underneath is white and shines through the large lace cutouts. With the white inner layer, my breasts and hips are accentuated, exactly the look I was going for. The boat-style neckline delightfully cuts across my clavicle. My breasts look like two ripe peaches itching to be bitten. I turn and view my back. The dress dips really low in a deep U shape, completely open. The scalloped edge does naughty things to the line of my back, making the dips in my lower back perfectly visible. Chase loves an exposed back. I can already imagine the tips of his fingers trailing along the bare skin and down my spine.

The dress lies daintily against the top of my knees. I step into my new heels. The heels are platform and add an additional five inches to my height. I plan to tower over "the Bitch" tonight. My hair falls in long mahogany-red curls around my face. Very circa 1940s Veronica Lake. An extra serum adds that much-needed dose of shine. One last swipe of "Perfect Peach" lip gloss, and I'm ready to dazzle.

I enter the living room, and Chase is on his cell phone. I listen for a moment.

"Yeah, we'll be leaving here shortly. Gillian's almost ready." He turns towards me and his mouth drops open. "Uh, yeah. Um, I'll see ya there," he says into the phone and hangs up. He roams slowly over my body and settles on my eyes.

"Gill… God, Gillian you take my breath away," Chase says in a breathy deep timber.

The sound fills me with warmth, spreading heat through my veins like a fine twenty-year-old whiskey.

Chase himself looks good enough to eat. He's wearing a black tuxedo, a white shirt, and a black vest. A black tie is tucked into the vest. He's incredibly handsome, and not for the first time, I'm reminded how incredibly lucky I am to have him. For a moment, I fantasize that it's my wedding day and Chase is standing there looking at me like I'm everything there ever was in the world. Except it's not my wedding day. But he's definitely looking at me with a reverence that makes my heart pound a heavy beat.

"I'm one lucky bastard," he says as he takes my hand and kisses my palm. He inhales the perfume at my wrist. "I love the way you smell," he says sweetly, placing a warm kiss against the tender skin.

I smile, and he pulls me toward him. My hands land on his finely muscled chest. I adjust his tie making sure it's perfect. It already is but doing something with my hands makes me feel more at ease.

"We're going to have fun tonight," he promises.

I doubt it. I keep that thought to myself.

"Shall we?" He holds out his elbow formally.

Grinning, I clasp my arm around his.

"Since the party is so large, we'll have Jack and Mr.

Campbell attending. That way, regardless of where we are, the bases are covered."

I roll my eyes but stay silent. I don't want to think about my stalker right now, but I'm happy he's taking precautions.

"Any more texts?" I ask.

Chase stiffens.

I look at him in warning, silently willing him to just tell me the truth and not keep something so important from me.

"Yes, as a matter of fact there has been one a day since you last received the flowers."

"And what did they say?"

He stops and places a hand to my chin. "Baby, I'm not going to tell you. Not because I don't want to be honest with you, but because I don't want those things in your head. They're in mine, and they are killing me. Okay?"

Besides telling me about his mom and dad, this is quite possibly the most honest and forthcoming he's been with me.

"I trust you to take care of me," I whisper.

He swallows. His gaze is so intense and holds mine for what feels like an eternity. Right there I feel it all. His love. His fear. His hatred of the person threatening me.

"I'll always take care of you, Gillian. No one will ever hurt you again," he promises.

And I know that if it's within his power, it's the truth. Only not everything will always be within in his power, regardless of how much money he has. Money isn't the end all be all. Sometimes there are really sick and twisted people in this world, and unfortunately, one of them wants a piece of me and I'm afraid he just might get it.

"Any leads on Justin?"

He grimaces and continues towards the door. "Unfortunately, no, but I have twenty men on it."

Twenty? Jesus! I nod as we make our way down the elevator. Our bodyguards are waiting.

Austin holds open my door. "You look lovely this evening, Ms. Callahan, ma'am," he says as I enter the stretch limo.

"Why thank you, Austin. You're very kind." I smile and slide into the car.

Chase claps Austin on the shoulder playfully. "You know she's taken, right?" He cocks his head and grins.

"Oh, yes, sir. I know she's your lady. I wasn't intending to…"

"He's kidding, Austin, relax." I shake my head. Poor guy. Chase, even when acting playful, can come off authoritative.

"Whew. Okay. Anything else, Mr. Davis, sir?" Austin says.

"As my lady says, relax, but not too much. She's priority number one. Nothing happens to her, got it?"

And there is my overprotective control freak. I was enjoying playful Chase far too much. I knew control freak Chase was just around the corner.

"Of course, no one but you gets to her," he says.

Chase grips his shoulder again. "Good man," he says and slaps the top of the limo. "Jack, we ready to shove off?" Chase enters the limo.

Austin gets into the passenger seat.

"We'll be there in thirty minutes, Mr. Davis," Jack replies.

The ride is smooth, and Chase holds my hand as we sit

in companionable silence. Eventually Chase takes one of his business calls. It really doesn't bother me. I thought his need to be available at all times to his work was going to drive a wedge between our relationship, but for the most part, he's really good at turning it off.

We arrive at the Davis mansion, and I see large white tents covering the grounds. Huge Chinese lantern-style lamps loop across the gardens in varying shades of white, blue, green, and pink. The limo stops, and Austin opens the door for us. We're greeted by waiters holding tall champagne flutes. I choose one of the pink ones, feeling a bit girly for my choice. We walk through a huge mansion-style home with people milling everywhere. Music wafts in the distance. Chase holds my hand, and I follow him through the throngs, silently taking in the opulent surroundings.

"Was this your childhood home?" I ask.

Chase nods and smiles.

"It's so...big and beautiful."

"My uncle taught me early on to enjoy the finer things in life."

He probably was literally fed with silver spoons. I imagine a cherub-faced little boy with brown locks falling into his eyes running around this huge house.

We exit to the garden, which isn't really a garden at all. It's the size of a football field, surrounded with lush greenery and flowers of all kinds. Marble statues litter the grass here and there. A giant fountain bursts water ten feet into the sky. Lights bounce off the water, making the streams look multicolored. Chase leads me to a large group of men in tuxedos. I can see his Uncle Charles in the center telling a story. Chase pushes through the people, and his uncle clasps him in a tight embrace.

"Chase, my boy," he says happily. "I see you brought the lovely Ms. Callahan this evening." He lets Chase go and grasps my hand, pulling it to his lips.

"Happy Birthday, Mr. Davis. Thank you for having me," I say.

"The pleasure is all mine, and you can call me Charles. I imagine 'Mr. Davis' gets cumbersome when you have your own Mr. Davis to contend with." He tips his head toward Chase.

He's obviously very fond of Chase, and it warms my heart to know how he came to live with his uncle early in his childhood.

"Chase speaks very highly of you," I offer.

He looks at Chase with a grin. "He does? Sharing my secrets, eh, Chase?"

So far I really like his family. Well, I haven't spent much time with Cooper aside from that one charity dinner. And his mother didn't seem too thrilled with my presence, but the rest of the Davis clan are top-notch.

Carson pops up behind me "Gillian, looking stunning as ever," he says as he comes up to hug me.

Kat is close behind him, and she is drop-dead gorgeous. She's in a form-fitting silver-sequined dress with a sparkling fringe cut at mid-thigh. Her legs go for days, coupled with strappy silver heels.

Wrapping my arms around her, I hug her. "Kat, wow. Did you make this one?" I ask, pulling back to assess her dress more closely.

"I did." She smiles wide. "If you look really close, you can see tiny pink sequins setting off the silver," she adds.

Bending over, I assess them up close finding what I expect, impeccable workmanship. She will definitely design for the stars one day.

"It's incredible. I'm digging the fringe! So hip, so now!" I gush.

"You're biased," she says lamely, but she can't hide the huge smile plastered on her face. "I just wish I'd had the chance to make your dress," she says with a pout. "Though Gucci does wonderful things for those curves. Damn girl! You are smokin' hot."

I smile wide as we spend a couple more minutes going over the fine details of our attire. Then Carson pulls Kat away to meet his family for the first time as his significant other. I stare off into the distance, holding onto the concrete banister. Chase is enjoying the company of his uncle and his friends, and I want him to feel comfortable without having me glued to his side. I sip from my glass and enjoy the view of the lush gardens and the smell of fresh jasmine in the air. The yard reminds me of what Shakespeare's *A Midsummer Night's Dream* would look like.

"You know, you're better looking than I expected."

A voice from behind me startles me enough to twirl around coming face-to-face with Megan "the Bitch" O'Brian. Clenching my teeth, I wait for her to continue, knowing she's about to spew something vile form her pretty pout.

"I am surprised by the similarities between us." She cocks her head to the side. "Guess he never did get over me. Which is good, *real* good." Her tone is scathing and smug.

I want to smash her perfect pointed face with my clutch. It's heavy enough to make a dent, or at the very least, scare the hell out of her.

Instead I choose to find out what she wants. "And why is that?" I ask, fully aware that I'm taking the bait.

"Because he's going to be mine again." Her response is confident and straight to the point. Briefly I consider smacking her but that will look poorly on me, not her. I'm honestly amazed by the audacity of this woman.

Megan continues undeterred. "Oh, I'm sure you're nice enough, obviously pretty enough, but I was his first love. I was the woman he was going to marry," she adds.

"You are his past, nothing but a distant memory." It feels good to dig into her, even though everything she's saying scrapes across my nerves like a metal scouring pad, feeding right into my insecurities.

"Ah, but you're living proof that he isn't over me. Why else would he choose to bring home a woman that could be my sister? He only dated blondes prior to you. I've been keeping tabs on him. I knew it was time to reenter his life when I saw a picture of the two of you a few months ago in the society pages. I knew then he wasn't over me." She smiles evilly.

"Think whatever you want. Chase loves me," I say with confidence.

"And you believe that? He tells every girl he wants to fuck that he loves her. He probably told you that you were his, right?"

My eyes go wide.

"You're a piece of ass to him. He probably fucked you saying, 'mine, mine, mine!'W"

I almost throw up when those words spill out of her perfect pink lips.

"Fuck you," I tell her and tear off down the stairs.

Tears build as the world as I know it crumbles. Holy shit. Everything she said, he did. Every single thing. He told me he loved me and then fucked me. He's only said it twice, but each time it was right before we made love or during. He's never said it in the cold light of day. I bump arms with several people as I'm trying to get as far away as I can. A clearing opens, and the moon shines down on me. I take a huge lungful of air, trying to catch my breath and calm the anxiety digging its evil claws into my heart and mind.

I think back to several of our intimate moments and the things he's said.

You are mine.

You. Are. My. Woman.

I close my eyes and let the tears fall as I relive so many times where he's *claimed* me. I believed every lie. He just wants a replacement for her…for Megan. What the hell am I going to do?

"Hey, Red," a deep voice whispers across my ear.

I back up quickly. My balance teeters as the spike of my stiletto gets caught in the cobblestone path.

Cooper's long arm reaches out and wraps around my waist, his hand against my bare back. "Well, now I've got you in my arms, what am I going to do with you?" He presents me with a devilish boy-like smile.

"Thank you for catching me." I pull away from him and wipe at the tears in my eyes.

"Why is such a beautiful woman crying at a happy occasion? Do I need to kick my cousin's ass?"

I smile. Maybe Cooper isn't as bad as Chase made him out to be.

"Because I will. Wouldn't be a hardship for me at all," he adds with machismo. "What's the matter, beautiful?"

I look over to where Megan was standing. She's still there, only this time Chase is with her. That didn't take long. He's smiling, and my heart is breaking. She puts her hand on his shoulder and slides it down his arm to his elbow. That one simple intimate touch is my undoing. Chase is willingly letting her touch him the way I would, the way a lover does. It's over.

"Um, nothing really. I just…" My shoulders fall and I start to sob.

He pulls me into an embrace. "Hey, hey, it's okay."

I spend moments crying into Cooper's chest.

He holds me loosely around the waist and gently caresses the naked skin of my lower back. The touch is too intimate and sends chills racing up my spine. That's when I realize I've leaned my face against his chest and he's whispering sweet nothings in my ear about how pretty I am, how I deserve someone better, someone like him. Holy shit. This is not happening.

I look up into Cooper's face, and he's staring at me with eyes heavy with lust. I've seen that look many times, but he's not the man I want.

"You don't need him. He'll only break your heart," he says.

"Get the fuck away from her." I hear Chase's booming voice about ten feet away.

Cooper pulls me close. "Why? You're the one who left her crying and heartbroken."

Chase looks at me, fear and anger at war in his ocean eyes. I'm certain my own eyes are swollen and red from crying, makeup smeared beyond recognition. My breath is erratic, and my nose is running. His eyes find mine and are questioning, but I can't hold his gaze, preferring to look away. I can see "the Bitch" hightailing it over here, running down the steps behind him.

"What the fuck are you talking about, Cooper?" Chase asks.

"You tell me, cuz. This beautiful woman is crying, and where were you?"

"With me," Megan says from the stairs just off our location. "Chase, honey, you don't need a sugary substitute when you can have the real thing." She comes up behind him and brings her hands to his biceps.

He shrugs her off. "Gillian, you're coming with me. Now." He comes over to me and pulls my hand. "And if you ever so much as touch her hand or a hair on her head, I will fucking ruin you, Coop. Stay away from my woman!" He makes to drag me up the stairs. His grip on my wrist is tighter than ever.

"Chase, you don't need her when you can have me," Megan says.

I try to pull away, not wanting to hear him pick her over me. I can't bear it. Chase holds me fast, not allowing a retreat. In fact, he pulls me to his side like he has so many times before.

Chase looks Megan up and down with a fierce scowl. "I've had you, and so has everyone else at this fucking party. You're a slut! I wouldn't touch you again with a ten-foot pole!"

Her eyes go wide.

"You broke my heart almost a decade ago. I've moved

on. Now you need to. Why don't you go fuck Cooper again? He's available." Chase continues up the stairs.

Fuck Cooper again? Oh my God. She slept with Cooper. Was it before or after their engagement? The details are extremely significant to me at this moment.

Chase doesn't slow down, and I regret my expensive purchase on these stilts as I sway and try to keep my balance. The cobblestone walk is proving extremely difficult, and I fear I'm going to break my ankle.

"Stop, Chase."

He continues to yank my arm, his grip viselike.

"God dammit, I'm going to fall if you don't slow the fuck down!" I scream and tug on his arm.

Instead of slowing down he stops, faces me, and pulls me up and over his shoulder fireman-style, my ass in the air and my head dangling over his back.

"I'm not giving you the chance to run this time," he says as he stomps through the garden and then the house.

People at the party stop and stare at the blatant spectacle. Each person's mouth hangs open. They are likely flabbergasted by the sight. Everyone except for his Uncle Charles and his cousin Carson, who instead are smiling like loons.

"Don't let her go, my boy!" his uncle calls.

Chase lifts his hand in a wave as he passes, his other hand firmly planted on my ass. I can see his mother sitting in her wheelchair by his uncle, absolutely furious with her son's caveman behavior.

We make it to the limo, and he hauls me into it.

"What the hell was that?" I ask as Jack speeds off. "Were you trying to embarrass me? Because if you were, it worked brilliantly!" I'm seething, ready to pluck his eyes out with my tweezers.

"What were you doing locked in an embrace with Cooper?" His tone is cold and accusatory.

"I wasn't locked in an embrace. Puh-leeze." It slips from my mouth with disdain. "He was comforting me after Megan 'the Bitch' O'Brian basically told me that our relationship was a sham!"

Chase grips his temples and ruffles a hand through his unruly hair. "And you believed her? After everything we've been through?" His eyes search mine. The tone of his voice is broken, sad even.

"I had no choice. She said things, Chase. Private things. Things that I thought were only between us, and she said you say them to every girl just to bed them!" My voice cracks.

"Gillian, I don't know what she told you, but I've never said anything to you that I didn't mean."

His eyes seem honest. He sounds like he's telling the truth, but my insecurities are running wild and I'm afraid.

"I need some time to think." I cross my arms over my chest protectively, huddle against the door, and look out the window. For the entire drive back, all I can hear in the limo is the sound of our strangled breaths.

Once we arrive at the penthouse, he follows me into his bedroom and pushes me against the wall. His body crowds mine, chest to chest, heart to heart. With our noses practically touching, I can see he's hurting, but so am I. This is too important to back down now. We have to have it out once and for all if we're ever going to move forward.

His breath stirs the wisps of hair from my check.

"Gillian, I'm not going to have that whore come between us. What we have is real. More real than anything I've ever known."

"She said you tell all the girls that. She said that you tell everyone that they are yours!" Tears form, and I choke back a sob.

He slams his hand into the wall behind my head, and it scares me. The response is too much like how Justin used to respond to me, using his fists to make a point. I flinch, and instinct brings my hands in front of my face defensively.

"Baby, I'm sorry. I don't want to scare you. I'd never hurt you. Never. It's just…this makes me so fucking angry."

I nod and settle my hands back at my sides. My breath is labored, coming in heaving gusts. My heart is beating so hard within me I fear it might pound right out of my chest. He brings me to the bed and sits me down. He does the one thing I never thought he'd do in a million years. He kneels at my feet. The position is not one of power and authority, but one of a man down on his knees in front of the woman he cherishes. He massages my thighs firmly as he reconnects with me.

There's a heaviness in the air that wasn't there before. The skin and hair on my forearms tingle, and chills run up my spine. He looks at me with so much love in his gaze I'm incapable of looking anywhere but at him.

Chase clasps my hands and with one thumb traces an infinity symbol. My eyes mist over at the gesture.

"Gillian, I want you. I've wanted you from the moment I laid eyes on you." His eyes fill with tears.

I'm shackled by the emotion he's admitting.

"I told you before, and I'll tell you again. You are *mine*.

I want you in my life, I want you in my bed, and I want you by my side. Always, forever, through infinity, baby." He cups my cheeks, his thumb caressing my cheekbones. For moments he stares into my eyes. "I love you, Gillian Grace Callahan. I will always love you. I will always run toward you and after you, no matter what."

"Chase—" I lick my lips.

"No, let me finish. What I had with Megan was over the night before our wedding when she fucked my cousin Cooper." His head bows and he takes a deep breath. "I couldn't wait until morning when we were going to get married. I had to kiss her goodnight. When I went to her room, I heard laughing and then..." He struggles for a moment. "I heard moaning."

It doesn't take a genius to know what comes next. I close my eyes, feeling the pain he must have felt that night.

"When I opened the door, Cooper was balls deep in the woman I was supposed to marry in the morning. I can't forget that image. I won't forgive her or him. I knew in that moment that she never truly loved me. I represented what she was supposed to marry, supposed to have in her life."

"I'm sorry, Chase." The tears start again and drip onto his hands.

He closes his eyes. "My feelings for you, Gillian, are so much stronger than anything I ever felt for her. Not having you in my life, by my side, would be the end of me. Don't you understand? I love you. I want to make you my wife," he pleads. "Don't leave me. Please promise me that you'll never leave me." A single tear tracks down his cheek.

I lean over and kiss it away, tasting the ocean of his sadness. "I won't leave you. I promise." I know this time that it's the truth. I could never leave him. I couldn't bear to be without him. He's a part of me. Chase will always be a part of me. There's no denying it now and nowhere I could run that he wouldn't find me and bring me home.

"Marry me?" he asks, searching my eyes.

"Chase, I'm not going to marry you right now. We've only been together a few months. Besides, you're just asking because of what happened this evening." I sigh, letting out the breath I've held since the moment the words "marry me" left his kissable pout.

"You think so?" He jumps up and goes into the closet. He comes back and kneels down in front of me once more. He pulls out a black velvet box, and my palms start to sweat. "You think this is spur of the moment, huh?" He shakes his head and smiles. "I already have the ring, gorgeous. I got it a couple weeks ago. I was waiting for the perfect opportunity. Now when you're questioning my love, my commitment, I'm willing to forego romance for reality. I want you forever. Please be my forever."

He opens the black velvet box, and a platinum diamond ring is nestled in the center. It's made of three lines of large bright sparkling diamonds that wrap completely around the circle. It's incredible, like nothing I've ever seen.

"Each band represents something special." His fingernail touches one delicate band. "One for our past, our present, and our future."

I spring my head up and search his eyes. Just like my soul sisters. The trinity. "I want to be a part of your everything. Marry me." His eyes sparkle and swirl, the most intense blue I've ever seen.

"Yes," I whisper.

He snaps his head up and his gaze holds mine. "Yes, as in yes, you'll marry me, or yes, you believe me?"

"Yes, I'll marry you, and yes, I believe you." I'm not at all shocked by the weight and depth of my answer. Chase and I were only ever meant to be together.

He puts the ring on my left hand and kisses it. "I'm going to make you so happy, Gillian, I swear!"

Those delicious lips slant over mine. He pours everything into this kiss, and I accept it all. His control freakiness, attitude, frustrations, overprotectiveness, sexiness, and most of all his undying love for me. Anything and everything he gives, I will own and give back in spades.

He pulls away quickly. "Let's get married tomorrow!" he says excitedly.

"No," I say flatly.

He blinks a few times. "Next week?" he says hopefully, layering on the sexy crooked grin.

"No. A year from now," I offer.

"An entire year? You want me to wait to make you mine for a year?" He sounds incredulous.

"If you love me, you'll wait." He knows my statement is final. He got me to agree to marriage. He's going to have to put in the time to prove his commitment.

"Move in with me then?" he barters. The man is always negotiating something. Probably why he's so insanely wealthy.

"Okay." It's a solid compromise.

"Okay?" Hope fills his tone.

"I'll move in with you. But you have to move Maria into one of your secure buildings that has video surveillance and a doorman—oh, and rent controlled."

"Done. She will not pay a dime!"

I take a deep breath. "That's not what I said." I roll my eyes.

"Baby, I'll give you the world." He kisses me and slides his hand up my leg to settle on the lacy fabric surrounding my thigh. "You're wearing stockings?"

I smile into his kiss.

He groans. "You know what they say about a woman who wears stockings? She's inviting a man into her most private—"

"Oh, shut up and kiss me!"

★ ★ ★ ★

I blow on my morning vanilla latte, courtesy of the lovely Bentley. Chase is munching on his fourth fresh-baked cookie. I actually watched him dunk the cookie into his coffee. Note to self…never share a cup of coffee with my fiancé. it's liable to have cookie crumbs in it. I watch Chase as he hums and flips through the pages of the Sunday paper. He's beyond happy this morning. After everything that happened last night, I still feel a bit raw and needy for his attention, but twirling my engagement ring around my finger repeatedly with my thumb definitely helps my insecurities. I love feeling the weight of it against my hand, knowing its meaning, anticipating our future together. It's the stuff true dreams are made of, and I'm going to enjoy every moment.

"A package has arrived for you, Ms. Callahan." Austin enters the room and sets the box on the living room table.

Chase snuggles into my side and kisses my neck. I hold

up my hand and look at my new engagement ring sparkling in the morning sunlight shining through the windows. He smiles against my neck.

"It looks good on you," he murmurs against my ear.

I turn, kiss him lightly, and then remove myself from Chase's grasp. He doesn't make it an easy escape. I package open the box pulling away the tissue paper. Inside I find a handful of black-and-white photos. They are all of Chase and me very close up. One was taken a month ago, and several others were taken over the past few weeks. In every picture, Chase's head is cut or crossed out with a deep red X across his image. My hands start to shake, and Chase jumps up and grabs the photos, scanning them quietly.

"Fuck! Jack!" he yells.

Both Jack and Austin race into the room.

Removing the soft fabric that's deep within the box, I catch my hand on something lacy along with a sticky substance. I pull it out and realize it's a pair of my underwear and a matching bra set in deep purple. I drop the items on the table and stare at my hand. There's white slimy gunk all over it. Chase grasps my wrist and takes a long look. His nostrils flare, and his face turns white-hot with rage. His jaw clenches, and that nasty tic in his jaw pounds out a beat along with his anger. Instantly, I know what the substance is. It's my admirer's semen.

I close my eyes trying to rein in the prickly spears of disgust, but my body has other plans. The shaking start out slow and turns into a full body quake in mere seconds. The stalker went into my apartment, found my undergarments, and jacked off on them before throwing them in a box to mail to me. Chase drags me to the kitchen and puts my hand under the water. He pours soap over my hands, and I scrub them. I grab the sponge and scrub roughly against my skin with the scratchy side until both hands are a deep red.

"Gillian, stop. It's off, you're clean," Chase says and pulls my hands away from the sink and kisses the entire surface of each one. "Take a few deep breaths."

He mimics me and we both take five deep breaths together. The panic lessens, and I'm much calmer as we walk back into the room.

"He's escalating." Jack holds the newest note in his hand.

"Read it," I demand.

"Baby, I don't think that's a good idea," Chase coos.

"Read it, Jack. Now!"

Chase wraps his arms around my waist, and I take comfort in his strength leaning back into his embrace fully.

"Go ahead, Jack," Chase says. "She needs to know what we're dealing with."

Bitch,

I told you that you couldn't hide from me. You will be mine. Nothing and no one will stand in the way of our reunion.

XOXO

I close my eyes and try to contain my temper. A burning hot rage sweeps across me, and I start to pace the room. The satin robe Chase gave me in New York trails behind me. I pick it up and slam it in a circle as I turn and pace the other direction. Traitorous tears build, and I'm ready to scream at the top of my lungs. Why now? Why is this happening to me? Haven't I suffered enough? Isn't it my turn to be happy? Tears pour down my cheeks, and I wipe them away, bristling with irritation.

"Baby, it's okay. I'm going to take care of you. Nothing is going to happen to you under my watch." He wraps his arms around me, pulling me into the safety of his love.

I nod against his chest and cling to him. I'm so tired of this.

"This ends here. Double the number of men. Jack, I want intel on this. Austin, she goes nowhere, and I mean *nowhere,* without you. You are officially her shadow. If you can't handle that responsibility, I'll find someone who can." His voice is tight, strained.

"Sir, I will do what it takes to keep her safe. I will protect her with my life." Austin stands tall and puffs out his chest. His jaw is stiff, his hands clench into fists.

Chase looks him up and down a moment. He gives him a manly nod that somehow communicates more than words would.

"Leave us," Chase says over my shoulder.

He brings his forehead down to mine. Fresh tears pool and fall as he holds me and we breathe together.

"Gillian, I will handle this. You are safe with me. We're going to have a long, beautiful future together. Okay?"

When he speaks with that finality in his voice, I believe him.

"Don't worry about this." Chase nuzzles my neck and lays a sweet kiss just behind my ear. "I love you," he whispers.

"I love you more." After I've calmed down and he's taken a round of ten breaths with me, I feel a bit more like myself.

We settle on the couch, and he holds me for a long time.

"Now can we please celebrate our engagement? I can't

wait to tell the girls." I smile as he cups the sides of my neck with both hands, tips his head back, and laughs. He's so beautiful when he's smiling.

"That sounds like an excellent idea. But first, let's celebrate privately." He waggles his eyebrows and smirks seductively before pulling me against his chest.

One hand tunnels into my hair at the nape tipping my head back for a slow and deep kiss. Shivers rush through my body and down to my toes.

Chase and I spend the rest of the morning celebrating our love. He's certain his team will solve the stalker issue sooner rather than later. For the first time in my life, I'm going to let someone else take care of me. Allow my safety and happiness to be protected in the hands of the man I love. No more living in the past and fearing the future. From now on, I will focus on the life I'm building with the people I love and feel secure in the knowledge that today, the present is beautiful.

The end…for now.

THE END

The Trinity Trilogy is continued in…

Mind

ALSO BY AUDREY CARLAN

The Calendar Girl Series

January (Book 1)
February (Book 2)
March (Book 3)
April (Book 4)
May (Book 5)
June (Book 6)
July (Book 7)
August (Book 8)
September (Book 9)
October (Book 10)
November (Book 11)
December (Book 12)

The Falling Series

Angel Falling
London Falling
Justice Falling

The Trinity Trilogy

Body (Book 1)
Mind (Book 2)
Soul (Book 3)

ACKNOWLEDGEMENTS

To my husband **Eric**—I will always love you more. Thank you for your unending support and encouraging me to chase after my dreams.

To my mentor **Jess Dee**—You were the first to tell me this novel needed serious work. That first critique started me on this journey. It was a moment in time that marked me forever. I'll always be in your debt for taking the time to give me advice, review my words, and tell me to keep chasing after my dream. I adore you and strive to one day be as good of a storyteller as I have found in you. Thank you, my friend. www.jessdee.com.

To my critique partner **Sarah Saunders**—Your belief in me is staggering. Thank you for seeing something special in my stories and wanting to participate in making them better. I love you, girlie.

To my editors—**Alfie Thompson**—Thank you for ripping this to shreds not once but twice! <grin> In the end, it made me a better writer. **Helen Hardt**—for making sure all the dangling bits were firmly back in their rightful place, thank you.

To my sisters **Jeana, Michele, and Denise**—I hope you find as much of Mom in this first book as I did. I'd like to think she was my muse for this novel, poking and prodding me along the way. I think she'd be proud of the end product.

To my beta readers:

Jeananna Goodall—My biggest fan. I'm not sure how the experience would be if I didn't have you cheerleading and anticipating every chapter as I write them. I so enjoy your love affair with my characters. It's as if they want to please you.

Ginelle Blanch—I'm pretty sure you win every award for finding the most unique errors. Without your keen eye for details I'd receive a lot more complaints about my grammar. Plus, I so look forward to reading your thoughts. You have such a way with words and your feedback saves my ass every time! Thank you, lady.

Heidi Ryan—Your betas are like opening up my own personal version of Chicago Manual of Style. You are now, and forever will be the Comma Queen. Thank you for taking the time to read and fix my errors. You are a sweetheart!

Emily Hemmer— Because my misery loves company and so does yours. I love that I have you to talk, vent, and share challenges and achievements. One day we'll be on that damned list, girlfriend! www.emilyhemmer.com

Additional special thanks to the following:

To **Audrey's Angels**—My official Audrey Carlan Street Team. I'm incredibly blessed to have the most amazing women to lift me up and cheer me on. It's not possible to thank you for everything you do for me. Mostly, thank you for being strong, beautiful women that support and care for one another. I heart you all big time!

To **Drue Hoffman**—Best blog tour chick in the universe! She does incredible book promoting services for authors with a special love for helping out the indies. Visit her site to view pricing and service offerings. You'll be happy you did. www.druesrandomchatter.com

To **Rhenna Morgan and MJ Handy**, thank you for your initial review, feedback, and support as I was wading my way through this monster.

And last but certainly not least, to the publishing team at **Waterhouse Press** for taking a chance on me and my stories, I'll always be grateful. Namaste.

ABOUT AUDREY CARLAN

Audrey Carlan lives in the sunny California Valley two hours away from the city, the beach, the mountains and the precious…the vineyards. She has been married to the love of her life for over a decade and has two young children that live up to their title of "Monster Madness" on a daily basis. When she's not writing wickedly hot romances, doing yoga, or sipping wine with her "soul sisters," three incredibly different and unique voices in her life, she can be found with her nose stuck in book or her Kindle. A hot, smutty, romantic book to be exact!

Any and all feedback is greatly appreciated and feeds the soul.
You can contact Audrey below:

E-mail: carlan.audrey@gmail.com
Facebook: facebook.com/AudreyCarlan
Website: www.audreycarlan.com